From now on

by

Frank L. Packard

Double 9
BOOKS

From now on
by Frank L. Packard

Copyright © 2023

All Rights reserved.

ISBN: 978-93-58018-77-6

Published by

DOUBLE 9 BOOKS

2/13-B, Ansari Road
Daryaganj, New Delhi – 110002
info@double9books.com
www.double9books.com
Tel. 011-40042856

ABOUT THE AUTHOR

Canadian author Frank L. Packard lived from February 2, 1877, until February 17, 1942. Frank L. Packard attended the Universities of Liège and McGill after being born in Montreal, Quebec. He was a civil engineer for the Canadian Pacific Railway when he was a young guy. His experiences as a railroad worker inspired him to write numerous train tales and later a series of mystery books, the most well-known of which included a character by the name of Jimmie Dale. He has some of his books adapted into movies. Frank Packard passed away in Lachine, Quebec, in 1942, and was laid to rest in Montreal's Mount Royal Cemetery. went to work as a civil engineer for the Canadian Pacific Railway as a young man. His experiences working on the railroad inspired him to write a number of mystery books, the most well-known of which included a character by the name of "Jimmie Dale," who made his debut in the 1917 book The Adventures of Jimmie Dale. By day, he was a wealthy playboy, but at night, he put on a disguise and went by the name The Grey Seal. He breaks into homes and businesses to open safes.

CONTENTS

BOOK I.
THE CHASE

I.
ONE HUNDRED THOUSAND DOLLARS

AWILD and prolonged roar came from every quarter of the race track. It swelled in volume. It came again and again. Pandemonium itself seemed loosed.

Outside the enclosure, a squat, fat man, the perspiration rolling in streams down his face, tugged at his collar with frantic, nervous jerks, as he leaned in over the side of a high-powered car, and with his other hand gripped at the arm of the young man in the driver's seat.

"Dave, listen to 'em! My God, listen to 'em!" snarled the fat man.

Dave Henderson, with the toe of his boot, moved the little black satchel that the other had dropped on the floor of the car farther to one side; and, by way of excuse for disengaging his arm, reached into his pocket for his cigarettes.

"I can hear 'em—even a yard away out here!" he said imperturbably. "Sounds like a great day for the bookies—not!"

The fat man secured his grip on Dave Henderson's arm again.

"I'm wiped out—every last cent—all I've made in years," he said hoarsely. "You get that, don't you? You know it! I'm cleaned out—and you don't seem to give a damn!"

"Why should I?" inquired Dave Henderson calmly. "I guess it's *their* turn, ain't it?"

Bookie Skarvan's red-rimmed little gray eyes narrowed, and he swallowed hard.

"I've played square, I have!" he whined. "And I'm wiped out!"

"Yes—square as hell!" amended Dave Henderson.

"You don't give a damn!" shrilled Bookie Skarvan. "That's like you! That's like the lot of you! Where would you have been if I hadn't taken you up—eh?"

"God knows!" said Dave Henderson dispassionately. "I'm not blaming you for trying to make a crook of me."

An apoplectic red heightened Bookie Skarvan's flushed and streaming face.

"Well, that's one thing I didn't make a bull of, at any rate!" he retorted viciously.

Dave Henderson shifted his cigarette from one corner of his mouth to the other with the tip of his tongue. There was a curious smile, half bitter, half whimsical, on his lips, as he leaned suddenly toward the other.

"I guess you're right, Bookie!" He shrugged his shoulders. "But I've only just found it out myself, so if you think there's any congrats coming to you and you're sore because you didn't get 'em before, you know why now."

The scowl on Bookie Skarvan's face deepened, then cleared abruptly, and the man forced a nervous, wheezy chuckle.

"You won't feel so blamed cool about it to-morrow morning when you come to size this up!" He was whining again, but plaintively now. "I'm wiped out, I tell you, and it's too hard a crack for Tydeman to give me any more backing after he's squared this up—so what are you going to do, eh?"

Dave Henderson glanced at the car's clock. It was already after three.

"I'm going up to 'Frisco—if I ever get started!" he said brusquely. "I've missed the train, as it is, and that means a ninety-mile run—and we're still wasting time! Get down to cases! You got Tydeman on the long distance— what did he say?"

"I couldn't help your missing the train!" Bookie Skarvan's voice had grown almost ingratiating. "There wasn't any use of you going until I knew Tydeman was at home, and unless I got hold of him before the banks closed, was there? And if I'd been able to get him at once we might have had time to arrange it by wire with a bank here—if they were carrying that much in ready cash—and you wouldn't have needed to go at all. But I didn't get him until just a few minutes ago. You know that! I couldn't help it, could I—and the run won't hurt you. You can grab the evening train back. I can stave this gang of wolves off until then by telling 'em Tydeman's making good."

"All right!" Dave Henderson was apparently much more intent upon the starting mechanism of the car, than he was upon either his companion or his companion's words. The engine was already purring softly when he looked up at Bookie Skarvan again. "Well, what's the arrangement?"

"Tydeman will have the money in cash at his house—one hundred thousand dollars. You go there and get it, and bring it back on the train tonight."

"Anything else?"

"No; that's all." Bookie Skarvan mopped at his face with the back of his sleeve, glanced in the direction of another sudden outburst of delirious cheering, and mopped at his face again. "That'll be another long shot—everybody's playing 'em—damn 'em! For God's sake, don't miss that train back, Dave! It leaves at nine o'clock. Some of these pikers that never turned a red in their lives before 'll be laying me out if I don't flash the long green then. You get me, Dave? I'll have all I can do to stave 'em off that long. I wish I could go with you and get out of here, but they'd think I was running away, and— —"

"I get you!" said Dave Henderson. "They all love Bookie Skarvan! Well, it's your car, and you've got a right there, but get off the step unless you're coming!" He threw in the clutch, and the car shot forward. "So-long, Bookie!" he flung out over his shoulder.

An hour passed. Out in the free sweep of country, the car was running at terrific speed. And now, from the road ahead, Dave Henderson's dark eyes, cool and self-reliant, strayed to the little black handbag at his feet as they had done many times before, while the tight lips parted slightly in a smile; and suddenly, over the rush of the wind and the roar of the speeding car, he spoke aloud.

"One hundred thousand dollars—*in cash*," said Dave Henderson meditatively. "Well, it looks like the chance I've been waiting for—what? Only I can't go and let old Tydeman hand it over to me and trust me with it, and then beat it and give him the doublecross, can I? Once he shoves it at me, and says, 'Dave, my boy, take this back to Skarvan,' I'm stung, and there's nothing doing! That's right, ain't it? Well then, what's the answer?"

The broad, muscular shoulders set a little more rigidly over the steering wheel, and the square jaws clamped in a sort of dogged defiance in the face of his self-propounded problem. His mind, as though seeking therefrom the solution he demanded, was reviewing the facts and circumstances that had placed that little black hand-bag, with its suggestive possibilities, at his feet. It had been a bad day for the bookmakers, and a particularly bad day for Bookie Skarvan—for it was the culmination of several extremely bad days for Bookie Skarvan. Shots at odds that were staggering had won again and again. There was absolutely no question but that the man was wiped out—a good many times over. True, Tydeman was coming to the rescue, but that did not put Bookie Skarvan on his feet again; it only paid the bills, and saved Bookie Skarvan from being used as a street cleaning device in the shape of a human mop! The curious thing about it was that Tydeman was in any way connected with Bookie Skarvan! Everybody knew that Skarvan was crooked from his boot soles up—except Martin K. Tydeman. But that was Tydeman's way! Tydeman must have been told often enough, but Tydeman wouldn't believe it. That was Tydeman's way! Once, years ago, Skarvan had tipped Tydeman off that one of his string was being "doctored." It did not matter that Skarvan had juggled his information, and had tried first to play both ends to the middle by blackmailing and then doublecrossing the man who had done the "doctoring"—Tydeman did not know that—and Tydeman from that moment was unshaken in his belief that there was no squarer man on the circuit than Bookie Skarvan. It had resulted in Tydeman becoming a silent partner of Bookie Skarvan—and the betting fraternity had been not a little pleased, for Tydeman's millions went up on the board better than even against Bookie Skarvan's trickiness.

Dave Henderson nodded his head. It was quite true. Martin K. Tydeman was getting to be quite an old man now, but Martin K. Tydeman was still hailed as the squarest, garnest sporting gentleman California had ever known—and it would be a little rough on that king of sports. It was too bad that it wasn't Bookie Skarvan! Skarvan was crooked from the ground up—and who knew it any better than he, Dave Henderson, who had worked for Skarvan for several years now? But, as it was, Tydeman would simply have to cough up a second hundred thousand out of his millions, that was all. No, it wasn't all! It depended entirely upon whether he, Dave Henderson, could get his hands on the money without accepting it as a trust from the old millionaire.

"You're a poor fool!" Dave Henderson informed himself, with a sharp laugh. "What's the difference? You pinch it either way, don't you?"

He shook his head, as the car tore forward.

"Mabbe," he muttered, "mabbe I am, and mabbe there ain't any difference—but there's nothing doing that way. I got a little reputation myself—left. No guy ever put a bean in my mitt that he didn't get a square deal on, and that's on the level—in spite of Skarvan! Damn Skarvan! He wouldn't have had a look-in on a two-bit bet for more seasons than one if I hadn't been running the cases for him—nobody'd have trusted him!"

Again Dave Henderson relapsed into silence. He drove in a purely mechanical way. His mind was rankling now in a sort of bitter speculation over the years that reached back as far as he could remember. They were not an altogether pleasing memory; and that was why he wanted, and not only wanted, but had made up his mind to have—one hundred thousand dollars. He did not remember either his father or his mother. They hadn't had any money, but he had an impression that they had been rather decent people— only they had died. He had been a kid when it happened—he didn't know how old—just a kid. Some one had put him in a school, an orphan school. It had been a hell of a place. And at ten he had run away. After that, beginning by making himself useful around one of the training stables, he had lived on the race courses ever since—and had risen to the heights of becoming Bookie Skarvan's clerk!

His jaws clamped hard. It was a piker life, but here was a chance to get out of it! He had been looking for the chance—and here it was—if he could get away with it. There had been lots of chances before, chances for a few thousand dollars—but the bet hadn't been good enough. He had even a little better than three thousand dollars himself, for that matter, and it was pulling interest, too; he had loaned it to Square John Kelly, who ran the Pacific Coral Saloon down on the Barbary Coast in 'Frisco. And he had a couple of hundred dollars in his pocket now, too, for that matter. But it was all chicken feed. He had won it, and he might win as much more again some time—or he might lose it. The game wasn't any good. It didn't get anywhere. Maybe it was the interest coming in on that three thousand that showed up where the odds stood on a hundred thousand. There wasn't anything else involved. Was it a good gamble? The interest on a hundred thousand would make a blooming gentleman of independent means out of him at one crack. Sure, it was worth the risk! If he got caught, well then—*good-night!* If he got away with it, well then—*zowie!*

Yes—but how? That was the question.

If he wouldn't go to Tydeman and let Tydeman trustfully hand the money over to him, how was he to get the cash into his possession? He was quite willing to accept the risk of pursuit and capture, given a few hours' start, he was quite willing to pit his wits against the machinery of the law, that was the gambling chance he ran; and it would be very simple to let Tydeman, in Tydeman's own library, say, assist in packing the little black hand-bag full of money, and then, instead of taking the train back to Stockton—to disappear. The strong jaws clamped harder. But—. nothing doing! Not that way! He'd go the limit, and he meant to have that hundred thousand, and he would have it, and, once decided upon getting it, he would drop in his tracks before he would give up the attempt, and he would drop in his tracks, if the attempt were successful, before he relinquished his grip on the money—but that way was *raw*. Rotten raw! To get away with a hundred thousand dollars was a sporting proposition, a gambling and a fighting chance, but to double-cross a man who placed that money in one's keeping in good faith was in Bookie Skarvan's line—not his!

Well then—how?

The miles and the minutes and the half-hours passed. Tight-lipped, the clean-shaven face set and hard, the dark eyes introspective as they held on the road ahead, Dave Henderson sat there, almost motionless, bent over the wheel. Once he stopped to replenish his supply of gasoline, and then the car roared on again, rocking in its speed. He drove perilously fast, in a sort of subconscious physical synchronism with his racing brain. One hundred thousand dollars—that was the stake. In another hour or so that hundred thousand dollars would be his—some way! There was no question about that! But how? There was something ironical in the fact that Tydeman was waiting to throw it at him, and that while he racked his mind for a method of getting the money into his possession, he must also rack his mind for a method that would prevent it being forced upon him! He laughed out sharply.

"Now wouldn't that sting you!" mumbled Dave Henderson. "Say, wouldn't that sting you!"

And then, abruptly, Dave Henderson stopped the car at the side of the road. He had it now—almost. It had come, the germ of it, in a flash. And now he wanted to think it out without the distraction of handling the machine. There came a smile, and the smile broadened—and he laughed again. There was a picture before his mind's-eye now that afforded him a grim sense of humor. He could see the great bare dormitory in the orphan school, a room whose walls were decorated with huge scrolled mottoes—and there was the one on the end wall with its great red painted letters, and the same old crack in the plaster that zigzagged its way through the words. Sure, he could see it! "Virtue Is Its Own Reward." He had never taken much stock in mottoes, but it looked now as though that one wasn't all to the bad! By refusing to allow himself to double-cross old Tydeman, he had now found a very much better way. He wouldn't have to take the risk of pursuit now if he had any luck, for the very simple reason that there wouldn't be any pursuit; and instead of it being a self-evident fact that he had got away with the money, he would not now appear in the affair at all.

He began to elaborate the germ very carefully in his mind. He knew old Tydeman's house well, almost every inch of it, for he had been there on errands for Skarvan many times. Tydeman had secured the money from the bank just before closing time, and had taken it to his home. Tydeman's habit was to dine about half-past six. These three facts woven together offered a most satisfactory solution to the problem. One hundred thousand dollars in bills of the denominations that Tydeman would be likely to call for in order to make it convenient for Bookie Skarvan's use, would be too bulky for Tydeman to carry around in his pocket. Therefore the money wouldn't be on Tydeman's person when the old millionaire sat down to his high-falutin' dinner with his butler at his elbow at half-past six. The money would be in the library most likely—and the library was accessible—thanks to the hedge that flanked the driveway to the house.

Dave Henderson selected another cigarette from his package, and lighted it thoughtfully. So far, so good! And the rest wasn't so dusty either! He had the whole thing now. As soon as he reached 'Frisco he would drive down to that shabby little street where he kept the shabby room in which he lived during the off seasons on the turf, and leave the car standing in front of the house. From his room he could easily gain the shed at the rear of the place, and from the shed he could gain the lane—and all this without the slightest chance of being observed. He should be able to go to Tydeman's house and return in, say, an hour, or an hour and a half at the outside. If any one noticed the car in front it would seem only natural that he had gone to his room to wash up and perhaps change his clothes after a ninety-mile run, especially in view of the fact that the train he was supposed to take back to Stockton did not leave until nine o'clock.

He leaned back in his seat, and blew a smoke ring into the air complacently.

"Sure!" observed Dave Henderson. "I guess I've got the odds switched— to a little better than even money. I'll be back with that hundred thousand and no one the wiser, but I've got to hide it somewhere—what? And I can't make the fool play of hiding it in my room."

Another smoke ring followed the first. Almost any place would do—so that it was easy to get at, and at the same time would not attract attention to him when he went back to it. Well—the shed, then? He nodded his head suddenly. Yes, of course—Mrs. Tooler's old pigeon-cote in the shed! It was the one place in a million! The money would be perfectly safe there, and he could get it again any time at a minute's notice. Again he nodded his head. The whole thing was as good as done now. After the money was hidden, he had only to get into the car, drive to Tydeman's house, mount the steps with the little black satchel in his hand—and request of Mr. Martin K. Tydeman, Esquire, the money that Bookie Skarvan had sent him for, and which he had motored a matter of some ninety miles to obtain!

Dave Henderson's lips parted in a sudden smile, though the outthrust, dogged jaw was in no degree relaxed. There would be one whale of a hullabaloo! But the last man who could by the wildest stretch of imagination have had anything to do with the robbery was—Dave Henderson!

After that, maybe he *would* accept a second hundred thousand from Tydeman—and take it back to Bookie Skarvan, too! That was all he had to do—play the game. In six months it would be soon enough to dig up and beat it out of the West for keeps. There wasn't any hurry. Being already a man of affairs, it would take him some time to get those affairs settled up! There was old Square John Kelly and that three thousand dollars, for instance. Kelly couldn't produce the cash at an instant's notice, it was invested in Kelly's business; but if he tipped old Kelly off that he was thinking of chucking up the West, Kelly would have it for him at the end of a few months. There wasn't any hurry.

Dave Henderson glanced at the car's clock—and flipped the butt of his cigarette away. It was ten minutes of five. He started the car forward again—but now he drove leisurely. The plan he had decided upon no longer demanded an excess of speed. He was getting in pretty close to 'Frisco, and he did not now want to reach the city until at least a few minutes after six.

There was something superbly insouciant about the man, as, far back in his seat, his hands rested in a sort of masterful negligence upon the steering wheel. Of ethics Dave Henderson knew little, and cared much less—ethics had been missing from the curriculum of the school in which he had been brought up. He wanted a hundred thousand dollars, because with a hundred thousand dollars he was fixed for life; and, having weighed the betting odds that stood between him and his goal, and having decided to accept those odds, it became simply a question of winning, or of being wiped out. If he got wiped out, he would neither whimper nor whine—he would simply swallow his medicine. He was taking a sporting chance—he was staking his liberty, quite possibly his life, against Martin K. Tydeman's hundred thousand dollars. And Tydeman could afford to lose. He wasn't for putting Tydeman, or any one else, on the rocks; that wasn't the sort of game he had any use for— but a hundred thousand to Tydeman was street-car fare. He admitted that he would have preferred it should have been some one other than Tydeman, in the sense that he possessed an unbounded admiration for Tydeman— for Tydeman, even though he was too old to take much of an active part in anything, was still the gamest sport on record. But it *was* Tydeman, it happened that it *was* Tydeman; and so, well—— Dave Henderson shrugged his shoulders.

"Step up, gentlemen, and place your bets!" murmured Dave Henderson softly. "And take a tip from me—bunch your wads on the dark horse!"

II.
THE THEFT

IT was in front of a shabby frame house in a shabby street that Dave Henderson stopped the car. It was five minutes after six. He lifted up the seat, and, leaning down, surreptitiously conveyed to his pocket a cold-chisel from the car's complement of tools. Lacking any of the accessories of a professional burglar, the chisel would make a most excellent substitute for a steel jimmy. He replaced the seat, picked up the little black hand-bag, alighted, entered the house, and from the musty hallway, after unlocking the door, stepped through into a room on the right. He closed the door behind him, and stood surveying his surroundings in a sort of half grim, half quizzical contempt.

It was possible that old Tooler upstairs, on hearing the car, and hearing him, Dave Henderson, enter the house, might come down; on the other hand, it was quite equally possible that old Tooler would not. It was, however, wise to wait a few minutes and see. That was part of the plan. He, Dave Henderson, was supposed to be here in his room while some one else made that little raid on Martin K. Tydeman's library! If, therefore, Tooler should come down, and find no one— — A shrug of his shoulders completed the obvious deduction.

His eyes traveled around the room. This was his home—that is, if he could claim a home anywhere, this was his home. It was dingy, comfortless and uninviting. There was only the one window that faced the street, and the window was inadequate, and the light seemed to be imbued with a niggardly hesitation about coming in at all—which was perhaps just as well. The furnishings weren't out of any prize collection!

He dug his hands impulsively into his side-pockets—and, one hand encountering the chisel, he smiled with a kind of cool, composed satisfaction. Between this barren and God-forsaken hole and this bit of steel there had been been a connection that was both intimate and pertinent. For nine years, ever since he had run away from school, the kind of existence this place stood for had got his goat—that was the reason why he had put the chisel in his pocket.

The room had served its purpose better than any other place of like circumstances and surroundings would have served him—he had, indeed, chosen this particular room very carefully—but the place had always got his goat. He had had to have a room somewhere—he had taken it here. There were many reasons why he had selected this one. It was cheap; and it was among the only class of people with whom he had ever had a chance to associate—the hangers-on of the race-tracks, the dance-hall crowd of the Barbary Coast, the night world of 'Frisco. He knew every one here—he knew the crooks and the lags of the underworld. These latter had time and again even tried to inveigle him into active membership in their fraternity. They wanted him. They had even paid him the compliment of telling him he would make the slickest crook in the United States. He had refused. The game didn't look good enough. It was all piker stuff. It wasn't morality that had held him back... his morality was the morality of his environment... nine years of it... what was morality anyhow?... as far as he could make out it was simply a question of whatever you do don't get caught. And he had seen some of the upper crust playing at morality, too! Sure, he knew what morality was—he had seen a lot of it in his nineteen years!

"Well, what do you know about that!" said Dave Henderson aloud, in a sort of surprised voice. "Sounds like I'm arguing with myself whether I ought to do this or not. Say, wouldn't that sting you! There's nothing to it! It's what you get for waiting—a lone hand that cops the sweepstakes, and sets you up for keeps like a nabob!"

He went to the door, opened it slightly, and listened. Upstairs he could hear Tooler moving about. That was another reason why he had, having once taken the room, remained on as the sole lodger in this house. Tooler minded his own business—and Mrs. Tooler couldn't help minding hers. Mrs. Tooler was a paralytic. They were a couple well beyond middle age, and, having been thrifty in their early days, had purchased this house here some fifteen years ago. The neighborhood, even if still a cheap neighborhood at that time, had been a little more refined in those days. It had changed for the worse since then, but having invested their savings the subsequent changes had to be borne, that was all. It hadn't apparently affected Tooler very much. The man was naturally sour anyhow, and Mrs. Tooler's illness hadn't changed him into what might be called, by any stretch of the imagination, genial! He was a mechanic of some sort; but his work had been spasmodic—Mrs. Tooler could not always be left alone.

Dave Henderson frowned. Tooler evidently wasn't coming down; but Tooler, for all that, must, if the necessity arose, be the means of establishing an alibi, and that required something of at least a definite recognition by Tooler of his, Dave Henderson's, presence. He stepped abruptly out into the hall.

"Heh, Tooler!" he called. "Tooler!"

A door opened somewhere above.

"Hello!" snapped a gruff voice.

"It's me," announced Dave Henderson.

"I heard you!" grunted Tooler.

"I just came in for a wash-up," explained Dave Henderson. "Came up in Skarvan's car. I'm going back to-night by train."

"All right!" Tooler grunted again.

"How's the wife?"

The only answer was the closing of a door upstairs. Dave Henderson smiled pleasantly, and re-entered his own room. When it came to sociability Tooler was a star! Well, so much the better! He had no complaint to register on that score—especially to-night! He crossed to where his trunk stood against the wall at the lower end of the room, opened the trunk, lifted out the tray, and from somewhere in the lower recesses possessed himself of an automatic pistol and a generous supply of reserve ammunition. With this in his pocket, he closed the trunk again, and, sitting down on the edge of the bed, unlaced and removed his shoes.

And now Dave Henderson, silent as a cat in his movements, his shoes tucked under one arm, the black hand-bag under the other, made his way out into the hall. The car standing in front of the house was mute evidence that he was still in his room. Later on, when he returned, in the course of an hour, say, he would call up to Tooler again to say that he was going. It was a perfectly good alibi!

He crept on along the hall, reached the back door, opened it cautiously without a sound, and stepped through into the shed that connected with the house. Here, he spent several minutes in a careful examination of the old pigeon-cote. He had never been very much interested in Mrs. Tooler's abandoned pigeon-cote before—he was very much interested in it now! There was a small side window in the shed, and it gave just light enough to enable him to see. It was many years since Mrs. Tooler had kept any pigeons, or anything else, save the bare threads of her life together; but the old pigeon-cote was still here at the end of the shed, just above the door that opened on the lane. It wasn't anything very elaborate, just a sort of ceiling platform, boarded in, and with a little door in it. Standing on the ground he could just reach up to the door, and he opened it tentatively. Yes, it would serve excellently. It was instantly accessible at any time, either from the house or from the lane, and certainly Mrs. Tooler's long-forgotten shelter for her bygone pets was not a thing to excite suspicion—especially in view of the fact that there never would be any suspicion excited on any score as far as he was concerned!

He put on his shoes again, and, opening the shed door at the rear, stepped out into the lane—and a moment later was walking quickly along a side street away from the house.

Martin K. Tydeman's house was on the Hill. Dave Henderson smiled a little grimly at the airy lightness of the empty black bag in his hand. It would be neither as light nor as empty on the way hack—if he had any luck! He pulled the slouch hat he was wearing a little farther down over his eyes. A man carrying a bag wasn't anything out of the ordinary, or anything to attract particular attention—he was much more concerned in avoiding the chance of personal recognition. And, anyway, the bag was a necessity. If the money, for instance, was in customary banded sheaves of banknotes, and loose, how else could he carry it? Not in his pockets—and he couldn't very well make a parcel of them in Tydeman's library! Of course, the bank might have made up a sealed package of the whole, but even then a sealed package would have to be kept out of sight.

The slouch hat was drawn down still a little lower, and by the less frequented streets Dave Henderson made his way along. At the expiration of some twenty minutes he had emerged, a block away, on the street upon which the millionaire's home fronted. The hurried pace was gone now, and he dropped into a leisurely and nonchalant saunter. It was a very select neighborhood. There was little or no traffic, and the majority of the houses possessed, to a greater or less extent, their own grounds. Tydeman's house, for example, was approached by a short driveway that was flanked on both sides by a high and thick hedge. Dave Henderson nodded his head complacently. He had pictured that driveway a dozen times on the run up from Stockton, and particularly he had pictured that hedge! It was a most convenient hedge! And it was exceedingly thoughtful of Martin K. Tydeman, Esquire, to have provided it! If one crouched low enough there was nothing, unless some one were especially on the watch, to prevent one reaching the library windows at the side-rear of the house, and of accomplishing this without the slightest chance of being seen.

He was close to the driveway entrance now, and his eyes swept narrowly up and down the street. For the moment there appeared to be no one in sight—and, with a quick side-step, he slipped suddenly in from the street under the shelter of the hedge.

He moved swiftly now, running, half bent over. It was a matter of but a few seconds—and now, darting across the driveway where it branched off to circle around to the front entrance, he gained the side wall of the house, and crouched, listening intently, beneath the window of the library.

A minute passed, another—there was no sound. He raised himself guardedly then to an upright position, pressing close against the wall, but keeping well back at one side of the window. The window sill was shoulder high, and now, edging forward inch by inch, he obtained a diagonal glance through the pane. The room, as far as he could see, for the portières within were but partially drawn, was unoccupied. It was what he had counted upon. Tydeman, if the millionaire were following his usual custom, was at dinner, and the dining room was on the other side of the house. No one of the household, either family or servants, would ordinarily have any occasion to be in the library at this hour. Ordinarily! A glint came into the dark eyes, and the eyes narrowed as in a dogged, uncompromising challenge—and then the shoulders lifted in a debonair shrug. Well, that was the chance he took! He was gambling anyhow!

His fingers crept to the window-sash, and tested it quietly. It would not move. Whether it was locked above or not, he did not know—the slight pressure that he was able to exert from the outside was at least not sufficient to lift it—but the improvised steel jimmy would quickly remedy that defect. He worked hurriedly now. The Western summer evenings were long and it was still light, and every minute he stood there was courting discovery. The edge of the chisel slipped in between the sill and the window-sash, and with the leverage the window was raised an inch or two. His question was answered.

It had not been locked at the top.

And now his fingers came into play again—under the window-sash. There was not a sound. The window went up easily and silently; and with a lithe, agile spring Dave Henderson swung himself up over the sill, dropped with a soft *pad* to the floor, and stood motionless, shrouded in one of the portières.

The room was empty. The door leading from the library, he could see as he peered out, was closed. From the other side of the door, muffled, there came a laugh, the murmur of voices, indeterminate little sounds. The set, straight lips relaxed a little. The way was quite clear. The chances in his favor were mounting steadily. The family was undoubtedly at dinner.

He made no sound as he stepped quickly now across the room. The rich, heavy pile of the velvet rug beneath his feet deadened his footfalls. And now he reached the massive flat-topped desk that stood almost in the center of the room. It was the most likely place, the natural place, for Tydeman to leave the money. If it was not here—again there came that debonair shrug—well then, he would look further—upstairs in Tydeman's bedroom, if necessary—or anywhere else, if necessary. One thing only was certain, and that was that, having started on the job, he would get the money, or they would get him—if he couldn't fight his way out. It was quite natural! Of course, he would do that! What else would he do? He had always done that! He had been brought up to it, hadn't he? Win or lose—he had always played win or lose. Cold feet and bet hedging was piker stuff—and that was in Bookie Skarvan's line, too, not his!

Keen, alert, his ears were sentinels against the slightest external sound. He was gnawing now in a sort of grim impatience at his lower lip, as he pulled open, drawer after drawer. Strange how his mind worked! The slickest crook in the U. S. A., they had said he would make. Well, perhaps he would, but, even so, it neither allured nor interested him. This was his first job—and his last. There was enough in this to see him through for the rest of his life. It wouldn't have been worth the risk otherwise, and he wouldn't have tackled it. Once East, and he could pretend to amass money little by little until no one would be surprised that he was worth a hundred thousand dollars. That was the trouble with the bunch he knew! Some of them had brains, but they worked their brains overtime—on small stuff—and they had to come again—to keep the living expenses going—and sooner or later they came once too often—and then it was the jug for theirs!

He bent down suddenly to a lower drawer that was locked—the only one that he had found locked—and pried it open with the cold chisel.

"Sure!" said Dave Henderson imperturbably under his breath. "I guess this looks like it—what? And all done up in a nice little package, too! Even more thoughtful of 'em than I had hoped!"

He took out a parcel from the drawer. It was securely tied with stout cord, and heavily sealed with great blobs of red wax that bore a bank's impression. There could indeed be but little doubt concerning the contents; but Dave Henderson, nevertheless, made a slight opening in one end of the wrapping paper—and disclosed to view crisp piles of brand-new yellowbacks. He nodded pleasantly to himself, as he consigned the package to the little black hand-bag.

It was what he had come for—and got—one hundred thousand dollars.

He closed the drawer, and knelt for an instant to examine it. Closed, it did not show enough of the chisel's work to attract attention; open, it at once became very apparent that the drawer had been forced. He smiled in satisfaction. That was exactly what he wanted! When, a little later, he drove up in Skarvan's car to the front door and requested the money, it was only then that it was likely to be missed for the first time; and certainly under such circumstances the last man on earth against whom any suspicion could arise would be himself. He had told himself that before. Well, why not repeat it? It was true, wasn't it?

He retreated to the window, lowered himself to the ground, and regained the street. The thing was done. He was in possession of one hundred thousand dollars. There had not been the slightest difficulty or obstacle. He hummed an air under his breath, as he went along. It had been very simple—more so even than he had expected. It had been almost tame!

III.
THE TRAP

DAVE HENDERSON lost no time on his return journey. Within some fifteen or twenty minutes after leaving the residence of Mr. Martin K. Tydeman, he slipped into the lane at the rear of the shabby house on the shabby street that he called his home, and, entering the shed, closed the door softly behind him. Here, it was but the work of an instant to take the sealed package of banknotes from the black hand-bag, reach up, slide the package in through the little door of the old pigeon-cote, push the package over into one corner, cover it with the chaff and old straw with which, relics of bygone days of occupancy, the bottom of the pigeon-cote was littered, and to close the little door again.

He stooped then, and, unlacing his shoes quickly, removed them. He had only one thing to guard against now, and his alibi was perfect, his possession of one hundred thousand dollars secure. Tooler must not hear him entering the house. Tooler must be morally convinced that he, Dave Henderson, had never left the house. As soon as he got back to his room again, he would put on his shoes, call up to Tooler that he was going, and, with the empty black hand-bag, get into his car—and drive up to Martin K. Tydeman's!

"Some uproar!" confided Dave Henderson to himself. "When I ask old Martin K. to fill the li'l old bag, and he goes for the cash, there'll be— — —"

His mental soliloquy ended abruptly. He had opened the door noiselessly that led into the house, and was creeping without a sound along the hallway toward the door of his room at the front of the house—and now suddenly he stood rigid and motionless. Was it fancy, his imagination playing tricks upon him, or had Tooler come down-stairs? It seemed as though he had caught the sound of a lowered voice; and it seemed as though it had come from his own room there along the hall.

And then he smiled sarcastically at himself, and began to creep forward again. He had complained of the whole thing being tame, and now he was getting an attack of nerves when it was all over! How could he have heard a lowered voice through the closed door of his room? It was a physical impossibility. And Tooler, in any case, was not in the habit of talking to *himself*! Tooler never talked to any one if he could help it. The man always seemed to be nursing a perennial grudge that he hadn't been born a mute!

Dave Henderson's smile broadened at his little conceit—and the next instant vanished entirely, as his lips compressed suddenly into a hard, straight line. He had halted for the second time, hugged now close against the wall. The door of his room was *not* closed, and it was *not* Tooler—and it was *not* nerves. The door was slightly ajar; and the words came quite audibly; and the guarded voice had a haunting familiarity about it:

"Sure, I grabbed the train, an' Bookie stalled on being able to get old Tydeman on the long-distance until after the train—an' me on it—was on our way. Tumble?"

Dave Henderson did not move. Into his face there had come, set in a grayish-whiteness, a look that mingled stunned amazement and a gathering fury. He had recognized that voice now—and, in a flash, what that voice meant. It was Runty Mott, a miserable little red-haired rat of a race-course tout and hanger-on. Runty Mott—Bookie Skarvan! He remembered very well indeed that Bookie Skarvan could not get Tyde-man on the long distance until after the train was gone!

Another voice chuckled in malicious assent.

"Take it from me"—it was Runty Mott again—"Bookie Skarvan's got some head! *Some* head! He was wiped out all right, but I guess this puts him on Easy Street again. Fifty thousand for him, an' we split the rest. Bookie says to me, he says, 'If Dave goes an' gets that money, an' disappears afterwards,'-he says, 'it's a cinch, with the ragged reputation he's got, that he stole it, an' beat it for parts unknown, an' if them parts unknown,' he says, 'is a nice little mound of earth somewhere in the woods about six feet long an' four feet deep, due to Dave having collided with a blackjack, I guess the police'll be concluding after a while that Dave was smart enough to give 'em the slip, an' get away with the coin for keeps. You grab the train for 'Frisco, Runty,' he says, 'an' wise up Baldy Vickers to what I say. You got a good two hours,' he says, 'to set the stage up there before Dave blows in.'"

Came that malicious chuckle again.

"An' the poor boob went an' cracked the crib himself!" ejaculated Runty Mott's companion—and chuckled once more.

"Sure!" said Runty Mott. "Bookie called the turn all right on the guy's reputation—he was born a crook. Well, it makes it all the easier, don't it? It might have been harder to get him when we wanted him if he'd just gone up there an' got the money on the level. As it is now, he's ducking his nut, trying to play innocent, an' he comes back here to make a nice fresh start up to old Tydeman's again. Only he didn't reckon on any one trailing him from the minute he got out of his car! I guess we got him—good. Spike telephoned ten minutes ago that Dave was on his way back. If he comes in by the shed, the boys'll see he don't get out that way again; an' if he comes in by the front he'll get a peach of a welcome home! Tumble? This is where he croaks—an' no noise about it—an' you look out that you swing the lead so's you won't have to swing it twice. We can carry him out through the shed, an' get the mortal remains away in a car with no one the wiser." Runty Mott was chuckling now quite as maliciously as his companion. "Can't you see the headlines in the papers! 'Promising Young Man Succumbs to Temptation.' Say, it's the safest thing that was ever pulled, an' — — —" He stopped suddenly. A low whistle sounded from the street in front. "Keep quiet!" cautioned Runty Mott. "He's coming in by the lane."

It was silent in the house—only the silence began to pound and throb, and become a world of riot and dismay, and make confused noises of its own. Crouched against the wall, Dave Henderson raised his hand to his forehead—and drew his hand away damp with beads of moisture. There was an overmastering rage, a tigerish ferocity upon him; but his brain, most curiously, was deadly cold in its composure, and was working now swift as lightning flashes, keen, alert, shrewd, active. The words he had just heard meant—*murder*. His murder! The very callousness of the words but lent a hideous sincerity to them. Also he knew Baldy Vickers—if any further proof was needed. Baldy Vickers was a gangster to whom murder was a trade; and Baldy Vickers with stakes in the thousands, when he would have committed any crime in the decalogue with greedy haste for a hundred-dollar bill, meant—murder.

He was stooping now, silently, with the utmost caution, slipping on his shoes. And now from the rear there came a faint sound, a low creaking, like the stealthy rending of wood. He knew what it meant: They were forcing the shed door—to follow him in here—to cut off his escape, and to assist if necessary in the work those two were waiting to perform in his room, which he was expected to enter.

His face was set, drawn in lines as hard as chiselled marble. And yet he could have laughed—laughed out in the bitterest mockeries. The game was up—even if he saved his life. He would be "wanted" for the theft of one hundred thousand dollars. He could not cover that up now. If he escaped Baldy Vickers and his pack, he would still be a fugitive from the law. And, worse still, he would be a fugitive empty-handed, chased like a mangy dog who had risked his all for a bone—and had dropped the bone in his flight! God, if he could only get back there and get that money! But there were footsteps coming now—his straining ears could hear them—they were coming nearer and nearer to the door that opened from the shed into the rear of the house. Fury surged upon him again. Skarvan! Bookie Skarvan! It was Skarvan, not Baldy Vickers, not that miserable, red-headed rat of a tout in there, that he would have sold his soul at that instant to settle with. It was Skarvan, the dirty Judas, not the others, who, smug and safe, had planned his, Dave Henderson's, murder in deliberate, coldblooded hellishness! Well, if he, Dave Henderson, lived, Bookie Skarvan would pay... an eye for an eye... that was God's law, wasn't it?... well, as certainly as God lived, Bookie Skarvan would pay... it was another incentive for him, Dave Henderson, to live now....

The brain works with incredible speed. Those footsteps had not yet quite reached the door leading into the hall. His shoes were on now; and now his eyes fell upon the empty black hand-bag which, to facilitate his movements in putting on his shoes, he had set down on the floor beside him, and there came, flickering suddenly over the tight-pressed lips, a curious smile. He might not get through; there was only one way to get through—his car out there in front—a dash for it, though it was certain that there would be others of Baldy Vickers' crowd lurking out there, too; he might not get through, but if he did, there was a way, too, to save that hundred thousand dollars, or, at least, to keep it from Bookie Skarvan's claws!

Into the dark, narrowed eyes there came a glint of humor—but it was grim, deadly humor. They believed, of course, that he had the money in the bag, since he would be credited with no object for having already disposed of it, the natural presumption being that, with the money once in his possession, he would make a run for it—and they must continue to believe that—be given no reason to believe otherwise. It was dangerous, an added risk, but if he pretended to fall unwarily into their trap, pretended to be unconscious that there was, for instance, a blackjack waiting for him in his room, their suspicions would never be aroused—and neither they nor any one else would ever suspect for an instant that the money was not still in the bag as he dashed from the house.

He was creeping forward again silently toward the door of his room. That was logical. They would expect that. They would expect him to creep in silently and stealthily, on account of Tooler upstairs—or, if they did not exactly expect it, it would explain itself in that very logical way to them afterwards.

Behind him now the door leading into the hall was being opened cautiously, so cautiously that he would not have heard it if he had not been listening for it, expecting it. But he was just at the edge of the jamb of his own door now. He straightened up, his hand reached out for the door handle, and, still retaining his grasp upon the knob and standing in full view upon the threshold, he pushed the door open to the extent of his outstretched arm. The slickest crook in the United States, they had said he would make! He would try and not disappoint them!

His eyes swept the interior in a flash. A burly figure was crouched low down against the wall within striking distance of the door, an ugly looking, leather-covered baton in his hand—Runty Mott was not in sight. It was for the fraction of a second that he stood there—no more—not long enough for that crouching figure to recover from its surprise.

"My God!" gasped Dave Henderson, in well-simulated dismay; and, leaping backward, pulled shut the door, and dashed for the door to the street.

There was a yell from the room; it was echoed by a shout, and the pound of racing feet from the rear of the hall. Dave Henderson wrenched the front door open—and slammed it behind him. A figure rose before him on the steps. His left hand, free, swung with all his body weight behind it, swung with a terrific blow to the point of a scrubby jaw that blocked his way—and the figure crumpled, and went down with a crash on the doorstep.

It was but a yard to the curb and his car. He threw himself into the driver's seat. Pandemonium seemed loosed now from the house. Up above, a second-story window was raised violently, and Tooler's head was thrust out; below, the front door was flung wide open, and, the red-headed little tout in the van, four men were racing down the steps. And then, over the chorus of unbridled blasphemy, there rose a shrill yell from Runty Mott, which was answered from somewhere down the street.

The car, like a mad thing stung into action, shot forward from the curb. A hand grasped at the car's side, and was torn loose, its owner spinning like a top and pitching to the sidewalk. Dave Henderson flung a glance over his shoulder—and his jaws clamped suddenly hard together. Of course! That shout of Runty Mott's! But he had not underestimated either Baldy Vickers' cunning, or Baldy Vickers' resourcefulness. He had rather expected it. A big, powerful gray car had swept around the corner of the first street behind him, and, slowing for an instant, was picking up Runty Mott and his companions.

And now Dave Henderson laughed a little in a sort of grim savagery. Well, the race was on—and on to a finish! He knew the men too well in that gray car behind him to delude himself for a moment with any other idea. They wanted that little black hand-bag, and they would get it if they could; and they would get him, if they could, at any cost. Again he laughed, and now with the laugh came that debonair lift to his shoulders. His brain was working in swift, lightning flashes. The only hope of shaking them off was in the open—if his car were the faster. And if it were not the faster? Well then, yes—there was still a chance—on a certain road he knew, the road he had traveled that afternoon—if he could make that road. It was a chance, a gambling chance, but the best chance—to win all—or lose all. There would be no hedging—it was all or nothing—win or lose. They would not dare use their revolvers here in the city streets, they could only cling close on his trail; and neither of them here in the city could put the respective speed of their cars to the test—but in the open, in the country— —

He looked over his shoulder again. The big gray car, some fifty yards in the rear, held five passengers. He could distinguish the little red-haired tout in the front seat beside the man who was driving, a short, thick-set man, whose cap was pulled down over his eyes—Baldy Vickers. He nodded his head. His glance had measured something else. By leaning forward in his seat and crouching low over the wheel, the back of his car seemed high enough, not to afford him absolute immunity, but to afford him at least a fair chance of protection once he elected to invite the shots that would be fired from the car behind. *

Then the thought came that by one of a dozen ways, by leaping from his car as he turned a corner, for instance, and darting into a building, he might give his pursuers the slip here in the city. But it was no good! The game was up! He was not only a fugitive from Baldy Vickers and his wolves, he was a fugitive now from the police. And if by some such means as that he managed to give Baldy Vickers the slip, there was still the police—and with a police drag-net out he cut his chances of escape by better than half if he remained in the city. It would not be long now before Tydeman, in view of his, Dave Henderson's, non-appearance, would become aware of the theft; and, granting that he eluded Baldy Vickers, the gangster, eager for revenge, would be the first to curry favor with the police—Baldy Vickers had only to state that one of his pals saw him, Dave Henderson, crawling out through Tydeman's library window. There was nothing to it! The game was up—even if he saved his life. Thanks to Bookie Skarvan! His jaws clamped again, and the knuckles of his hands stood out in white knobs as they clenched in sudden passion on the wheel. Thanks to Bookie Skarvan! By God, that alone was worth living for—to settle with Bookie Skarvan!

Like some sinister, ominous thing, silently, attracting no attention from the passers-by, the big gray car maintained its distance fifty yards behind. That grim humor, deadly in its cold composure, was upon Dave Henderson again. He meant to be taken by neither Baldy Vickers, nor by the police; nor did he intend that a certain package containing one hundred thousand dollars in cash should fall into the hands of either Baldy Vickers or the police! Some day, even yet, he might find use for that particular package himself!

Block after block was traversed, corner after corner was turned, as Dave Henderson threaded his way through the streets, heading steadily for the outskirts of the city, and the road on which he had already traveled ninety miles that day. And fifty yards behind came on that big gray car. They were well content, no doubt—the occupants of that car! He was playing their game for them! He was playing the fool! In the city their hands were tied! Out in the country they would be free to do something more than merely follow silently behind him! Well, that was all quite true—perhaps! But out in the country, if he got away from them, he would not at least jump from the pot into the fire and have the police at his heels the very next instant; and, besides, there was that hundred thousand dollars! The further away he got from 'Frisco the more inviolate became Mrs. Tooler's old pigeon-cote!

Fifty yards! He glanced behind him again. It was still fifty yards—*start*. Well, fifty yards was fifty yards, and he might as well take it now. He was well in the outskirts, the houses were becoming scattered, an open road was ahead, and — —

He bent suddenly low over the wheel, and flung the throttle wide. The car leaped forward like a thoroughbred answering to the spur. There was a burst of yells from behind—and then silence, save for the rush of the wind, the creak of the swaying, lurching car, and the singing throb of the sixty horse-power engine, unleashed now, in full stride under the lash.

A mile, two miles—the speed was terrific. There was no sound from behind—just the roar of his own car in his ears. The houses were fewer now— it was the open country. Another mile! He was at his absolute maximum of speed now. He straightened up slightly, and shot a quick glance over his shoulder. The big gray car was fifty yards behind.

A shot rang out—and then a fusillade of them. He was low over the wheel again, his jaws set rigidly. Was it fifty yards? He was not sure, he was not sure but that it was less—he was only sure that it was not more.

The shots ceased for a moment. A car, coming in the opposite direction, had taken to the extreme edge of the road, half into the ditch. He had a flash of a woman's face, as he swept by—great dark eyes that stared out of a death-white face—a beautiful face even in its terror—it haunted him, that face.

A furious, sustained racketing, like a thousand echoes reverberating through a rocky, high-walled canon, stilled the roaring sweep of the wind, and the roaring of his car. He shot through the main street of a town like a meteor, and laughed out like a madman. A dog escaped by the fraction of an inch, and, tail down, scurried with a sharp yelp for the sidewalk; there was a dash for horses' heads at the curbs; people rushed to doorways and windows, peering out; women screamed; men yelled hoarsely; a fat woman, retreating wildly as she was about to cross the road, dropped a laden basket-to shake her fist in panic fury. It was kaleidoscopic—it was gone.

The shots came again. Another town was passed—still another. The big gray car was not fifty yards behind now—it was less than thirty—so near that now there came from time to time an exultant yell.

Dave Henderson's face was drawn, tense, its lines hard, sharp, strained; but in the dark eyes was still that smoldering light of grim, debonair humor. The race was almost at an end—he knew that now. He knew now that he could not shake off that gray streaking thing behind. It gained only by inches, they were well matched, the two cars, and it was a good race; but a few more miles would end it as those inches lengthened into feet and yards.

Well, then, since he could not escape this way, there was still the other way; and if that failed, too, in the last analysis he had a revolver in his pocket. But it was not likely to fail, that other way. He had banked on it almost from the moment he had made his escape from the Toolers' house. As between himself, Dave Henderson, and the hundred thousand dollars, Baldy Vickers, if Baldy Vickers could not get both, would very obviously and very earnestly prefer the hundred thousand dollars. His lips tightened in a sort of merciless irony. Well, Baldy Vickers would have a chance at least to exercise his preference! A few miles farther on, just a few miles, the road, in a wooded tract, made an abrupt, almost right-angled, turn. He remembered that turn— and he had banked on that, too, if by then speed alone should have failed him! He could hold out that much longer. The inches did not accumulate fast enough to overtake him before he reached that turn—he was not afraid of that—but every one of those inches made of him a better target.

He was motionless, like a figure carved in stone, as he hung over the wheel. The car rocked to the furious pace—but it did not swerve. A swerve meant the gift of another of those inches to that gray thing behind. He held the center of the road, driving with all the craft and cunning that he knew, his arms like steel bands, his fingers locked in an iron grip upon the wheel.

He did not look behind him now. It was useless. Nearer and nearer the gray car was creeping up, he was well aware of that; but, also, nearer and nearer came that wooded stretch ahead. He could see it now—a mile down the road. But a mile at this rate of speed did not take long to cover.

The shouts grew more exultant behind him; the shots came thicker. Murderers! The angry hum of a bullet past his ear roused a fury in his soul that was elemental, primal, and he cursed now under his breath. Murderers... six feet of earth... in cold blood... or if they winged him, the car, amuck, slanting from the road to up-end itself, would do their bloody work for them... Bookie Skarvan... some day, if he lived through this... Bookie Skarvan... it was strange that all their shots had missed... even if the back of his car was a protection... they wouldn't have many more chances... the woods and the turn of the road were just ahead now, and...

There was a crash, the splintering of glass, and a bullet shattered the wind-shield scarcely a hair's-breadth to the right of his head. A demoniacal yell of triumph went up from behind. They had him now—and, with him, one hundred thousand dollars! Again that grimace of merciless irony was twisting at Dave Henderson's lips. It was the psychological moment, not only because that wood was just ahead, but because, realizing that his chances were desperate now, he would logically be expected to sacrifice anything— even that hundred thousand dollars—to save himself.

Something, like the flick of a fiery lash, bringing a hot, burning sensation, was laid suddenly across his leg above the knee. It did not hurt very much—a bullet deflected probably from the rim of the steering wheel—but they had hit him at last. He laughed savagely—and snatched at the empty black hand-bag, and hurled it with all his might far out across the side of the road.

A chorused yell answered his act. He looked back—and laughed again. It had not failed! They were stopping. Wolves! Again he laughed. And like wolves with slavering fangs they were after their prey! It would give him a minute, perhaps two—but that was enough!

The car swept on, and rounded the turn, and the trees blotted out the view of the road behind. He jammed on the brakes, slewed the car half around, full across the road, and leaping from it, dashed in amongst the trees. The foliage was thick. He ran on. He was safe for the moment here in the woods; and presently it would be dark, and he would make across country to the railroad, and work his way East.

The roar of the gray car coming on again at full speed reached him. He laughed as he ran, harshly, without mirth. They wanted vengeance now— vengeance because he had not let them murder him! Well, he did not mean to disappoint them! He had disappointed them once—with an empty bag! He would not disappoint them again! It was perfectly logical that there should be—vengeance. There was hardly room to stop that car around the turn!

A wild cry, echoed by another, and still another, shrill in terror, rang out from the road over the roar of the speeding car—and then a terrific crash—a scream—silence.

He had stopped mechanically. The wolves wouldn't bother him any more. It wasn't Baldy Vickers now, that smash would have taken the fight out of Baldy Vickers, if it hadn't taken anything more—it was the police. He clenched his hands in sudden, passionate fury. He was safe from Baldy Vickers here in the woods, anyhow; but, for all that, he had played and lost. He was a hunted man now. He was not whining, he had played and lost—only he had played against stacked cards. The face of Bookie Skarvan rose before him, and his hands clenched the tighter. He swept a knotted fist fiercely across his eyes. What was the use of that—now! Not now! He had something else besides Bookie Skarvan to think of now; there was the police, and—yes—his leg! It was burning hot, and it hurt now. He glanced downward. His trouser-leg was soaked with blood. His teeth gritted together—and he plunged on again through the woods.

IV.
TWO THOUSAND DOLLARS'
REWARD—DEAD OR ALIVE

THREE days, and four nights—was that it?

It was hard to remember. It hadn't even been easy to get the little food he had had; it had been impossible to get his wound dressed, save in the rough, crude, wholly inadequate way in which he had been able to dress it himself—with pieces torn from his shirt and underclothing. They had hunted him like a mad beast. Those cursed police placards were everywhere! Everywhere! TWO THOUSAND DOLLARS' REWARD—DEAD OR ALIVE. The police had acted quickly, quicker than he had ever thought they could act! Joe Barjan, Lieutenant Barjan of the 'Frisco plain-clothes squad, would have had a hand in this. Queer! He'd given Barjan tips on the races, straight tips, honest tips, in the old days—not this kind of a race. Barjan and he used to get along all right together. Funny business!

It was dark, pitch black—save only for a moon-ray-that flickered and danced across the flooring of the bouncing, jolting boxcar, and that came in through the half-open, rattling door. He should have closed that door more tightly when he had crawled in. It had got loose again. Well, no matter! It couldn't do any harm for the moment, except for the noise it made, a noise that beat a devil's tattoo on his aching head. But that didn't matter, either. It wasn't as bad as the clatter and jangle and damnable everlasting creaking of the car—and he couldn't stop the car from creaking anyhow. When the train began to slow down for the next stop, he would go over and shut the door again. It was an effort to move—uselessly—before he had to.

Three days, and four nights—was that it? It was hard to remember. But he must have put many miles, hundreds of them, between himself and 'Frisco. And he had lived through hell—alternately beating his way in some boxcar such as this, and hiding in the woods, or where he could. But the boxcars were mostly for the night—mostly for the night—it was safer. Damn those police circulars, and that reward! Every one was on the hunt for him—every one—two thousand dollars. How far East would he have to go and not find one of the haunting things nailed upon a station wall! The drag-net *couldn't* reach out all the way—there was a limit—a limit to everything.

His brain caught at the last phrase—a limit to everything. His lips were cracked and dry, and he touched them with his tongue.

"No!" He shook his head, whispering hoarsely a dogged defiance. "No limit—win or lose—all the Way—no limit."

Through hell! The whole countryside was hell! They wouldn't even let him buy food. Well, he had stolen it—what he had had. They had nearly trapped him the second time he had tried to buy food—the night following his escape—in a little grocery store—a big, raw-boned, leering man who ran the place—the man hadn't got the two thousand dollars' reward—no, not much of a fight—he had knocked the man out, and run for it—that was all. After that he hadn't tried to buy any food—he had stolen it—only he hadn't stolen very much. It was hard to get. It was even hard to get water, a drink of water sometimes. It didn't run everywhere. There weren't ponds and lakes and rivers everywhere. He couldn't ask anybody for a glass of water. There had been a ditch that afternoon. It had been muddy and slimy. Since then there had been nothing. He would have sold his soul for a few of those drops that had splashed in lavish abundance from the spout of the water-tank at the station earlier that night when he had crawled into the car here—he had seen the fireman on the back of the tender manipulating the spout, and he had heard the water splash.

He spoke hoarsely again.

"I'm shot full of fever, that's what I am," he said. "I'm shot full of it."

Sprawled out on the floor of the car, he shifted his position a little; and, tight-locked though his lips were, there came an irrepressible moan of pain. God, how his eyes burned; how hot his head was, and how it throbbed and ached! The throbs kept devilish time, marching time, like the tramp of feet to the beat of the drum, to that ceaseless, brutal throbbing in his leg. He hadn't looked at his leg to-day—it had been bad enough yesterday. What was the use! He couldn't do anything. He hadn't even any water—there wasn't any use dressing it with that slimy, muddy stuff he had drunk. It would have to get better—or worse.

He touched his lips with his tongue again. There didn't seem to be any moisture on his tongue; it was thick and big in his mouth, so it couldn't be dried up, but there wasn't any moisture on it. Would the car never stop its jolting, and that infernal *clack-clack, clackety-clack!* There was abominable pain in every jolt, it seemed to shake his leg the way a mold of jelly would shake;

it seemed to shake and vibrate to the bone itself. Sometimes it brought nausea and faintness.

Perhaps there *was* a limit! He had lain exhausted for a long time, bathed in sweat from his exertions, when he had climbed and clawed his way into the car. He remembered now—that was why he hadn't shut the door tightly. He must be getting pretty near his limit to go down like a lump of putty just through climbing from the track into a boxcar. He clenched his hands in fierce denial. No! No limit—it was win or lose—no hedging—it was all the way—even against stacked cards.

Stacked cards! The pain was gone momentarily in a sweep of fury that brought him up from his back to sway like a pendulum upon his elbows with the swaying of the car. He owed Bookie Skarvan for this. He owed it to Bookie Skarvan that he was a hunted, wounded thing. He owed every thrust of pain that caught at and robbed him of his breath to Bookie Skarvan. He owed it to Bookie Skarvan that he was an outcast for the rest of his life. He owed Bookie Skarvan for as damnable and callous an attempt to murder him as was ever hatched in a human brain. And they had left Bookie Skarvan to him! His laugh rang loud and hollow, a bitter, sinister sound, unbridled in its deadly passion, through the car. They had left Bookie Skarvan to him! It was good to think of that—very good, like a drink of water, icy water, with the beads frosting on the long glass. They had left Bookie Skarvan to him. Well, he would not change the story they had told! He would promise them that. Not by a word! They had left Bookie Skarvan to him!

He knew the story. Last night in a switchman's shanty in a railroad yard he had found a newspaper—the story was there. Baldy Vickers and Runty Mott, who had been sitting in the front seat of the big gray car, were in the hospital from the smash; the others had not been much hurt. Bookie Skarvan's car had been identified, what there was left of it, and that formed an implicating link between him, Dave Henderson, and Baldy Vickers' crowd. Runty Mott and Vickers, being forced therefore to explain, had told a story that was almost true—but they hadn't split on Bookie Skarvan—they had left Bookie Skarvan out of it. The story was enough of a confession, smacked enough of State's evidence to let them out of any criminal proceedings, even if there had been any really definite charge that could be brought against them. They hadn't stolen the money! The story rang true because it was *almost* true—only they had left Bookie Skarvan out of it.

Runty Mott, according to the newspaper, had been the spokesman. Runty said he had overheard Bookie Skarvan and Dave Henderson at the race-course, when they were making arrangements to get the money from Tydeman. He, Runty Mott, had taken the train for 'Frisco, and had put it up to

Baldy Vickers. Then they had followed Dave Henderson, meaning to take the money from him the first chance they got. But Dave Henderson had handed them a jolt by crawling in through Tydeman's library window, and stealing it himself. After that they had figured the easiest place to grab the coin was in Dave Henderson's room, when he sneaked back there with the black hand-bag. And Dave Henderson had walked right into their trap, only they hadn't heard him coming any more than he, in turn, had been wise to the fact that they were there, and in the showdown he had managed to jump through the front door and reach his car. He had the money in the black hand-bag with him. They had chased him in the other car that the police had found smashed up, and had nearly got him, when he threw the black hand-bag out of the car. They stopped to pick it up, and found out the trick he had played on them. The hand-bag was empty; he still had the money in his car. They took up the chase again—and crashed into the other machine where Dave Henderson had left it blocking the road just around a sharp turn.

Dave Henderson's laugh rang with a devil's mirth through the boxcar again. That was all! They hadn't split on a pal. They had left the pal to him. Runty Mott had told the story—and Runty Mott's story went! He, Dave Henderson, wouldn't change it! They didn't know, and Bookie Skarvan didn't know, *that he knew*. They had left Bookie Skarvan to him—and they had made Mrs. Tooler's pigeon-cote as safe as a vault.

The slue of the car on a curve flung him with a savage wrench from his elbows to his back again, and he groaned in agony. Red flashes danced before his eyes, and nausea came once more, and faintness—and he lay for a long time still. It seemed as though he no longer had any power to move; even the pain seemed to have become subordinate to a physical sense of weakness and impotence that had settled upon him. His head grew dizzy and most strangely light.

There came the blast of the engine whistle, the grind and thump of buffer beams, the shriek of the brake-shoes biting at the wheel tires, the sickening sensation of motion being unsmoothly checked. His mind did not grasp the significance of this for a moment—and then with a frantic effort he struggled to his feet.

The door! The car door! He must close it—he must close the door. The train was stopping. If any one passed by outside and saw the door open, and looked in, he was caught. He was too weak to fight any more; too weak to run any more. He must close the door.

He could not stand. The car swayed, and bumped, and lurched too much! No one could stand with the car jolting around in circles like that! He dropped to his knees. He could crawl, then. The door! The car door! It must be closed—even if he had to drag himself to it.

It wasn't far to the door—just a few feet. It was the pain in his leg that made him faint, but he could get that far—just to the door. He touched his lips with his tongue again. They weren't dry now, his lips, and there was a curious taste upon them, and they hurt. They tasted of blood. That was funny! His teeth must have sunk into his lips somehow. But he was almost at the door now—yes, he could reach it now. Only he couldn't close it when he was lying flat down like this. He would have to get up—on his knees at least.

His hand swept across his eyes, and pressed fiercely upon his forehead. The moon-ray wavered in through the door in jagged, glancing streaks—he had to shut that moon-ray out—to make it black here in the car. Strange! It was growing black now, even though he had not shut the door—perhaps it was a cloud—the moon passing behind a cloud. His body seemed to sway, to be out of control, and his knees, instead of balancing him, crumpled suddenly beneath him, pitching him forward, face downward, on the floor of the car—and something seemed to snap inside his head, and it was black, all blackness.

Repose, comfort, ineffable luxuriousness, something soft and soothing supporting his body, and a freedom from the excruciating, unbearable, intolerable pain that he had been enduring! He was dreaming! He dared not open his eyes. It was a dream. If he opened his eyes he would dispel the illusion, and the pain would come again.

It seemed as though he had been upon a great journey that was crowded with a multitude of strange, fantastic scenes and happenings. He could not remember them all distinctly; they jumbled together in his memory—the orphan school, the race-track, Square John Kelly and three thousand dollars in the Pacific Coral Saloon on the Barbary Coast, all conglomerated into one.

He remembered only one thing distinctly, and that was because it had happened so often. He was in a great, gloomy forest, and always just ahead of him was Bookie Skarvan. He did not know why it was, but he could always see Bookie Skarvan in the darkness, though Bookie Skarvan could not see him. And yet he could never quite reach that fat, damnable figure that kept flitting around the trees. Bookie Skarvan was not running away, because Bookie Skarvan did not even know that he was being followed—and yet Bookie Skarvan always eluded him.

If he was dreaming now, it was at least a very vivid dream. He remembered. He had just fallen unconscious on the floor of the car. Well, then, he must get the door shut, if he was to escape. Yes, the pain might come again if he moved, it would take all his will power to shatter this blessed restfulness, and he was still very tired; but he had no choice—it was win or lose—all the way—no limit.

He opened his eyes. He did not understand at first; and then he told himself quite simply that of course he could not still be lying on the floor of that lurching car, and at the same time feel these soft things all around his body. He was in bed—in a white bed, with white covers—and there was a screen around his bed. And around the corner of the screen he could see other beds—white beds with white covers. It must be a hospital ward. There was some one sitting in a chair beside the foot of his bed—no, not a nurse; it was a man. The man's face for the moment was turned slightly away. He studied the face. It seemed familiar. His eyes opened a little wider. Yes, it was familiar! A cry surged upward from his soul itself, it seemed—and was choked back. His hands, clenched fiercely, relaxed. There came a queer smile to twist his lips.

The man at the foot of the bed was looking at him now. It was Barjan, Lieutenant Joe Barjan, of the 'Frisco plain-clothes squad.

The man spoke:

"Hello, Dave!"

"Hello, Joe!"

There was silence.

The other spoke again:

"Tough luck, Dave! Sorry to grab you like this. Feeling better?"

"Some," said Dave Henderson.

Barjan nodded his head.

"It was touch and go with you," he said. "Bad leg, bad fever—you've been laying like a dead man since the night they found you in the freight car." Dave Henderson made no reply. There wasn't any door to shut now, and he wouldn't have to move now... until he went away with Joe there... back to 'Frisco. He wasn't squealing... stacked cards... a new deal with a new pack perhaps... some day... he wasn't squealing... but he couldn't fight any more... not now... he couldn't fight... he was too weak.

"I've been hanging around two or three days waiting for you to come out of dreamland, so's I could ask you a question," said Barjan pleasantly. "Come across, Dave! Where'd you put that little package you had with you when you beat it from the car, and handed Baldy the broken ribs?"

Dave Henderson smiled. He was very weak, miserably weak, it was an effort to talk; but his brain, because there wasn't any pain, was clear—clear enough to match Barjan's.

"Come again?" said Dave Henderson.

"Aw, can that!" A tinge of impatience had crept into the police officer's voice. "We got the whole story. Runty Mott and Baldy Vickers opened up—wide."

"I read about them in the papers," said Dave Henderson. "They said enough without me butting in, didn't they?"

"You mean," said Barjan sharply, "that you won't come across?"

"What's the use!" said Dave Henderson. "Their story goes, doesn't it? I wouldn't spoil a good story. They said I took the money, and if you believe them, that goes. I'm through."

"No good!" snapped Barjan. "You'd better open up on where that money is, or it will go hard with you!"

"How hard?" inquired Dave Henderson.

"I dunno," said Barjan grimly. "Five years."

Five years! How long was five years? His mind was growing tired now, too, like his body. He forced himself to the effort of keeping it active. It was a long way from where Baldy Vickers had broken his ribs, and where they thought he, Dave Henderson, had last had the money, to Mrs. Tooler's old pigeon-cote! And a hundred thousand dollars in five years was twenty thousand dollars a year—salary, twenty thousand dollars a year. Five years! It was win or lose, wasn't it? No hedging! Five years—five years before he could settle with Bookie Skarvan!

He spoke aloud unconsciously:

"It's a long time to wait."

"You bet your life, it is!" said Barjan. "Don't fool yourself! It's a hell of a long time in the pen! And if you think you could get away with the wad when you get out again, you've got another think coming, too! Take it from me!"

"I wasn't thinking about the money," said Dave Henderson slowly. "I was thinking about that story." He closed his eyes. The room was swimming around him. Five years—chalked up to Bookie Skarvan! His hand on the coverlet clenched, and raised and fell impotently to the coverlet again. He was conscious that Barjan was leaning over the bed to catch his words, because he wasn't speaking very loud. "I was thinking it was a long time to wait—to get even."

A woman's voice seemed to come drifting out of space... that would be the nurse, of course... a woman's voice....

"That's all very well! You may be a police officer, but you had no business to make him talk. He is not strong enough to stand any excitement, and——"

The voice drifted off into nothingness.

BOOK II.
FIVE YEARS LATER

I.
CONVICT NO. 550

FROM somewhere far along the iron gallery, a guard's boot-heel rang with a hollow, muffled, metallic sound;' from everywhere, as from some strange, inceptive cradle, the source out of which all sounds emanated, and which, too, was as some strange sounding-board that accentuated each individual sound as it was given birth, came a confused, indeterminate, scarcely audible rupture of the silence that never ceased its uneasy, restless murmur. It was like water simmering in a caldron—only the water was a drear humanity, and the caldron was this gray-walled, steel-barred place.

A voice, low, quite inarticulate, falling often to little more than a whisper, mumbled endlessly on. That was the old bomb-thrower, old Tony Lomazzi, the lifer, in the next cell. The man was probably clinging to the bars of his door, his face thrust up against them, talking, talking, talking—always talking to himself. He did not disturb anybody. Everybody was used to it; and, besides, the man did not talk loudly. One even had to listen attentively to catch the sound of his voice at all. It had become a habit, second nature; the man was incorrigible. Presently the guard would come along, and perhaps rap the old man on the knuckles; after that Lomazzi would retire to his cot quite docilely. It had been that way night after night, week after week, month after month, year after year.

Dave Henderson laid the prison-library book, that he had been fingering absently, down on the cot beside him. It was still early evening in early summer, and there was still light in the cell, though hardly enough to read by; but he had not been reading even when there had been better light. His mind was too active to-night. And now there was a curiously wistful smile on his face. He would miss that stumbling, whispering voice. A most strange thing to miss! Or was it the old man himself whom he would miss? Not to-morrow, not even next week, there still remained sixty-three days—but sixty-three days, with all the rest of the five years behind them, gone, served, wiped out, were like to-morrow; and, as against a lifer's toll, it was freedom, full born and actually present. Yes, he would miss Tony Lomazzi. There was a bond between the old man and himself. In almost the first flush of his entry into the penitentiary he had precipitated a fight amongst his fellow convicts on account of old Tony. Two of them had gone into the hospital, and he, Dave Henderson, had gone into the black hole.

He sat suddenly bolt upright on his cot. He had not forgotten the horror of those days of solitary confinement. He was not likely to forget them—the silence, the blackness. The silence that came at last to scream and shriek at him in myriad voices out of the blackness until he was upon the verge of screaming and shrieking back in raving, unhinged abandon; the blackness that was as the blackness of the pit of hell, and that came at last to be peopled with hideous phantom shapes that plagued him until, face down on his cot, he would dig his fists into his eyes that he might not see—the blackness! His hands clenched hard as the memory of it surged upon him; but a moment later he laughed a little under his breath. It had been bad, bad enough; but he wasn't there *now*, was he? Old Tony hadn't deluged him with any excessive thanks. The old man had simply called him a fool—but there had been a difference after that. On the march out from the cells, old Tony was always the man behind him, and old Tony's shoulder touch in the lock-step wasn't as perfunctory as it had been before. And there had been years of that. Yes, he would miss old Tony Lomazzi!

Instinctively he turned his head in the direction of that voice that whispered through the bars of the adjoining cell, and his face, lean and hard, softened, and, tinging the dead-white prison pallor, a flush crept into his cheeks. The man was a lifer. A lifer! God, he knew what that meant! Five years of a living hell had taught him that. Five years that were eternities piled upon eternities, and they were only a short step along the path toward the only goal to which a lifer could look forward—death!

Yes, he knew! The massed eternities, that were called five years by those who walked outside in the sunlight, where men laughed, and women smiled, and children played, had taught him why old Tony Lomazzi clung to the bars and whispered.

Five years! Was it only five years since he had stood in the dock in that courtroom, and the judge had sentenced him to—five years? The scene was vivid and distinct enough! Even the ages that spanned the gulf between the now and then could not efface that scene, nor dim it, nor rob it of a single stark and naked detail. Tydeman had been there—Martin K. Tyde-man, that prince of royal sports. Tydeman was about the only man in that courtroom whose presence had made him uneasy; and yet Tydeman, too, was the only man in that courtroom who had been friendly toward him. It was probably due to the old millionaire's plea for leniency that the sentence had been five years, and not ten, or fifteen, or twenty, or whatever it might be that the erect, spare little figure on the bench, with the thin, straight lips, had had the right to pronounce. And Tydeman was dead now.

Dave Henderson stirred uneasily on the edge of the cot. He drew his hand slowly across his eyes. He had wished from the start, hadn't he, that it might have been some one else rather than Martin K. Tydeman? But it *had* been Tydeman's money, and the hundred thousand dollars alone was all that had counted, and Tydeman was dead now, had been dead two or three years, and on that score that ended it—didn't it?

The dark eyes, that had wavered abstractedly around the cell, narrowed suddenly, and from their depths a smoldering fire seemed to leap as suddenly into flame. But there was another score that was not ended! Bookie Skarvan! Baldy Vickers, Runty Mott and the rest of Baldy's gang had lied speciously, smoothly, ingeniously and with convincing unanimity. They had admitted the obvious—quite frankly—because they could help themselves. They had admitted that their intention had been to steal the hundred thousand dollars themselves. But they hadn't stolen it—and that let them out; and they proved that he, Dave Henderson, had—and that saved their own hides. Also they had not implicated Bookie Skarvan.

Their story had been very plausible! Runty Mott "confessed" that, on the morning of the crime, he had overheard Bookie Skarvan and Dave Henderson making their arrangements at the race course to get Tydeman to put up the money to tide Bookie Skarvan over the crisis. He, Runty Mott, had then left at once for San Francisco, put the deal up to Baldy Vickers and Baldy's gang, and they had waited for Dave Henderson to arrive. Naturally they had watched their proposed prey from the moment of his arrival in the city, intending to rob him when the money was in his possession and before he got back to the race course that night; but instead of Tydeman turning the money over to Dave Henderson, as they had expected, Dave Henderson had completely upset their plans by stealing the money himself, and this had resulted in the prisoner's attempted getaway, and the automobile chase which represented their own efforts to intercept him.

The dark eyes were almost closed now, but the gleam was still there— only now it was half mocking, half triumphant, and was mirrored in a grim smile that flickered across his lips. He had not denied their story. To every effort to obtain from him a clue as to the whereabouts of the stolen money, he had remained as mute and unresponsive as a stone; cajolery, threats, the hint of lighter sentence if restitution were made, he had met with silence. He had not even employed a lawyer. The court had appointed one. He had refused to confer with the lawyer. The lawyer had entered a perfunctory plea of "not guilty."

The grim smile deepened. There had been very good reasons why he had refused to open his lips at that trial—three of them. In the first place, he was guilty; in the second place, there was Bookie Skarvan, who had no suspicion that he, Dave Henderson, knew the truth that lay behind Runty Mott's story; and in the third place—there was one hundred thousand dollars. There was to be no hedging. And he had not hedged! That was his creed. Well, it had paid, hadn't it, that creed? The hundred thousand dollars was almost his now—there were only sixty-three days left. He had bought it with his creed, bought it with five years wrung in blood and sweat from his life, five years that had turned his soul sick within him. He had paid the price. Five years of sunlight he had given for that hundred thousand dollars, five years that had sought to bring the slouch of slavery and subjugation to his shoulders, a cringe into his soul, a whimper into his voice, and——

He was on his feet, his hands clenched until his knuckles cracked. And he stood there for a long time staring at the barred door, and then suddenly he shrugged his shoulders, and relaxed, and laughed in a low, cool way. But he had won, hadn't he, even on that score? It was not often that the penitentiary would do for a man what this devil's hole had done for him! He had entered it a crude, unpolished assistant to a crooked bookmaker, his education what he had acquired before he had run away from an orphan school at ten; and he could leave the place now, given the clothes and the chance, and pass anywhere for a gentleman—thanks in a very large measure to Charlie Millman.

Dave Henderson began to pace slowly up and down his cell. Millman had never understood, of course, just why he had had so apt a pupil. He had never explained to Millman that it had been from the very beginning his plan to rise to the level of a hundred thousand dollars that was waiting for him when he got out! Millman knew, of course, what he, Dave Henderson, was up for; but that was about all. And Millman had perhaps, and very naturally so, attributed his, Dave Henderson's, thirst for polish and education to the out-cropping of the inherent good that in him was, the coming to the surface finally of his better nature. And so Millman, up for two years, had proved a godsend, for there hadn't been much progress made along the lines of "higher education" until Millman had come into the prison.

He liked Millman; and somehow Millman seemed to like him. A gentleman from the tip of his fingers was Millman—and he took his medicine like a gentleman. Millman wasn't the name that was entered on the prison books—there it was Charlie Reith.

It was strange that Millman should have given him his confidence; he could never quite understand that, except that it had seemed to come gradually as their friendship grew, until finally it was almost the basis of that friendship itself. He had come to trust Millman as he had never trusted any other man, and he had come to believe in Millman as the soul of courtesy and honor. And yet he had not been quite as open with Millman as Millman had been with him; he had not spread his cards upon the table, and Millman had never asked to see them; and somehow he liked the man all the better for that. It was not that he did not trust the other; it was because his confidence was not the sort of confidence to give to an *honest* man—and Millman was honest. There was a queer twist to it all!

Dave Henderson smiled grimly again. It wouldn't be *fair* to make an honest man a party to the secret of where that money was, for instance, would it—to make an honest man an accomplice after the fact? And there was no doubt of Millman's clean-cut, courageous honesty. The prison stripes could not change that!

He knew Millman's story: A nasty bit of work on the Barbary Coast, and viciously clever. Millman, a stranger in the city, and en route for a long trip through the South Seas, had been inveigled by a woman's specious plea for help into a notorious resort on the night in which a much-wanted member of the underworld was hard put to it to give the police the slip—and Millman had unsuspectingly made himself the vehicle of the other's escape.

The details were sordid; the woman's story pitifully impressive; and Millman's chivalry had led him, innocent of the truth, to deprive the plain-clothes squad of the services of one of their best men for the period of several months—while one of the slickest counterfeiters in the United States, and the woman with him, had made good their getaway. It didn't look innocent in the eyes of the police, and Millman had stood for two years—convicted as Charles Reith—to save the name of Charles Millman, and those that belonged to him back in New York. He had been found in a very unsavory place, and no amount of explanation could purify those surroundings. Millman had never said so in so many words, but he was buying a little woman's peace of mind back there in New York with two years' hard labor. And meanwhile he was supposed to be somewhere on a trading schooner in the out-of-the-way isles of the Pacific, or something like that—maybe it was Borneo on a hunting trip—he, Dave Henderson, didn't remember just precisely how the other had fixed it. It didn't matter! The point was that they had made Millman one of the convict librarians in the prison, and Millman had become his tutor and his friend. Well, Millman was another he would miss. The day after to-morrow Millman's time was up, and Millman would be gone. He was glad for Millman's sake.

Five steps and a half from the rear wall of the cell to the steel-barred door, and five and a half steps back again—over and over. He was unaccountably restless to-night both in body and mind. He had spent his five years, less the time that had been manumitted for good conduct, and less the sixty-three days that still remained, not altogether to his own disadvantage in an educational sense. In that respect he was satisfied he was now ready to leave the prison and make the most of that hundred thousand dollars—not as a "raw skate," blowing it to the winds, but as one who would make it pay dividends on those five years of servitude that represented its purchase price. It was enough, that amount, for the rest of his life, if he took care of it. It meant comfort, independence, luxury. He didn't want any more. That was the amount he had already fixed and decided upon even before the opportunity had come to take it. It was his first job—but it was equally his last. And it was his last because he had waited until, at the first attempt, he had got all he wanted. He wasn't coming back to the penitentiary any more. He was going out for good—in sixty-three days.

Sixty-three days! He wanted no piker, low-brow life at the end of those sixty-three days when he got out. He had had enough of that! That was one reason why he had taken the money—to pitch that one seamy room at Tooler's and the rotten race-track existence into the discard, and he was ready now, equipped, to play the part he meant to play. He had spent the years here learning not to eat with his knife, either literally or metaphorically. But there were only sixty-three days left, and there was still *one* thing he hadn't done, one problem still left unsolved, which of late had been growing into nightmare proportions. In the earlier years of his sentence he had put it aside—until the time came. That time was here now—and the problem was still aside.

He had made all other preparations. He had even communicated secretly, by means of a fellow convict who was going out, discharged, with Square John Kelly of the Pacific Coral Saloon in San Francisco, with whom he had invested his savings—that three thousand dollars at six per cent. And he had had foresight enough to do this months ago in order to give Kelly time to pull the money out of his business and have it ready in cash; for he wasn't quite sure where the law stood on this point. Failing to recover the proceeds of the Tydeman robbery, the law might confiscate those savings—if the law knew anything about them. But the law didn't—and wouldn't. Square John had sent back word that everything was all right.

But there was still one problem left to solve—the way, once he was a free man again and outside these walls, of getting that hundred thousand dollars away from under the noses of the police and then giving the police the slip. And this, grown to monumental proportions in the last few months, rose before him now like some evil familiar that had taken possession of both his waking and sleeping hours. And there came upon him now, as it had come again and again in these last months, that scene in the hospital when he had first opened his eyes to consciousness and they had rested on the face of the man who had run him to earth—Barjan, Lieutenant Joe Barjan, of the 'Frisco plainclothes squad. And Joe Barjan's words were ringing in his ears now; ringing, somehow, with a cursed knell in them:

"Don't fool yourself! It's a hell of a long time in the pen! And if you think you could get away with the wad when you get out again, you've got another think coming too! Take it from me!"

An acute sense of the realization of the *tangibility* of his surroundings seized upon him and brought a chill to his heart. That hard, unyielding cot; these walls, that caged him within their few scanty feet of space; his keepers' voices, that lashed out their commands; the animals, of which he was one, that toiled upon the eternal treadmill of days whose end but foretold another of like horror and loathing to come! Barjan had told the truth; more of the truth than Barjan ever knew, or could know, that he had told. It had been a hell of a long time. Long! His face, as he still paced the cell, grayed under the prison pallor. God, it had been long! Years of damnable torment that had shut him out from the freedom that he loved! It had been a price beyond all reckoning that he had paid for that hundred thousand dollars. But he had paid it! He had paid it—paid it! He had gone all the way—gone the limit. Was Barjan, right in one thing, right in that other thing as well—that at the end they would beat him?

His hands curled into knotted lumps. There were not enough Barjans for that though the world were peopled with Barjans! The thought had brought a chill of dread for a moment, that was all. He had paid the price; he was not likely to forget what that price had been; and he would never yield up what that price had bought. True, he had no plan for this last play of his worked out in detail, but he would find a way—because he must. He was probably exaggerating what the police would, or could do, anyhow! At first when he had come into the penitentiary, they had tried to trap, sometimes to wheedle him into disclosing where the money was, though they had long since given up those tactics and left him to himself. But suppose the police did watch him now when he got out. He could afford to wait—to wait a long while—until the police got tired, perhaps, or perhaps came to the conclusion that, after all, they had got the wrong man. They would not forget that, though he had refused to say anything at the trial, he had not been so mute in his attitude toward Runty Mott and Baldy Vickers, who had "sent him up;" and Barjan would not forget, either, that in the hospital that day, with scarcely strength to speak, he had threatened to get even with the gangster and the Runt. There was a psychological factor in this. If he, Dave Henderson, made no effort to get the money, showed no sign that he had any knowledge of its whereabouts, might not the police in time come to the far from illogical conclusion that they might better have watched—five years ago—the men who had so glibly acted as witnesses for the State, the men who had, admittedly, themselves attempted to steal the money? It wasn't unreasonable, was it? And he could afford to wait. The three thousand dollars from Square John Kelly would keep him going for quite a while! He was a fool to let this thing madden his brain with its constant torturing doubts. It was their move—not his.

From far along the iron gallery again a boot-heel rang with a dull, metallic sound. It was the guard, probably, coming to rap old Tony Lomazzi over the knuckles. Dave Henderson stopped his restless pacing, and stood still in the center of the cell to listen. No, the old bomb-thrower wasn't talking any longer; there wasn't any sound at all except that boot-heel ringing on the iron flooring. The sound came nearer, and Dave Henderson frowned in a puzzled way. The guard was not alone, in any case. He could distinguish the footsteps of two men now. It wasn't usual at this hour for any one to be out there with the guard. What was in the wind? The warden, perhaps, making an unexpected round, or — —

His hands gripped suddenly hard and tight—but he did not move. There came flashing over him once more the scene in that hospital ward of five years ago. The cell door had opened and closed. A man had entered. The guard's footsteps died away outside. The man spoke:

"Hello, Dave!"

It was Barjan, Lieutenant Joe Barjan, of the 'Frisco plain-clothes squad. It *was* the scene of five years ago. That was exactly what Barjan had said then: "Hello, Dave!" And he had answered: "Hello, Joe!" But he did not answer now.

"This is a little irregular, Dave," said Barjan pleasantly; "but I wanted to have a quiet little chat with you, you know, before"—he stepped forward and clapped his hand on Dave Henderson's shoulder, and laughed—"well, before you changed your address." Dave Henderson made no reply. He moved back from the other, and sat down on the edge of his cot.

"There's a couple of things I want to say to you," said Barjan, still pleasantly. "And the first of them is that I want to tell you on the level just where you stand. You're going out of here pretty soon now, Dave. I guess you've got a better line on that than I have—eh?" He laughed again good-humoredly. "Got the days counted, haven't you, Dave?"

No answer. Dave Henderson's eyes were fixed on the ungainly lines of the toe of his prison boot.

"Oh, come on, now, Dave!" Barjan's tones were still hearty and jocular, but the heartiness and jocularity, as though disconcerted, lacked some of their original spontaneity. "Loosen up! You've been a clam for five years. That's long enough. I've come up here to-night to play square with you. You know that whatever I say goes with both of us. I know you aren't holding anything against me personally just because I happened to be the one who put the bracelets on you, and back of that we used to be pretty good friends. I haven't forgotten the tips you used to give me in the old days—and don't you think I have, either! Remember when that old skeleton with the horse-hair cover pranced away with a forty-to-one shot? Bonnie Lass, her name was—or was it Boney? Remember? She got the hee-haw—but my missus got the swellest outfit of gewgaws and fixings the old girl ever had before or since. You wised me up to that, Dave."

No answer. There seemed to be something curiously significant in the uncouthness and the coarseness of that boot toe—but the significance was irritatingly elusive in its application.

There was silence for a moment. Barjan walked the length of the cell, and back again.

"All right," he said, halting in front of the cot. "Maybe we'll get along better on another tack. I'm not beating about the bush, Dave"—his voice was a little harder, crisper, sterner—"I want to know where that hundred thousand dollars is. But I told you that I'd put you straight first on where you stand. Now, listen! We've played both ends to the middle. We believed that the story Runty Mott and Baldy Vickers told was true; but both men had a record, and you can't be sure of a crook on his own say-so. We didn't take any chances, and so we're sure now. Those men were watched—not for a couple of weeks, or a couple of months, but for the last four years. They don't know where the money is, and they never did know what you did with it after you handed them that automobile smash and beat it for the woods. Get that? It's up to you! And now, get this: I told you in the hospital that day, you remember, that you could never get away with it, and that's as true as I'm standing here talking to you now. You've got some brains, Dave—use 'em now for your own sake. From the moment you step outside these walls you're a marked man, and not for just a little while either, but for all your life. They'll never let up on you, Dave. Let that sink in! And it ain't only just old Joe Barjan you've got to fool. Talking racey, Dave, your number's up on the board on every police track in this country from one end to the other. You can't beat that kind of a game. I'm talking straight, and you know it. Come on now, Dave, pry them lips of yours apart, and come across!" Dave Henderson's lips parted—but it was only to touch them with the tip of his tongue. They were dry. His eyes were still on that coarse, ungainly toe. Its significance had taken concrete form now. He knew now what it meant. It typified a living hell of five long years, a ghastly hell and a ghastly price paid for that hundred thousand dollars—years that had left a stench in his nostrils that would live as long as he lived—years that piled the daily, never-ending details of petty persecutions, of loathsome associations, of miserable discomforts, of haggard dreariness, of heart sickness, of bitterness that was the bitterness of gall, into one overwhelming mass of horror from which the soul recoiled, blanched, seared, shrivelled. And it went back further than that. It went back to a night of the long, long ago, eternities ago, a night when, in physical torture and anguish from his wound, his teeth had sunk into his lips, and he had become blood-fanged like the hunted animal at bay he was, and he had endured until the blackness came. That was what it meant, this rough, heavy ungraceful clod of a prison boot upon his foot! It meant that he had gone the limit, that he had never hedged, that he had paid the price, all of it—all of it—except only the sixty-three days that were left.

"Ain't you going to say anything, Dave?"

Tony Lomazzi must have shuffled his way back to the bars of his cell door. The old Italian was whispering and muttering again. If one listened very intently, one could hear him. There was no other sound.

Barjan cleared his throat.

"Look here," he said slowly, "what's the use, Dave? I've showed you that you're bound to lose, and that on that score it don't pay. And it don't pay any way you want to look at it. You don't have to go out of here a marked man, Dave. There ain't any truth in that—that the police never give a guy a chance to go straight again. There ain't anything in that. It's all up to the guy himself. You come across, make good on that money, and I'll guarantee you'll get the squarest deal any man ever got. Why, it would be proof in itself that you meant to go straight, Dave, and everybody'd fall over himself to give you the glad hand. You can see that, can't you, Dave? Don't you want to look the other fellow in the eye for the rest of your life? Don't you want to be a free man? You've got a lot of years ahead of you. Ain't you ever thought of a home, and kiddies, maybe? It don't pay, Dave—the other way don't. You've got the chance now to make good. What do you say?"

Tony Lomazzi was still muttering. Strange the guard was letting the old bomb-thrower have so much license to-night! Tony seemed to be chattering louder than he had ever chattered in all the years he had occupied that next cell there!

Barjan laughed a little in a low, but not unpleasant way.

"Well, then, listen again, Dave," he said. "I got one more thing to tell you. You know what I've said is right. You come across, and I'll see that you get your chance—and you don't have to wait for it, either, Dave. I've got it all fixed, I've got the papers in my pocket. You come across, and you walk out of here a free man with me right now—to-night!" He leaned forward and slapped Dave Henderson's shoulder again. "To-night, Dave—get that? Right now—tonight—this minute! What do you say?"

It was true! The tentative plan he had half formulated was no good! He realized that now. To lay low and wait was no good—Barjan had made that clear. The hope that the police might veer around to the belief that Runty Mott and Baldy Vickers were, after all, the men to watch, was no good either—Barjan had made that equally clear. There didn't seem to be any way out—and his number was up on the board on every police track in the country. Yes, that was true, too. He lifted his eyes from the toe of his boot for the first time, and met Barjan's eyes, and held the other's for a long minute in a steady gaze.

And then Dave Henderson spoke—for the first time.

"You go to hell!" he said.

II.
WOLVES ON THE SCENT

GUARDS on the raised platforms at either end of the room, guards circulating amongst the striped figures that toiled over the work benches, guards watching everywhere. They aroused a new and sullen fury in Dave Henderson's soul. They seemed to express and exemplify to-day in a sort of hideous clearness what Barjan had told him last night that he might expect in all the days to follow.

His number was up on the board!

He had not slept well last night. Barjan did not know it, but Barjan had struck a blow that had, in a mental way, sent him groggy to the ropes. He was groggy yet. His mind was in confusion. It reached out in this direction—and faltered, not quite sure of itself; it groped out in another direction—and faltered. It seemed to have lost its equilibrium and its poise. He had never expected that the whole world would turn its back while he walked from the penitentiary to Mrs. Tooler's pigeon-cote and tucked that package of a hundred thousand dollars under his arm. In that sense Barjan had told him nothing new. But nevertheless Barjan had struck home. He could not tell just where in the conversation, at just precisely what point, Barjan had done this, nor could he tell in any concrete way just what new difficulties and obstacles Barjan had reared up. He had always expected that it was up to him to outwit the police when he got away from these cursed guards. But his mind was haggard this afternoon. He had lashed it, driven it too hard through the night and through the morning. It had lost tenacity; it would not define. The only thing that held and clung there, and would not be dislodged, was the unreal, a snatch of nightmare out of the little sleep, fitful and troubled, that he had had. He was swimming across a dark, wide pool whose banks were all steep and impassable except at one spot which was very narrow, and here a figure worked feverishly with a pile of huge stones, building up a wall against him. He swam frantically, like a madman; but for every stroke he took, the figure added another stone to the wall; and when he reached the edge of the bank the wall was massive and high, and Barjan was perched on the top of the wall grinning at him.

He raised his hand, and drew it across his eyes. The clatter and clamor in the carpenter shop here around him was unendurable. The thud of a hammer jarred upon him, jangling his nerves; the screech of the bandsaw, a little way down the shop, was like the insane raving of some devil, with a devil's perverted sense of humor, running up and down a devil's scale. There were sixty-two days left.

His eyes fell upon old Tony Lomazzi a few benches away. Showing under Tony's cap, the hair, what there was of it, was silver—more nearly silver than it had somehow ever seemed to be before. Perhaps the prison barber had been a little late in getting around to the old man this time, perhaps it was because it was a little longer, perhaps that was it. It was strange though, rather queer! His eyes, arrested now, held on the other, and he seemed to be noticing little details that had never attracted his attention before. His own hands, that mechanically retained their grip upon the plane he had been using, were idle now. Certainly those old shoulders over there were more bowed and bent than he had ever seen them before. And the striped form was very frail; the clothes hung on it as clothes hang on a scarecrow. There was only the old fellow's side face in view, for the other's back was partially turned, but it appeared to possess quite a new and startling unfamiliarity. It wasn't the gray-white, unhealthy pallor—old Tony wasn't the only one who had that, for no one had ever claimed that there was any analogy between a penitentiary and a health resort—but the jowl was most curiously gaunt, and drawn inward as though the man were sucking in his cheeks, and yet the skin seemed to be stretched tight and hard as a drum-head. Very curious! It must be because he couldn't see the sharp little black eyes, full of fire, that put life and soul into that scarecrow frame.

Old Tony turned, and their eyes met. The old man lifted his hand as though to wipe his mouth—and there was a little flirt of the fingers in Dave Henderson's direction. It was the old, intimate, little signal that had passed between them unnumbered times in the thousand years that they had spent together here in the penitentiary's carpenter shop—but he had been quite wrong about the eyes. Something seemed to have filmed across them, veiling their luster. And suddenly Dave Henderson swallowed hard. Sixty-two days! Old Tony hadn't much more than that. Perhaps another year at the outside, and the old lifer would be free, too.

Dave Henderson's mind reverted to Lieutenant Joe Barjan, of the plain-clothes squad. It was perfectly true that playing a lone hand against the police of all America was a desperate game—desperate in the sense that success was in jeopardy. That was what made his brain confused and chaotic now. He was afraid—not of Barjan, not of all the police in the United States in a physical way, he had never hedged a bet, and the five years that he had now paid would goad him on more than ever to face any physical risk, take any physical chance—but he was afraid now, sick with fear, because his mind would not respond and show him clearly, definitely the way to knock Barjan and his triumphant grin from off that nightmare wall, and——

A guard's voice snapped sharply at his elbow.

Yes, of course! He had been standing idle for a few seconds—perhaps an hour. Automatically he bent over the bench, and automatically his plane drew a neat, clean shaving from the work in front of him.

The guard's voice snapped again.

"You're wanted!" said the guard curtly. "There's a visitor to see you."

Dave Henderson turned away from the bench, and followed the guard; but the act was purely mechanical, born out of the years of discipline and obedience. A visitor—for him! There was no one in the outside world, not a soul, who cared for him; not many even, to whom his existence was of enough interest to cause a second thought—except Barjan. And Barjan had visited him yesterday. Another visitor—to-day! Well, whoever it was, the visitor had been in no hurry about it! The little attention was certainly belated! His lips thinned bitterly. Whoever it was had waited almost five years. He had never had a visitor before—except the police. It was an event! The bitterness grew deeper, and rankled. He had asked for no human touch, or thought, or consideration; he had asked for none, and he had given none; he had made his own bed, and he had not whined because it had proved to be a rack of torture. He was not whining now, and he had no desire to change the rules of the game that he himself had elected to play. This was no visitor—it was an intruder!

But curiosity, as he crossed the prison yard and entered the main building, tempered the sullen antagonism that had flared up in his soul. Who was it that was waiting for him there along the corridor in the wire-netted visitor's room, where, like some beast with its keeper pacing up and down in front of the cage, he was to be placed on exhibition? He searched his brain for an answer that would be even plausible. Not Square John Kelly. Kelly *might* have come if Kelly had been left to himself, but Kelly was the one man he had warned off from the beginning—there was that matter of three thousand dollars, and caution had prompted him to avoid any sign of intimacy between them. There was no one else. Even Kelly, perhaps, wasn't a friend any more. Kelly would, perhaps, simply play square, turn over the three thousand dollars— and then turn his back. It wouldn't be Tooler. The only thing that interested Tooler was to see that he collected his room rent regularly—and there would be some one else paying rent now for that front room at Tooler's! No, there was no one else. Leaving a very keen regard for old Tony Lomazzi aside, he had only one friend that he knew of whom he could really call a friend, only one man that he could trust—and that man was a convict too! It was ironical, wasn't it?—to trust a convict! Well, he could trust Millman—only it wouldn't be fair to Millman.

He lagged a little behind the guard as they approached the visitor's room, a sudden possibility dawning upon him. Perhaps it *was* Millman! Millman's time was up to-morrow, and to-morrow Millman was going away. He and Millman had arranged to say good-by to one another at the library hour to-day after work was over; but perhaps, as a sort of special dispensation, Millman had obtained permission to come here.

Dave Henderson shrugged his shoulders, impatient with himself, as the guard opened a door and motioned him to enter. It was absurd, ridiculous! Who had ever heard of one prisoner visiting another in this fashion! There wouldn't have been any satisfaction in it anyhow, with a guard pacing up and down between them! Well, then, who was it?

The door closed behind him—he was subconsciously aware that the door had closed, and that the guard had left him to himself. He was also subconsciously aware that his hands had reached out in front of him and that his fingers were fiercely laced in the interstices of the heavy steel-wire netting of the enclosure in which he stood, and that faced another row of steel-wire netting, separated from his own only by the space that was required to permit the guard to pace up and down between the two—only the guard hadn't come in yet from the corridor to take up his station there. There was only a face peering at him from behind that other row of netting—a fat face—the face was supposed to be smiling, but it was like the hideous grin of a gargoyle. It was the same face, the same face with its rolls of fat propped up on its short, stumpy neck. There wasn't any change in it, except that the red-rimmed gray eyes were more shifty. That was the only change in five years—the eyes were more shifty. He found that his mouth was dry, curiously dry. The blood wasn't running through his veins, because his fingers on the wire felt cold—and yet he was burning, the soul of him suddenly like some flaming furnace, and a mad, passionate fury had him in its grip, and a lust was upon him to reach that stumpy neck where the throat was, and—and—— He had been waiting five years for that—and he was simply smiling, just as that other face was smiling. Why shouldn't he smile! That fat face was Bookie Skarvan's face.

"I guess you weren't looking to see me, Dave?" said Skarvan, nodding his head in a sort of absurd cordiality. "Maybe you thought I was sore on you, and there's no use saying I wasn't. That was a nasty crack you handed me. If

Tydeman hadn't come across with another bunch of coin on the jump, those pikers down at the track would have pulled me to pieces. But I didn't feel sore long, Dave—that ain't in me. And that ain't why I kept away."

The man was quite safe, of course, on account of these wire gratings, and on account of the guard who was somewhere out there in the corridor. It was very peculiar that the guard was not pacing up and down even now in this little open space between Bookie Skarvan and himself—very peculiar! Bookie was magnanimous—not to be sore! He wanted to laugh out in a sort of maniacal hysteria, only he would be a fool to do that because there were sixty-two days left before he could get his fingers around that greasy, fat throat, and he must not *scare* the man off now. He had a debt to pay—five years of prison, those days and nights and hours of torment when he had been a wounded thing hounded almost to his death. Certainly, he owed all that to this man here! The man had cunningly planned to have him disappear by the *murder* route, hadn't he? And he owed Bookie Skarvan for that too! If it hadn't been for that he would have got away with the money, and there wouldn't have been five years of prison, or those hours of physical torment, or— —

He lifted his hand and brushed it heavily across his forehead. He was quite cool now, perfectly in control of himself. The man didn't have even a suspicion that he, Dave Henderson, knew these things. He mustn't put the other on his guard—there were still sixty-two days during which these prison walls held him impotent, and during which another, warned, could get very far out of reach. Yes, he was quite cool now. He was even still smiling, wasn't he? He could even play the man like a hooked fish. It wasn't time to land the other yet. But it was strange that Bookie Skarvan should have come here at all. Bookie wasn't a fool; he hadn't come here for nothing. What was it the man wanted?

"Ain't you glad to see me, Dave?" demanded Bookie Skarvan quite jocularly. "'Cause, if you ain't now, you will be before I go."

"What do you mean?" inquired Dave Henderson coolly.

"Notice anything queer about what's doing here right at this minute?" Bookie's left eye closed in a significant wink. "Sure, you do! There ain't any guard butting in, Dave. Get me? Well, I fixed it like that."

Dave Henderson relapsed into the old vernacular.

"Spill it!" he invited. "I'm listening."

"Attaboy!" Bookie grinned. "You bet you're listening! We ain't forgotten those years you and me spent together, have we, Dave? You know me, and I know you. I kept away from here until now, 'cause I didn't want 'em to get the right dope on the betting—didn't want 'em to think there was any chance of us playing up to each other."

"You mean you didn't want them to get wise that you were a crook, too," suggested Dave Henderson imperturbably.

Bookie Skarvan had no false modesty—his left eyelid drooped for the second time.

"You got the idea, Dave," he grinned again. "They've got to figure I'm straight—that's the play. That's the play I've been making in waiting five years—so's they'd be sure there wasn't nothing between us. Now you listen hard, Dave. All you've handed the police is a frozen face, and that's the right stuff; but I got a dead straight tip they're going to keep their eyes on you till hell's a skating pond. They're going to get that money—*or else you ain't!* See? Well, that's where I stepped in. I goes to the right source, and I says: 'Look here, you can't do nothing with Dave. Let me have a try. Maybe I can handle him. He worked for me a good many years, and I know him better than his mother would if he had one. He's stubborn, stubborn as hell, and threats ain't any good, nor promises neither; but he's a good boy, for all that. You let me have a chance to talk to him privately, and maybe I can make him come across and cough up that money. Anyway, it won't do any harm to try. I always liked Dave, and I don't want to see him dodging the police all his life. Tydeman's dead, and, though it was really Tydeman's money, I was a partner of Tydeman's, and if anybody on earth can get under Dave's shell I can.'" Bookie put his face closer to his own particular stretch of wire netting. He lowered his voice. "That's the reason I'm here, and that's the reason the guard—ain't!"

There was almost awe and admiration in Dave Henderson's voice.

"You've got your nerve with you!" he said softly.

Bookie Skarvan chuckled in his wheezy way.

"Sure!" he said complacently. "And that's why we win. You get the lay, don't you?" He was whispering now. "You can't get that cash *alone*, Dave. I'm telling you straight they won't let you. But they won't watch *me!* You know me, Dave. I'll make it a fair split—fifty-fifty. Tell me where the money is, and I'll get it, and be waiting for you anywhere you say when you come out; and I'll fix it to hand over your share so's they'll never know you got it—I got to make sure it's fixed like that for my own sake, you can see that. Get me, Dave? And I go out of here now and tell the warden it ain't any good, that I can't get you to talk. I guess that looks nifty enough, don't it, Dave?" #

There was a fly climbing up the wire netting. It zigzagged its course over the little squares. It was a good gamble whether, on reaching the next strand, it would turn to the right or left, or continue straight ahead. Dave Henderson watched it. The creature did no one of those things. It paused and frictioned its front legs together in a leisurely fashion. After that it appeared to be quite satisfied with its position—and it stayed there.

"Poor Bookie!" murmured Dave Henderson. "Sad, too! I guess it must be softening of the brain!"

Bookie Skarvan's face blotched suddenly red—but he pressed his face still more earnestly against the wire barrier.

"You don't get it!" he breathed hoarsely. "I'm giving you a straight tip. Barjan's waiting for you. The police are waiting for you. You haven't got a hope. I tell you, you can't get that money alone, no matter where you put it."

"I heard you," said Dave Henderson indifferently.

There was silence for a moment.

A sort of anxious exasperation spread over Skarvan's face, then perplexity, and then a flare of rage.

"You're a fool!" he snarled. "You won't believe me! You think I'm trying to work you for half of that money. Well, so I am, in a way—or I wouldn't have come here. But I'm earning it. Look at the risk I'm taking—five years, the same as you got. You crazy fool! Do you think I'm bluffing? I tell you again, I know what I'm talking about. The police'll never give you a look-in. You got to have help. Who else is there but me? It's better to split with me than lose the whole of it, ain't it?"

"You haven't changed a bit in five years, Bookie." There was studied insolence in Dave Henderson's voice now. "Not a damned bit! Run along now—beat it!"

"You mean that?" Bookie Skarvan's eyes were puckered into slits now. "You mean you're going to turn me down?"

"Yes!" said Dave Henderson.

"I'll give you one more chance," whispered Skarvan. "*No!*"

Bookie Skarvan's fat fingers squirmed around inside his collar as though it choked him.

"All right!" His lips were twitching angrily. "All right!" he repeated ominously. "Then, by God, *you'll* never get the money—even if you beat the police! Understand? I'll see to that! I made you a fair, straight offer. You'll find now that there'll be some one else besides you and Barjan out for that coin—and when the showdown comes it won't be either you or Barjan that gets it! And maybe you think that's a bluff, too!"

"I never said I knew where the money was," said Dave Henderson—and smiled—and shrugged his shoulders. "Therefore you ought to stand just as good a chance as Barjan—or I. After I got wounded I kind of lost track of things, you know."

"You lie!" said Skarvan fiercely. "I—I———" He checked himself, biting at his lips. "I'll give you one more chance again. What's your last word?"

"You've got it, Bookie," said Dave Henderson evenly.

"Then take mine!" Skarvan rasped. "I'll go now and tell the warden you wouldn't say anything. If you try to put a crimp in me by reporting my offer, I'll say you lied. I don't mind taking chances on my word being believed against the word of a convict and a thief who is known to be playing tricky! You get that? And after that—God help you!"

The man was gone....

Presently, Dave Henderson found himself back in the carpenter shop. The band-saw was shrieking, screeching insanely again. He had smiled in there in the visitor's room at Bookie Skarvan; he had even been debonair and facetious—he wasn't that way now. He could mask his face from others; he couldn't mask his soul from himself. It seemed as though his courage were being drained away from him, and in its place were coming a sense of final, crushing defeat. Barjan's blow of last night had sent him groggy to the ropes; but the blow Bookie Skarvan had just dealt had smashed in under his guard and had landed on an even more vital spot.

Skarvan's veiled threat hadn't veiled anything. The veil was only too transparent! "God help you!" meant a lot. It meant that, far more dangerous to face, even more difficult to outwit than the police, there was now to be aligned against him the criminal element of San Francisco. It meant Baldy Vickers and Runty Mott, and Baldy Vickers' gang. It meant the men who had already attempted to murder him, and who would be eager enough to repeat that attempt for the same stake—one hundred thousand dollars. With the police it would have been, more than anything else, the simple thrust and parry of wits; now, added to that, was a physical, brutish force whose danger only a fool would strive to minimize. There were dives and dens in the underworld there, as he knew well enough, where a man would disappear from the light of day forever, and where tortures that would put the devil's ingenuity to shame could be applied to make a man open his lips. He was not exaggerating! It was literally true. And if he were once trapped he could expect no less than that. They had already tried to murder him once! Naturally, they had entered into his calculations before while he had been here in prison; but they had not seemed to be a very vital factor. He had never figured on Bookie Skarvan setting that machinery in motion again—he had only figured on getting his own hands on Bookie Skarvan himself. But he saw it now; and he realized that, once started again, they would stop at nothing to get that money. Whether Bookie Skarvan would have abided by his offer, on the basis that he would get more out of it for himself that way, or whether it was simply a play to discover the whereabouts of the money and then divide up with his old accomplices, did not matter; it was certain now that Bookie Skarvan would be content with less rather than with none, and that the underworld would be unleashed on his, Dave Henderson's, trail. The police—and now the underworld! It was like a pack of wolves and a pack of hounds in chase from converging directions after the same quarry; the wolves and the hounds might clash together, and fall upon one another—but the quarry would be mangled and crushed in the mêlée.

The afternoon wore on. At times Dave Henderson's hands clenched over his tools until it seemed the tendons must snap and break with the strain; at times the sweat of agony oozed out in drops upon his forehead. Bookie Skarvan was right. He could not get that money *alone*. No! No, that was wrong! He could get it alone, and he would get it, and then fight for it, and go under for it, all hell would not hold him back from that, and Bookie Skarvan and some of the others would go under too—but he could not get *away* with the money alone. And that meant that these five years of prison, five years of degradation, of memories that nauseated him, five years that he had wagered out of his life, had gone for nothing! God, if he could only turn to some one for help! But there was no one, not a soul on earth, not a friend in the world who could aid him—except Millman.

And he *couldn't* ask Millman—because it wouldn't be fair to Millman.

His face must have grown haggard, perhaps he was acting strangely. Old Tony over there had been casting anxious glances in his direction. He took a grip upon himself, and smiled at the old bomb-thrower. The old Italian looked pretty bad himself—that pasty whiteness about the old fellow's face had a nasty appearance.

His mind went back to Millman, working in queer, disconnected snatches of thought. He was going to lose Millman, too... Millman was going out tomorrow.... It had always been a relief to talk to Millman.... He had never told Millman where the money was, of course, but Millman knew what he, Dave Henderson, was "in" for.... The library hour wasn't far off, and it would help to talk to Millman now.... Only Millman was going out to-morrow—? and he was to bid Millman good-by.

This seemed somehow the crowning jeer of mockery that fate was flinging at him—that to-morrow even Millman would be gone. It seemed to bring a snarl into his soul, the snarl as of some gaunt, starving beast at bay, the snarl of desperation flung out in bitter, reckless defiance.

He put his hands to his face, and beneath them his jaws clamped and locked. They would never beat him, he would go under first, but—but— —

Time passed. The routine of the prison life went on like the turning of some great, ponderous wheel that moved very slowly, but at the same time with a sort of smooth, oiled immutability. It seemed that way to Dave Henderson. He was conscious of no definite details that marked or occupied the passage of time. The library hour had come. He was on his way to the library now— with permission to get a book. He did not want a book. He was going to see Millman, and, God knew, he did not want to see Millman—to say good-by.

Mind, body and soul were sick—sick with the struggle of the afternoon, sick with the ceaseless mental torment that made his temples throb and brought excruciating pain, and with the pain brought almost physical nausea; sick with the realization that his recompense for the five years of freedom he had sacrificed was only—wreckage, ruin and disaster.

He entered the little room. A guard lounged negligently against the wall. One of the two convict librarians was already busy with another convict—but it wasn't Millman who was busy. He met Millman's cool, steady, gray eyes, read a sudden, startled something in them, and moved down to the end of the sort of wooden counter away from the guard—and handed in his book to be exchanged.

"What's the matter, Dave?" Millman, across the counter, back half turned to the guard, spoke in a low, hurried voice, as he pretended to examine the book. "I never saw you look like this before! Are you sick?"

"Yes," said Dave Henderson between his teeth. "Sick—as hell! I'm up against it, Charlie! And I guess it's all over except for one last little fight."

"What book do you want?" said Millman's voice coolly; but Millman's clean-cut face with its strong jaw tightening a little, and Millman's clear gray eyes with a touch of steel creeping into them, said: "Go on!"

"The police!" Dave Henderson spoke through the corner of his mouth without motion of the lips. "Barjan was here last night. And I got another tip to-day. The screws are going on—to a finish."

"You mean they're going to see that you don't get that money?"

Dave Henderson nodded curtly.

"Why not give it up then, Dave, and start a clean sheet?" asked Millman softly.

"Give it up!" The red had come into Dave Henderson's face, there was a savage tightening of his lips across his teeth. "I'll never give it up! D'ye think I've rotted here five years only to *crawl* at the end? By God! No! I'll get it—if they get me doing it!" His hoarse whisper caught and choked suddenly. "But it's hell, Charlie—hell! Hell to go under like that, just because there isn't a soul on God's wide earth I can trust to get it for me while they're watching me!" Millman turned away, and walked to the racks of books at the rear of the room.

Dave Henderson watched the other in a numbed sort of way. It was a curious kind of good-by he was saying to Millman. He wasn't quite sure, for that matter, just what he had said. He was soul sick, and body sick. Millman was taking a long while over the selection of a book—and he hadn't even asked for a book, let alone for any particular one. What did it matter! He didn't want anything to read. Reading wasn't any good to him any more! Barjan and Bookie Skarvan had——

Millman was leaning over the counter again, a book in his hand.

"Would you trust *me*, Dave?" he asked quietly.

"You!" The blood seemed to quicken, and rush in a mad, swirling tide through Dave Henderson's veins. "Do you mean that, Charlie? Do you mean you'll help me?"

"Yes," said Millman. "If you want to trust me, I'll get that money for you. I'm going out to-morrow. But talk quickly! The guard's watching us and getting fidgety. Where is it?"

Dave Henderson rubbed his upper lip with the side of his forefinger as though it itched; the remaining fingers, spread out fanlike, screened his mouth.

"In the old pigeon-cote—shed back of Tooler's house where I used to live—you can get into the shed from the lane."

Millman laid the book on the counter—and pushed it toward Dave Henderson.

"All right," he said. "They won't be looking for it in New York. You've two months more here. Make it the twenty-fourth of June. That'll give you time enough. I'll be registered at the St. Lucian Hotel—New York—eight o'clock in the evening—June twenty-fourth. I'll hand the money over to you there, and——"

"You there, Five-Fifty"—the guard was moving toward them from across the room—"you got your book, ain't you?"

Dave Henderson picked up the book, and turned toward the door.

"Good-by!" he flung over his shoulder.

"Good-by!" Millman answered.

III.
BREAD UPON THE WATERS

IT was dark in the cell, quite dark. There was just the faint glimmer that crept in from the night lights along the iron galleries, and came up from the main corridor two tiers below. It must have been hours since he had left Millman in the prison library—and yet he was not sure. Perhaps it was even still early, for he hadn't heard old Tony talking and whispering to himself through the bars to-night yet.

Dave Henderson's head, cupped in hands whose fingers dug with a brutal grip into the flesh of his cheeks, came upward with a jerk, and he surged to his feet from the hinged shelf that he called cot and bed. What difference did it make whether it was dark or light, or late or early, or whether old Tony had babbled to himself or not! It was pitifully inconsequential. It was only his brain staggering off into the byways again, as though, in some sneaking, underhand way, it wanted to steal rest and respite.

His hands went up above his head, and held there, and his fists clenched. He was the fool of fools, the prince of fools! He saw it now! His laugh purled low, in hollow mirth, through the cell—a devil's laugh in its bitter irony. Yes, he saw it now—when it was too late.

Millman! Damn Millman to the pit! Damn Millman for the smoothest, craftiest hypocrite into whom God had ever breathed the breath of life! He had been trapped! That had been Millman's play, two years of cunning play—to win his confidence; two years of it, that always at the end the man might get that hundred thousand dollars. And he had fallen into Millman's trap!

He did not believe Millman's story, or in Millman's innocence now—when it was too late! He couldn't reach Millman now. There were bars of iron, and steel doors, and walls of stone between himself and Millman's cell; and in the morning Millman would be gone, and Millman would have sixty-two—no, sixty-one days—to get that money and put the width of the world between them before he, Dave Henderson, was free.

Sixty-one days! And in the space of one short moment, wrecking all that the toil and agony of years was to have stood for, he had told Millman what

Millman wanted to know! And that was the moment Millman had been waiting for through two long years with cunning patience—and he, Dave Henderson, because he was shaken to the soul with desperation, because he was alone with his back to the wall, in extremity, ready to grasp at any shred of hope, and because he was sick in body, and because the sudden, overwhelming uplift at Millman's offer had numbed and dulled his faculties in a mighty revulsion of relief, had fallen into the traitor's trap.

And it had been done so quickly! The guard had been there and had intervened, and there hadn't been time for his mind to win back its normal poise and reason logically. He hadn't reasoned in that brief instant; he had only caught and grasped the outflung hand of one whom, for two years, he had trusted and believed was a friend. He hadn't reasoned then; he had even stepped out of the prison library more lighthearted than he had been almost from the moment they had put these striped clothes upon him five years before; but he had barely stood locked in his cell here again when, like some ghastly blight falling upon him, reason had come and left him a draggled weakling, scarcely able physically to stand upon his feet. And then that had passed, and he had been possessed of an insensate fury that had bade him fling himself at the cell door, and, with superhuman strength, wrench and tear the bars asunder that he might get at Millman again. He had checked that impulse amidst the jeers and mockeries of impish voices that rang in his ears and filled the cell with their insane jabberings—voices that laughed in hellish glee at him for being a fool in the first place, and for his utter impotence in the second.

They were jeering and chuckling now, those insane demon voices!

He swung from the center of the cell, and flung himself down on the cot again. They might well mock at him, those voices! For two years, though he had had faith in Millman, he had kept the secret of the hiding place of that money to himself because, believing Millman to be an honest man, it would have been unfair to Millman to have told him, since, as an honest man, Millman then would either have had to inform the authorities—or become a dishonest man. It was clear enough, wasn't it? And logical enough? And yet in one unguarded moment he had repudiated his own logic! He had based all, his faith and trust and confidence in Millman, on the belief that Millman was an honest man. Well, an *honest* man wouldn't voluntarily aid and abet a thief in getting away with stolen money, nor make himself an accomplice after the fact, nor offer to help outwit the police, nor agree to participate in what amounted to stealing the money for a second time, and so make of himself a criminal! And if the man was then *dishonest*, and for two years had covered that dishonesty with a mask of hypocrisy, it was obvious enough, since the hypocrisy had been solely for his, Dave Henderson's, benefit, that Millman had planned it all patiently from the beginning, and now meant to do him cold, to get the money and keep it.

He could not remain still. He was up on his feet again from the cot. Fury had him in its grip once more. Five years! Five years of hell in this devil's hole! And a branded name! He had thrown everything into the balance—all he had! And now—*this!* Tricked! That was it—tricked! Tricked by a Judas!

All the passion of the man was on the surface now. Lean and gaunt, his body seemed to crouch forward as though to spring; his hands, with fingers crooked like claws reaching for their prey, were outstretched before him. Sixty-one days' start Millman had. But Millman would need more than that! The only man in the world whom he had ever trusted, and who had then betrayed him, would need more than sixty-one days to escape the reckoning that was to come. Millman might hide, Millman might live for years in lavish ease on that money, and in the end there might be none of that money left, but sooner or later Millman would pay a bigger price than—a hundred thousand dollars. He would get Millman. The world wasn't big enough for the two of them. And when that day came— —

His muscles relaxed. The paroxysm of fury left him, and suddenly he moaned a little as though in bitter hurt. There was another side to it. He could not help thinking of that other side. There had been two years of what he had thought was friendship—and the friendship had been hypocrisy. It was hard to believe. Perhaps Millman meant to play square after all, perhaps Millman would keep that rendezvous in New York on June twenty-fourth at eight o'clock in the evening at the St. Lucian Hotel. Perhaps Millman would. It wasn't only on account of the money that he hoped Millman would—there were those two years of what he had thought was friendship.

He leaned suddenly against the wall of the cell, the palms of his hands pressed against it, his face crushed into his knuckles. No! What was the use of that! Why try to delude himself again? Why try to make himself believe what he *wanted* to believe? He could reason now coolly and logically enough. If Millman was honest he would not do what he had offered to do; and being, therefore, dishonest, his apparent honesty had been only a mask, and the mask had been only for his, Dave Henderson's, benefit, and that, logically, could evidence but one thing—that Millman had deliberately set himself to win the confidence that would win for Millman the stake of one hundred thousand dollars. There was no other conclusion, was there?

His head came up from his hands, and he stood rigid, tense. Wait! Wait a minute, until his brain cleared. There was another possibility. He had not thought of it before! It confused and staggered him now. Suppose that

Millman stood in with the police! Suppose that the police had used Millman for just the purpose that Millman had accomplished! Or—why not?—suppose that Millman was even one of the police himself! It was not so tenable a theory as it was to assume that Millman had acted as a stool-pigeon; but it was, even at that, well within the realm of possibility. A man would not count two years ill spent on a case that involved the recovery of a hundred thousand dollars—nor hesitate to play a convict's part, either, if necessary. It had been done before. Until Barjan had come last night, the police had made no sign for years—unless Millman were indeed one of them, and, believing at the last that he was facing failure, had called in Barjan. Millman hadn't had a hard time of it in the penitentiary. His education had been the excuse, if it were an excuse, for all the soft clerical jobs. Who was to know if Millman ever spent the nights in his cell?

Dave Henderson crushed his fists against his temples. What did it matter! In the long run, what did it matter! Crook, or informant, or an officer, Millman had wrecked him, and he would pay his debt to Millman! He laughed low again, while his teeth gnawed at his lip. There was Barjan and Bookie Skarvan—and now Millman! And Baldy Vickers and the underworld!

There wasn't much chance, was there? Not much to expect now in return for the eternities in which he had worn these prison stripes, not much out of the ruin of his life, not much for the all and everything he had staked and risked! Not much—only to make one last fight, to make as many of these men pay as dearly as he could. Fight! Yes, he would fight. He had never hedged. He would never hedge. They had him with his back to the wall. He knew that. There wasn't much chance now; there wasn't any, if he looked the situation squarely in the face. He stood alone, absolutely alone; there was nowhere to turn, no single soul to turn to. His hand was against every other man's. But he was not beaten. They would never beat him. A knife thrust or a black-jack from Bookie Skarvan's skulking pack, though it might end his life, would not beat him; a further term here behind these walls, though it might wither up the soul of him, would not beat him!

And Millman! Up above his head his hands twisted and knotted together again, and the great muscular shoulders locked back, and the clean, straight limbs grew taut. And he laughed. And the laugh was very low and sinister. A beast cornered was an ugly thing. And the dominant instinct in a beast was self-preservation—and a leap at its enemy's throat. A beast asked no quarter—and gave none. Fie was a beast. They had made him a beast in here, an animal, a numbered thing, not a man; they had not even left him with a name—just one of a herd of beasts and animals. But they had not tamed him. He was alone, facing them all now, and there wasn't much chance because the odds were overwhelming; but if he was alone, he would not go *down* alone, and—

He turned his head suddenly, and his hands dropped to his sides. There had come a cry from somewhere. It was not very loud, but it rang in a startling way through the night silence of the prison. It was a cry as of sudden fear and weakness. It came again; and in a bound Dave Henderson reached the bars of his door, and beat upon them furiously with his fists. He would get into trouble for it undoubtedly, but he had placed that cry now. Old Tony wasn't whispering tonight. There was something wrong with the old bomb-thrower. Yes, he remembered—old Tony's strange appearance that afternoon. He rattled again and again on the bars. Old Tony was moaning now.

Footsteps on the run sounded along the iron gallery. A guard passed by; another paused at the door.

"Get back out of there!" growled the guard. "Beat it! Get back to your cot!"

Dave Henderson retreated to the center of the cell. He heard old Tony's door opened. Then muffled voices. And then a voice that was quite audible— one of the guard's:

"I guess he's snuffed out. Get the doc—and, yes, tell the warden, if he hasn't gone to bed yet."

Snuffed out! There was a queer, choking sensation in Dave Henderson's throat. A guard ran along the gallery. Dave Henderson edged silently close up to the door of his cell again. He couldn't see very much—only a gleam of light from Lomazzi's cell that fell on the iron plates of the gallery. There was no sound from within the other cell now.

Snuffed out! The thought that old Tony was dead affected him in a numbed, groping sort of way. It had come with such startling suddenness! He had not grasped it yet. He wondered whether he should be sorry or glad for old Tony—death was the lifer's goal. He did not know. It brought, though, a great aching into his own soul. It seemed to stamp with the ultimate to-night the immeasurable void in his own life. Old Tony was the last link between himself and that thing of priceless worth that men called friendship. Millman had denied it, outraged it, betrayed it; and now old Tony had swerved in his allegiance, and turned away at the call of a greater friend. Yes, death could not be anything but a friend to Tony. There seemed to be no longer any doubt of that in his mind.

Footsteps, several of them, came again along the iron gallery, racketing through the night, but they did not pass his cell this time; they came from the other direction, and went into Lomazzi's cell. It was strange that this should have happened to-night! There would be no more shoulder-touch in the lock-step for the few days that were left; no smile of eyes and lips across the carpenter shop; no surreptitious, intimate little gestures of open-hearted companionship! It seemed to crown in an appalling way, to bring home to him now with a new and appalling force what, five minutes ago, he had thought he had already appreciated to its fullest and bitterest depths—loneliness. He was alone—alone—alone.

The murmur of voices came from the other cell. Time passed. He clung there to the bars. Alone—without help! The presence of death seemed to have infused itself into, and to have become synonymous with that thought. It seemed insidiously to eat into his soul and being, to make his mind sick and weary, whispering to him to capitulate because he was alone, ringed about with forces that would inevitably overwhelm his puny single-handed defiance—because he was alone—and it would be hopeless to go further alone—without help.

He drew back suddenly from the door, conscious for the first time that he must have been clutching and straining at the bars with all his strength. His fingers, relaxed now, were stiff, and the circulation seemed to have left them. A guard was opening the door. Behind the guard, that white-haired man was the warden. He had always liked the warden. The man was stern, but he was always just. He did not understand why the warden had come to his cell.

It was the warden who spoke:

"Lomazzi is dying. He has begged to be allowed to say good-by to you. I can see no objection. You may come."

Dave Henderson moistened his lips with the tip of his tongue.

"I—I thought I heard them say he was dead," he mumbled.

"He was unconscious," answered the warden briefly. "A heart attack. Step quickly; he has not many minutes."

Dave Henderson stepped out on the iron gallery; and paused an instant before the door of the adjoining cell. A form lay on the cot, a form with a pasty-colored face, a form whose eyes were closed. The prison doctor, a hypodermic syringe still in his hand, stood a little to one side. Dave Henderson swept his hand across his eyes—there was a sudden mist there that blurred the scene—and, moving forward, dropped down on his knees beside the cot.

A hand reached out and grasped his feebly; the dark eyes opened and fixed on him with a flicker of the old fire in their depths; and the lips quivered in a smile.

Old Tony was whispering—old Tony always talked and whispered to himself here in his cell every night—but old Tony never disturbed anybody— it was hard to hear old Tony even when one listened attentively. Dave Henderson brushed his hand across his eyes again, and bent his head to the other's lips to catch the words.

"You make-a da fool play when you come in here, Dave—for me. But I never, never forget. Old Tony no forget. You no make-a da fool play when you go out. Old Tony knows. You need-a da help. Listen—Nicolo Capriano— 'Frisco. You understand? Tony Lomazzi send-a you. Tony Lomazzi take-a da life prison for Nicolo. Nicolo will pay back to Tony's friend. You did not think that"—the voice was growing feebler, harder to understand, and it was fluttering now—"that, because old Tony call-a you da fool, he did—did not— remember—and—and——"

Some one disengaged Dave Henderson's hand from the hand that was clasped around it, and that had suddenly twitched and, with a spasmodic clutch, had seemed as though striving to maintain its hold.

The prison doctor's voice sounded muffled in the cell:

"He is dead."

Dave Henderson looked up at the touch of a guard's hand on his shoulder. The guard jerked his head with curt significance in the direction of the door.

BOOK III.
PATHS OF THE UNDERWORLD

I.
THE DOOR ON THE LANE

WAS that a shadow cast by the projection of the door porch out there across the street, or was it *more* than a shadow? It was true that, to a remarkable degree, one's eyes became accustomed to the murk, almost akin to blackness, of the ill-lighted street; but the mind did not accommodate itself so readily—a long and sustained vigil, the brain spurred into abnormal activity and under tense strain, produced a mental quality of vision that detracted from, rather than augmented, the dependence to be placed upon the physical organs of sight. It peopled space with its own imaginations; it created, rather than descried. Dave Henderson shook his head in grim uncertainty. He could not be sure what it was out there. With the black background of the unlighted room behind him he could not be seen at the window by any one on the street, which was two stories below, and he had been watching here since it had grown dark. In that time he had seen a dozen shadows that he could have sworn were not shadows—and yet they were no more than that after all. He was only sure of one thing—that out there somewhere, perhaps nowhere within eye range of his window, perhaps even half a block away, but somewhere, some one was watching. He had been sure of that during every hour of his new-found freedom, since he had reached 'Frisco that noon. He had been sure of it intuitively; but he had failed signally to identify any one specifically as having dogged or followed him.

Freedom! He laughed a little harshly. There weren't any stone walls any more; this window in front of him wasn't grated, nor the door of the room steel-barred, nor out there in the corridor was there any uniformed guard— and so it was freedom.

The short, harsh laugh was on his lips again. Freedom! It was a curious freedom, then! He could walk at will out there in the streets—within limits.

But he did not dare go yet to that shed where Mrs. Tooler's old pigeon-cote was. The money probably wasn't there anyhow—Millman almost certainly had won the first trick and had got away with it; but it was absolutely necessary that he should be sure.

He had freedom; but he had dared go nowhere to procure a steel jimmy, for instance, or a substitute for a steel jimmy, with which to force that shed door; nor had he dared to go anywhere and buy a revolver with which to arm himself, and of which he stood desperately in need. He had only a few dollars, but he knew where, under ordinary circumstances, he could obtain those things without any immediate outlay of money—only it was a moral certainty that every move he made was watched. If he procured, say, a chisel, if he procured, say, a revolver, he was not fool enough to imagine such facts would be hidden long from those who watched. They would be suspicious facts. It was his play now to create no suspicion. He could make no move until he had definitely and conclusively identified and placed those who were watching him; and then, with that point settled, it should not be very hard to throw the watchers off the track long enough to enable him to visit Mrs. Tooler's pigeon-cote, and, far more important, his one vital objective now, old Tony Lomazzi's friend—Capriano.

His jaws locked. He meant to force that issue tonight, even if he could not discriminate between shadows and realities out there through the window! He had a definite plan worked out in his mind—including a visit to Square John Kelly's. He hadn't been to Square John's yet. To have gone there immediately on reaching San Francisco would have been a fool play. It would have been, not only risky for himself, but risky for Square John; and he had to protect Square John from the searching and pertinent questions that would then have certainly ensued. He was going there to-night, casually, as simply to one of many similar places—that was part of his plan!

And now he smiled in mingled bitterness and menace. The underworld had complimented him once on being the possessor of potentialities that could make of him the slickest crook in the United States. He had not forgotten that. The underworld, or at least a section of it in the persons of Baldy Vickers and his gang, was leagued against him now, as well as the police. He would strive to merit the underworld's encomium!

He turned suddenly away from the window, walked in the darkness to the table in the center of the room, and, groping for his hat, made his way to the door. He had not expected much from this vigil at the window, but there had always been the possibility that it would be productive, and the earlier hours of the evening could have been employed in no better way. It was dark enough now to begin his night's work in earnest. It must be between half-past nine and ten o'clock.

There was a dim light in the corridor, but, dim though it was, it did not hide the ragged, threadbare state of the carpet on the hallway and stairs, nor the lack of paint, or even of soap and water, on doors and woodwork. Pelatt's Hotel made no pretentious claims. It was as shabby as the shabby quarter in which it was located, and as shabby as the shabby patrons to whom it catered. But there were not many places where a man with close-cropped hair and wearing black clothes of blatant prison cut could go, and he had known Pelatt in the old days, and Pelatt, in lieu of baggage, hadn't demanded any cash in advance—he had even advanced Dave Henderson a little cash himself.

Dave Henderson reached the ground floor, and gained the street through a small, dingy office that was for the moment deserted. He paused here for an instant, the temptation strong upon him to cross the street and plunge into those shadows at the side of that porch just opposite to him. His lips grew tight. The temptation was strong, almost overpoweringly strong. He would much rather fight that way!

And then he shrugged his shoulders, and started along the street. Since he had left the penitentiary, he had not given the slightest sign that he had even a suspicion he was being watched; and, more than ever, he could not afford to do so now. There were two who could play at the game of laying traps! And, besides, the chances were a thousand to one that there were nothing but shadows over there; and there were the same odds that some one who was not a shadow would see him make the tell-tale investigation. He could not afford to take a chance. He could not afford to fail now. He had to identify beyond question of doubt the man, or men, who were on his trail, if there were any; or, with equal certainty, establish it as a fact that he was letting what he called his intuition run away with him.

There came a grim smile to his lips, as he went along. Intuition wasn't all he had to guide him, was it? Barjan had not minced words in making it clear that he would be watched; and Bookie Skarvan had made an even more ominous threat! Who was it tonight, then—the police, or the underworld, or both?

He had given no sign that he had any suspicions. He had gone to Pelatt's openly; after that, in an apparently aimless way, as a man almost childishly interested in the most trivial things after five years of imprisonment, he had roamed about the streets that afternoon.

But his wanderings had not been entirely aimless! He had located Nicolo Capriano's house—and, strangely enough, his wanderings had quite inadvertently taken him past that house several times! It was in a shabby quarter of the city, too. Also, it was a curious sort of house; that is, it was a curious sort of house when compared with its neighbors. It was one of a row of frame houses in none too good repair, and it was the second house from the corner—the directory had supplied him with the street and number. The front of the house differed in no respect from those on each side of it; it was the rear that had particularly excited his attention. He had not been able to investigate it closely, of course, but it bordered on a lane, and by walking down the cross street one could see it. It had an extension built on that reached almost to the high fence at the edge of the lane, and the extension, weather-beaten in appearance, looked to be almost as old as the house itself. Not so very curious, after all, except that no other house had that extension—and except that, in view of the fact that one Nicolo Capriano lived there, it was at least suggestive. Its back entrance was extremely easy of access!

Dave Henderson turned abruptly in through the door of a saloon, and, leaning against the bar—well down at the far end where he could both see and be seen every time the door was opened—ordered a drink.

He had thought a good deal about Nicolo Capriano in the two months since old Tony Lomazzi had ended his life sentence. He hadn't "got" it all at the moment when the old bomb-thrower had died. It had been mostly old Tony himself who was in his thoughts then, and the reference to Capriano had seemed no more than just a kindly thought on old Tony's part for a friend who had no other friend on earth. But afterwards, and not many hours afterwards, it had all taken on a vastly different perspective. The full significance of Tony's words had come to him, and this in turn had stirred his memories of earlier days in San Francisco; and he remembered Nicolo Capriano.

The barkeeper slid a bottle and whisky glass toward him. Dave Henderson half turned his back to the street door, resting his elbow negligently on the bar. He waited for a moment until the barkeeper's attention was somewhat diverted, then his fingers cupped around the small glass, completely hiding it; and the bottle, as he raised it in the other hand, was hidden from the door by the broad of his back. He poured out a few drops—sufficient to rob the glass of its cleanness. The barkeeper looked around. Dave Henderson hastily set the bottle down, like a child caught in a misdemeanor, hastily raised the glass to his lips, threw back his head, and gulped. The barkeeper scowled. It was the trick of the saloon vulture—not only a full glass, but a little over for good measure, when, through practice, the forefinger and thumb became a sort of annex to the rim. Dave Henderson stared back in sullen defiance, set the glass down on the bar, drew the back of his hand across his lips—and went out.

He hesitated a moment outside the saloon, as though undecided which way to go next, while his eyes, under the brim of his slouch hat, which was pulled forward almost to the bridge of his nose, scanned both sides of the street and in both directions. He moved on again along the block.

Yes, he remembered Nicolo Capriano. Capriano must be a pretty old man now—as old as Tony Lomazzi.

There had been a great deal of talk about a gang of Italian black-handers in those days, when he, Dave Henderson, was a boy, and Capriano had been a sort of hero-bandit, he remembered; and there had been a mysterious society, and bomb-throwing, and a reign of terror carried on that had paralyzed the police. They had never been able to convict Nicolo Capriano, though it was common knowledge that the police believed him to be the brains and front of the organization. Always something, or some one, had stood between Capriano and prison bars—like Tony Lomazzi, for instance!

He did not remember Lomazzi's trial, nor the details of the particular crime for which Lomazzi was convicted; but that, perhaps, had put an end to the gang's work. Certainly, Capriano's activities were a thing of the past; it was all a matter of years ago. Capriano was never heard of now; but even if the man through force of circumstances, was obliged to live a retired existence, that in no way robbed him of his cleverness, nor made him less valuable as a prospective ally.

Capriano was the one man who could help him. Capriano must still possess underground channels that would be of incalculable value in aiding him to track Millman down.

His fists, hidden in the side pockets of his coat, clenched fiercely. That was it—Millman! There wasn't a chance but that Millman had taken the money from the pigeon-cote. He would see, of course, before many more hours; but there wasn't a chance. It was Millman he wanted now. The possibility that had occurred to him in prison of Millman being a stool-pigeon, or even one of the police, no longer held water, for if the money had been recovered it would be publicly known. It hadn't been recovered. Therefore, it was Millman he must find, and it was Nicolo Capriano's help he wanted. But he must protect Capriano. He would owe Capriano that—that it should not be known there was anything between Nicolo Capriano and Dave Henderson. Well, he was doing that now, wasn't he? Neither Square John Kelly nor Nicolo Capriano would in any way be placed under suspicion through his visits to them to-night!

The saloons appeared to be Dave Henderson's sole attraction in life now. He went from one to another, and he passed none by, and he went nowhere else—and he left a trail of barkeepers' scowls behind him. One drink in each place, with five fingers curled around the glass, hiding the few drops the glass actually contained, while it proclaimed to the barkeeper the gluttonous and greedy imposition of the professional bum, wore out his welcome as a customer; and if the resultant scowl from behind the bar was not suggestive enough, it was augmented by an uncompromising request to "beat it!" He appeared to be possessed of an earnest determination to make a night of it— and also of an equally earnest determination to get as much liquor for as little money as possible. And the record he left behind him bore unimpeachable testimony to that purpose!

He appeared to grow a little unsteady on his feet; he was even lurching quite noticeably when, an hour later, the lighted windows of Square John Kelly's Pacific Coral Saloon, his first real objective, flung an inviting ray across his path. He stood still here full in the light, both of the window and a street lamp, and shook his head in well-simulated grave and dubious inebriety. He began to fumble in his pockets. He fished out a dime from one, and a nickel from another—a further and still more industrious search apparently proved abortive. For a long time he appeared to be absorbed in a lugubrious contemplation of the two coins that lay in the palm of his hand—but under his hat brim his eyes marked a man in a brown peaked cap who was approaching the door of the saloon. This was the second time in the course of the last half hour—since he had begun to show signs that the whisky was getting the better of him—that he had seen the man in the brown peaked cap!

There were swinging wicker doors to the saloon, and the man pushed these open, and went in—but he did not go far. Dave Henderson's lips thinned grimly. The bottom of the swinging doors was a good foot and a half above the level of the sidewalk—but, being so far gone in liquor, he would hardly be expected to notice the fact that the man's boots remained visible, and that the man was standing there motionless!

Dave Henderson took the street lamp into his confidence.

"Ol' Kelly," said Dave Henderson thickly. "Uster know Kelly—Square John. Gotta have money. Whatsh matter with touching Kelly? Eh—whatsh matter with that?"

He lurched toward the swinging doors. The boots retreated suddenly. He pushed his way through, and stood surveying the old-time familiar surroundings owlishly. The man with the brown cap was leaning against the bar close to the door; a half dozen others were ranged farther down along its length; and at its lower end, lounging against the wall of the little private office, was a squat, paunchy man with a bald head, and florid face, and keen gray eyes under enormously bushy gray eyebrows. It was Kelly, just as Kelly used to be—even to the massive gold watch chain stretched across the vest, with the massive gold fraternity emblem dangling down from the center.

"'Ello, Kelly!" Dave Henderson called out effusively, and made rapid, though somewhat erratic progress across the room to Kelly's side. "Glad t'see you, ol' boy!" He gave Kelly no chance to say anything. He caught Kelly's hand, and pumped it up and down. "Sure, you know me! Dave Henderson—ol' days at the track, eh? Been away on a vacation. Come back—broke." His voice took on a drunkenly confidential tone—that could be heard everywhere in the saloon, "Shay, could I see you a minute in private?"

A man at the bar laughed. Dave Henderson wheeled belligerently. Kelly intervened.

Perplexity, mingling with surprise and disapproval, stamped Kelly's florid face.

"Yes, I know you well enough; but I didn't expect to see you like this, Dave!" he said shortly. He jerked his hand toward the door of the private office. "I'll talk to you in there."

Dave Henderson entered the office.

Kelly shut the door behind them.

"You're drunk!" he said sternly.

Dave Henderson shook his head.

"No," he said quietly. "I'm followed. Do you think I'm a fool, John? Did you ever see me drunk? They're shadowing me, that's all; and I had to get my money from you, and keep your skirts clean, and spot the shadow, all at the same time."

Kelly's jaw sagged helplessly.

"Good God!" he ejaculated heavily. "Dave, I———"

"Don't let's talk, John—now," Dave Henderson interrupted. "There isn't time. It won't do for me to stay in here too long. 'You've got my money ready, haven't you?"

Kelly nodded—still a little helplessly.

"Yes," he said; "it's ready. I've been looking for you all afternoon. I knew you were coming out today." He went over to a safe in the corner, opened it, took out a long envelope, and handed the envelope to Dave Henderson. "It's all there, Dave—and five years' interest, compounded. A little over four thousand dollars—four thousand and fifteen, as near as I could figure it. It's all in five-hundreds and hundreds, except the fifteen; I didn't think you'd want to pack a big wad."

"Good old Square John!" said Dave Henderson softly. He opened the envelope, took out the fifteen dollars, shoved the large bills into his pocket, tucked a five-dollar bill into another pocket, and held out the remaining ten to Kelly. "Go out there and get me ten dollars from the cash register, John, will you?" he said. "Let them see you doing it. Get the idea? I'd like them to know you came across, and that I've got something to spend."

Kelly's eyes puckered in an anxious way, as they scrutinized Dave Henderson's face; but the anxiety, it was obvious enough, was all for Dave Henderson.

"You mean there's some one out there now?" he asked, as he moved toward the door.

"Yes," said Dave Henderson, with a grim little smile. "See if you know that fellow with the brown peaked cap up at the front end of the bar."

Kelly was gone a matter of two or three minutes. He came back and returned the ten dollars to Dave Henderson.

"Know the man?" asked Dave Henderson.

"Yes," said Kelly. "His name's Speen—he's a plain-clothesman." He shook his head in a troubled way, and suddenly laid both hands on Dave Henderson's shoulders. "Dave, what are you going to do?"

Dave Henderson laughed shortly.

"Do you want to know?" He flung out the words in a sort of bitter gibe. "Well, I'll tell you—in confidence. I'm going to blow the head off a *friend* of mine."

Dave Henderson felt the hands on his shoulders tighten.

"What's the use, Dave?" said Square John Kelly quietly. "I suppose it has something to do with that Tydeman wad; but what's the use? You've got four thousand dollars. Why not start clean again? The other don't pay, Dave, and——" He stopped.

Dave Henderson's face had hardened like flint.

"There's a good deal you don't know," he said evenly. "And I guess the less you know the safer you'll be. I owe you a lot, John; and the only way I can square it now is to tell you to stand from under. What you say, though I know you mean it, doesn't make any dint in five years of hell. I've got a debt to pay, and I'm going to pay it. Maybe I'll see you again—maybe I won't. But even a prison bird can say God bless you, and mean it; and that's what I say to you.

They won't have any suspicions that there's anything of any kind between you and me; but they'll naturally come here to see if they can get any information, when that fellow Speen out there turns in his report. You can tell them you advised me to start clean again, and you can tell them that I swear I don't know where that hundred thousand dollars is. They won't believe it, and you don't believe it. But let it go at that! I don't know what's going to break loose, but you stand from under, John. I'm going now—to get acquainted with Mr. Speen. It wouldn't look just right, in my supposed condition, for you to let me have another drink in your place, after having staked me; but I've got to make at least a bluff at it. You stay here for a few minutes—and then come out and chase me home." He held out his hand, wrung Square John Kelly's in a hard grip, turned abruptly away—and staggered out into the barroom.

Clutching his ten dollars in his hand, and glancing furtively back over his shoulder every step or two, Dave Henderson neared the door. Here, apparently reassured that his benefactor was not watching him, and apparently succumbing to an irresistible temptation, he sidled up to the bar—beside the man with the brown peaked cap.

"Kelly's all right—s'il right," he confided thickly to the other. "Ol' friend. Never turns down ol' friend in hard luck. Square John—betcher life! Have a drink?"

"Sure!" said the man in the brown peaked cap.

The drink was ordered, and as Dave Henderson, talking garrulously, poured out his whisky—a genuine glassful this time—he caught sight, in the mirror behind the bar, and out of the corner of his eye, of Kelly advancing down the room from the private office. And as he lifted his glass, Kelly's hand, reaching from behind, caught the glass, and set it back on the bar.

"You promised me you'd go home, and cut this out!" said Kelly in sharp reproof. "Now, go on!" He turned on the detective. "Yes, and you, too! Get out of here! You ought to know better! The man's had enough! Haven't you got anything else to do than hang around bumming drinks? I know you, and I've a mind to report you! Get out!"

Dave Henderson slunk out through the door without protest. On the sidewalk the man with the brown peaked cap joined him.

"Kelly's sore." Dave Henderson's tones were heavy with tolerant pity and magnanimous forgiveness. "Ol' friend—be all right to-morrow. Letsh go somewhere else for a drink. Whatsher shay?"

"Sure!" said the man in the brown peaked cap.

The detective was complacently agreeable to all suggestions. It was Dave Henderson who acted as guide; and he began a circuit of saloons in a direction that brought him sensibly nearer at each visit to the street and house occupied by one Nicolo Capriano. In the same block with Capriano's house he had noticed that there was also a saloon, and if Capriano's house had an exit on the lane, so, likewise, it was logical to presume, had the saloon. And that saloon now, barring intermediate stops, was his objective. But he was in no hurry. There was one point on which he had still to satisfy himself before he gave this man Speen the slip in that saloon and, by the lane, gained the rear door of Nicolo Capriano's house. He knew now that he was dealing with the police; but was Speen detailed *alone* to the case, or did Speen have assistance at hand in the background—assistance enough, say, to have scared off any move on the part of Bookie Skarvan's and Baldy Vickers' gang, of whom, certainly, he had seen nothing as yet?

A half hour passed. Several saloons were visited. Dave Henderson no longer cupped his hand around his glass. Having had nothing to start with, he could drink frankly, and a shaky hand could be trusted to spill any over-generous portions. They became confidential. He confided to Speen what Speen already knew—that he, Dave Henderson, *was* Dave Henderson, and just out from the penitentiary. Speen, stating that his name was Monahan, reciprocated with mendacious confidences that implied he was puritanical in neither his mode of life nor his means of livelihood—and began to throw out hints that he was not averse to a share in any game that Dave Henderson might have on hand.

Dave Henderson got along very badly now between the various oases that quenched his raging thirst. He leaned heavily on Speen, he stumbled frequently, and, in stumbling, obtained equally frequent views of both sides of the street behind him. No one seemed to be paying any attention to his companion or himself, and yet once or twice he had caught sight of skulking figures that, momentarily at least, had aroused his suspicions. But in this neighborhood there were many skulking figures! Again he could not be sure; but the saloon in Capriano's block was the next one ahead now, and certainly nothing had transpired that would seem to necessitate any change being made in his plans.

Speen, too, was feigning now a certain degree of intoxication. They reached the saloon, reeled through the door arm in arm, and ranged up alongside the bar.

Dave Henderson's eyes swept his surroundings, critical of every detail. It was an unpleasant and dirty place; and the few loungers, some seated at little tables, some hanging over the bar itself, were a hard and ugly looking lot.

The clientele, however, interested Dave Henderson very little—at the rear of the room, and but a few yards from the end of the bar, there was an open door, disclosing a short passage beyond, that interested him a great deal more! Beyond that passage was undoubtedly the back yard, and beyond that again was the lane. He had no desire to harm Speen, none whatever; but if any one of a dozen pretexts, that he might make to elude the man for the moment or two that was necessary to gain the yard unobserved, did not succeed, and Speen persisted in following him out there into the yard—well, so much the worse for Speen, that was all!

He was arguing now with Speen, each claiming the right to pay for the drink—but his mind was sifting through those dozen pretexts for the most plausible one to employ. He kept on arguing. Customers slouched in and out of the place; some sat down at the tables, some came to the bar. One, a hulk of a man, unshaven, with bull-breadth shoulders, with nose flattened over on one side of his cheek, stepped up to the bar beside Speen. Speen's back was turned, but the man grinned hospitably at Dave Henderson over Speen's shoulder, as he listened to the argument for a moment.

"Put away your money, son, an' have a drink with me," he invited.

Speen turned.

The grin on the battered face of the newcomer faded instantly, as he stared with apparently sudden recognition into Speen's face; and a black, ugly scowl spread over the already unhandsome features.

"Oh, it's you, is it?" he said hoarsely, and licked his lips. "By God, you got a nerve to come down here—you have! You dirty police spy!"

Speen was evidently not easily stampeded. He eyed the other levelly.

"I guess you've got the wrong man, haven't you?" he returned coolly enough. "My name's Monahan, and I don't know you."

"You lie!" snarled the other viciously. "Your name's Speen! And you don't know me—*don't you?*"

"No!" said Speen.

"You don't, eh?" The man thrust his face almost into Speen's. "You don't remember a year ago gettin' me six months on a fake plant, either, I suppose!"

"No!" said Speen.

"You don't, eh?" snarled the man again. "A hell of a bad memory you've got, ain't you? Well, I'll fix it for you so's you won't forget me so easy next time, and——-"

It came quick, without warning—before Dave Henderson could move. He saw a great, grimy fist whip forward to the point of Speen's jaw, and he caught a tiny reflected gleam of light from an ugly brass knuckleduster on one of the fingers of the clenched fist; and Speen's knees seemed to crumple up under him, and he went down in a heap to the floor.

Dave Henderson straightened up from the bar, a hard, grim smile twisting across his lips. It had been a brutal act. Speen might be a policeman, and Speen, lying there senseless, solved a certain little difficulty without further effort on his, Dave Henderson's, part; but the brutality of the act had him in its grip. There was a curious itching at his finger tips for a clutch that would maul this already battered bruiser's face beyond recognition. His eyes circled the room. The men at the tables had risen to their feet; some were pushing forward, and one, he saw over his shoulder, ran around the far end of the bar and disappeared. Speen lay inert, a huddled thing on the floor, a crimson stream spilling its way down over the man's white collar.

The twisted smile on Dave Henderson's lips deepened. The bruiser was watching him like a cat, and there was a leer on the other's face that seemed to possess some hidden significance. Well, perhaps he would change that leer, with whatever its significance might be, into something still more unhappy! He moved a few inches out from the bar. He wanted room for arm-play now, and——

The street door opened. Four or five men were crowding in. He caught a glimpse of a face among them that he knew—a little wizened face, crowned with flaming red hair—Runty Mott.

And then the lights went out.

Quick as a lightning flash Dave Henderson dropped to his hands and knees. There was a grunt above him, as though from the swing of a terrific blow that, meeting with no resistance, had over-reached itself in midair— then the forward lunge of a heavy body, a snarl, an oath, as the bruiser stumbled over Dave Henderson's crouched form—and then a crash, as Dave Henderson grappled, low down at the other's knees, and the man went to the floor. But the other, for all his weight and bulk, was lithe and agile, and his arms, flung out, circled and locked around Dave Henderson's neck.

The place was in pandemonium. Feet scuffled; chairs and tables toppled over in the darkness. Shouts, yells and curses made a din infernal. Dave Henderson wrenched and tore at the arms around his neck. He saw it all now—all. The police had trailed him; Baldy Vickers' gang had trailed the police. The bruiser was one of the gang. They had to get rid of the police, in the person of Speen, to cover their own trail again before they got him,

Dave Henderson. And they, too, had thought him drunk, and an easy prey. With Speen unconscious from a quarrel that even Speen, when he recovered, would never connect with its real purpose, they meant to kidnap him, Dave Henderson, and get him away in the confusion without any of the innocent bystanders in the place knowing what was going on. That was why the lights had gone off—that man he had seen running around the upper end of the room—he remembered now—the man had come in just behind the bruiser—that accounted for the lights—they wouldn't dare shoot—he had that advantage—dead, he wasn't any good to them—they wanted that— hundred—thousand—dollars.

He was choking. Instead of arms, steel fingers had sunk into his throat. He lunged out with all his strength. His fist met something that, though it yielded slightly, brought a brutal twinge of pain across his knuckles. His fist shot out again, whipped to its mark with everything that was in him behind the blow; and it was the bruiser's face he hit. He hit it again, and, over the mad fury that was upon him, he knew an unholy joy as his blows crashed home.

The steel fingers around his throat relaxed and fell away. He staggered to his feet.

A voice from somewhere close at hand spoke hoarsely:

"Scrag him, Mugsy! See that he's knocked cold before we carry him out!"

There was no answer from the floor.

Dave Henderson's lips were no longer twisted in a smile, they were thinned and straight; he knew why there was no answer from the floor! He crouched, gathering himself for a spring. Dark, shadowy forms were crowding in around him. There was only one chance—the door now, the rear door, and the lane! Voices growled and cursed, seemingly almost in his ears. They had him hemmed against the bar without knowing it, as they clustered around the spot where they expected he was being strangled into unconsciousness on the floor.

"Mugsy, d'ye hear! Damn you, d'ye hear! Why don't you——"

Dave Henderson launched himself forward. A wild yell went up. Hands clutched at him, and tore at his clothing, and struck at his face; forms flung themselves at his shoulders, and clung around his legs. He shook them off— and gained a few yards. He was fighting like a madman now—and now the darkness was in his favor.

They came on again in a blind rush. The door could not be far away! He stumbled over one of the small tables, recovered himself, and, snatching up the table, whirled it by one of its legs in a sweep around his head. There was a smash of impact that almost knocked the table from his grasp—and, coincidentally, a scream of pain. It cleared a space about him. He swung again, whirling the table around and around his head, gaining impetus—and suddenly sent it catapulting from him full into the shadowy forms in front of him, and, turning, made a dash for the end of the room.

He reached the wall, and groped along it for the door. The door! Where was it? He felt the warm, blood trickling down over his face. He did not remember when that had happened! He could not see—but they would turn on the lights surely now in an instant if they were not fools—and he must find the door first or he was trapped—that was his only chance—the place was a bedlam of hideous riot—curse the blood, it seemed to be running into his eyes now—Runty Mott—if only he could have settled with the skulking——

His fingers touched and felt around the jamb of the open door—and he surged, panting, through the doorway. The short passage ended in another door. He opened this, found the yard in front of him, dashed across it, and hurled himself over the fence into the lane.

The uproar, the yells, the furious shouts from behind him seemed suddenly to increase in volume. He ran the faster. They had turned the lights on—and found him gone! From somewhere in the direction of the street there came the shrill cheep-cheep of a patrolman's whistle. Yes, he quite understood that, too—there would be a riot call pulled in a minute, but that made little difference to him. It was the gangsters, who were now probably pouring out of the saloon's back door in pursuit of him, with whom he had to reckon. But he should be safe now—he was abreast of Capriano's house, which he could distinguish even in the darkness because the extension stuck out like some great, black looming shadow from the row of other houses.

There was a gate here somewhere, or a door in the fence, undoubtedly; but he had no time to hunt for gate or door, perhaps only to find it locked! The fence was quicker and easier. He swung himself up, and over—and, scarcely a yard away, found himself confronted with what looked like an enclosed porch or vestibule to the Italian's back door.

He was quick now, but equally silent in his movements. From the direction of the saloon, shouts reached him, the voices no longer muffled, but as though they were out in the open—in the back yard of the saloon perhaps, or perhaps by now in the lane itself. He stepped inside the porch, and knocked softly on the door. He knocked again and again. It seemed as though the seconds dragged themselves out into immeasureable periods of time. He swept the blood out of his eyes once more, and, his ears strained laneward, continued to knock insistently, louder and louder.

A light footstep, hurried, sounded from within. It halted on the other side of the closed door. He had a feeling that somehow, even through that closed door, and even in the darkness, he was under inspection. The next instant he was sure of it. Above his head a small incandescent bulb suddenly flooded the porch with light, and fell full upon him as he stood there, a ghastly object, he realized, with blood-stained face, and torn and dishevelled clothes.

From behind the closed door came a girl's startled gasp of dismay and alarm; from up the lane now unmistakably came the pound of racing feet.

"Quick!" whispered Dave Henderson hoarsely. "I'm from Tony Lomazzi. For God's sake, put out that light!"

II.
SANCTUARY

THE light in the porch went out. From within, as though with slow, dubious hesitation, a key turned in the lock. The door opened slightly, and from a dark interior the girl's voice reached Dave Henderson again.

"Tony Lomazzi sent you, you say!" she exclaimed in a puzzled way; and then, a sudden apprehension in her voice: "You are all covered with blood — what is the matter? What do you want?"

From the lane, the sound of pounding, racing feet seemed almost opposite the Italian's porch now. Dave Henderson, without ceremony, pushed at the door. It yielded, as the girl evidently retreated backward abruptly, and he stepped inside, closed the door softly behind him, and, feeling for the key, turned it swiftly in the lock. He could see nothing, but out of the darkness near him came a sharp, quick-drawn intake of breath.

"I'm sorry!" said Dave Henderson quietly. "But it was a bit of a close call. I'm not quite sure whether they are running after me, or running from the police, but, either way, it would have been a little awkward if I had been seen."

She seemed to have regained her composure, for her voice, as she spoke again, was as quiet and as evenly modulated as his own.

"What do you want?" she asked once more. "Why did Tony Lomazzi send you here?"

He did not answer at once. From somewhere in the front of the house, muffled, but still quite audible, there came the voices of two men—one high-pitched, querulous, curiously short-breathed, the other with a sort of monotonous, sullen whine in it. He listened automatically for an instant, as his eyes searched around him. It was almost black inside here as he stood with his back to the door, but, grown more accustomed to the darkness now, he could make out a faint, blurred form, obviously that of the girl, a few feet away from him.

"I want to see Nicolo Capriano," he said.

It was her turn now to pause before she answered.

"Is it necessary?" she asked finally.

"To me—yes," said Dave Henderson.

"My father has already had far too much excitement to-night," she said in a low voice. "He is a very sick man. There is some one with him now. If you could give me the message it would be better. As for any help you need, for you appear to be hurt, I will gladly attend to that myself. You may be assured of that, if you come from Tony Lomazzi."

She was Nicolo Capriano's daughter, then! It struck him as a passing thought, though of no particular consequence, that she spoke excellent English for an Italian girl.

"I'm afraid that won't do," said Dave Henderson seriously. "It is practically a matter of life and death to me to see Nicolo Capriano, and——"

From the front of the house the querulous voice rose suddenly in a still higher pitch:

"Teresa! Teresa!"

"Yes, I am coming!" the girl cried out; and then, hurriedly, to Dave Henderson: "Wait here a moment. I will tell him. What is your name?"

Dave Henderson smiled a little queerly in the darkness.

"If he is alone when you tell him, it is Dave Henderson," he said dryly. "Otherwise, it is Smith—John Smith."

She was gone.

He listened as her footsteps died away in the darkness; and then he listened again at the door. There was still a great deal of commotion out there in the lane, but certainly there was nothing to indicate that he and Nicolo Capriano's back porch had in any way been suspected of having had anything in common; it was, rather, as though the entire saloon up there had emptied itself in haste into the lane, and was running pell-mell in an effort to be anywhere but in that vicinity when the police arrived. Well, so much the better! For the moment, at least, he had evaded the trap set for him both by Bookie Skarvan's pack and by the police—and the next move depended very largely upon Nicolo Capriano, or, perhaps even more, upon this daughter of his, since the old man, it seemed, was sick. The girl's name was apparently Teresa—which mattered very little. What mattered a great deal more was that she evidently had her wits about her—an inheritance possibly from the old man, whose reputation, in his day, as one of the coolest and shrewdest of those outside the pale of the law, was at least substantiated by the fact that he had been able to stand off the police for practically a lifetime.

Dave Henderson raised his hand, and felt gingerly over his right temple. The blood had stopped flowing, but there was a large and well-defined lump there. He did not remember at just what particular stage of the fight that had happened. From his head, his hand felt over his clothing. He nodded a little ruefully to himself. He had come off far from scathless—his coat had almost literally been torn from his back.

Voices reached him again from the front of the house; he heard the girl speaking quietly in Italian; he heard some response in the sullen whine that he had remarked before; and then the street door opened and closed. There was silence then for what seemed a long time, until finally he caught the sound of the girl's step coming toward him again.

"My father will see you," she said. "But I want to warn you again that he is a very sick man—sicker than he imagines he is. It is his heart."

"Yes," said Dave Henderson.

"Come with me, then," she said tersely. "There is a door here—the passage turns to the right. Can you see?"

It was a queer place—with its darkness, and its twisted passage! Quite queer for so small and ordinary a dwelling—but, if rumor were true, it had been queerer still in the years gone by! A grim smile crossed Dave Henderson's lips, as he followed the shadowy form of his conductor. It augured well, at all events! The surroundings at least bore out Nicolo Capriano's record, which was a record much to be desired by a man in his, Dave Henderson's, straits.

The light from an open door beyond the turn in the passage dispelled the darkness. The girl was standing there now, motioning him to enter—but suddenly, for a moment, he stood and stared at her. This was queer, too! Everything about the place was queer! Somehow he had pictured in the darkness an Italian girl, pretty enough perhaps in a purely physical way, with gold rings in her ears, perhaps, such as the men wore, and slatternly, with feet shod in coarse, thick boots; the only kind of an Italian girl he had ever remembered having seen—a girl that hauled at the straps of a hand-organ, while the man plodded along the streets between the shafts. She wasn't like that, though—and he stared at her; stared at the trim, lithe, daintily dressed little figure, stared at the oval face, and the dark, steady, self-reliant eyes, and the wealth of rich, black hair that crowned the broad, white forehead, and glinted like silken strands, as the light fell upon it.

The color mounted in her cheeks.

And then, with a start, he pushed his hand across his eyes, and bit his lips, and flushed a deeper red than hers.

Her eyes, that had begun to harden as they met his gaze, softened in an instant, and she smiled. His confusion had been his apology, his acquittal of any intended offense.

She motioned again to him to enter, and, as he stepped forward across the threshold, she reached in and rested her hand on the doorknob.

"You can call when you need me, father," she said—-and closed the door softly.

Dave Henderson's eyes swept the room with a swift, comprehensive glance; and then held steadily on a pair of jet-black eyes, so black that they seemed to possess no pupils, which were in turn fixed on him by a strange-looking figure, lying on a quaint, old-fashioned, four-poster bed across the room. He moved forward and took a chair at the bedside, as the other beckoned to him.

So this was Nicolo Capriano! The man was propped upright in bed by means of pillows that were supported by an inverted chair behind them; both hands, very white, very blue under the nails of the long, slender fingers, lay out-stretched before him on an immaculately white coverlet; the man's hair was silver, and a white beard and mustache but partially disguised the thin, emaciated condition of his face. But it was the eyes that above all else commanded attention. They were unnaturally bright, gleaming out from under enormously white, bushy eyebrows; and they were curiously inscrutable eyes. They seemed to hold great depths beneath which might smolder a passion that would leap without warning into flame; or to hold, as they did now, a strange introspective stare, making them like shuttered windows that gave no glimpse of the mind within.

"I am Nicolo Capriano," said the man abruptly, and in perfect English. "My daughter tells me that you gave your name as Dave Henderson. The name seems familiar. I have heard it somewhere. I remember, it seems to me, a little matter of one hundred thousand dollars some five years ago, for which a man by that name went to the penitentiary."

Dave Henderson's eyes wandered for a moment around the room again. He found himself wondering at the man's English—as he had at the girl's. Subconsciously he was aware that the furnishings, though plain and simple and lacking in anything ornate, were foreign and unusual, but that the outstanding feature of the room was a sort of refreshing and immaculate cleanliness—like the coverlet. He forced his mind back to what Nicolo Capriano had said.

Were all his cards to go face up on the table for Nicolo Capriano to see?

He had intended to make no more of a confidant of the other than was absolutely necessary; but, equally, he had not expected to find in Nicolo Capriano a physically helpless and bed-ridden man. It made a difference—a very great difference! If Millman, for instance, had been bed-ridden, it— — He caught himself smiling a little mirthlessly.

"That's me—Dave Henderson," he said calmly.

The old Italian nodded his head.

"And the hundred thousand dollars has never been recovered," he observed shrewdly. "The police are interested in your movements, eh? It is for that reason you have come to me, is it not so? And Tony Lomazzi foresaw all this—and he sent you here?"

"Yes," said Dave Henderson—and frowned suddenly. It was bothering him again—the fact that this Italian and his daughter should speak English as though it were their own tongue.

Nicolo Capriano nodded his head again. And then, astutely:

"Something is disturbing you, my young friend," he said. "What is it?"

Dave Henderson straightened in his chair with a little start—and laughed shortly. Very little, evidently, escaped Nicolo Capriano!

"It's not much," he said. "Just that you and your daughter speak pretty good English for Italians."

Nicolo Capriano smiled softly.

"I should speak pretty good English," he said; "and Teresa should speak it even better. We both learned it as children. I, in a certain part of London, as a boy; and Teresa here in San Francisco, where she was born. Her mother was American, and, though I taught Teresa Italian, we always spoke English while her mother was alive, and afterwards my daughter seemed to think we should continue to do so." He shrugged his shoulders. "But you came from Lomazzi," he prompted. "Tell me about Lomazzi. He is well?"

"He is dead," said Dave Henderson quietly.

The thin hands, outstretched before the other, closed with a quick twitching motion—then opened, and the fingers began to pluck abstractedly at the coverlet. There was no other sign of emotion, or movement from the figure on the bed, except that the keen, black eyes were veiled now by half closed lids.

"He died—fifteen years ago—when he went up there—for life"—the man seemed to be communing with himself. "Yes, yes; he is dead—he has been dead for fifteen years." He looked up suddenly, and fixed his eyes with a sharp, curiously appraising gaze on Dave Henderson. "You speak of actual death, of course," he said, in a low tone. "Do you know anything of the circumstances?"

"It was two months ago," Dave Henderson answered. "He was taken ill one night. His cell was next to mine. He was my friend. He asked for me, and the warden let me go to him. He died in a very few minutes. It was then, while I was in the cell, that he whispered to me that I would need help when I got out, and he told me to come to you, and to say that he sent me."

"And to the warden, and whoever else was in the cell, he said—nothing?"

"Nothing," said Dave Henderson.

Nicolo Capriano's eyes were hidden again; the long, slim fingers, with blue-tipped nails, plucked at the coverlet. It was a full minute before he spoke.

"I owe Tony Lomazzi a great debt," he said slowly; "and I would like to repay it in a little way by helping you since he has asked it; but it is not to-day, young man, as it was in those days so long ago. For fifteen years I have not lifted my hand against the police. And it is obviously for help from the police that you come to me. You have served your term, and the police would not molest you further except for a good reason. Is it not so? And the reason is not far to seek, I think. It is the money which was never recovered that they are after. You have it hidden somewhere. You know where it is, and you wish to outwit the police while you secure it. Am I not right?"

Dave Henderson glanced at the impassive face propped up on the pillows. Old Nicolo Capriano in no way belied his reputation for shrewdness; the man's brain, however physically ill he might be otherwise, had at least not lost its cunning.

"Yes," said Dave Henderson, with a short, sudden laugh, "you are right— but also you are wrong. It is the police that I want to get away from, and it is on account of that money, which, it is also true, I hid away before I went up; but it is not only the police, it is the gang of crooks who put me in wrong at the trial who are trying to grab it, too—only, as it stands now, I don't know where the money is myself. I trusted a fellow in the jug, who got out two months ahead of me—and he did me."

The white bushy eyebrows went up.

"So!" ejaculated the old Italian. "Well, then, what is the use!"

"A whole lot!" returned Dave Henderson grimly. "To get the fellow if I can! And I can't do that with the police, and a gang of crooks besides, at my heels, can I?"

Nicolo Capriano shook his head meditatively.

"I have my daughter to think of," he said. "Listen, young man, it has not been easy to stand square with the police during these years as it is, and that without any initiative act on my part that would stir them up against me again. Old associations and old records are not so easily got rid of. I will give you an example. There was a man here to-night—when you came. His name is Ignace Ferroni. He was one of us in the old days—do you understand? When the trouble came for which Tony Lomazzi suffered, Ignace managed to get away. I had not seen him from that day to this. He came back here to-night for help—for a very strange kind of help. He was one of us, I have said, and he had not forgotten his old ways. He had a bomb, a small bomb in his pocket, whose mechanism had gone wrong. He had already planted it once to-night, and finding it did not explode, he picked it up again, and brought it to me, and asked me to fix it for him. It was an old feud he had with some one, he would not tell me who, that he had been nursing all this time. I think his passion for vengeance had perhaps turned his head a little. I refused to have anything to do with his bomb, of course, and he left here in a rage, and in his condition he is as likely to turn on me as he is to carry out his original intention. But, that apart, what am I to do now? He was one of us, I cannot expose him to the police—he would be sentenced to a long term. And yet, if his bomb explodes, to whom will the police come first? To me!" Nicolo Capriano suddenly raised his hands, and they were clenched—and as suddenly caught his breath, and choked, and a spasm of pain crossed his face. The next instant he was smiling mirthlessly with twitching lips. "Yes, to me—to me, whom some fool amongst them once called the Dago Bomb King, which they will never forget! It is always to me they come! Any crime that seems to have the slightest Italian tinge—and they come to Nicolo Capriano!" He shrugged his shoulders. "You see, young man, it is not easy for me to steer my way unmolested even when I am wholly innocent. But I, too, do not forget! I do not forget Tony Lomazzi! Tell me exactly what you want me to do. You think you can find the man and the money if you can throw the police and the others off your trail?"

"Yes!" said Dave Henderson, with ominous quiet. "That's my job in life now! If I could disappear for three or four days, I guess that's all the start I'd need." There was a tolerant smile now on the old bomb king's lips.

"Three or four days would be a very easy matter," he answered. "But after that—what? It might do very well in respect to this gang of crooks; but it would be of very little avail where the police are concerned, for they would simply do what the crooks could not do—see that every plain-clothesman and officer on this continent was on the watch for you. Do you imagine that, believing you know where the money is, the police will forget all about you in three or four days?"

"No," admitted Dave Henderson, with the same ominous quiet; "but all I ask is a fighting chance." Nicolo Capriano stared in speculative silence for a moment.

"You have courage, my young friend!" he said softly. "I like that—also I do not like the police. But three or four days!" He shook his head. "You do not know the police as I know them! And this man you trusted, and who, as I understand, got away with the money, do you know where to find him?"

"I think he is in New York," Dave Henderson answered.

"Ah! New York!" Nicolo Capriano nodded. "But New York is a world in itself. He did not give you his address, and then rob you, I suppose!"

Dave Henderson did not answer for a moment. What Nicolo Capriano said was very true! But the rendezvous that Millman had given was, on the face of it, a fake anyhow. That had been his own opinion from the start; but during the two years Millman and he had been together in prison there had been many little inadvertent remarks in conversation that had, beyond question of doubt, stamped Millman as a New Yorker. Perhaps Millman had remembered that when he had given the rendezvous in New York—to give color to its genuineness—because it was the only natural place he could propose if he was to carry out logically the stories he had told for two long years.

"You do not answer?" suggested Nicolo Capriano patiently.

It was on Dave Henderson's tongue to lay the whole story bare to the date, day and hour of that hotel rendezvous, but instead he shook his head. He was conscious of no distrust of the other. Why should he be distrustful! It was not that. It seemed more an innate caution, that was an absurd caution now because the rendezvous meant nothing anyhow, that had sprung up spontaneously within him. He felt that he was suddenly illogical. Fie found himself answering in a savage, dogged sort of way.

"That's all right!" he said. "I haven't got his address—but New York is good enough. He spilled too much in prison for me not to know that's where he hangs out. I'll get him—if I can only shake the police."

Nicolo Capriano's blue-tipped fingers went straggling through the long white beard.

"The police!" He was whispering—seemingly to himself. "It is always the police—a lifetime of the cursed police—and I have my daughter to think of—but I do not forget Tony Lomazzi—Teresa would not have me forget."

He spoke abruptly to Dave Henderson. "Tell me about to-night. My daughter says you came here like a hunted thing, and it is very evident that you have been in a fight. I suppose it was with the police, or with this gang you speak of; but, in that case, you have ruined any chance of help from me if you have led them here—if, for instance, they are waiting now for you to come out again."

"I do not think they are waiting!" said Dave Henderson, with a twisted smile. "And I think that the police end of to-night, and maybe some of the rest of it as well, is in the hospital by now! It's not much of a story—but unless that light in your back porch, which was on for about two seconds, could be seen up the lane, there's no one could know that I am here."

The old Italian smiled curiously.

"I do not put lights where they act as beacons," he said whimsically. "It does not show from the lane; it is for the benefit of those *inside* the house. Tell me your story."

"It's not much," said Dave Henderson again. "The police shadowed me from the minute I left the penitentiary to-day. To-night I handed them a little come-on, that's all, so as to make sure that I had side-tracked them before coming here. And then the gang, Baldy Vickers' gang——"

"Vickers—Baldy Vickers! Yes, yes, I know; they hang out at Jake Morrissey's place!" exclaimed the old bomb king suddenly. "Runty Mott, and——"

"It was Runty Mott that butted in to-night," said Dave Henderson, with a short laugh. "I had the fly-cop going, all right. I let him pick me up in a saloon over the bar. He thought I was pretty drunk even then. We started in to make a night of it—and the fly-cop was going to get a drunken man to spill all the history of his life, and incidentally get him to lead the way to where a certain little sum of money was! Understand? I kept heading in this direction, for I had looked the lay of the land over this afternoon. That saloon up the street was booked as my last stopping place. I was going to shake the fly-cop there, and——" Dave Henderson paused.

Nicolo Capriano was leaning forward in his bed, and there was a new, feverish light in the coal-black eyes—like some long-smoldering flame leaping suddenly into a blaze.

"Go on!" he breathed impatiently. "Go on! Ah! I can see it all!"

"Runty Mott and his crowd must have been trailing me." Dave Henderson smiled grimly. "They thought both the fly-cop and myself were drunk. But to cover their own game and make their play at me they had to get the fly-cop out of the road first. One of the gang came into the saloon, faked a quarrel with the fly-cop, and knocked him out. I didn't know what was up until then, when I caught sight of Runty Mott and the rest of his crowd pushing in through the door." Dave Henderson's smile grew a little grimmer. "That's all! They started something—but they didn't finish it! They had it all framed up well enough—the lights switched off, and all that, so as to lay me out and kidnap me, and then stow me away somewhere and make me talk." He jerked his hand toward his torn garments. "There was a bit of a fight," he said quietly. "I left them there pawing the air in the dark, and I was down here in your porch before any of them got out to the lane. I fancy there's some little row up there now on account of that fly-cop they put to sleep."

Nicolo Capriano's hand reached out, and began to pat excitedly at Dave Henderson's sleeve.

"It is like the old days!" he said feverishly. "It is like the young blood warming up an old man's veins again. Yes, yes; it is like the old days back once more! Ah, my young friend, if I had had you on the night that Tony Lomazzi was trapped, instead of—but that is too late, eh? Yes—too late! But you are clever, and you use your head, and you have the courage. That is what I like! Yes, assuredly, I will help you, and not only for Tony Lomazzi's sake, but for your own. You shall have your chance, your fighting chance, my young friend, and you will run down your man" —his voice was rising in excitement—"and the money—eh! Yes, yes! And Nicolo Capriano will help you!" He raised his voice still higher. "Teresa! Here, Teresa!" he shouted.

The door opened; the girl stood on the threshold.

"Father," she said reprovingly, "you are exciting yourself again."

The old bomb king's voice was instantly subdued.

"No, I am not! You see—my little one! You see, I am quite calm. And now listen to me. This is Tony Lomazzi's friend, and he is therefore our friend. Is it not so? Well, then, listen! He is in need of help. The police must not get him. So, first, he must have some clothes instead of those torn ones. Get him some of mine. They will not fit very well—but they will do. Then you will telephone Emmanuel that I have a guest for him who does not like the police, a guest by the name of Smith—that is enough for him to know. And tell Emmanuel that he is to come with his car, and wait a block below the lane. And after that again you will go out, Teresa, and let us know if all is safe, and if there is still any police, or any one else, in the lane. Eh? Well, run then!"

"Yes," she said. She was looking at Dave Henderson now, and there was a friendly smile in the dark, steady eyes, though she still addressed her father. "And what news does he bring us of Tony?"

"You will know by and by, when there is time," her father answered with sudden brusqueness. "Run, now!"

She was back in a few moments with an armful of clothes; then once more left the room, this time closing the door behind her.

Nicolo Capriano pointed to a second door at the side of the room.

"There is the bathroom, my young friend," he said crisply. "Go in there and wash the blood off your face, and change your clothes."

Dave Henderson hesitated.

"Do you think it is safe for her, for your daughter, to go out there?" he demurred. "There was more of a row than perhaps I led you to imagine, and the police——"

"Safe!" The old Italian grinned suddenly in derision. "Listen, my young friend, you need have no fear. My daughter is a Capriano—eh? Yes, and like her father, she is more than a match for all the police in San Francisco. Go now, and change! It will not take Emmanuel long to get here."

It took Dave Henderson perhaps ten minutes to wash and bathe his bruises, and change into the Italian's clothes. At the expiration of that time, he surveyed the result in a small mirror that hung on the wall. The clothes were ready-made, and far from new; they were ill-fitting, and they bulged badly in places. His appearance was not flattering! He might have passed for an Italian navvy in hard luck and—— He smiled queerly, as he turned from the mirror and transferred the money he had received from Square John Kelly, together with his few belongings, from the pockets of his discarded suit to those of the one he now had on. He stepped out into the bedroom.

Nicolo Capriano in turn surveyed the metamorphosis critically for a moment—and nodded his head in approval.

"Good!" ejaculated the old bomb king. "Excellent!" He rubbed his thin fingers together. "Yes, yes, it is like the old days again! Ha, ha, old Nicolo still plays a hand in the game, and old Nicolo's head is still on his shoulders. Three or four days! That would be easy even for a child! Emmanuel will take care of that. But we must do better than that—eh? And that is not so simple! To hide away from the police is one thing, and to outwit them completely is another! Is it not so? You must give the old man, whose brain has grown rusty because it has been so long idle, time to think, eh? It will do you no good if you always have to hide—eh? But, listen, you will hide while old Nicolo thinks—you understand? You can trust Emmanuel—but tell him nothing. He keeps a little restaurant, and he will give you a room upstairs. You must not leave that room, you must not show yourself, until you hear from me. You quite understand?"

"You need not worry on that score!" said Dave Henderson grimly.

"Good!" cried the old Italian again. "Only my daughter and myself will know that you are there. You can leave it to old Nicolo to find a way. Yes, yes"—excitement was growing upon the man again; he rocked his body to and fro—"old Nicolo and the police—ha, ha! Old Nicolo, who is dying in his bed—eh? And— —" His voice was hushed abruptly; he lowered himself back on his pillows. "Here is Teresa!" he whispered. "She will say I am exciting myself again. Bah! I am strong again with the old wine in my veins!" His hands lay suddenly quiet and composed on the coverlet before him, as the door opened, and the girl stood again on the threshold. "Well, my little one?" he purred.

"Emmanuel has come," she said. "There are some police up in Vinetto's saloon, but there is no one in the lane. It is quite safe."

Nicolo Capriano nodded.

"And Emmanuel understands?"

"Yes," she said.

"Go, then!" The old Italian was holding out his hand to Dave Henderson. "Go at once! My daughter will take you to Emmanuel."

Dave Henderson caught the other's hand.

"Yes, but look here," he said, a sudden huskiness in his voice, "I— —"

"You want to thank me—eh?" said the old bomb king, shaking his head. "Well, my young friend, there will be time enough for that. You will see me again—eh? Yes! When old Nicolo sends for you, you will come. Until then—you will remember! Do not move from your room! Now, go!"

Teresa spoke from the doorway.

"Yes, hurry, please!" she said quietly. "The lane was empty a few minutes ago, but— —" She shrugged her shoulders significantly.

Dave Henderson, with a final nod to the propped-up figure in the bed, turned and followed Teresa along the passage, and out into the porch. Here she bade him wait while she went out again into the lane; but in a minute more she called out to him in a whisper to join her.

They passed out of the lane, and into the cross street. A little ahead of them, Dave Henderson could see a small car, its hood up, standing by the curb.

She stopped suddenly.

"Emmanuel has seen me," she said. "That is all that is necessary to identify you." She held out her hand. "I—I hope you will get out of your danger safely."

"If I do," said Dave Henderson fervently, "I'll have you and your father to thank for it."

She shook her head.

"No," she said. "You will have to thank Tony Lomazzi."

He wanted to say something to detain her there for a moment or two longer, even under those most unauspicious of circumstances—but five years of prison had not made him glib of tongue, or quick of speech. She was very pretty—but it was not her prettiness alone that made her appeal. There was something of winsomeness about the lithe, graceful little figure, and something to admire in the quiet self-reliance, and the cool composure with which, for instance, she had just accepted the danger of possible, and decidedly unpleasant, interference by the police in the lane.

"But I can't thank Tony Lomazzi, since he is dead," he blurted out—and the next instant cursed himself for a raw-tongued, blundering fool. In the rays of the street lamp a little way off, he saw her face go deathly white. Her hand that was in his closed with a quick, involuntary clutch, and fell away—and there came a little moan of pain.

"Dead!" she said. "Tony—dead!" And then she seemed to draw her little form erect—and smiled—but the great dark eyes were wet and full of tears.

"I——" Her voice broke. "Good-night!" she said hurriedly—and turned abruptly away.

He watched her, gnawing viciously at his lip, cursing at himself again for a blundering fool, until she disappeared in the lane; and then he, too, turned, and walked to the waiting car.

A man in the driver's seat reached out and opened the door of the tonneau.

"Me Emmanuel," he said complacently, in broken English. "You no give-a da damn tor da police anymore. I gotta da room where you hide—safe. See? Over da restaurant. You eat, you sleep, you give-a da cops da laugh."

Dave Henderson stepped into the car. His mind was in a chaotic whirl. A thousand diverse things seemed struggling for supremacy—the police and Runty Mott—Millman—Capriano, the queer, sick Capriano—the girl, the girl with the wondrous face, who cried because Tony Lomazzi was dead—a thousand things impinging in lightning flashes that made a vortex of his brain. They found expression in a sort of debonair facetiousness.

"Some boy, Emmanuel!" he said—and flung himself down on the seat. "Go to it!"

III.
NICOLO CAPRIANO PLAYS HIS CARDS

NICOLO CAPRIANO'S eyes were closed; the propped-up form on the pillows was motionless—only the thin fingers plucking at the coverlet with curiously patient insistence bore evidence that the man was not asleep.

Suddenly he smiled; and his eyes opened, a dreamy, smoldering light in their depths. His hand reached out for the morning paper that lay on the bed beside him, and for the second time since Teresa had brought him the paper half an hour before, he pored for a long while over a leading "story" on the front page. It had nothing to do with the disturbance in Vinetto's saloon of the night before; it dealt with a strange and mysterious bomb explosion in a downtown park during the small morning hours, which, besides awakening and terrifying the immediate neighborhood, had, according to the newspaper account, literally blown a man, and, with the man, the bench on which he had evidently been sitting under an arc light, to pieces. The victim was mutilated beyond recognition; all that the police had been able to identify were fragments of a bomb, thus establishing the cause of the accident, or, more likely, as the paper hinted, murder.

"The fool!" Nicolo Capriano whispered. "It was Ignace Ferroni—the fool! And so he would not listen to old Nicolo—eh?" He cackled out suddenly, his laugh shrill and high echoing through the room. "Well, perhaps it is as well, eh, Ignace? Perhaps it is as well—perhaps you will be of some service, Ignace, now that you are dead, eh, Ignace—which is something that you never were when you were alive!"

He laid the paper down, and again his eyes closed, and again the blue-tipped fingers resumed their interminable plucking at the coverlet—but now he whispered constantly to himself.

"A hundred thousand dollars.... It is a great deal of money.... We worked for much less in the old days—for very much less.... I am old and sick, am I?... Ha, ha!... But for just once more, eh—just once more—to see if the old cunning is not still there.... And if the cards are thrust into one's hands, does it not make the fingers itch to play them!... Yes, yes, it makes young again the blood in the old veins.... And Tony is dead.... Yes, yes, the young fellow is clever, too—clever enough to find the money again if the police do not meddle with him.... And the gang, Baldy Vickers' gang—bah!—they are already no longer to be considered—they have not long arms, they do not reach far—they do not reach to New York—eh—where the police reach—and where old Nicolo Capriano reaches, too.... Ignace—the fool!.... So he would not listen, to me, eh—and he sat out there under the park light trying to fix his old bomb, and blew himself up.... The fool—but you have no reason to complain, eh, Nicolo?.... It will bring the police to the door, but for once they will be welcome, eh?.... They will not know it—but they will be welcome.... We will see if Nicolo Capriano is not still their match!"

Outside somewhere in the hall he could hear Teresa moving about, busy with her morning work. He listened intently—not to his daughter's movements, but for a footstep on the pavement that, instead of passing by, would climb the short flight of steps to the front door.

"Well, why do they not come—eh?" he muttered impatiently. "Why do they not come?"

He relapsed into silence, but he no longer lay there placidly with his eyes closed. A strange excitement seemed to be growing upon him. It tinged the skin under his beard with a hectic flush, and the black eyes glistened and glinted abnormally, as they kept darting objectiveless glances here and there around the room.

Perhaps half an hour passed, and then the sick man began to mutter again:

"Will they make me send for them—the fools!" He apostrophized the foot of the bed viciously. "No, no—it would not be as safe. If they do not come in another hour, there will be time enough then for that. You must wait, Nicolo. The police have always come before to Nicolo Capriano, if they thought old Nicolo could help them—and with a bomb—ha, ha—to whom else would they come—eh?—to whom————-"

He was instantly alert. Some one was outside there now. He heard the door bell ring, and presently he heard Teresa answer it. He caught a confused murmur of voices. The thin fingers were working with a quick, jubilant motion one over the other. The black eyes, half closed again, fixed expectantly on the door of the room opposite to the foot of the bed. It opened, and Teresa stepped into the room.

"It is Lieutenant Barjan, father," she said, in a low tone. "He wants to talk to you about that bomb explosion in the park."

"So!" A queer smile twitched at the old bomb king's lips. He beckoned to his daughter to approach the bed, and, as she obeyed, he pulled her head down to his lips. "You know nothing, Teresa—nothing! Understand? Nothing except to corroborate anything that I may say. You did not even know that there had been an explosion until he spoke of it. You know nothing about Ignace. You understand?"

"Yes," she said composedly.

"Good!" he whispered. "Well, now, go and tell him that I do not want to see him. Tell him I said he was to go away. Tell him that I won't see him, that I won't be bothered with him and his cursed police spies! Tell him that"—he patted his daughter's head confidentially—"and leave the door open, Teresa, little one, so that I can hear."

"What do you mean to do, father?" she asked quickly.

"Ha, ha—you will see, my little one—you will see!" Capriano patted her head again. "We do not forget our debt to Tony Lomazzi. No! Well, you will see! Tell the cunning, clever Barjan to go away!"

He watched as she left the room; and then, his head cocked on one side to listen, the blue-tipped fingers reached stealthily out and without a sound slid the newspaper that was lying in front of him under the bed covers.

"I am very sorry," he heard Teresa announce crisply; "but my father positively refuses to see you."

"Oh, he does—does he?" a voice returned in bland sarcasm. "Well, I'm very sorry myself then, but I guess he'll have to change his mind! Pardon me, Miss Capriano, if I——"

A quick, heavy step sounded in the hallway. Nicolo Capriano's alert and listening attitude was gone in a flash. He pushed himself up in the bed, and held himself there with one hand, and the other outflung, knotted into a fist, he shook violently in the direction of the door, as the figure of the plain-clothesman appeared on the threshold.

Old Nicolo Capriano was apparently in the throes of a towering passion.

"Get out of here!" he screamed. "Did my daughter not tell you to get out! Go away! I want nothing to do with you! Curse you—and all the rest of the police with you! Can you not leave old Nicolo Capriano to die in peace—eh?"

"That's all right!" said Barjan coolly. He glanced over his shoulder. Teresa was standing just outside in the hall behind him. "Pardon me," he said again—and closed the door upon her. "Now then"—he faced Nicolo Capriano once more—"there's no use kicking up all this dust. It won't get you anywhere, Nicolo. There's a little matter that I want to talk to you about, and that I'm going to talk to you about whether you like it or not—that's all there is to it."

And we'll get right to the point. What do you know about that affair in the park last night?"

Nicolo Capriano sank back on his pillows, with a furious snarl. He still shook his fist at the officer.

"What should I know about your miserable affairs!" he shouted. "I know nothing about any park! I know nothing at all! Why do you not leave me in peace—eh? For fifteen years this has gone on, always spying on Nicolo Capriano, and for fifteen years Nicolo Capriano has not lifted a finger against the law."

"That is true—as far as we know," said Barjan calmly. "But there's a little record that goes back beyond those fifteen years, Nicolo, that keeps us a little chummy with you—and you've been valuable at times, Nicolo."

"Bah!" Nicolo Capriano spat the exclamation viciously at the other.

"About last night," suggested Barjan patiently. "It's rather in your line. I thought perhaps you might be able to give us a little help that would put us on the right track."

"I don't know what you're talking about!" snapped Nicolo Capriano.

"I'm talking about the man that was blown to pieces by a bomb." Barjan was still patient.

Nicolo Capriano's eyes showed the first gleam of interest.

"I didn't know there was any man blown up." His tone appeared to mingle the rage and antagonism that he had first exhibited with a new and suddenly awakened curiosity. "I didn't know there was any man blown up," he repeated.

"That's too bad!" said Barjan with mock resignation—and settled himself deliberately in a chair at the bedside. "I guess, then, you're the only man in San Francisco who doesn't."

"You fool!" Nicolo Capriano rasped in rage again. "I've been bed-ridden for three years—and I wish to God you had been, too!" He choked and coughed a little. He eyed Barjan malevolently. "I tell you this is the first I've heard of it. I don't hang about the street corners picking up the news! Don't sit there with your silly, smirking police face, trying to see how smart you can be! What information do you expect to get out of me like that? When I know nothing, I can tell nothing, can I? Who was the man?"

"That's what we want to know," said Barjan pleasantly. "And, look here, Nicolo, I'm not here to rile you. All that was left was a few fragments of park bench, man, arc-light standard, and a piece or two of what was evidently a bomb."

"What time was this?" Nicolo Capriano's eyes were on the foot of the bed.

"Three o'clock this morning," Barjan answered.

The old bomb king's fingers began to pluck at the coverlet. A minute passed. His eyes, from the foot of the bed, fixed for an instant moodily on Barjan's face—and sought the foot of the bed again.

Barjan broke the silence.

"So you do know something about it, eh, Nicolo?" he prodded softly.

"I didn't know anything had happened until you said so," returned Nicolo Capriano curtly. "But seeing it has happened, maybe I——" He cut his words off short, and eyed the plain-clothesman again. "Is the man dead?" he demanded, with well-simulated sudden suspicion. "You aren't lying to me—eh? I trust none of you!"

"Dead!" ejaculated Barjan almost hysterically. "Good God—dead! Didn't I tell you he was blown into unrecognizable atoms!"

The sharp, black eyes lingered a little longer on Barjan's face. The result appeared finally to allay Nicolo Capriano's suspicions.

"Well, all right, then, I'll tell you," he said, but there was a grudging note still in the old bomb king's voice. "It can't do the man any harm if he's dead. I guess you'll know who it is. It's the fellow who pulled that hundred thousand dollar robbery about five years ago on old man Tydeman—the fellow that went by the name of Dave Henderson. I don't know whether that's his real name or not."

"What!" shouted Barjan. He had lost his composure. He was up from his chair, and staring wildly at the old man on the bed. "You're crazy!" he jerked out suddenly. "Either you're lying to me, or you're off your nut! You——"

Nicolo Capriano was in a towering rage in an instant.

"You get out of here!" he screamed. "You get to hell out of here! I didn't ask you to come, and I don't give a damn whether it was Dave Henderson or a polecat! It's nothing to do with me! It's your hunt—so go and hunt somewhere else! I'm lying, or I'm off my nut, am I? Well, you get to hell out of here! Go on!" He shook a frantic fist at Barjan, and, choking, coughing, pulled himself up in bed again, and pointed to the door. "Do you hear? Get out!"

Barjan shifted uneasily in alarm. Nicolo Capriano's coughing spell had developed into a paroxysm that was genuine enough.

"Look here," said Barjan, in a pacifying tone, "don't excite yourself like that. I take back what I said. You gave me a jolt for a minute, that's all. But you've got the wrong dope somehow, Nicolo. Whoever it was, it wasn't Dave Henderson. The man was too badly smashed up to be recognized, but there was at least some of his clothing left. Dave Henderson was followed all day yesterday by the police from the minute he left the penitentiary, and he didn't buy any clothes. Dave Henderson had on a black prison suit—and this man hadn't."

Nicolo Capriano shrugged his shoulders in angry contempt.

"I'm satisfied, if you are!" he snarled. "Go on—get out!"

Barjan frowned a little helplessly now.

"But I'm not satisfied," he admitted earnestly. "Look here, Nicolo, for the love of Mike, keep your temper, and let's get to the bottom of this. For some reason you seem to think it was Dave Henderson. I know it wasn't; but I've got to know what started you off on that track. Those clothes——"

"You're a damn fool!" Nicolo Capriano, apparently slightly mollified, was jeering now. "Those clothes—ha, ha! It is like the police! And so old Nicolo is off his nut—eh? Well, I will show you!" He raised his voice and called his daughter. "Teresa, my little one," he said, as the door opened and she appeared, "bring me the clothes that young man had on last night."

"What's that you say!" exclaimed Barjan in sudden excitement.

"Wait!" said Nicolo Capriano ungraciously.

Teresa was back in a moment with an armful of clothing, which, at her father's direction, she deposited on the foot of the bed.

Nicolo Capriano waved her from the room. He leered at Barjan.

"Well, are those the clothes there that you and your police are using to blindfold your eyes with, or are they not—eh? Are those Dave Henderson's clothes?"

Barjan had already pounced upon the clothing, and was pawing it over feverishly.

"Good God—yes!" he burst out sharply.

"And the clothes that the dead man had on—let me see"—Nicolo Capriano's voice was tauntingly triumphant, as, with eyes half closed, visualizing for himself the attire of one Ignace Ferroni, he slowly enumerated the various articles of dress worn by the actual victim of the explosion. He looked at Barjan maliciously, as he finished. "Well," he demanded, "was there enough left of what the man had on to identify any of those things? If so——" Nicolo Capriano shrugged his shoulders by way of finality.

"Yes, yes!" Barjan's excitement was almost beyond his control. "Yes, that is what he wore, but—good Lord, Capriano!—what does this mean? I don't understand!"

"About the clothes?" inquired Nicolo Capriano caustically. "But I should know what he had on since they were *my* clothes—eh? And you have only to look at the ones there on the bed to find out for yourself why I gave him some that, though I do not say they were new, for I have not bought any clothes in the three damnable and cursed years that I have lain here, were at least not all torn to pieces—eh?"

Barjan was pacing up and down the room now. When the other's back was turned, Nicolo Capriano permitted a sinister and mocking smile to hover on his lips; when Barjan faced the bed, Nicolo Capriano eyed the officer with a sour contempt into which he injected a sort of viciously triumphant self-vindication.

"Come across with the rest!" said Barjan abruptly. "How did Dave Henderson come here to you? And what about that bomb? Did you give it to him?" Nicolo Capriano's convenient irascibility was instantly at his command again. He scowled at Barjan, and his scranny fist was flourished under Barjan's nose.

"No, I didn't!" he snarled. "And you know well enough that I didn't. You will try to make me out the guilty man now—eh—just because I was fool enough to help you out of your muddle!"

Barjan became diplomatic again.

"Nothing of the kind!" he said appeasingly. "You're too touchy, Nicolo! I know that you're on the square all right, and that you have been ever since your gang was broken up and Tony Lomazzi was caught. That's good enough, isn't it? Now, come on! Give me the dope about Dave Henderson."

Nicolo Capriano's fingers plucked sullenly at the coverlet. A minute passed.

"Bah!" he grunted finally. "A little honey—eh—when you want something from old Nicolo! Well, then, listen! Dave Henderson came here last night in those torn clothes, and with his face badly cut from a fight that he said he had been in. I don't know whether his story is true or not—you can find that out for yourself. I don't know anything about him, but this is what he told me. He said that his cell in the prison was next to Tony Lomazzi's; that he and Tony were friends; that Tony died a little while ago; and that on the night Tony died he told this fellow Henderson to come to me if he needed any help."

"Yes!" Barjan's voice was eager. He dropped into the chair again, and leaned attentively over the bed toward Nicolo Capriano. "So he came to you through Tony Lomazzi, eh? Well, so far, I guess the story's straight. I happen to know that Henderson's cell was next to Lomazzi's. But where did he get the bomb? He certainly didn't have it when he left the prison, and he was shadowed— —"

"So you said before!" interrupted Nicolo Capriano caustically. "Well, in that case, you ought to know whether the rest of the story is true, too, or not. He said he met a stranger in a saloon last night, and that they chummed up together, and started in to make a night of it. They went from one saloon to another. Their spree ended in a fight at Vinetto's place up the block here, where Henderson and his friend were attacked by some of Baldy Vickers' gang. Henderson said his friend was knocked out, and that he himself had a narrow squeak of it, and just managed to escape through the back door, and ran down the lane, and got in here. I asked him how he knew where I lived, and he said that during the afternoon he had located the house because he meant to come here last night anyway, only he was afraid the police might be watching him, and he had intended to wait until after dark." Nicolo Capriano's eyelids drooped to hide a sudden cunning and mocking gleam that was creeping into them. "You ought to be able to trace this friend of Henderson's if the man was knocked out and unconscious at Vinetto's, as Henderson claimed—and if Henderson was telling the truth, the other would corroborate it."

"We've already got him," said Barjan, with a hint of savagery in his voice. The "friend," alias a plain-clothesman, had proved anything but an inspiration from the standpoint of the police! "Go on! The story is still straight. You say that Dave Henderson said he intended to come here anyway, quite apart from making his escape from Vinetto's. What for?"

Nicolo Capriano shrugged his shoulders.

"Money, I dare say," he said tersely. "The usual thing! At least, I suppose that's what he had originally intended to come for—but we didn't get as far as that. The fight at Vinetto's seemed to have left him with but one idea. When he got here he was in a devil's rage. The only thing that seemed to be in his mind was to get some clothes that wouldn't attract attention, instead of the torn ones he had on, and to get out again as soon as he could with the object of getting even with this gang of Baldy's. He said they were the ones that 'sent him up' on account of their evidence at his trial, and that they were after him again now because of the stolen money that they believed he had hidden somewhere. He was like a maniac. He said he'd see them and everybody else in hell before they got that money, and he swore he'd get every last one of that gang—and get them in a bunch. I didn't know what he meant then. I tried to quiet him down, but I might as well have talked to a wild beast. I tried to get him to stay here and go to bed—instead, he laughed at me in a queer sort of way, and said he'd wipe every one of that crowd off the face of the earth before morning. I began to think he was really crazy. He put on the clothes I gave him, and went out again."

Barjan nodded.

"You don't know it," he said quietly; "but that's where the police lost track of him—when he ran in here."

"I didn't even know the police were after him," said Nicolo Capriano indifferently. "He came back here again about two o'clock this morning, and he had a small clockwork bomb with him. The fool!" Nicolo Capriano cackled suddenly. "He had found Baldy's gang all together down in Jake Morrissey's, and he had thrown the thing against the building. The fool! Of course, it wouldn't go off! He thought it would by hitting it against something. The only way to make it any good was to open the casing and set the clockwork. When he found it didn't explode, he picked it up again, and brought it back here. He wanted me to fix it for him. I asked him where he got it. All I could get out of him was that Tony Lomazzi had told him where he had hidden some things. Ha, ha!" Nicolo Capriano cackled more shrilly still, and began to rock in bed with unseemly mirth. "One of Tony's old bombs! Tony left the young fool a legacy—a bomb, and maybe there was some money, too. I tried to find out about that, but all he said was to keep asking me to fix the bomb for him. I refused. I told him I was no longer in that business. That I went out of it when Tony Lomazzi did—fifteen years ago. He would listen to nothing. He cursed me. I did not think he could do any harm with the thing—and I guess he didn't! A young fool like that is best out of the way. He went away cursing me. I suppose he tried to fix it himself under that arc light on the park bench." Nicolo Capriano shrugged his shoulders again. "I would not have cared to open the thing myself—it was made too long ago, eh? The clockwork might have played tricks even with me, who once was——"

"Yes," said Barjan. He stood up. "I guess that's good enough, and I guess that's the end of Dave Henderson—and one hundred thousand dollars." He frowned in a meditative sort of way. "I don't know whether I'm sorry, or not," he said slowly. "We'd have got him sooner or later, of course, but——" He pointed abruptly to the prison clothes on the bed. "Hi, take those," he announced briskly; "they'll need them at the inquest."

"There's some paper in the bottom drawer of that wardrobe over there," said Nicolo Capriano unconcernedly. "You can wrap them up."

Barjan, with a nod of thanks, secured the paper, made a bundle of the clothes, and tucked the bundle under his arm.

"We won't forget this, Nicolo," he said heartily, as he moved toward the door.

"Bah!" said Nicolo Capriano, with a scowl. "I know how much that is worth!"

He listened attentively as Teresa showed the plain-clothesman out through the front door. As the door closed again, he called his daughter.

"Listen, my little one," he said, and his forefinger was laid against the side of his nose in a gesture of humorous confidence. "I will tell you something. Ignace Ferroni, who was fool enough to blow himself up, has become the young man whom our good friend Tony Lomazzi sent to us last night."

"Father!" Her eyes widened in sudden amazement, not unmixed with alarm.

"You understand, my little one?" He wagged his head, and cackled softly. "Not a word! You understand?"

"Yes," she said doubtfully.

"Good!" grunted the old bomb king. "I think Barjan has swallowed the hook. But I trust no one. I must be sure—you understand—sure! Go and telephone Emmanuel, and tell him to find Little Peter, and send the scoundrel to me at once."

"Yes, father," she said; "but— —"

"It is for Tony Lomazzi," he said.

She went from the room.

Nicolo Capriano lay back on the pillows, and closed his eyes. He might have been asleep again, for the smile on his lips was as guileless as a child's; and it remained there until an hour later, when, after motioning Teresa, who had opened the door, away, he propped himself up on his elbow to greet a wizened, crafty-faced little rat of the underworld, who stood at the bedside.

"It is like the old days to see you here, Little Peter," murmured Nicolo Capriano. "And I always paid well—eh? You have not forgotten that? Well, I will pay well again. Listen! I am sure that the man who was killed with the bomb in the park last night was a prison bird by the name of Dave Henderson; and I told the police so. But it is always possible that I have made a mistake. I do not think so—but it is always possible—eh? Well, I must know, Little

Peter. The police will investigate further, and so will Baldy Vickers' gang—
they had it in for the fellow. You are a clever little devil, Little Peter. Find out
if the police have discovered anything that would indicate I am wrong, and
do the same with Baldy Vickers' gang. You know them all, don't you?"

The wizened little rat grinned.

"Sure!" he said, out of the corner of his mouth. "Youse can leave it to me,
Nicolo. I'm wise."

Nicolo Capriano patted the other's arm approvingly, and smiled the man
away.

"You have the whole day before you, Little Peter," he said. "I am in no
hurry."

Once more Nicolo Capriano lay back on his pillows, and closed his eyes,
and once more the guileless smile hovered over his lips.

At intervals through the day he murmured and communed with himself,
and sometimes his cackling laugh brought Teresa to the door; but for the most
part he lay there through the hours with the placid, cunning patience that the
school of long experience had brought him.

It was dusk when Little Peter stood at the bedside again.

"Youse called de turn, Nicolo," he said. "Dat was de guy, all right. I got
next to some of de fly-cops, an' dey ain't got no doubt about it. Dey handed
it out to de reporters." He flipped a newspaper that he was carrying onto
the bed. "Youse can read it for yerself. An' de gang sizes it up de same way.
I pulled de window stunt on 'em down at Morrissey's about an hour ago.
Dey was all dere—Baldy, an' Runty Mott, an' all de rest—an' another guy,
too. Say, I didn't know dat Bookie Skarvan pulled in wid dat mob. Dey was
fightin' like a lot of stray cats, an' dey was sore as pups, an' all blamin' de
other one for losin' de money. De only guy in de lot dat kept his head was
Bookie. He sat dere chewin' a big fat cigar, an' wigglin' it from one corner
of his mouth to de other, an' he handed 'em some talk. He give 'em hell for
muss-in' everything up. Say, Nicolo, take it from me, youse want to keep yer
eye peeled for him. He says to de crowd: 'It's a cinch dat Dave Henderson's
dead, thanks to de damned mess youse have made of everything,' he says;
'an' it's a cinch dat Capriano's story in de paper is straight—it's too full of de
real dope to be anything else. But if Dave Henderson told old Ca-priano dat
much, he may have told him more—see? Old Capriano's a wily bird, an' wid
a hundred thousand in sight de old Dago wouldn't be asleep. Anyway, it's
our last chance—dat Capriano got de hidin' place out of Dave Henderson.
But here's where de rest of youse keeps yer mitts off. If it's de last chance, I'll
see dat it ain't gummed up. I'll take care of Capriano myself.'"

Little Peter circled his lips with his tongue, as Nicolo Capriano extracted a banknote of generous denomination from under his pillow, and handed it to the other.

"Very good, Little Peter!" he said softly. "Yes, yes—very good! But you have already forgotten it all—eh? Is it not so, Little Peter?"

"Sure!" said Little Peter earnestly. "Sure—youse can bet yer life I have!"

"Good-by then, Little Peter," said Nicolo Capriano softly again.

He stared for a long while at the door, as it closed behind the other—stared and smiled curiously, and plucked with his fingers at the coverlet.

"And so they would watch old bed-ridden Nicolo, would they—while Nicolo watches—eh—somewhere else!" he muttered. "Ha, ha! So they will watch old Nicolo—will they! Well, well, let them watch—eh?" He looked around the room, and raised himself up in bed. He began to rock to and fro. A red tinge crept into his cheeks, a gleam of fire lighted up the coal-black eyes. "Nicolo, Nicolo," he whispered to himself, "it is like the old days back again, Nicolo—and it is like the old wine to make the blood run quick in the veins again."

IV.
THE MANTLE OF ONE IGNACE FERRONI

UP and down the small, ill-furnished room Dave Henderson paced back and forward, as, not so very long ago, he had paced by the hour from the rear wall of his cell to the barred door that opened on an iron gallery without. And he paced the distance now with the old nervous, pent-up energy that rebelled and mutinied and would not take passively to restraint, even when that restraint, as now, was self-imposed.

It had just grown dark. The window shade was tightly drawn. On the table, beside the remains of the supper that Emmanuel had brought him some little time before, a small lamp furnished a meager light, and threw the corners of the room into shadow.

He had seen no one save Emmanuel since last night, when he had left Nicolo Capriano's. He had not heard from Nicolo Capriano. It was the sense of personal impotency, the sense of personal inactivity that filled him with a sort of savage, tigerish impatience now. There were many things to do outside in that world beyond the drawn window shade—and he could only wait! There was the pigeon-cote in Tooler's shed, for instance. All during the day the pigeon-cote had been almost an obsession with him. There was a chance— one chance in perhaps a million—that for some reason or other Millman had not been able to get there. It was a gambling chance—no more, no less—with the odds so heavily against Millman permitting anything to keep him from getting his hands on a fortune in ready cash that, from a material standpoint, there was hardly any use in his, Dave Henderson, going there. But that did not remove the ever present, and, as opposed to the material, the intangible sense of uncertainty that possessed him. He expected to find the money gone; he would be a fool a thousand times over to expect anything else. But he had to satisfy himself, and he would—if that keen old brain of Nicolo Capriano only succeeded in devising some means of throwing the police definitely off the trail.

But it was not so easy to throw the police definitely off the trail, as Nicolo Capriano himself had said. He, Dave Henderson, was ready to agree in that with the crafty old Italian; and, even after these few hours, cooped up in here, he was even more ready to agree with the other that the mere hiding of himself away from the police was utterly abortive as far as the accomplishment of any conclusive end was concerned.

It was far from easy; though, acting somewhat as a panacea to his impatience, the old Italian had inspired him with faith as being more than a match for the police, and yet— —

He gnawed at his lips. He, too, had not been idle through the day; he, too, had tried to find some way, some loophole that would enable him, once he went out into the open again, to throw Barjan, and all that Barjan stood for, conclusively and forever off his track. And the more he had thought of it, the more insurmountable the difficulty and seeming impossibility of doing so had become. It had even shaken his faith a little in Nicolo Capriano's fox-like cunning proving equal to the occasion. He couldn't, for instance, live all his life in disguise. That did very well perhaps as a piece of fiction, but practically it offered very little attraction!

He frowned—and laughed a little harshly at himself. He was illogical again. He had asked only for three or four days, for a fighting chance, just time enough to get on Millman's trail, hadn't he? And now he was greedy for a permanent and enduring safe-conduct from the police, and his brain mulled and toiled with that objective alone in view, and he stood here now employed in gnawing his lips because he could not see the way, or see how Nicolo Capriano could find it, either. He shrugged his shoulders. As well dismiss that! If he could but reach Millman—and, after Millman, Bookie Skarvan— just to pay the debts he owed, then— —

His hand that had curled into a clenched fist, with knuckles showing like white knobs under the tight-stretched skin, relaxed, as, following a low, quick knock at the door, Emmanuel stepped into the room.

"I gotta da message for you from Nicolo," Emmanuel announced; "an' I gotta da letter for you from Nicolo, too. You get-a damn sick staying in here, eh? Well, Nicolo say you go to his place see him tonight. We take-a da car by-an'-by, an' go."

"That's the talk, Emmanuel!" said Dave Henderson, with terse heartiness. "You're all right, Emmanuel, and so is your room and your grub, but a little fresh air is what I am looking for, and the sooner the better!"

He took the envelope that Emmanuel extended, crossed over to the lamp, and turned his back on the other, as he ripped the envelope open. Nicolo Capriano's injunction had been to say nothing to Emmanuel, and— — He was staring blankly at the front page of the evening newspaper, all that the envelope contained, and which he had now unfolded before him. And then he caught his breath sharply. He was either crazy, or his eyes were playing him tricks. A thrill that he suppressed by an almost superhuman effort of will, a thrill that tore and fought at the restraint he put upon it, because he was afraid that the mad, insane uplift that it promised was but some fantastic hallucination, swept over him. There was a lead pencil circle drawn around the captions of one of the columns; and three written words, connected to the circle by another pencil stroke, leaped up at him from the margin of the paper:

"You are dead."

He felt the blood surging upward in his veins to beat like the blows of a trip-hammer at his temples. The words were not blurred and running together any more, the captions, instead, inside that circle, seemed to stand out in such huge startling type that they dominated the entire page:

MAN BLOWN TO PIECES BY BOMB IDENTIFIED
MYSTERY IS EXPLAINED
DAVE HENDERSON, EX-CONVICT,
VICTIM OF HIS OWN MURDEROUS INTENTIONS

Dave Henderson glanced over his shoulder. Behind him, Emmanuel was clatteringly piling up the supper dishes on the tray. He turned again to the newspaper, and read Nicolo Capriano's story, all of it now—and laughed. He remembered the old Italian's tale of the man Ignace Ferroni and his bomb. Nicolo Capriano, for all his age and infirmity, was still without his peer in craft and cunning! The ingenious use of enough of what was true had stamped the utterly false as beyond the shadow of a suspicion that it, too, was not as genuine as the connecting links that held the fabric together. He warmed to the old Italian, an almost hysterical admiration upon him for Nicolo Capriano's guile. But transcending all other emotions was the sense of freedom. It surged upon him, possessing him; it brought exhilaration, and it brought a grim, unholy vista of things to come—a goal within possibility of reach now—Millman first, and then Bookie Skarvan. He was free—free as the air. He was dead. Dave Henderson had passed out of the jurisdiction of the police. To the police he was now but a memory—he was dead.

"You are dead." A queer tight smile thinned his lips, as his eyes fell again upon the penciled words at the margin of the paper.

"It's no wonder they never got anything on old Capriano!" he muttered; and began to tear the paper into shreds.

He was free! He was dead! He was impatient now to exercise that freedom. He could walk out on the streets with no more disguise than these cast-off clothes he had on, plus the brim of his hat to shade his face—for Dave

Henderson was dead. Neither Bookie Skarvan, nor Baldy Vickers would be searching for a dead man any more—nor would the police. He swung around, and faced Emmanuel.

"I am to go to Nicolo Capriano's, eh?" he said. "Well, then, let's go; I'm ready."

"No make-a da rush," smiled Emmanuel. "Capriano say you gotta da time, plenty time. Capriano say come over by-an'-by in da car."

Dave Henderson shook his head impatiently.

"No; we'll go now," he answered.

Emmanuel in turn shook his head.

"I gotta some peep' downstairs in da restaurant," he said. "I gotta stay maybe an hour yet."

Dave Henderson considered this for a moment. He could walk out on the streets now quite freely. It was no longer necessary that he should be hidden in a car. But Nicolo Capriano had told Emmanuel to use the car. Emmanuel would not understand, and he, Dave Henderson, had no intention of enlightening the other why a car was no longer necessary. Neither was Emmanuel himself necessary—there was Mrs. Tooler's pigeon-cote. If he went there before going to Nicolo Capriano! His brain was racing now. Yes, the car, *without Emmanuel*, would be a great convenience.

"All right!" he said crisply. "You stay here, and look after your restaurant. There's no need for you to come. I'll take the car myself."

"You drive-a da car?" asked Emmanuel dubiously. Dave Henderson laughed quietly. The question awakened a certain and very pertinent memory. There were those who, if they chose to do so, could testify with some eloquence to his efficiency at the wheel of a car!

"Well, I have driven one," he said. "I guess I can handle that old bus of yours."

"But"—Emmanuel was still dubious—"Capriano say no take-a da risk of being seen on——"

"I'm not looking for any risk myself," interposed Dave Henderson coolly. "It's dark now, and there's no chance of anybody recognizing me while I'm driving a car. Forget it, Emmanuel! Come on! I don't want to stick around here for another hour. Here!"—from his pocket he produced a banknote, and pushed it across the table to the other.

Emmanuel grinned. His doubts had vanished.

"Sure!" said Emmanuel. He tiptoed to the door, looked out, listened, and jerked his head reassuringly in Dave Henderson's direction. "Getta da move on, then! We go down by da back stairs. Come on!"

They gained the back yard, and the small shed that did duty for a garage— and in a few moments more Dave Henderson, at the wheel of the car, was out on the street.

He drove slowly at first. He had paid no attention to the route taken by Emmanuel when they had left Nicolo Capriano's the night before, and as a consequence he had little or no idea in what part of the city Emmanuel's restaurant was located; but at the expiration of a few minutes he got his bearings, and the speed of the car quickened instantly.

V.
CON AMORE

TEN minutes later, the car left at the curb half a block away, Dave Henderson was crouched in the darkness at the door of old Tooler's shed that opened on the lane. There was a grim set to his lips. There seemed a curious analogy in all this—this tool even with which he worked upon the door to force it open, this chisel that he had taken from the kit under the seat of Emmanuel's car, as once before from under the seat of another car he had taken a chisel—with one hundred thousand dollars as his object in view. He had got the money then, and lost it, and had nearly lost his life as well, and now————

He steeled himself, as the door opened silently under his hand; steeled himself against the hope, which somehow seemed to be growing upon him, that Millman might never have got here after all; steeled himself against disappointment where logic told him disappointment had no place at all, since he was but a fool to harbor any hope. And yet—and yet there were a thousand things, a thousand unforeseen contingencies which might have turned the tables upon Millman! The money *might* still be here. And if it were! He was dead now—and free to use it! Free! His lips thinned into a straight line.

The door closed noiselessly behind him. The flashlight in his hand, also borrowed from Emmanuel's car, played around the shed. It was the same old place, perhaps a little more down-at-the-heels, perhaps a little dirtier, a little more cumbered up with odds and ends than it had been five years before, but there was no other change. And there was the door of the pigeon-cote above him, that he could just reach from the ground.

He moved toward it now with a swift, impulsive step, and snarled in sudden anger at himself, as he found his hand trembling with excitement, causing the flashlight to throw a jerky, wavering ray on the old pigeon-cote door. What was the use of that! He expected nothing, didn't he? The pigeon-cote would be empty; he knew that well enough. And yet he was playing the fool. He knew quite well it would be empty; he had prepared himself thoroughly to expect nothing else.

He reached up, opened the door, and felt inside. His hand encountered a moldy litter of chaff and straw. He reached further in, with quick eagerness, the full length of his arm. He remembered that he had pushed the package into the corner, and had covered it with straw.

For a minute, for two full minutes, his fingers, by the sense of touch, sifted through the chaff, first slowly, methodically, then with a sort of frantic abandon; and then, in another moment, he had stooped to the floor, seized an old box, and, standing upon it, had thrust head and shoulders into the old pigeon-cote, while the flashlight's ray swept every crevice of the interior, and he pawed and turned up the chaff and straw where even it lay but a bare inch deep and only one bereft of his senses could expect it to conceal anything.

He withdrew himself from the opening, and closed the pigeon-cote door again, and stood down on the floor. He laughed at himself in a low, bitter, merciless way. He had expected nothing, of course; he had expected only to find what he had found—nothing. He had told himself that, hadn't he? Quite convinced himself of it, hadn't he? Well, then, what did it matter? His hands, clenched, went suddenly above his head.

"I paid five years for that," he whispered. "Do you hear, Millman—five years—five years! And I'll get you—Millman! I'll get you for this, Millman— are you listening?—whether you are in New York—or hell!"

He put the box upon which he had stood back in its place, went out of the shed, closed the door behind him, and made his way back to the car. He drove quickly now, himself driven by the feverish, intolerant passion that had him in its grip. He was satisfied now. There were not any more doubts. He knew! Well, he would go to Nicolo Capriano's, and then—his hands gripped fiercely on the steering wheel. He was dead! Ha, ha! Dave Henderson was dead—but Millman was still alive!

It was not far to Capriano's. He left the car where Emmanuel had awaited him the night before, and gained the back porch of Nicolo Capriano's house.

Teresa's voice from the other side of the closed door answered his knock.

"Who's there?" she asked.

He laughed low, half in facetiousness, half in grim humor. He was in a curious mood.

"The dead man," he answered.

There was no light in the porch to-night. She opened the door, and, as he stepped inside, closed it behind him again. He could not see her in the darkness—and somehow, suddenly, quite unreasonably, he found the situation awkward, and his tongue, as it had been the night before, awkward, too.

"Say," he blurted out, "your father's got some clever head, all right!"

"Has he?" Her voice seemed strangely quiet and subdued, a hint of listlessness and weariness in it.

"But you know about it, don't you?" he exclaimed. "You know what he did, don't you?"

"Yes; I know," she answered. "But he has been waiting for you, and he is impatient, and we had better go at once."

It was Tony Lomazzi! He remembered her grief when he had told her last night that Tony was dead. That was what was the matter with her, he decided, as he followed her along the passageway. She must have thought a good deal of Tony Lomazzi—more even than her father did. He wished again that he had not broken the news to her in the blunt, brutal way he had—only he had not known then, of course, that Tony had meant so much to her. He found himself wondering why now. She could not have had anything to do with Tony Lomazzi for fifteen years, and fifteen years ago she could have been little more than a child. True, she might perhaps have visited the prison, but— —

"Well, my young friend—eh?" Nicolo Capriano's voice greeted him, as he followed Teresa into the old Italian's room. "So Ignace Ferroni has done you a good turn—eh? And old Nicolo! Eh—what have you to say about old Nicolo? Did I not tell you that you could leave it to old Nicolo to find a way?"

Dave Henderson caught the other's outstretched hand, and wrung it hard.

"I'll never forget this," he said. "You've pulled the slickest thing I ever heard of, and I— —"

"Bah!" Nicolo Capriano was chuckling delightedly.

"Never mind the thanks, my young friend. You owe me none. The old fingers had the itch in them to play the cards against the police once more. And the police—eh?—I do not like the police. Well, perhaps we are quits now! Ha, ha! Do you know Barjan? Barjan is a very clever little man, too—ha, ha!—Barjan and old Nicolo have known each other many years. And that is what Barjan said—just what you said—that he would not forget. Well, we are all pleased—eh? But we do not stop at that. Old Nicolo does not do things by halves. You will still need help, my young friend. You will go at once to New York—eh? That is what you intend to do?"

"Yes," said Dave Henderson.

Nicolo Capriano nodded.

"And you will find your man—and the money?"

"Yes!" Dave Henderson's lips thinned suddenly. "If he is in New York, as I believe he is, I will find him; if not—then I will find him just the same."

Again Nicolo Capriano nodded.

"Ah, my young friend, I like you!" he murmured. "If I had had you—eh?—fifteen years ago! We would have gone far—eh? And Tony went no farther than a prison cell. But we waste time—eh? Old Nicolo is not through yet—a Capriano does not do things by halves. You will need help and friends in New York. Nicolo Capriano will see to that. And money to get to New York—eh? You will need some ready money for that?"

Dave Henderson's eyes met Teresa's. She stood there, a slim, straight figure, just inside the door, the light glinting on her raven hair. She seemed somehow, with those wondrous eyes of hers, to be making an analysis of him, an analysis that went deeper than a mere appraisal of his features and his clothes—and a little frown came and puckered the white brow—and, quick in its wake, with a little start of confusion, there came a heightened tinge of color to her cheeks, and she lowered her eyes.

"Teresa, my little one," said Nicolo Capriano softly, "go and get some paper and an envelope, and pen and ink."

Dave Henderson watched her as she left the room.

Nicolo Capriano's fingers, from plucking at the counterpane, tapped gently on Dave Henderson's sleeve.

"We were speaking of money—for your immediate needs," Nicolo Capriano suggested pleasantly.

Dave Henderson shook his head.

"I have enough to keep me going for a while," he answered.

The old bomb king's eyebrows were slightly elevated.

"So! But you are just out of prison—and you said yourself that the police had followed you closely."

Dave Henderson laughed shortly.

"That wasn't very difficult," he said. "I had a friend who owed me some money before I went to the pen—some I had won on the race-track. I gave the police the slip without very much trouble last night in order to get here, and it was a good deal more of a cinch to put it over them long enough to get that money."

"So!" said Nicolo Capriano again. "And this friend—what is his name?"

Dave Henderson hesitated. He had seen to it that Square John Kelly was clear of this, and he was reluctant now, even to this man here to whom he owed a debt beyond repayment, to bring Square John into the matter at all; yet, on the other hand, in this particular instance, it could make very little difference. If Square John was involved, Nicolo Capriano was involved a hundredfold deeper. And then, too, Nicolo Capriano might very well, and with very good reason, be curious to know how he, Dave Henderson, could, under the circumstances, have come into the possession of a sum of money adequate for his present needs.

"I'd rather keep his name out of it," he said frankly; "but I guess you've got a right to ask about anything you like, and if you insist I'll tell you."

Nicolo Capriano's eyes were half closed—and they were fixed on the foot of the bed.

"I think I would like to know," he said, after a moment.

"All right! It was Square John Kelly," said Dave Henderson quietly—and recounted briefly the details of his visit to the Pacific Coral Saloon the night before.

Nicolo Capriano had propped himself up in bed. He leaned over now as Dave Henderson finished, and patted Dave Henderson's shoulder in a sort of exultant excitement.

"Good! Excellent!" he exclaimed. "Ah, my young friend, I begin to love you! It brings back the years that are gone. But—bah!—I shall get well again— eh? And I am not yet too old—eh? Who can tell—eh?—who can tell! We would be invincible, you and I, and——" He checked himself, as Teresa reentered the room. "Yes, yes," he said. "Well, then, as far as money is concerned, you are supplied; but friends—eh?—are sometimes more important than money. You have found that out already—eh? Listen, then, I will give you a letter to a friend in New York whom you can trust—and I promise you he will stop at nothing to carry out my orders. You understand? His name is Georges Vardi, but he is commonly known as Dago George; and he, too, was one of us in the old days. You will want somewhere to go. He keeps a little hotel, a very *quiet* little hotel off the Bowery, not far from Chatham Square. Any one will tell you there where to find Dago George. You understand?"

"Yes," said Dave Henderson.

Nicolo Capriano motioned his daughter abruptly to a small table on the opposite side of the bed.

"Teresa will write the letter, and put it in Italian," he said, as she seated herself at the table. "I do not write as easily as I used to. They say old Nicolo is a sick man. Well, maybe that is so, but old Nicolo's brain is not sick, and old Nicolo's fingers can at least still sign his name—and that is enough. Ha, ha, it is good to be alive again! Well"—he waved his hand again toward his daughter—"are you ready, my little one?"

"Yes, father," she answered.

"To Dago George, then," he said. "First—my affectionate salutations."

Her pen scratched rapidly over the paper. She looked up.

"Yes, father?"

Nicolo Capriano's fingers plucked at the coverlet.

"You will say that the bearer of this letter—ah! Yes!" He turned with a whimsical smile to Dave Henderson. "You must have a name, eh, my young friend—since Dave Henderson is dead! We shall not tell Dago George everything. Fools alone tell all they know! What shall it be?"

Dave Henderson shrugged his shoulders.

"Anything," he said. "It doesn't matter. One is as good as another. Make it Barty Lynch."

"Yes, that will do. Good!" Nicolo Capriano gestured with his hand in his daughter's direction again. "You will say that the bearer of this letter is Barty Lynch, and that he is to be treated as though he were Nicolo Capriano himself. You understand, my little one? Anything that he asks is his—and I, Nicolo Capriano, will be responsible. Tell him, my little one, that it is Nicolo Capriano's order—and that Nicolo Capriano has yet to be disobeyed. And particularly you will say that if our young friend here requires any help by those who know how to do what they are told and ask no questions, the men are to be supplied. You understand, Teresa?"

She did not look up this time.

"Yes, father."

"Write it, then," he said. "And see that Dago George is left with no doubt in his mind that he is at the command of our young friend here."

Teresa's pen scratched rapidly again across the paper.

Nicolo Capriano was at his interminable occupation of plucking at the counterpane.

Dave Henderson pushed his hand through his hair in a curiously abstracted sort of way. There seemed to be something strangely and suddenly unreal about all this—about this man, with his cunning brain, who lay here in this queer four-poster bed; about that trim little figure, who bent over the table there, and whose profile only now was in view, the profile of a sweet, womanly face that somehow now seemed to be very earnest, for he could see the reflection of a puckered brow in the little nest of wrinkles at the corner of her eye.

No, there wasn't anything unreal about her. She was very real.

He remembered her as she had stood last night on the threshold there, and when in the lighted doorway he had seen her for the first time. He would never forget that—nor the smile that had followed the glorious flood of color in her cheeks, and that had lighted up her eyes, and that had forgiven him for his unconscious rudeness.

That wasn't what was unreal. All that would remain living and vibrant, a picture that would endure, and that the years would not dim. It was unreal that in the space of a few minutes more everything here would have vanished forever out of his existence—this room with its vaguely foreign air, this four-poster bed with its strange occupant, whose mental vitality seemed to thrive on his physical weakness, that slimmer figure there bending over the table, whose masses of silken hair seemed to curl and cluster in a sort of proudly intimate affection about the arched, shapely neck, whose shoulders were molded in soft yielding lines that somehow invited the lingering touch of a hand, if one but had the right.

His hand pushed its way again through his hair, and fumbled a little helplessly across his eyes. And, too, it was more than that that was unreal. A multitude of things seemed unreal—the years in the penitentiary during which he had racked his brain for a means of eluding the police, racked it until it had become a physical agony to think, were now dispelled by this man here, and with such ease that, as an accomplished, concrete fact, his mind somehow refused to accept it as such. He was dead. It was very strange, very curious! He sank back a little in his chair. There came a vista of New York— not as a tangible thing of great streets and vast edifices, but as a Mecca of his aspirations, now almost within his grasp, as an arena where he could stand unleashed, and where the iron of five years that had entered his soul should have a chance to vent itself. Millman was there! There seemed to come an unholy joy creeping upon him. Millman was there—and he, Dave Henderson, was dead, and in Dave Henderson's place would be a man in that arena who had friends now at his back, who could laugh at the police. Millman! He felt the blood sweep upward to his temples; he heard his knuckles crack, as his hand clenched in a fierce, sudden surge of fury. Millman! Yes, the way was clear to Millman—but there was another, too. Bookie Skarvan!

His hand unclenched. He was quite cool, quite unconcerned again. Teresa had finished the letter, and Nicolo Capriano was reading it now. He could afford to wait as far as Bookie Skarvan was concerned—he could not afford to wait where Millman was concerned. And, besides, there was his own safety. Bookie Skarvan was here in San Francisco, but the further he, Dave Henderson, got from San Francisco for the present now, and the sooner, the better it would be. In a little while, a few months, after he had paid his debt to Millman—he would pay his debt to Bookie Skarvan. He was not likely to forget Bookie Skarvan!

His eyes fell on Teresa. He might come back to San Francisco in a few months. With ordinary caution it ought to be quite safe then. Dave Henderson would have been dead quite long enough then to be utterly forgotten. They would not be talking on every street corner about him as they were to-night, and— —

Nicolo Capriano was nodding his head approvingly over the letter.

"Yes, yes!" he said. "Excellent! With this, my young friend, you will be a far more important personage in New York than you imagine. Old Nicolo's arm still reaches far." He stared for a moment musingly at Dave Henderson through half closed eyes. "You have money, and this letter. I do not think there is anything else that old Nicolo can do for you—eh?—except to give you a little advice. You will leave here shortly, and from that moment you must be very careful. Anywhere near San Francisco you might be recognized. Travel only by night at first—make of yourself a tramp and use the freight trains, and hide by day. After two or three days, which should have taken you a good many miles from here, you will be able to travel more comfortably. But still do not use the through express trains—the men on the dining and sleeping cars have all started from here, too, you must remember. You understand? Go slowly. Be very careful. You are not really safe until you are east of Chicago. I do not think there is anything else, unless—eh?—you are armed, my young friend?"

Dave Henderson shook his head.

"So!" ejaculated Nicolo Capriano, and pursed his lips. "And it would not be safe for you to buy a weapon to-night—eh?—and it might very well be that to-night you would need it badly. Well, it is easily remedied." He turned to his daughter. "Teresa, my little one, I think we might let our young friend have that revolver upstairs in the bottom of the old box—and still not remain defenseless ourselves—eh? Yes, yes! Run and get it, Teresa."

She rose from her seat obediently, and turned toward the door—but her father stopped her with a quick impulsive gesture.

"Wait!" he said. "Give me the pen before you go, and I will sign this letter. Dago George must be sure that it came from Nicolo Capriano—eh?"

She dipped the pen in the ink, and handed it to him. Nicolo Capriano propped the letter on his knees, as he motioned her away on her errand. His pen moved laboriously across the paper. He looked up then, and beckoned Dave Henderson to lean over the bed.

"See, my young friend," he smiled—and pointed to his cramped writing. "Old Nicolo's fingers are old and stiff, and it is a long while since Dago George has seen that signature—but, though I am certain he would know it again, I have made assurance doubly sure. See, I have signed: 'Con Amore, Nicolo Capriano.' You do not know Italian—eh? Well, it is a simple phrase, a very common phrase. It means—'with love.' But to Dago George it means something else. It was a secret signal in the old days. A letter signed in that way by any one of us meant—'trust to the death!' You understand, my young friend?" He smiled again, and patted Dave Henderson's arm. "Give me die envelope there on the table."

He was inserting the letter in the envelope, as Teresa entered the room again. He sealed the envelope, reached out to her for the revolver which she carried, broke the revolver, nodded as he satisfied himself that it was loaded— and handed both envelope and weapon to Dave Henderson. He spread out his hands then, and lifted his shoulders in a whimsical gesture of finality.

"It is only left then to say good-by—eh?—my young friend—who was the friend of Tony Lomazzi. You will have good luck, and good fortune, and— —"

Dave Henderson was on his feet. He had both of the old Italian's hands in his.

"I will never forget what you have done—and I will never forget Nicolo Capriano," he said in a low tone, his voice suddenly choked.

The old bomb king's eyelids fluttered down. It was like a blind man whose face was turned to Dave Henderson.

"I am sure of that, my young friend," he said softly. "I am sure that you will never forget Nicolo Capriano. I shall hear of you through Dago George." He released his hands suddenly. His eyes opened—they were inscrutable, almost dead, without luster. "Go," he said, "I know what you would say. But we are not children to sob on one another's neck. Nicolo is not dead yet. Perhaps we will meet again—eh? We will not make a scene—Teresa will tell you that it might bring on an attack. Eh? Well, then, go! You will need all the hours from now until daylight to get well away from the city." He smiled again, and waved Dave Henderson from the bed.

In an uncertain, reluctant way, as though conscious that his farewell to the old Italian was entirely inadequate, that his gratitude had found no expression, and yet conscious, too, that any attempt to express his feelings would be genuinely unwelcome to the other, Dave Henderson moved toward the door. Teresa had already passed out of the room, and was standing in the hall. On the threshold Dave Henderson paused, and looked back.

"Good-by, Nicolo Capriano!" he called.

The old Italian had sunk back on the pillows, his fingers busy with the counterpane.

"The wine of life, my young friend"—it was almost as though he were talking to himself—"ha, ha!—the wine of life! The old days back again—the measured blades—the fight, and the rasp of steel! Ha, ha! Old Nicolo is not yet dead! Good-by—good-by, my young friend! It is old Nicolo who is in your debt; not you in his. Good-by, my young friend—good-by!"

Teresa's footsteps were already receding along the passageway toward the rear door. Dave Henderson, with a final wave of his hand to the old Italian, turned and walked slowly along the hall. He heard the porch door ahead of him being opened. He reached it, and halted, looking around him. It was dark, as it always was here, and he could see nothing—not even a faint, blurred outline of Teresa's form. Surprised, he called her name softly. There was no answer—only the door stood wide open.

He stepped out into the porch. There was still no sign of her. It was very strange! He called her again—he only wanted to say good-by, to thank her, to tell her, as he had told her father, that he would not forget. And, yes, to tell her, too, if he could find the words, that some day he hoped that he might see her again. But there was no answer.

He was frowning now, piqued, and a little angry. He did not understand—only that she had opened the door for him, and in some way had deliberately chosen to evade him. He did not know why—he could find no reason for it. He moved on through the porch. Perhaps she had preceded him as far as the lane.

At the lane, he halted again, and again looked around him—and stood there hesitant. And then there reached him the sound of the porch door being closed and locked.

He did not understand. It mystified him. It was not coquetry—there was no coquetry in those steady, self-reliant eyes, or in that strong, sweet face. And yet it had been deliberately done, and about it was something of finality—and his lips twisted in a hurt smile, as he turned and walked from the lane.

"Beat it!" said Dave Henderson to himself. "You're dead!"

VI.
THE HOUSE OF MYSTERY DRAWS ITS BLINDS

TERESA'S fingers twisted the key in the lock of the porch door that she had closed on Dave Henderson. There was a queer, tight little smile quivering on her lips.

"There was no other way," she whispered to herself. "What could I do? What could I say?"

Behind her, and at one side of the passage, was a small panel door, long out of use now, a relic of those days when Nicolo Capriano's dwelling had been a house of mystery. She had hidden there to let Dave Henderson pass by; she closed it now, as she retraced her steps slowly to her father's room. And here, on the threshold, she paused for a moment; then reached in quietly to close the door, and retire again. Her father lay back on the bed, his eyes closed, and his hands, outstretched on the coverlet, were quiet, the long, slim fingers motionless. He was asleep. It was not uncommon. He often did that. Sleep came at the oddest times with the old man, even if it did not last long, and——

"Teresa—eh—what are you doing?" Nicolo Capriano's eyes half opened, and fixed on his daughter. "Eh—what are you doing?"

"I thought you were asleep, father," she murmured. "Asleep! Bah! I have been asleep for fifteen years—is that not long enough? Fifteen years! Ha, ha! But I am awake now! Yes, yes, old Nicolo has had enough of dreams! He is awake now! Come here, Teresa. Come here, and sit by the bed. Has our clever young friend gone?"

"Yes, father," she told him, as she took the chair at the bedside.

Nicolo Capriano jerked his head around on his pillows, and studied her face for a moment, though his black eyes, with their smoldering, introspective expression, seemed not at all concerned with her.

"And what do you think of him—eh—Teresa, my little one—what do you think of him?"

She drew back in her chair with a little start.

"Why—what do you mean, father?" she asked quickly.

"Bah!" There was a caustic chuckle in the old bomb king's voice. "We do not speak of love—I suppose! I do not expect you to have fallen in love just because you have seen a man for a few minutes—eh? Bah! I mean just what I say. I called him clever. You are a Capriano, and you are clever; you are the cleverest woman in San Francisco, but you do not get it from your mother—you are a Capriano. Well, then, am I right? He is clever—a very clever fellow?"

Her voice was suddenly dull.

"Yes," she said.

"Good!" ejaculated Nicolo Capriano. "He was caught five years ago, but it was not his fault. He was double-crossed, or he would never have seen the inside of a penitentiary. So you agree, then, that he is clever? Well, then, he has courage, too—eh? He was modest about his fight at Vinetto's—eh? You heard it all from Vinetto himself when you went there this morning. Our young friend was modest—eh?"

Teresa's eyes widened slightly in a puzzled way. She nodded her head.

"Yes," she said.

"Good!" said Nicolo Capriano—and the long, slim fingers began to twine themselves together, and to untwine, and to twine together again. "Well, then, my little one, with his cleverness and his courage, he should succeed—eh—in New York? Old Nicolo does not often make a mistake—eh? Our young friend will find his money again in New York—eh?"

She pushed back her chair impulsively, and stood up.

"I hope not," she answered in a low voice.

"Eh?" Nicolo Capriano jerked himself sharply up on his pillows, and his eyes narrowed. "Eh—what is that you say? What do you mean—you hope not!"

"It is not his money now any more than it was before he stole it," she said in a dead tone. "It is stolen money."

"Well, and what of it?" demanded Nicolo Capriano. "Am I a fool that I do not know that?" Sudden irascibility showed in the old Italian's face and manner; a flush swept his cheeks under the white beard, the black eyes grew lusterless and hard—and he coughed. "Well, am I a fool?" he shouted.

She looked at him in quick apprehension.

"Father, be careful!" she admonished. "You must not excite yourself."

"Bah!" He flung out his hand in a violent gesture. "Excite myself! Bah! Always it is—'do not excite yourself!' Can you find nothing else to say? Now, you will explain—eh?—you will explain! What is it about this stolen money that Nicolo Capriano's daughter does not like? You hear—I call you Nicolo Capriano's daughter!"

It was a moment before she answered.

"I do not like it—because it has made my soul sick to-night." She turned her head away. "I hid behind the old panel when he went out. I do not like it; I hate it. I hate it with all my soul! I did not understand at first, not until your talk with him to-night, that there was any money involved. I thought it was just to help him get away from the police who were hounding him even after his sentence had been served, and also to protect him from that gang who tried to get him in Vinetto's place—and that we were doing it for Tony's sake. And then it all seemed to come upon me in a flash, as I went toward the door to let him out to-night—that there was the stolen money, and that I was helping him, and had been helping him in everything that was done here, to steal it again. I know what I should have done. It would have done no good, it would have been utterly useless; I realized that—but I would have been honest with myself. I should have protested there and then. But I shrank from the position I was in. I shrank from having him ask me what I had to do with honesty, I, who—and you have said it yourself but a moment ago—I, who was Nicolo Capriano's daughter; I, who, even if I protested on one score, had knowingly and voluntarily done my share in hoodwinking the police on another. He would have had the right to think me mad, to think me irresponsible—and worse. I shrank from having him laugh in my face. And so I let him go, because I must say that to him or nothing; for I could not be hypocrite enough to wish him a smiling good-by, to wish him good fortune and success—I couldn't—I tell you, I couldn't—and so—and so I stepped behind the panel, and let him pass."

Nicolo Capriano's two hands were outthrust and clenched, his lips had widened until the red gums showed above his teeth, and he glared at his daughter.

"By God!" he whispered hoarsely, "it is well for you, you kept your mouth shut! Do you hear, you—you——-" A paroxysm of coughing seized him, and he fell back upon the pillows.

In an instant, Teresa was bending over him anxiously.

He pushed her away, and struggled upward again, and for a moment he shook his fists again at his daughter—and then his eyes were half veiled, and his hands opened, and he began to pat the girl's arm, and his voice held a soft, purring note.

"Listen! You are not a fool, my little one. I have not brought you up to be a fool—eh? Well, then, listen! We have a little money, but it is not much. And he will get that hundred thousand dollars. Do you understand? He is clever, and he has the courage. Do you think that I would have tricked the police for him, otherwise? Eh—do you think old Nicolo Capriano does not know what he is about?"

She stared at him, a sort of dawning dismay in her eyes.

"You mean," she said, and the words seemed to come in a hard, forced way from her lips, "you mean that if he gets that money again, you are to have a share?"

"A share! Ha, ha!" The old Italian was rocking backward and forward in glee. "No, my little one, not a share—Nicolo Capriano does not deal in shares any more. All—my little one—all! One hundred thousand dollars—all! And my little black-eyes will have such gowns as——"

"Father!" It came in a startled, broken cry of amazed and bitter expostulation.

Nicolo Capriano stopped his rocking, and looked at her. A sudden glint of fury leaped from the smoldering eyes.

"Bah!" he said angrily. "Am I mistaken after all? Is it that you are your mother—and not a Capriano! Perhaps I should not have told you; but now you will make the best of it, and behave yourself, and not play the child—eh? Do you think I risked myself with the police for nothing! Yes—all! All—except that I must pay that leech Dago George something for looking after our young friend—*con amore*—*con amore*, Nicolo Capriano—eh?—since I signed the letter so."

She stood an instant, straight and tense, but a little backward on her heels, as though she had recoiled from a blow that had been struck her—and then she bent swiftly forward, and caught both her father's wrists in her strong young grasp, and looked into his eyes for a long minute, as though to read deep into his soul.

"You signed that letter *con amore*!" Her voice was colorless. "You signed it—*con amore*—the code word of the old, horrible, miserable days when this house was a den of outlaws, the code word that marked out the victim who was to be watched and hounded down!"

The old bomb king wrenched himself still further up in bed. He shook his wrists free.

"What is it to you!" he screamed in a blaze of fury—and fell into a second, and more violent paroxysm of coughing—and now caught at his breast with his thin, blue-tipped fingers, and now in unbridled passion waved his arms about like disjointed flails. "Yes—I signed it that—*con amore*. And it is the old signal! Yes, yes! And Dago George will obey. And he will watch our young friend—watch—watch—watch! And in the end—bah!—in the end our young friend will supply Nicolo Capriano with that hundred thousand dollars. Ha! And in the end we will see that our young friend does not become troublesome. He is a pawn—a pawn!" Old Nicolo's face, between rage and coughing, had grown a mottled purple. "A pawn! And when a pawn has lost its usefulness—eh?—it is swept from the board—eh? *Con amore!* The old days again! The finger of Nicolo Capriano lifted—and the puppets jump! *Con amore!* I will see that Dago George knows what to do with a young man who brings him Nicolo Capriano's letter! Ha, ha! Yes, yes; I will take care of that!"

She had not moved, except to grow a little straighter in her poise, and except that her hands now were clenched at her sides.

"I cannot believe it!" Her voice was scarcely above a whisper. "I cannot believe it! I cannot believe that you would do this! It is monstrous, horrible!"

It seemed as though Nicolo Capriano could not get his breath, or at least one adequate enough to vent the access of fury that swept upon him. He choked, caught again at his breast, and hooked fingers ripped the nightdress loose from his throat.

"Out of the room!" he screamed at last. "Out of it! I will teach you a chit of a girl's place! Out of it!"

"No; I will not go out—not yet," she said, and steadied her voice with an effort. "I will not go until you tell me that you will not do this thing. You can't do it, father—you can't—you can't!" Even the semblance of calmness was gone from her now, and, instead, there was a frantic, almost incoherent pleading in her tones. "He came—he came from Tony Lomazzi. Father, are you mad? Do you not understand? He came from Tony Lomazzi, I tell you!"

"And I tell you to get out of this room, and hold your tongue, you meddling little fool!" screamed Nicolo Capriano again. "Tony Lomazzi! He came from Tony Lomazzi, did he? Damn Tony Lomazzi—damn him—damn him! What do I owe Tony Lomazzi but the hell of hate in a man's soul that comes only in one way! You hear! It was the prison walls only that saved Lomazzi from my reach—from these fingers of mine that are strong, strong at the throat, and never let go! Do you think I was blind that I could not see, that I did not know—eh?—that I did not know what was between your mother and that accursed Lomazzi! But he died—eh?—he died like a rat gnawing, gnawing at walls that he could not bite through!"

Teresa's face had gone suddenly a deathly white, and the color seemed to have fled her lips and left them gray.

"It is a lie—a hideous lie!" she cried—and all the passion of her father's race was on the surface now. "It is a lie! And you know it is—you know it is! My mother loved you, always loved you, and only you—and you broke her heart—and killed her with the foul, horrible life of crime that seethed in this house! Oh, my God! Are you trying to make me hate you, hate *you*, my father! I have tried to be a good daughter to you since she died. She made me promise that I would, on that last night. I have tried to love you, and I have tried to understand why she should have loved you—but—but I do not know. It is true that Tony Lomazzi loved her, but, though he was one of you in your criminal work, his love was the love of a brave, honest man. It is true, perhaps, that it was for her, rather than for you, that it was because of his love, a great, strong, wonderful love, and to save her from horror and despair because she loved *you*, that he gave his life for you, that he went to prison in your stead, voluntarily, on his own confession, when he was less guilty than you, and when the police offered him his freedom if he would only turn evidence against you, the man they really wanted. But that is what he did, nevertheless. He kept you together." She was leaning forward now, her eyes ablaze, burning. "That was his love! His love for my mother, and for me—yes, for me—for he loved me too, and I, though I, was only a little girl, I loved Tony Lomazzi. And he gave his life—and he died there in prison. And now—now—you mean to betray his trust—to betray his friend who believed in you because he believed in Tony, who trusted you and sent him here. And you tricked him, and tricked the police for your own ends! Well, you shall not do it! You shall not! Do you hear? You shall not!"

Nicolo Capriano's face was livid. A fury, greater than before, a fury that was unbalanced, like the fury of a maniac, seized upon him. He twisted his hands one around the other with swift insistence, his lips moved to form words—and he coughed instead, and a fleck of blood tinged the white beard.

"You dare!" he shrieked, catching for his breath. "You, a girl, dare talk to me like that, to me—Nicolo Capriano! I shall not—eh? You say that to me! I shall not! And who will stop me?"

"I will!" she said, through tight lips. "If you will not stop it yourself—then I will. No matter what it costs, no matter what it means—to you, or to me—I will!"

Nicolo Capriano laughed—and the room rang with the pealing laughter that was full of unhinged, crazy, shuddering mirth.

"Fool!" he cried. "You will stop it—eh? And how will you stop it? Will you tell the police? Ha, ha! Then you, too, would betray dear Tony's friend! You would tell the police what they want to know—that Dave Henderson can be found in New York, and that he has gone there to get the money back. Or perhaps you will write another letter—and tell Dago George to pay no attention to my orders? Ha, ha! And it is too bad that our young friend himself has gone, and left you no address so that you could intercept him!"

Teresa drew back a little, and into her eyes came trouble and dismay. And Nicolo Capriano's laugh rang out again—and was checked by a spasm of coughing—and rang out once more, ending in a sort of triumphant scream.

"Well, and what do you think now about stopping it—eh? Do you imagine that Nicolo Capriano sees no farther than his nose? Stop it! Bah! No one will stop it—and, least of all, you!"

She seemed to have overcome the dismay that had seized upon her, though her face had grown even whiter than before.

"It is true, what you say," she said, in a low, strained voice. "But there is one way left, one way to find him, and warn him, and I will take that way."

"Hah!" Nicolo Capriano glared at her. His voice dropped. "And what is that way, my little one?" he purred, through a fit of coughing. "Old Nicolo would like to know."

"To go where Dave Henderson is going," she answered. "To go where he can be found, to go to New York, to keep him from going to Dago George's, or, if I am too late for that, to warn him there before Dago George has had time to do him any harm, and——"

Her words ended in a startled cry. Nicolo Capriano's long, slim fingers, from the bed, had shot out, locked about her waist, and were wrenching at her in a mad-man's fury.

"You—you would do that!" the old Italian screamed. "By God! No! No! No! Do you hear? No!" His hands had crept upward, and, with all his weight upon her, he was literally pulling himself out of the bed. "No!" he screamed again. "No! Do you hear? No!"

"Father!" she cried out frantically. "Father, what are you doing? You will kill yourself!"

The black eyes of the old man were gleaming with an insane light, his face was working in horrible contortions.

"Hah!" He was out of the bed now, struggling wildly with her. "Hah! Kill myself, will I? I would kill you—*you*—before I would let you meddle with my plans! It is the old Nicolo again—Nicolo Capriano of the years when——"

The room seemed to swirl around her. The clutching fingers had relaxed. It was she now who struggled and grasped at the man's body and shoulders—to hold him up. He was very heavy, too heavy for her. He seemed to be carrying her downward with him—until he fell back half across the bed. And she leaned over him then, and stared at him for a long time through her hands that were tightly held to her face—and horror, a great, blinding horror came, and fear, a fear that robbed her of her senses came, and she staggered backward, and stumbled over the chair at the bedside, and clutched at it for support.

She did not speak. Nicolo Capriano had left his bed for the first time in three years—to die.

Her father was dead. That was the theme of the overwhelming horror, and the paralyzing fear that obsessed her brain. It beat upon her in remorseless waves—horror—fear. Time did not exist; reality had passed away. She was in some great, soundless void—soundless, except for that strange ringing in her ears. And she put her hands up to her ears to shut out the sound. But it persisted. It became clearer. It became a tangible thing. It was the doorbell.

Habit seemed to impel her. She went automatically to the hall, and, in a numbed sort of consciousness, went along the hall, and opened the door, and stared at a short, fat man, who stood there and chewed on the butt of a cigar that dangled from one corner of his mouth.

"My name's MacBain," said Bookie Skarvan glibly. "And I want to see Nicolo Capriano. Very important. You're his daughter, aren't you?"

She did not answer him. Her brain floundered in that pit of blackness into which it had been plunged. She was scarcely aware of the man's presence, scarcely aware that she was standing here in the doorway.

"Say, you look scared, you do; but there's nothing to be scared about," said Bookie Skarvan ingratiatingly. "I just want to see Nicolo Capriano for a few minutes. You go and tell him a reporter wants to see him about that bomb explosion, and 'll give him a write-up that'll be worth while."

She drew back a little, forcing herself to shake her head.

"Aw, say, go on now, there's a good girl!" wheedled Bookie Skarvan. "The paper sent me here, and I've got to see him. There's nothing for you to look so white about. I'm only a reporter. I ain't going to hurt him—see?"

Teresa shivered. How cold the night was! This man here—what was it he had said? That he wanted to see Nicolo Capriano? Strange that words came with such curious difficulty to her tongue—as though, somehow, she had been dumb all her life, and was speaking now for the first time.

"Nicolo Capriano is dead," she said—and closed the door in Bookie Skarvan's face.

BOOK IV.
THE IRON TAVERN

I.
THE RENDEZVOUS

THE metamorphosis in Dave Henderson's appearance since the night, nine days ago, when he had left San Francisco and Nicolo Capriano's house, had been, by necessity, gradual; it had attained its finished state now, as he stepped from a train to one of the sub-level station platforms in the City of New York. Then, he had been attired in one of the old Italian's cast-off and ill-fitting suits, an object neither too respectable nor presentable; now, the wide-brimmed soft hat was new and good, and the dark tweed suit, of expensive material, was that of a well-groomed man.

It had taken time—all this. Nor had it been entirely simple of accomplishment, in spite of the ample funds received from Square John Kelly, funds that now, wary of unsavory corners into which a certain business that he had on hand might lead him here in New York, he had taken the precaution to secrete about his person in a money belt beneath his underclothing.

He had scarcely needed old Nicolo Capriano's warning to be careful. Dave Henderson had not changed so much in five years in prison that he could take liberties with the risk of recognition in that section of the country where, in the days before, he had been so familiar a figure on the local race-tracks. He had made his way out of California, and considerably beyond California, in the same way that, once before, he had attempted to elude the police—and on which former occasion would have succeeded, he was quite satisfied, had it not been for the wound that had finally robbed him of consciousness and placed him at their mercy.

He had traveled during three nights, and only at night, in boxcars, and on freight trains, stealing his way. But there had been no hurry. The night of the twenty-fourth of June, the date of the rendezvous that Millman had given him, had not been very far off, and though it had always obtruded itself upon him and never allowed itself to be forgotten from the moment he had heard it from Millman's lips, he had consistently told himself that the twenty-fourth of June was a consideration to be entirely disregarded. Since Millman was a thief and had double-crossed him, the rendezvous was blatantly a fake. It existed only as a sort of jeering, ironical barb with which Millman at times, out of the nowhere, like a specter, grinning maliciously, prodded and made devil's sport of him. He had no concern with Millman's twenty-fourth of June! He would meet Millman in due time—two hemispheres were not big enough, or wide enough apart, to prevent that—but the meeting would be by his, not Millman's, appointment.

And then he had passed out of the more critical danger zone, and got further east. But, even then, he had taken no chances. Dave Henderson was dead—the creation of one Barty Lynch was not a matter to be trifled with. He had taken no chances; if anything, he had erred on the side of extreme caution. The abrupt transition into respectability by one in misfitting, threadbare garments, and who looked, moreover, a disreputable tramp from his nights in the boxcars, was only to invite suspicion at any ordinary store where he might attempt to buy clothes. A second-hand suit, therefore, of fairly creditable appearance, first replaced Nicolo Capriano's discarded garments; later, at a more exclusive establishment still further east, in Chicago, to be exact, this was exchanged for the attire he now wore—while, here and there, he had stocked a dress-suit case with needed requirements. He had been deliberately leisurely in his progress east once he had felt it safe to dispense with his boxcar mode of travel—and this, actually, as a sort of defiance and challenge flung down by his common sense to that jeering prod with which Millman, and Millman's cynical rendezvous, plagued him in spite of himself. The evening of June twenty-fourth at the St. Lucian Hotel in New York was of no particular interest to him! It had taken him a week to reach Chicago. It was nine days now since he had left Nicolo Capriano's house. Nine days! He was now in New York, standing here on one of the station platforms—and it was the evening of the twenty-fourth of June!

He looked at his watch, as he made his way to the main section of the station. It was seven-thirty. He deposited his dress-suit case in the parcel-room, and went out to the street. Here, he asked a policeman to direct him to the St. Lucian Hotel.

He smiled a little grimly as he walked along. The much vaunted challenge of his common sense had gone down to rout and defeat, it seemed! He was on his way now to the St. Lucian Hotel—and he would be there at eight o'clock on the evening of June twenty-fourth. He laughed outright at himself, suddenly, mirthlessly.

Well, why not! And why not be entirely honest with himself? Despite self-argument to the contrary, he knew all along that he would be at the rendezvous at the appointed time. He was a fool—undoubtedly a fool. Nothing could come of it except, possibly, to afford Millman, if Millman had elected to watch from some safe vantage point in hiding, an amusing spectacle.

He was a fool—he offered nothing in defense of himself on that score. But, too, as far as any results had been obtained, he had been a fool to go searching the old pigeon-cote for the money, when he had beforehand already persuaded himself in his own mind that the money was gone! It was the same thing over again now—the elimination of doubt, that would always have crept insidiously into his mind; the substitution of doubt, however ill-founded, for an established certainty. He had felt better for that visit to the old pigeon-cote; he would feel better, even at the expense of pampering again to fantastic doubts, for his visit to the St. Lucian Hotel to-night. Millman would not be there, any more than the money had been in the pigeon-cote; but, equally, he, Dave Henderson, would have established that fact beyond the reach of any brain quibbling which, of late, had been, it seemed, so prone to affect him.

He stopped again to ask directions from an officer, and to ask this time another question as well—a question prompted by a somewhat unpleasant possibility which, having once decided to keep the rendezvous, he could not now ignore. What kind of a place *was* this St. Lucian Hotel?

"One of the best," the officer answered. "There you are—two blocks ahead, and one to the left."

Dave Henderson smiled with a sort of patient tolerance at himself. The locality alone should have been sufficient answer to his question. It was not the setting, very far from it, for a trap! His hand, that had un consciously closed around the stock of his revolver in the side pocket of his coat, was withdrawn and swung now at his side, as he walked along again.

He looked at his watch once more, as he turned the corner indicated. It was five minutes to eight. A half block ahead of him he saw the hotel. He walked slowly now, the short distance remaining. "The St. Lucian Hotel. Eight o'clock in the evening. June twenty-fourth." The words seemed to mock at him now, and the gibe to sting. He had fallen for it, after all! He could call himself a fool again if he wished, but what was the use of that? It was obvious that he was a fool! He *felt* like one, as he passed a much bedecked functionary at the doorway, and found himself standing a moment later in the huge, luxuriously appointed rotunda of the hotel. He was not even recompensed by novelty, as he stared aimlessly about him. It was just the usual thing—the rug-strewn, tiled floor; the blaze of lights; the hum of talk; the hurry of movement; the wide, palm-dotted corridors, whose tables were crowded with men and women in evening dress at after-dinner coffee; the deep lounging chairs in his more immediate vicinity; the strains of an orchestra trying to make itself heard above the general hubbub.

A clock from the hotel desk behind him began to chime the hour. He turned mechanically in that direction, his eyes seeking the timepiece—and whirled suddenly around again, as a hand fell upon his shoulder. The police! The thought flashed swift as a lightning stroke through his mind. Somewhere, somehow he had failed, and they had found him out, and— —

The rotunda, the lights, seemed to swirl before him, and then to vanish utterly, and leave only a single figure to fill all the space, a figure in immaculate evening clothes, a figure whose hand tightened its shoulder-grip upon him, a figure whose clear, gray eyes stared into his and smiled.

He touched his lips with the tip of his tongue.

"Millman!" he said hoarsely. "You!"

"Well," said Millman easily, "this is the St. Lucian Hotel; it's eight o'clock, and June twenty-fourth—who did you expect to meet here?"

"You," said Dave Henderson—and laughed unnaturally.

Millman's gray eyes narrowed, and his face clouded suddenly.

"What's the matter with you, Dave?" he demanded sharply.

Dave Henderson's hands, at his sides, were clenched. Millman—this was Millman! Millman, whom he hadn't expected to meet here! Millman, whom he had promised himself he would track down if it took a lifetime, and, once found, would settle with as he would settle with a mad dog! And Millman was here, smiling into his face! His mind groped out through a haze of bewilderment that robbed him of the power to reason; his tongue groped for words. It was as though he were dazed and groggy from a blow that had sent him mentally to his knees. He did not understand.

"There's nothing the matter with me," he said mechanically.

He felt Millman's hand close on his arm.

"Come on up to my rooms," said Millman quietly. "It's a little public here, isn't it?"

Dave Henderson did not disengage his arm from the other's hold, but his hand slipped unostentatiously into his coat pocket. A rift seemed to come breaking through that brain fog, as he silently accompanied Millman to the elevator. He had dismissed the probability of such a thing but a few minutes before, had even jeered at himself for considering it, but, in spite of the eminent respectability of the St. Lucian Hotel, in spite of its fashion-crowded corridors and lobby, the thought was back now with redoubled force—and it came through the process of elimination. If Millman was a crook, as he undoubtedly was, and had secured the money, as he undoubtedly had, why else should Millman be here? There seemed to be no other way to account for Millman having kept the rendezvous. Strange things, queer things, had happened in hotels that were quite as enviable of reputation as the St. Lucian—perhaps it was even the *safest* place for such things to happen, from the perpetrator's standpoint! His lips were tight now. Well, at least, he was not walking blindfold into—a trap!

They had ascended in silence. He eyed Millman now in cool appraisal, as the elevator stopped, and the other led the way and threw open the door to a suite of rooms. There was quite a difference between the prison stripes of a bare few months ago and the expensive and fashionably tailored evening clothes of to-night! Well, Millman had always claimed he was a gentleman, hadn't he? And he, Dave Henderson, had believed him—once! But that did not change anything. Millman was no less a crook for that! From the moment Millman had gone to that pigeon-cote and had taken that money, he stood out foursquare as a crook, and—— Dave Henderson felt his muscles tauten, and a chill sense of dismay seize suddenly upon him. There was still another supposition—one that swept upon him now in a disconcerting flash. Suppose Millman had *not* gone to that pigeon-cote, suppose it was *not* Millman who had taken the money, suppose that, after all, it had been found by some one else, that Tooler, for instance, had stumbled upon it by chance! And, instead of Millman having it, suppose that it was gone forever, without clue to its whereabouts, beyond his, Dave Henderson's, reach! It was not impossible—it was not even improbable. His brain was suddenly in turmoil—he scarcely heard Millman's words, as the other closed the door of the suite behind them.

"The family is in the country for the summer months," said Millman with a smile, as he waved his hand around the apartment; "and I have gone back to my old habit—since I have been free to indulge my habits—of living here during that time, instead of keeping a town house open, too. Sit down there, Dave, by the table, and make yourself comfortable."

It sounded plausible—most plausible! Dave Henderson scowled. Across his mind flashed that scene in the prison library when Millman had been plausible before—damnably plausible! His mind was in a sort of riot now; but, through the maze of doubt and chaos, there stood out clearly enough the memory of the hours, and days, and weeks of bitter resolve to "get" this man who now, offensively at his ease, and smiling, was standing here before him.

And then Dave Henderson laughed a little—not pleasantly.

Well, he was face to face with Millman now. It would be a showdown anyhow. Trap, or no trap, Millman would show his hand. He would know whether Millman had got that money, or whether somebody else had! He would know whether Millman was straight—or whether Millman was a crook!

He jerked his shoulders back sharply; his fingers closed a little more ominously on the revolver in his coat pocket. Was he quite crazy? Had he lost all sense of proportion? The chances were a thousand to one that it *was* Millman who had looted the pigeon-cote; the chances were one in a thousand that it could have been any one else.

"Yes," he said coolly. "Nice rooms you've got here, and a bit of a change from—out West!" He jerked his head abruptly toward a door across the room. "I notice you've got a closed door there. I hope I'm not butting in, if you're entertaining friends, or anything like that!" He laughed again—raucously now. His nerves seemed suddenly to be raw and on edge. Millman was favoring him with what, whether it was genuine or not, was meant for a blank stare.

"Friends?" said Millman questioningly. And then his gray eyes softened. "Oh, I see!" he exclaimed. "It's hard to get over the habit, isn't it? No; there's no one there. But perhaps you'd feel better satisfied to look for yourself."

"I would!" said Dave Henderson bluntly.

"Go ahead, then!" invited Millman readily, and waved his hand toward the door.

"I'll follow *you*," said Dave Henderson curtly.

Millman turned toward the door, hesitated, and stopped.

"Dave, what's the matter with you?" he demanded for the second time.

"Nothing much!" replied Dave Henderson. "But we'll get this over first, eh? Go on, let's see the rest' of this suite of yours. It's good to know that an old pal is enjoying such pleasant surroundings."

Without a word, Millman stepped across the room, and opened the door in question. It led into a bedroom, and from there to a bathroom; there was nothing else. Dave Henderson inspected these in silence. He eyed Millman, frowning in a renewed perplexity, as they returned to the outer room.

"All right!" he said gruffly. "You win the first trick. But how about a certain little package now? I'll trouble you to hand that over, Millman!"

Millman shook his head in a sort of tolerant expostulation.

"As we used to say 'out there,' I don't get you, Dave!" he said slowly. "You are acting very strangely. I've been looking forward to this meeting— and you haven't even a handshake for an old friend. I don't understand."

"I don't myself!" returned Dave Henderson evenly. "There's a whole lot of things that don't fit. But it's five years since I've seen that package, and maybe I'm a trifle over-anxious about it. Suppose you come across with it!"

Millman shrugged his shoulders a little helplessly.

"You're a queer card, Dave," he said. "Of course, I'll come across with it! What else in the world are we here for to-night?" He stepped to the table, pulled a drawer open, and produced a neatly tied parcel, which he laid on the table. "I took it out of the vault to-day, so as to have it ready for you to-night."

From the package, Dave Henderson's eyes lifted, and held Millman's in a long stare. It was as though, somehow, the ground had been swept from under his feet. He had expected anything but the package. Logically, from every conclusion based on logic, Millman should not be handing over that package now. And this act now was so illogical that he could account for it on no other basis than one of trickery of some sort. He tried to read the riddle in the other's eyes; he read only a cool, imperturbable composure. His hand still toyed with the revolver in his pocket.

"There's an outside wrapper on it, I see," he said in a low voice. "Take it off, Millman."

Millman's brows knitted in a sort of amused perplexity.

"You're beyond me to-night, Dave," he said, as he stripped off the outer covering. "Utterly beyond me! Well, there you are!"

The package lay there now on the table, intact, as it had been on the night it had found a hiding-place in the old pigeon-cote. The original brown-paper wrapper was still tied and sealed with its several bank seals in red wax; the corner, torn open in that quick, hasty examination in Martin K. Tydeman's library, still gaped apart, disclosing the edges of the banknotes within. It was the package containing one hundred thousand dollars, intact, untouched, undisturbed.

Dave Henderson sat down mechanically in the chair behind him that was drawn up close to the table. His hand came from his pocket, and, joined by the other, cupped his chin, his elbows resting on the table's edge, as he stared at the package.

"I'm damned!" said Dave Henderson heavily.

His mind refused to point the way. It left him hung up in midair. It still persisted in picturing the vengeance he had sworn against this man here, in picturing every stake he owned flung into the ring to square accounts with this man here—and the picture took on the guise now of grotesque and gigantic irony. But still he did not understand. That picture had had its inception in a logical, incontrovertible and true perspective. It was strange! He looked up now from the package to Millman, as he felt Millman's hand fall and press gently upon his shoulder. Millman was leaning toward him over the table.

"Well, Dave," said Millman, and his smile disarmed his words, "you've treated me as though I were a thug up to the moment I opened that package, and now you act as though the sight of it had floored you. Perhaps you'll tell me now, if I ask you again, what's the matter?"

Dave Henderson did not answer for a moment. His hand went into his pocket and came out again—with his revolver balanced in its palm.

"I guess I made a mistake," he said at last, with a queer smile. "Thug is right! I was figuring on pulling this on you—in another way."

Millman drew a chair deliberately up to the opposite side of the table, and sat down.

"Go on, Dave," he prompted quietly. "I'm listening."

Dave Henderson restored the weapon to his pocket, and shrugged his shoulders in a way that was eloquent of his own perturbed state of mind.

"I guess you'll get the point in a word or two," he said slowly. "The story you told me in the pen, and the way you acted for two years made me believe you, and made me think you were straight. Understand? And then that afternoon before you were going out, and I was up against it hard—you know—I told you where this money was. Understand? Well, I had hardly got back to my cell when I figured you had trapped me. If you were straight you wouldn't touch that money, unless to do me in by handing it back to the police, for it would be the same thing as stealing it again, and that would make a crook of you; if you were a crook then you weren't playing straight with me to begin with, since the story you told me was a lie, and the only reason I could see for that lie was to work me up to spilling the beans so that you could cop the loot and give me the slip. Either way, it looked raw for me, didn't it? Well, when I got out, the money *hadn't* gone back to the police, but it *had* gone! I swore I'd get you. Don't make any mistake about that, Millman—I swore I'd get you. I didn't expect to meet you here to-night. I called myself a fool even for coming. You were either straight or a crook, and there wasn't much room left for doubt as to which it was. See, Millman?"

Millman nodded his head gravely.

"I see," he said, in the same quiet tones. "And now?"

Dave Henderson jerked his hand toward the package of banknotes that lay on the table before him.

"I guess that's the answer, isn't it?" he said, with a twisted smile. "There's the hundred thousand dollars there that you pinched from the old pigeoncote." He shoved out his hand impulsively to Millman. "I'm sorry, Millman. Shake! I've been in wrong all the time. But I never seemed to get that slant on it before; that you were—a straight crook."

Millman's gray eyes, half amused, half serious, studied Dave Henderson for a long minute, as their hands clasped.

"A straight crook, eh?" he said finally, leaning back again in his chair. "Well, the deduction is fairly logical, Dave, I'll have to admit. And what's the answer to that?"

Dave Henderson jerked his hand toward the package of banknotes again.

"There's only one, isn't there?" he returned. "You've got a stake in that coin now. A fair share of it is yours, and I'll leave it to you to say what you want."

Millman lighted a cigarette before he answered.

"All right!" he said, with a curious smile, as his eyes through the spiral of blue smoke from the tip of his cigarette fixed on Dave Henderson again. "All right! I'll accept that offer, Dave. And I'll take—all, or none."

Dave Henderson drew sharply back in his chair. There was something in Millman's voice, a significance that he did not like, or quite understand, save that it denied any jocularity on Millman's part, or that the other was making a renunciation of his claim through pure generosity. His eyes narrowed. The money was here. Millman had come across with it. Those facts were not to be gainsaid; but they were facts so utterly at variance with what months of brooding over the matter had led him to expect they should be, that he had accepted them in a sort of stunned surprise. And now this! Was he right, after all—that there was some trickery here?

"What do you mean—all, or none?" he said, a hint of menace creeping into his voice.

"Just that," said Millman, and his tones were low and serious now. "Just what I said—all, or none."

Dave Henderson laughed shortly.

"Then I guess it'll be—none!" he said coolly.

"Perhaps," admitted Millman slowly. "But I hope not." He leaned forward now, earnestly, over the table. "Dave," he said steadily, "let us get back to the old pal days again when we believed in each other, just man to man, Dave; because now you've got a chip on your shoulder. I don't want to knock that chip off; I want to talk to you. I want to tell you why I committed what you have rightly called theft in going to that pigeon-cote and taking that money. And I want to try and make you understand that my life in prison and the story that I told you there, in spite of the fact that I have 'stolen' the money now, was not a lie. There is not a soul on this wide earth, Dave, except yourself, who knows that Charles Millman served two years in the penitentiary with prison stripes on his back. If it were known I think it would mean ruin to me, certainly in a social sense, very probably in a commercial sense as well. And yet, Dave, I would rather you knew it than that you didn't. Does that sound strange? Well, somehow, I've never pictured the flaring headlines that would be in every paper in this city if I were exposed—because, well, because I couldn't picture it—not through you, Dave—and that's the only way it could come about. And so you see, Dave, I did not ask you for faith in me without reposing my own faith in you in the same full measure."

Dave Henderson's brows gathered. He stared at the other. It was like the Charlie Millman of old talking now. But the whole business was queer—except that the money lay here now within reach of his hand after five years of hell and torture. He made no comment.

"And so, Dave, what could I do?" Millman went on. "As far as I could see then, and as far as I can see now, I had no choice but to offer to get that money from its hiding-place. I knew you meant literally what you said when you swore you'd fight for it if all the police in America were blocking your way, and that you'd either get it or go down and out. I knew you'd do that; I knew the police *would* watch you, and I feared for you either physical harm or another long prison sentence. And so I took the money and shared your guilt. But, Dave, once I was committed to that act, I was committed to another as well—I hadn't any choice there, either—I mean, Dave, the return of the money to the estate where it belongs."

Dave Henderson was on his feet. His face, that had softened and relaxed as Millman was speaking, was suddenly hard and set again, and now a red, angry flush was dyeing his cheeks. He choked for his words.

"What's that you say!" he rasped out. "Return it!" He laughed raucously. "Have you been drinking, Millman—or are you just crazy?"

A strange, whimsical smile crept to Millman's lips. "No," he said. "I guess I'm what you called me—just a straight crook. I can't see any other way out, Dave. I've stolen the money too, and it's up to me as well as you. It's got to go back."

"By God—no!" said Dave Henderson through his teeth. "No! You understand—no!"

Millman shook his head slowly.

"Dave, it's no good," he said quietly. "Apart from every other consideration, it won't get you anywhere. Listen, Dave, I——"

"No!" Dave Henderson interrupted savagely. "You can cut that out! You're going to preach; but that's no good, either! You're going to pull the goody-goody stuff, and then you're going to tell me that sooner or later I'll be caught, anyhow. Well, you can forget it—the preaching, because I don't want to listen to you; and the other, because there's nothing to it now." He leaned across the table, and laughed raucously again, and stared with cynical humor at the other. "I'm dead—see? Dave Henderson is dead. A friend of mine pulled the trick on them in 'Frisco. They think Dave Henderson is dead. The book is closed, slammed shut forever—understand? I'm dead—but I've got this money now that I've fought for, and paid for with the sweat of hell, and it's going to pay me back now, Millman! Understand? It's going to pay the dividends now that I've earned—and that, by God, no man is going to take away from me!"

"Good old Dave!" said Millman softly. "That's what's the matter with you—you'd drop in your tracks before you'd let go. If only you weren't looking through the wrong glasses, Dave, you'd fight just as hard the other way. No, I don't want to preach to you, and I'm not going to preach; but there's a great big bond, two years of prison together, between you and me, and I want you to listen to me. You were never meant for a crook, Dave. There's not a crooked thing in the world about you, except this one distorted brain kink that's got hold of you. And now you're in wrong. Look at it from any angle that you like, and it doesn't pay. It hasn't paid you so far—and it never will."

"Hasn't it!" snapped Dave Henderson. "Well, maybe not! But that's because it hasn't had the chance. But the chance is here now, and it's all bust wide open. You can forget everything else, Millman, except just this, and then you'll understand once for all where I stand: Here's the money—and I'm dead!"

"Your soul isn't," said Millman bluntly.

Dave Henderson's jaws set.

"That's enough!" he flung out curtly. "Once for all—no!"

Millman did not answer for a moment, nor did he look at Dave Henderson—his eyes, through the curling cigarette smoke, were fixed on the package of banknotes.

"I'm sorry, Dave," he said at last, in a low, strained way. "I'm sorry you won't take the biggest chance you'll ever have in your life, the chance you've got right now, of coming across a white man clean through. I thought perhaps you would. I hoped you would, Dave—and so I'm sorry. But that doesn't alter my position any. The money has got to go back to the estate, and it is going back."

For an instant Dave Henderson did not move, then he thrust his head sharply forward over the table. The red had flooded into his face again, and his eyes were hard and full of menace.

"That's better!" he said through tight lips. "You're talking a language now that I understand! So that money is going back, is it? Well, you've talked a lot, and I've listened. Now you listen to me, and listen hard! I don't want to hurt you, Millman, as God is my judge, I don't want to hurt you, but it will be one or the other of us. Understand, Millman? One or the other of us, if you start anything like that! You get me, Millman? You've called a showdown, and that goes; but, by God, unless you've got a better hand than I have, you'll never send that money back!"

Millman's hand was resting on the package of banknotes. He pushed it now quietly across the table to Dave Henderson.

"Not this, Dave," he said simply. "You settled that when I asked for all or none. This is yours—to do with as you like. Don't misunderstand me, Dave; don't make any mistake. You can put that package under your arm and leave here this minute, and I'll not lift a finger to stop you, or, after you are gone, say a word, or make any move to discredit your assumed death, or bring the police upon your heels. I told you once, Dave—do you remember?—that you could trust me. But, Dave, if you won't return the stolen money, then I will. I haven't any choice, have I? I stole it, too."

Dave Henderson stared, frowning, into the steel-gray eyes across the table.

"I don't get you!" he said shortly. "What do you mean?"

"Just what I say, Dave," Millman answered. "That if you won't return it yourself, I will pay it back out of my own pocket."

For a minute Dave Henderson eyed the other incredulously, then he threw back his head and laughed, but it was not a pleasant laugh.

"You will, eh!" he said. "Well, if you feel that way about it, go to it! Maybe you can afford it; I can't!"

"Yes," said Millman soberly, "as far as that goes, I am a rich man, and I can afford it. But, Dave, I want to say this to you"—he was standing up now—"the richest man in the world couldn't afford to part with a nickel as well as you could afford to part with that hundred thousand dollars there. It isn't money that you've got at stake, Dave. Well, that's all. Either you pay—or I do. It's up to you, Dave."

Dave Henderson's hands were clenching and unclenching, as he gripped at the edge of the table. Vaguely, dimly, he sensed an awakening something within him which seemed to be striving to give birth to some discordant element that sought to undermine and shake his resolution. It was not tangible yet, it was confused; his mind groped out in an effort to grasp it in a concrete way so that he might smother it, repudiate it, beat it down.

"No!" he shot out.

Millman shook his head.

"I don't ask you for an answer to-night," he said gravely. "I don't think you're ready to give an answer now, and be fair to yourself. It's a pretty big stake, Dave. You'll never play for a bigger—and neither will I. I'm staking a hundred thousand dollars on the Dave Henderson I know—the chap that's dead for a while. It doesn't matter much now whether the money is back in the hands of the estate in a day, or a week, or a month from now. Take a month, Dave. If at the end of a month the estate has not received the money from you—and I shall know whether it has or not—it will receive a hundred thousand dollars in cash from me, anonymously, with the statement that it is to square the account for which Dave Henderson was convicted."

Dave Henderson raised a clenched hand, and swept it, clenched, across his eyes. He had it now! He understood that thing within him that seemed quite as eager to offer battle as he was to give it. And it was strong, and insidious, and crafty. He cursed at it. It took him at a disadvantage. It placed him suddenly on the defensive—and it angered him. It placed him in a position that was not a nice one to defend. He cursed at it; and blind fury came as his defense. And the red that had surged into his face left it, and a whiteness came, and his lips thinned into a straight line.

"Damn you, Millman!" he whispered hoarsely. "I get you now! Damn you, you've no right to put the screws on me like this! Who asked you to offer your money as a sacrifice for me—to make me out a white-livered cur if I turned you down! But it doesn't go, understand? It's blackmail, that's what it is! It may be whitewashed with holiness, but it's blackmail just the same—and you can go to hell with it!"

He snatched up the package of banknotes, whipped the outer wrapping around it, and tucked it under his arm—and paused, as though awaiting or inviting some action on Millman's part. But Millman neither moved nor spoke. And then Dave Henderson, with a short laugh, crossed to the door, wrenched it open, stepped out of the room, and slammed the door behind him.

II.
THE FIRST GUEST

BLIND to his surroundings, mechanically retracing his steps to the railway station, Dave Henderson swung along the street. He walked as though he would outwalk his thoughts—fast, indifferent to all about him. He clung stubbornly to the fury in which he had sought refuge, and which he had aroused within himself against Millman. He clung to this tenaciously now, because he sensed a persistent attempt on the part of some unwelcome and unfamiliar other-self to argue the pros and cons, both of Millman's motives and Millman's acts; an attempt, that sought to introduce a wedge doubt into his mind, that sought to bring about a wavering of purpose with the insidious intent of robbing him, if it could, of the reward that was now within his grasp.

Within his grasp! He laughed out sharply, as he hurried along. It was *literally* within his grasp! The reward was his now—his absolutely, concretely, tangibly—the hundred thousand dollars was in this innocent-looking parcel that was at this precise moment tucked under his arm. He laughed out again. There was enough in that one fact to occupy his mind and attention, and to put to utter rout and confusion those other thoughts that endeavored to make cunning and tricky inroads upon him. It shattered and swept aside, as though by the waving of some magical wand, every mental picture he had drawn of himself in New York, every plan that he had made for his sojourn here.

He had been prepared to spend weeks and months of unceasing effort to run Millman to earth; he had planned to rake the dens and dives of the underworld, to live as one of its sordid and outlawed inhabitants, if necessary, in order to get upon Millman's track; he had meant to play Millman at his own game until he had trapped Millman and the final showdown came. And, instead, he had scarcely been in New York an hour, and he was walking now along the street with the hundred thousand dollars under his arm, with Millman no longer a vicious and stealthy antagonist to be foiled and fought wherever he might be found—with nothing to do now but spend or employ this money under his arm as his fancy or his judgment dictated, free of all hindrance or restraint, for Millman was no longer a source of danger or concern, and Dave Henderson was dead to the world in general and to the police in particular, and that left Barty Lynch as the unfettered possessor of one hundred thousand dollars!

Millman had given him a month, and—ah! he was back on that tack, was he? He clenched his hand. No! A month represented time, and it was time in a purely abstract way that he was considering now; it had nothing to do with Millman, or Millman's "month," It would take time to make new plans and new arrangements. He did not intend to act hastily.

He had come by that money by too brutally hard a road not to realize the worth of every cent of it. He needed time now to think out the future carefully. He was not a fool—to scatter that money to the winds. A thousand times in prison he had buoyed himself up with the knowledge that in the returns from that sum of money lay independence for life. That was what he had taken it for in the first place! It meant, safely invested, a minimum of five thousand dollars a year. He could get along very well, even luxuriously, on five thousand a year! He had only now to decide where and how he should invest that money; and he needed only now the time to arrive at that decision without any undue haste that might afterwards be bitterly regretted. Would he go to Australia, or to South America, for example, and begin life anew there as a gentleman of independent means? Or somewhere in Europe, perhaps? It needed time now to make this decision, and, as a natural corollary, a temporary abode was required, an abode where he could feel quite secure, both as regards his money, and as against any eleventh-hour trick of fate that might disclose his identity and spill the fat into the fire.

Well, he had had that latter problem solved for him from the first, hadn't he? There was Dago George's; and in his pocket was Nicolo Capriano's letter that was an "open sesame" to Dago George's hospitality, and, more vital still, to Dago George's fidelity. He was going there now, as soon as he got his dress-suit case again from the station which now loomed ahead of him down the block.

His thoughts reverted to Nicolo Capriano, and, from the old Italian, to the old Italian's daughter. Teresa! He had not forgotten Teresa! Again and again, in those jolting boxcars, and during his flight from San Francisco, there had come a mental picture in which those fearless eyes had met his, and he had seen her smile, and watched the color mount and crimson her face as it had done on that occasion when he had first seen her.

He had not forgotten Teresa, he had not tried to; he had even invited those mental pictures of her. It was like some fragrant and alluring memory that had seemed to ding to him, and he had dung to it. Some day he wanted to see Teresa again—and she was the only woman toward whom he had ever felt that way. He wasn't in love with her, that was ridiculous, unless he had fallen in love with her since he had left her! But of one thing he was distinctly conscious, and that was that her attitude on that last night, when she had let him go in so strange a way, still plagued and tormented him. It was as though she had slammed the door of her presence in his face, and he wanted to see her again—some time—and——

Queer fancies crept into his brain. The old Italian said he was getting better. Perhaps Nicolo Capriano would like Australia, or South America—or perhaps Europe!

Dave Henderson shrugged his shoulders a little helplessly, and smiled ironically at himself, as he reached and entered the station. It was Nicolo Capriano alone, of course, of whom he was thinking! But—he shrugged his shoulders again—his immediate business now was to get to this Dago George!

He secured his dress-suit case from the parcel-room, deposited the package of banknotes in the dress-suit case, and sought a taxi. That was the easiest and most convenient way of reaching Dago George's. He did not know either in what direction or how far he had to go, and somehow, both physically and mentally, he suddenly, and for the first time, realized that he was tired.

"Chatham Square," he told the starter, as he climbed into the taxi; and then, as the car moved forward, he leaned over and spoke to the chauffeur: "There's a fellow called Dago George who keeps a place right near there," he said. "I don't know exactly where it is; but I guess you can find it, can't you?"

"Sure!" said the chauffeur heartily, with an extra tip in sight, "Sure! Leave it to me!"

Dave Henderson settled himself comfortably back on the seat, and relaxed. The strain of the days since he had left San Francisco, the strain of the days since the prison doors had opened and let him free, the strain of the five years behind those pitiless walls of stone and those bars of steel was gone now. The money was his, in his sole possession, here in the dress-suit case at his feet. It was the end of the bitter struggle. It was finished. He could let go now, and relax luxuriously. And, besides, he was tired.

He refused to think of Millman, because it irritated him. He refused to think of anything now, because his brain was like some weary thing, which, with a sigh of relief, stretched itself out and revelled in idleness. His future, Nicolo Capriano, Teresa—all these could wait until to-morrow, until a night's sleep, the first he would have known for many nights that was not haunted by distracting doubts and problems, should bring him fresh to the consideration of his new plans.

He lighted a cigarette and smoked, and watched the passing crowds and traffic through the window. He had only to present his letter to Dago George, and turn in for the night, with the feeling, also for the first time in many nights, of absolute security.

Dave Henderson continued to gaze out of the window. The localities through which he passed did not seem to improve. He smiled a little. He knew nothing about New York, but this was about what he had expected. Dago George was not likely either to reside or conduct his business in a very exclusive neighborhood!

Finally the taxi stopped, but only to permit the chauffeur to ask directions from a passer-by on the sidewalk. They went on again then, turned a corner, and a moment later drew up at the curb.

"I guess this is the place all right," announced the chauffeur.

A glance confirmed the chauffeur's statement. Across the somewhat dingy window of a barroom, as he looked out, Dave Henderson read in large, white, painted letters, the legend:

THE IRON TAVERN

GEORGES VARDI, PROP.

That was Dago George's name, he remembered Nicolo Capriano had told him—Georges Vardi. He alighted, paid and dismissed the chauffeur, and stood for an instant on the sidewalk surveying the place.

It was a small and old three-story frame building. The barroom, to which there was a separate entrance, bordered on a lane at his right; while, almost bisecting the building, another door, wide open, gave on a narrow hall—and this, in turn, as he could see through the end window at his left, gave access to the restaurant, such as it was, for at several small tables here the occupants were engaged in making a belated dinner. Above, there was a light or two in the second story windows, the third story was in complete darkness.

It was certainly not over-prepossessing, and he shrugged his shoulders, half in a sort of philosophical recognition of a fact that was to be accepted whether or no, and half in a sort of acquiescent complacence. It was the sort of a place he wanted for the present anyhow!

Dave Henderson chose the restaurant entrance. An Italian waiter, in soiled and spotted apron, was passing along the hall. Dave Henderson hailed the man.

"I want to see Dago George," he said.

The waiter nodded.

"I tell-a da boss," he said.

Again Dave Henderson surveyed the place—what he could see of the interior now. It had evidently been, in past ages, an ordinary dwelling house. The stairs, set back a little from the entrance, came down at his right, and at the foot of these there was a doorway into the barroom. At his left was the restaurant which he had already seen through the window. Facing him was the narrow hall, quite long, which ended in a closed door that boasted a fanlight; also there appeared to be some other mysterious means of egress under the stairs from the hall, an entrance to the kitchen perhaps, which might be in the cellar, for the waiter had disappeared in that direction.

The door with the fanlight at the rear of the hall opened now, and a tall, angular man, thin-faced and swarthy, thrust out his head. His glance fell upon Dave Henderson.

"I'm Dago George—you want to see me?" His voice, with scarcely a trace of accent, was suave and polite—the hotel-keeper's voice of diplomacy, tentatively gracious pending the establishment of an intruder's identity and business, even though the intrusion upon his privacy might be unwelcome.

Dave Henderson smiled, as he picked up his dress-suit case and stepped forward. He quite understood. The proprietor of The Iron Tavern, though he remained uninvitingly upon the threshold of the door, was not without tact!

"Yes," said Dave Henderson; and smiled again, as he set down his dress-suit case in front of the blocked doorway, and noted an almost imperceptible frown cross Dago George's face as the other's eyes rested on that article. His hand went into his pocket for Nicolo Capriano's letter—but remained there. He was curious now to see, or, rather, to compare the reception of a stranger with the reception accorded to one vouched for by the old bomb king in San Francisco. "Yes," he said; "I'd like to get a room here for a few days."

"Ah!" Dago George's features suddenly expressed pain and polite regret. "I am so sorry—yes! I do not any longer keep a hotel. In the years ago—yes. But not now. It did not pay. The restaurant pays much better, and the rooms above for private dining parties bring the money much faster. I am desolated to turn you away; but since I have no rooms, I have no rooms, eh? So what can I do?"

Dave Henderson studied the other's face complacently. The man was not as old as Nicolo Capriano; the man's hair was still black and shone with oil, and in features he was not Nicolo Capriano at all; but somehow it *was* Nicolo Capriano, only in another incarnation perhaps. He nodded his head. He was not sorry to learn that The Iron Tavern was ultraexclusive!

"That's too bad," he said quietly. "I've come a long way—from a friend of yours. Perhaps that may make some difference?"

"A friend?" Dago George was discreetly interested.

"Nicolo Capriano," said Dave Henderson.

Dago George leaned suddenly forward, staring into Dave Henderson's eyes.

"What!" he exclaimed. "What is that you say? Nicolo Capriano!" He caught up the dress-suit case from the floor, and caught Dave Henderson's arm, and pulled him forward into the room, and closed the door behind them. "You come from Nicolo Ca-priano, you say? Ah, yes, my friend, that is different; that is *very* different. There may still be some rooms here, eh? Ha, ha! Yes, yes!"

"You may possibly already have heard something from him about me," said Dave Henderson. "Barty Lynch is the name."

Dago George shook his head.

"Not a word. It is long, very long, since I have heard from Nicolo Capriano. But I do not forget him—no one forgets Nicolo Capriano. And you have come from Nicolo, eh? You have some message then—eh, my friend?"

Dave Henderson extended the old bomb king's letter.

Dago George motioned to a chair, as he ripped the envelope open.

"You will excuse, while I read it—yes?" he murmured, already engrossed in its contents.

Dave Henderson, from the proffered chair, looked around the room. It was blatantly a combination of sleeping room and office. In one corner was a bed; against the wall facing the door there was a safe; and an old roll-top desk flanked the safe on the other side of the only window that the room possessed. His eyes, from their cursory survey of his surroundings, reverted to Dago George. The man had folded up the letter, and was stretching out his hands effusively.

"Ah, it is good!" Dago George ejaculated. "Yes, yes! Anything—anything that I can do for you is already as good as done. I say that from my heart. You are Barty Lynch—yes? And you come from the old master? Well, that is enough. A room! You may be sure there is a room! And now—eh— you have not perhaps dined yet? And what else is there? It is long, very long! You may be sure there is a room! And now—eh—you have not perhaps dined yet? And what else is there? It is long, very long, since I have heard from the old master the old master? Well, that is enough. A room! You may be sure there is a room! "

Dave Henderson laughed.

"There is nothing else—and not even that," he said. "There was a dining-car on the train to-night. There's not a thing, except to show me my room and let me turn in."

"But, yes!" exclaimed Dago George. "Yes, that, of course! But wait! The old master! It is long since I have heard from him. He says great things of you; and so you, too, are a friend of Nicolo Capriano. Well, then, it is an occasion, this meeting! We will celebrate it! A little bottle of wine, eh? A little bottle of wine!"

Dave Henderson shook his head.

"No," he said, and smiled. "As a matter of fact, I'm rather all in; and, if you don't mind, I'll hit the hay to-night pronto."

Dago George raised his hands protestingly.

"But what would Nicolo Capriano say to me for such hospitality as that!" he cried. "So, if not a bottle, then at least a little glass, eh? You will not refuse! We will drink his health—the health of Nicolo Capriano! Eh? Wait! Wait!" And he rushed pell-mell from the room, as though his life depended upon his errand.

Dave Henderson laughed again. The man with his volubility and effervescence amused him.

Dago George was back in a few minutes with a tray and two glasses of wine. He offered one of the glasses with an elaborate bow to Dave Henderson.

"It is the best in my poor house," he said, and held the other glass aloft to the light. "To Nicolo Capriano! To the old master! To the master of them all!" he cried—and drank, rolling his wine on his tongue like a connoisseur.

Dave Henderson drained his glass.

"To Nicolo Capriano!" he echoed heartily.

"Good!" said Dago George brightly. "One more little glass? No? You are sure? Well, you have said that you are tired—eh? Well, then, to make you comfortable! Come along with me!" He picked up the dress-suit case, opened the door, and led the way into the hall He was still talking as he mounted the stairs. "There will be many things for us to speak about, eh? But that will be for to-morrow. We are perhaps all birds of a feather—eh—or Nicolo Capriano perhaps would not have sent you here? Well, well—to-morrow, my friend, if you care to. But I ask nothing, you understand? You come and you go, and you talk, or you remain silent, as you wish. Is it not so? That is what Nicolo Capriano writes—and it is enough." He paused at the second-story landing. "You see," he said, waving his hand around the dimly lighted passage. "Little private dining-rooms! But there is no business to-night. Another flight, my friend, and perhaps we shall find better accommodations there."

It was as the other had said. Partially opened doors showed the three or four small rooms, that opened off the hall, to be fitted up as dining-rooms. Dave Henderson made no comment, as he followed the other up the next flight of stairs. He was tired. He had been telling himself lazily so from the moment he had taken the taxi. He was acutely aware of it now. It was the relaxation, of course—but he had become of a sudden infernally sleepy.

Dago George unlocked a door at the head of the third floor landing, entered, deposited the dress-suit case on the floor, and turned on the light. He handed the key of the room to Dave Henderson.

"It is plain, it is not rich," he said apologetically; "but the bed is good, and you will be quiet here, my friend, very *quiet*—eh?—you can take my word for that."

"It looks good to me, all right!" said Dave Henderson, and stifled a yawn. "I certainly owe you my best thanks."

Dago George shrugged his shoulders in expostulation.

"But it is nothing!" he protested. "Do you not come from Nicolo Capriano? Well, that is enough. But—you yawn! No, no; do not try to hide it! It is I who am to blame. I talk—and you would rest. But, one thing, my friend, before I go. It is my curiosity. The letter—it is signed by Nicolo Capriano, and I know the signature well—but it is written by a woman, is it not? How is that? I am curious. But perhaps you do not know?"

"Yes," Dave Henderson answered, and yawned frankly this time, and smiled by way of apology. "It was his daughter who wrote it. Nicolo Capriano is sick."

"Sick!" repeated Dago George. "I did not know! But it is so long since I have heard from him—yes? He is not very sick, perhaps?"

"I don't know," replied Dave Henderson sleepily. "He's been laid up in bed for three years now, I think."

"Godam!" ejaculated the Italian. "Is that so! But to-morrow—eh?—we will talk to-morrow. Goodnight, my friend! Good-night—and sleep well!"

"Good-night!" responded Dave Henderson.

He closed and locked the door as Dago George went out, and, sitting down on the edge of the bed, looked at his watch. It was a quarter to ten.

"I'll stretch out for ten minutes before I turn in," said Dave Henderson to himself—but at the end of ten minutes Dave Henderson was asleep.

III.
THE SECOND GUEST

IN the hallway of The Iron Tavern, as Dago George descended the stairs from Dave Henderson's room, a slim little figure in black, heavily veiled, stood waiting. Beside her, the greasy waiter, who had previously conveyed Dave Henderson's message to the proprietor, bowed and scraped and wiped his hands on his spotted apron, and pointed to Dago George on the stairs.

"Dat-a da boss," he announced.

A taxi chauffeur had already deposited two valises in the hall, and had retired. Outside, as the taxi moved away, another taxi, a short, but discreet, distance up the block, started suddenly out from the curb, as its fare, a fat man who chewed upon the butt of a cigar, dug with pudgy fingers into his vest pocket, and handed his chauffeur an address.

"Baggage and all—that's good enough!" said the fat man to himself; and to the chauffeur: "Beat it—and beat it fast!"

The waiter retired from the hall. The almost imperceptible frown on Dago George's face at sight of the valises, was hidden by an ingratiating smile as he hurried forward.

"Madam," he inquired, "you desire to see me?" The little figure in black nodded her head.

"Yes—in private," she answered quietly.

"Ah!" Dago George bowed profoundly. "But, yes—certainly! This way, then, if you please, madam."

He led the way into the rear room, and closed the door.

The little figure in black raised her veil.

"Do you not know me?" she asked.

Dago George stared for a long minute into her face. He shook his head.

"I am desolated!" he murmured apologetically. "It is my memory that is unbelievably stupid, madam."

"I am Teresa Capriano," she said.

Dago George moved closer. He stared again into her face, and suddenly into his own there came the light of recognition.

"You—the so-little Teresa—the little bambino!" he cried. "But, yes—yes, it is true!" He caught both her hands, and began to pat them effusively. "Is it possible? Yes, yes! I begin to see again the little girl of the so-many years ago! Ah, no; Dago George has not forgotten, after all! The little Teresa! The little bandit queen! Eh? And you—do you remember that we called you that?" He led her to a chair, and seated her. "Well, well, the little Teresa! And your father, my good friend Nicolo—I had heard that he was sick. He is better— yes? And he is perhaps here, too, in New York?"

"My father is dead," Teresa answered in a low voice.

"Dead!" Dago George drew back, and stared again, but in a curiously bewildered way now. "Dead!" he repeated. "You say that Nicolo Capriano is—dead?"

"Yes," she said, and turned her face away from his gaze—only to raise her eyes again, and watch the man covertly, narrowly, as he now began to walk rapidly up and down the room with quick, nervous strides. Her hands tightened a little on the arms of her chair. Here was the end of that long race across the continent, the goal of those fearsome, harried days of haste in San Francisco while her father lay dead. Was she first or last in that frantic race? What did Dago George know? A thousand times she had pictured this scene, and planned for it every word and act that was to be hers—but it was actuality now, and the room for an instant seemed to swirl around her. *She* remembered Dago George—as one of the most crafty, callous and unscrupulous of the lawless band over whom the man who had been her father had reigned as king. The letter! Had Dago George received it—yes or no? Had Dave Henderson reached here before her? Was he already in danger; or did it require but just a simple bit of acting on her part to undo the treachery of which her father had been guilty—a simple story, for instance, that she was on her way to her father's people in Italy, which would enable her to stay here in this place unsuspected until Dave Henderson came, and she could intercept him, and warn him before any harm was done? Which was it? She dared not ask. If Dago George knew nothing, he must at all costs continue to know nothing. A hint, and Dago George, if he were the Dago George of old, would be like a bloodhound on the scent, and, exactly as though Dago George had actually received her father's letter, Dave Henderson would be the quarry. But if, on the other hand, the letter had already been delivered, well, then—then there was another rôle to play. She dared not ask; not until Dago George had shown his hand, not until she was sure of her own ground.

She turned her head away again; Dago George had halted abruptly in front of her chair.

"Dead!" he said uneasily. "You say that Nicolo Capriano, that your father, is dead?"

Teresa nodded without looking up.

Dago George, as abruptly as he had halted, turned and paced the length of the room and back again, and abruptly halted once more in front of her. He leaned toward her, one hand now laid over his heart.

"I am unpardonable!" he said softly. "I say nothing to you of your so-great grief. I do not sympathize. I am heartless! But you will forgive! It is the shock of my own grief for the loss of my friend from which I have not recovered. I bleed for you in your deep sorrow. My poor little bambino! But you understand—yes—do you not?"

Teresa's hands, in her lap now, toyed with one of her gloves which she had taken off. She did not look up.

"Yes, yes," murmured Dago George. "You understand! But we will speak no more of that now—it is but to depress us both. There are other things— that you have come all this way from San Francisco, and that you have come immediately to me, for you have but just arrived in New York to-night, is it not so?"

"Yes," Teresa answered. "The train was very late. I came here at once from the station."

"Then, thanks to your train being late," said Dago George, with a significant lowering of his voice, "I think I can tell you why you came. If you had been an hour earlier, it would have been you who would have had to tell me. Eh? Is it not so? There was a letter—eh? A letter which you wrote for Nicolo Capriano, for your father—is it not so?"

The blood seemed suddenly to Teresa to grow hot, and as suddenly to grow chill and cold in her veins. Dago George had answered her question. Dave Henderson had already delivered the letter! It brought fear; but it brought, too, a sense of relief. The road was clear now before her. It was her wits against Dago George—to draw, and win, and hold the other's full and unreserved confidence, to make herself appear essential to Dago George— for an hour—a week—a month—until she could reach Dave Henderson, wherever he might be, and meanwhile checkmate any move that this man here might make. She glanced furtively, with well simulated caution, around her.

"Yes," she said, in a guarded voice. "You are right. It is the letter that brought me. What else? My father died the night it was written. He had no time to communicate with you. I do not know all, but I know enough, I think, to make the matter sure. There is a great deal of money at stake, and so I came."

"Ah!" Dago George was whispering excitedly now. "Wait! Wait a minute, my little bambino!" He ran to the door, opened it, looked out, closed and locked it again, and, crossing the room, pulled the half drawn roller shade down to the window sill. He drew a chair close up to Teresa's, and sat down. "It is better to be sure, is it not? Yes, yes! And we will continue to speak English, eh? It is less understood here. Ah, my little bambino! You are your father's daughter! Yes, yes! Nicolo Capriano is not dead! Well, the letter, eh? There is money in it, much money in it, you say?"

"Yes," she replied. Her voice sharpened, and became a little imperious. "Yes, there is money in it, provided you have not lost sight of the man who brought the letter to you."

Dago George rubbed his hands together softly.

"Have no fear of that!" he whispered eagerly. "Dago George did not serve under Nicolo Capriano for nothing! The young man is upstairs, and safely asleep. He came perhaps a little more than half an hour ago. We had a little glass of wine together, and—" He shrugged his shoulders, and made a significant little circling motion with his thumb and forefinger.

Teresa's eyebrows lifted in frank impatience.

"What do you mean by that?" she asked sharply.

Again Dago George shrugged his shoulders.

"Have I not said that he is—asleep?" he smiled.

"Drugged!" exclaimed Teresa.

"But, yes—naturally! What would you have?" smiled Dago George.

Teresa's glove slipped from her lap to the floor. She was deliberate and long in picking it up.

"But why?" There was irritation and censure in her voice now, as she looked up at him and frowned.

"I don't see why! You know nothing of the reasons that prompted my father to write that letter. Why should you drug him? What could you expect to accomplish by that, except to excite his suspicions when he wakes up?"

"Ah, but you do me an injustice, my little bambino!" said Dago George smoothly. "It was but a pinch of the drug, a drug that I know very well, and that never plays tricks on me. He has had but enough to last for four or five hours, and he will experience no ill effects when he wakes up. You can trust Dago George for that. And as for why—what else could I do? It was precisely because I had had no word from Nicolo Capriano, and because it was all a mystery to me, except that the letter was signed *con amore*. Eh? You know well enough what that means, and that it was not to be disobeyed. The man must never leave my sight or hands until the little game, whatever it was, was played out. Is it not so? It was also necessary that, having nothing further from the old master to guide me, I should look this Signor Barty Lynch over for myself—yes? Is it not so, my little bambino?"

Teresa preserved her frown.

"Perhaps," she admitted, with well assumed unwillingness. "Well?"

Dago George drew a little closer.

"Well, he is safe upstairs, then. You see that Dago George had his head about him, after all, eh? And now—the letter! What is it that the old master was about to do?"

Teresa's mind was working swiftly. Dave Henderson was upstairs, drugged, but safe so far. It might be hours before he could make any move; but by morning surely, by morning before daylight, he could get away, and until then she must stay here. There was only one way she could do that without arousing suspicion, and at the same time have freedom of action—as an ally, an indispensable ally, of this man here. There was only one dominating consideration, therefore, to guide her in what, or how much, she told Dago George, for once Dave Henderson had slipped away that was the last Dago George would ever see of him, or her; and the consideration involved was, that, while she knew Dago George too well to trust him in the smallest degree, Dago George must be made to trust *her* in the fullest measure, and from the strongest of all reasons from Dago George's standpoint—that of self-interest. And the surest way to accomplish that was to tell Dago George enough of the truth to, at one and the same time, arouse his cupidity and leave him in a sense dependent upon her cooperation for his future activities.

"I can only tell you what I heard them saying to each other that night when I wrote that letter for my father," she said deliberately. "But that is enough, I think; anyway, it was enough to decide me to come here to you. My father, of course, intended to communicate with you—in just what way, I do not know—but he died that same night. The only thing, then, that I could see to do was to get here without a moment's delay, and I left San Francisco immediately after my father's burial. You understand?"

"Yes, yes!" Dago George nodded his head vigorously in assent. "But, of course! Yes, yes, my little bambino! Well—and then?"

She leaned forward impressively toward Dago George.

"This Barty Lynch stole some money," she said, in a quick, eager voice; "a great deal of money, thousands; I heard them speak of a hundred thousand. My father had helped him to get away from the police; that is why he trusted my father. But this money was stolen again from Barty Lynch by a man who Barty Lynch said had run here to New York for cover. That is what has brought Barty Lynch here—to find that man, and get the money back. You see? Once Barty Lynch gets hold of the money again, he—but that is why my father gave him a letter to you, and— —-"

"Signed it *con amore* broke in Dago George," whispering feverishly, and almost as though speaking to himself. "Yes, yes! I see! It is the hand of the old master, and it has lost none of its cunning! Yes, yes! I see! There is no risk! It is stolen money to begin with! Signor Barty Lynch has no recourse to the law! And even if Signor Barty Lynch *disappeared*—eh?—who is to know the difference, since he has already arranged things so nicely in hiding himself away from the police! Eh? Yes! It is excellent, superb! Is it not so?"

Teresa's face was impassive.

"Yes, except that we have not got that money yet!" she said curtly. "It may not be as easy as it looks. That is why I am here—to help; and also"—she stared Dago George levelly in the face—"to see that Dago George does not get more than his share."

The Italian's hands were raised instantly in protestation.

"But, my little bambino—that you should say that!" He shook his head in an aggrieved way. "I am hurt that you should think I forget Nicolo Capriano, though he is dead, or that you should think I would do anything like that."

"Nor do I think so," she answered steadily. "I warn you, that is all. We shall work all the better together if we understand to begin with that Nicolo Capriano's daughter, though Nicolo Capriano is dead, has still some power; and if we understand that this is Nicolo Capriano's plan, and not yours, and that the division will be made on the same basis that Nicolo Capriano would have made it."

"It is Nicolo himself speaking," murmured Dago George. He was smiling now. "I had no thought of anything but that. It is understood. I could ask for nothing better."

"Very well!" she said. "There is nothing to be done at first then, but to watch him in everything he does here in New York. You have plenty of men you can depend upon—I know that; but I think I can do more, or at least as much, as they can, and certainly with all of us working together we should succeed. He is in a room upstairs, you say. You have another one next to his that is empty, perhaps? Yes? Well, that is good. I will take it. He will be surprised to see me here, but he will not be suspicious. He believes that you were a very intimate friend of my father. Naturally, then, it would be at the house of that intimate friend that I would come to stay when, owing to my father's death, I am making arrangements to sail to my father's people back in Italy. Barty Lynch trusted my father absolutely. That is plain. He therefore trusts me equally. It may not even be necessary to watch him; he is even more likely than not—if he is played right—to make a confident of me."

Dago George rubbed his hands together excitedly. "Yes," he cried. "It is superb! I salute you. You do credit to Nicolo Capriano! Ah, my little bambino, you have your father's brains!"

Teresa, with a prettily imperious nod of her head, rose from her chair.

"It is getting late," she said. "It must be nearly eleven o'clock, and I have had a long journey. Since he is drugged, he is safe for the time being, and there is nothing more to be done to-night. To-morrow we can begin our work. Take me to my room."

"Yes—it is superb!" Dago George repeated exultantly. He bowed Teresa to the door, and, picking up the valises, led the way upstairs. He chuckled with perverted humor, as they passed Dave Henderson's door. "He is in there," he said; "but we must not disturb his rest, eh? He said he was very tired!" He ushered Teresa into the next room, and turned on the light. "If there is anything that the little bambino requires?"—his head and hands gestured eloquently.

Teresa was looking around the none too clean, and none too well furnished, room.

"Nothing!" she said.

Dago George Retreated to the door. He cleared his throat, and hesitated, and shuffled a little awkwardly with his feet.

"It is that the little bambino will know that I am thinking of her great sorrow, though I have said little, that I speak of it again," he said softly. "The master has been long dead? It is true you have told me he died on the night you wrote that letter for him, but the letter"—he produced it from his pocket, and scanned it earnestly—"yes, I am right—it bears no date."

"My father died nine days ago," Teresa answered tersely, and half turned away her head.

"Ah, yes! Nine days ago!" Dago George shook his head sorrowfully, as he backed across the threshold. "The old master! It is very sad! Nine days ago! It is very sad! I wish you repose, my little bambino. Good-night!"

Teresa closed and locked the door behind Dago George—and stood still for an instant listening. Dago George's footsteps died away on the stairs below. She moved a little then, and stood with her ear pressed against the partition of the next room. There was no sound. And then she began to walk slowly about the room, and a few minutes later, the time that it would ordinarily have taken her to prepare for bed, she turned out the light—and sat down in a chair, fully dressed, and stared into the blackness.

She pressed her hand a little wearily across her eyes. She was here now at the end of those thousands of miles, every one of which had seemed to yawn as some impassable gulf between her and her goal; she was here now, and, in spite of her fears, she had reached that goal—in time. She had even outwitted—for the moment anyhow—Dago George. True, Dave Henderson lay there in that next room drugged, but she was not too late. She smiled a little ironically. In a purely literal sense she was too early! She dared not make a move now for perhaps hours yet, not until she was sure the house was closed for the night, and that Dago George—she did not trust Dago George— had gone to bed.

And so she must sit here and stare into the blackness. She would not fall asleep; there was no fear of that. She could not sleep. Already thoughts and memories, as myriad in divergence as they were in numbers, were crowding upon her, and goading her brain into an abnormal and restless activity.

She twisted her hands together now in her lap. She remembered, and she could not forget, the horror and the fear of that night when her father had died, and of the days thereafter when she had performed—alone—the last duties that had devolved upon her. Yes, it had been alone. She had lied to Dago George. It had been alone! If Nicolo Capriano had had friends and been powerful in life, Nicolo Capriano had been alone in death. She had lied to Dago George; there had been no heritage of power. She had lied—but then her whole life was a lie!

A low sound, a bitter moan, came suddenly from her lips. It was not the Teresa now who had faced Dago George with cool complacence in the room below. She slipped from the chair to her knees, and buried her face in her hands. It was the black hour, of which she had known so many since that fearful night, that surged and swept upon her now again. It whirled scenes and thoughts of the past, and pictures of the future, before her like some bewildering and tormenting kaleidoscope. She could not define to herself her feelings relative to her father's death; grief seemed to mingle indissolubly with bitter abhorrence at his act of treachery. But in another way her father's death meant something to her that she was coming to grasp more clearly. It seemed to release her from something, from—from a tangled life.

All her life had been a lie. She was the daughter of a criminal, and all her life had been a lie; her environment had been a lie. In big things, in little things, it had been a lie. She had lied to herself that night when she had let this man in the next room here go without a word of protest from her lips to carry out a criminal act. She had been a coward that night, and it had shamed her. She had owed something to her father, a loyalty to her father; perhaps, fundamentally, that was the basis for her refusal to face the issue squarely that night; perhaps it was because the habit of years, the lies, and only lies, that had been lived around her, had strangled her and weakened her. Perhaps it was that; but if so, and if she had owed and given loyalty to her father, then she had given more than loyalty—she had given her soul. And her soul turned miserably away from this pitiful landscape of life upon which now she was forcing it to gaze.

But this was a picture of the past, for if it were true, or in any degree true, her father's death had brought her release—her father was dead. And so she faced the future—alone. In so many a different sense—alone. She was alone now, a free agent to mold her own life, and the test was before her; whether the lie, for example, she had acted that night when she had sent Dave Henderson away, was the outcome of things extraneous to her soul, or inherent in that soul itself. Her hands, that clasped her face, tightened. Thank God, she knew! Thank God, that from the moment her brain had staggered out of its blind pit of horror and darkness on that night, she had seen the way clearly lighted before her! Her first duty was to save the man in the next room from her father's treachery, and she was here now to do that; but she was here, too, to do something else. She could, and would, stand between Dave Henderson and the personal harm that threatened him through the trust he had reposed in Nicolo Capriano, and she would do this at any cost and at any sacrifice to herself; but she could not, and she would not, connive at anything that would tend to keep the stolen money from the possession of its rightful owners.

Her hands lifted now and pressed hard against her temples, which had begun to throb. Yes, and she must do even more than that. There had been not only treachery on her father's part toward Dave Henderson, there had been treachery and trickery toward the police in an effort to cover up the stolen money; and, tacitly at least, she had been an accomplice in that, and therefore morally she was as much a thief as that man next door, as much a thief as her father had intended to be—unless now, with all her strength, with all her might, she strove to undo and make restitution for a crime in which she had had a part. If it lay within her power, not adventitiously, not through haphazard, but through the employment toward that end of every faculty of brain and wit and courage she possessed, she had no choice now but to get possession of that money and return it to the authorities. Her conscience was brutally frank on that point, and brutally direct; there was no room to temporize, no halfway course—and here was the final, ultimate and supreme test.

Her face in the darkness whitened. Her lips moved silently. It was strength and help she asked now. Her mind was already made up. She would fight for, and, in any way or by any means that offered, get that money, and return it. And that meant that *she* must watch Dave Henderson, too. There was no other way of getting it. He alone knew where it was, and since it was not to be expected that he would voluntarily give it up, there seemed left but one alternative—to *take* it from him.

Her mind was almost overpoweringly swift now in its flow of tormenting thoughts. It seemed an impossible situation that she should warn him of danger from one source, only to do to him again what—no! His life was not in danger with her; that was the difference. But—but it was not easy to bring herself to this. She was alone now, with no bonds between herself and any living soul, except those strange, incongruous bonds between herself and that man in the next room whom she was, in the same breath, both trying to save and trying to outwit. Why was it that he was a thief? They could have been friends if he were not a thief; and she would have been so glad of a friend now, and she had liked him, and he did not look like a thief. Perhaps her mother had liked Nicolo Capriano in the early days, and perhaps Nicolo Capriano then had not looked like a thief, and perhaps her mother had counted on turning Nicolo Capriano into an honest man, and ——

Teresa rose abruptly to her feet. She felt the hot color flood her face. She saw the man as he had stood that first night on the threshold of her father's room, and he had looked at her so long and steadily—and there had been no offence in his look. She caught her breath sharply. Her mind was running riot! It must not do that! She had many things to accomplish tonight, and she would need all her wits.

She forced her thoughts violently into another channel. How long would it be before this Iron Tavern closed for the night, and Dago George was in bed and asleep? She did not trust Dago George! She knew him as one utterly without scruples, and one who was insidiously crafty and dangerously cunning. She began to rehearse again the scene that she had had with him— and suddenly drew herself up tensely. Why, at the last moment as he had left the room, had he reverted to her father's death, and why had he waited until then, when it should naturally have been one of his first questions, to inquire—so plausibly—when her father's death had taken place?

Her lips grew suddenly hard. Nine days! She had told him nine days. Was there any significance in that—to Dago George, or to herself? She had been delayed in leaving San Francisco by her father's funeral. Dave Henderson had left there several days earlier, but he had only arrived here at Dago George's to-night. True, the difference in time might be accounted for through Dave Henderson's presumed necessity of travelling under cover; but, equally, it might not. Had Dago George thought of that—as she was thinking of it now? Was it possible that Dave Henderson had *already* got that money, and had come here for refuge with it; that it was now, at this moment, in that next room there, and that, below stairs, Dago George, too, was sitting, waiting for the hours to pass, and sleep to come to all but himself!

She went mechanically to the window, and stood for a moment staring out upon a vista of dark, shadowy buildings that made jagged, ill-defined points against the sky-line—and then, with a sudden start, she raised the window cautiously, soundlessly, inch by inch, and leaned out. Yes, she was right! The iron platform of a fire-escape was common to her room and to the room next door.

For another moment she stood there, and then returned softly across the room to her chair.

"It is too early yet!" she whispered—and, with her chin in her hands, settled back in her chair, and stared into the blackness.

IV.
THE THIRD GUEST

BOOKIE SKARVAN, alias the fat man in the taxicab who chewed on the butt of his cigar, leaned back in his seat, and nibbed his pudgy hands together in a sort of gratified self-applause.

"Baggage and all," repeated Bookie Skarvan to himself. "I guess that's good enough—what? I guess that's where she's going to hang out, all right. And I guess the place looks the part! The Iron Tavern—eh?" He read the window sign, as his taxi rolled by. "Well, leave it to Bookie! I guess I'll blow back there by-and-by and register—if the rates ain't too high! But there ain't no hurry! I've been sticking around now for five years, and I guess I can take a few minutes longer just to make sure the numbers go up right on the board this time!"

Bookie Skarvan, with the adroit assistance of his tongue, shifted the cigar butt to the other corner of his mouth. He expectorated on the floor of the taxi—and suddenly frowned uneasily. He had had uneasy moments more than once on his late trip across the continent, but they were due, not so much to the fear that anything was wrong with his "dope-sheet," as they were to the element of superstition which was inherent in him as a gambler—so far he had not had any luck with that hundred thousand dollars, in the theft of which he had been forestalled by Dave Henderson five years ago. That was what was the matter. He was leery of his luck.

He chewed savagely. He had an attack of that superstition now—but at least he knew the panacea to be employed. At times such as these he communed and reasoned patiently with himself. He communed with himself now.

"Sure, she knows where the money is! She's the dark horse, and the long shot—and I got the tip and the inside dope, ain't I? Sure, she's the play!" he reassured himself. "She hustled that funeral along something fierce. And she went tearing around like a wet hen raising money, letting things go and grabbing at any old price until she'd got enough to see her through, and then she suddenly locks the house up and beats it like hell. 'Twasn't natural, was it? She was in *some hurry*—believe me! What did she do it for—eh? Well, I'll tell you, Bookie—on the quiet. What Nicolo Capriano knew, she knew. And Nicolo Capriano wasn't the bird to let one hundred thousand dollars get as close to his claws as it did without him taking a crack at it. If you ask me, Nicolo pulled Dave Henderson's leg for the dope; and if you ask me, Nicolo was the guy who handed out that bomb, and he did it to bump Dave Henderson off—same as I figured to do once—and cop the loot for himself. Mabbe I'm wrong—but I guess I'm not. And I guess the odds weren't too rotten to stake a ride on across the country, I guess they weren't!"

Bookie lifted a fat hand, pushed back his hat, and scratched ruminatively at the hair over his right temple.

"Dave must have had a pal, or he must have slipped it to some one that time Baldy chased him in the car. It must have been that—he slipped it to some one during them days the bulls was chasing him, and whoever it was mabbe has been keeping it for him here in New York. So she beats it for New York—what? It don't figure out any other way. He didn't go nowhere and get it after he got out of prison, *I* know that. And he got killed the same night, and he didn't have it then. Sure, Capriano bumped him off! Sure, my hunch is good for the limit! Dave fell for the Lomazzi talk, and goes and puts his head on Nicolo's bosom so's to give the police the go-by, and Nicolo sucks the orange dry and heaves away the pip! And then the old geezer cashes in himself, and the girl flies the coop. Mabbe she don't know nothing about it"—Bookie Skarvan stuck his tongue in his cheek, and grinned ironically—"oh, no, mabbe she don't! And I guess there ain't any family resemblance between the old man and the girl, neither—eh?—oh, no, mabbe not!"

The taxi stopped abruptly. The chauffeur reached around and dexterously opened the door.

"Here you are!" he announced briefly.

Bookie Skarvan looked out—upon a very shabby perspective. With the sole exception of a frankly dirty and disreputable saloon, designated as "O'Shea's," which faced him across the sidewalk, the neighborhood appeared to consist of nothing but Chinese tea-shops, laundries, restaurants, and the like; while the whole street, gloomy and ill-lighted, was strewn with unprepossessing basement entrances where one descended directly from the sidewalk to the cellar level below.

Bookie Skarvan picked up his hand-bag, descended to the sidewalk, paid and dismissed the chauffeur, and pushed his way in through the swinging doors of the saloon.

"I guess I ain't drinking—not here!" confided Bookie Skarvan to himself, as he surveyed the unkempt, sawdust-strewn floor and dirty furnishings, and a group of equally unkempt and hard-looking loungers that lined the near end of the bar. "No, I guess not," said Bookie to himself; "but I guess it's the place, all right."

He made his way to the unoccupied end of the bar. The single barkeeper that the place evidently boasted disengaged himself from the group of loungers, and approached Bookie Skarvan.

"Wot's yours?" he inquired indifferently.

Bookie Skarvan leaned confidentially over the rail, "I'm looking for a gentleman by the name of Smeeks," he said, and his left eyelid drooped, "Cunny Smeeks."

The barkeeper's restless black eyes, out of an unamiable and unshaven face, appraised Bookie Skarvan, and Bookie Skarvan's well-to-do appearance furtively.

"It's a new one on me!" he observed blandly. "Never heard of him!"

Bookie Skarvan shifted his cigar butt—with his tongue.

"That's too bad!" he said—and leaned a little further over the bar. "I've come a long way to see him. I'm a stranger here, and mabbe I've got the wrong place. Mabbe I've got the wrong name too"—Bookie Skarvan's left eyelid twitched again—"mabbe you'd know him better as the Scorpion?"

"Mabbe I would—if I knew him at all," said the barkeeper non-committally. "Wot's your lay? Fly-cop?"

"You're talking now!" said Bookie Skarvan, with a grin. He pulled a letter from his pocket, and pushed it across the bar. "You can let the Scorpion figure out for himself how much of a fly-cop I am when he gets his lamps on that. And it's kind of important! Get me—friend?"

The barkeeper picked up the plain, sealed envelope—and twirled it meditatively in his hands for a moment, while his eyes again searched Bookie Skarvan's face.

"Youse seem to know yer way about!" he admitted finally, as though not unfavorably impressed by this later inspection.

Bookie Skarvan shoved a cigar across the bar.

"It's straight goods, colonel," he said. "I'm all the way from 'Frisco, and everything's on the level. I didn't blow in here on a guess. Start the letter on its way, and let the Scorpion call the turn. If he don't want to see me, he don't have to. See?"

"All right!" said the barkeeper abruptly. "But I'm tellin' youse straight I ain't seen him to-night, an' I ain't sayin' he's to be found, or that he's stickin' around here anywhere."

"I'll wait," said Bookie Skarvan pleasantly.

The barkeeper walked down the length of the bar, disappeared through a door at the rear for a moment, and, returning, rejoined the group at the upper end of the room.

Bookie Skarvan waited.

Perhaps five minutes passed. The door at the rear of the bar opened slightly, the barkeeper sauntered down in that direction, and an instant later nodded his head over his shoulder to Bookie Skarvan, motioning him to come around the end of the bar.

"Cunny'll see youse," he announced, stepping aside from the doorway to allow Bookie Skarvan to pass. "De Chink'll show youse de way." He grinned suddenly. "I guess youse are on de level all right, or youse wouldn't be goin' where youse are!"

The door closed behind him, and Bookie Skarvan found himself in a narrow, dimly-lighted passage. A small, wizened Chinaman, in a white blouse, standing in front of him, smiled blandly.

"You fliend of Scorpy's—that allee same belly glood. You come," invited the man, and scuffled off along the had.

Bookie Skarvan followed—and smiled to himself in complacent satisfaction. Cunny Smeeks, alias the Scorpion, was, if surroundings were any criterion, living up to his reputation—which was a not insignificant item on Bookie Skarvan's "dope-sheet"—as one of the "safest," as well as one of the most powerful criminal leaders in the underworld of New York.

"Sure!" said Bookie Skarvan to himself. "That's the way I got the dope—and it's right!"

The passage swerved suddenly, and became almost black. Bookie Skarvan could just barely make out the flutter of the white blouse in front of him. And then the guide's voice floated back:

"Allee same stlairs here—you look out!"

Cautioned, Bookie Skarvan descended a steep flight of stairs warily into what was obviously, though it was too dark to see, a cellar. Ahead of him, however, there appeared, as through an opening of some sort, a faint glow of light again, and toward this the white blouse fluttered its way. And then Bookie Skarvan found himself in another passage; and a strange, sweetish odor came to his nostrils; and strange sounds, subdued whisperings, rustlings, the dull ring of metal like coin thrown upon a table, reached his ears. And there seemed to be doors now on either side, and curtained hangings, and it was soft and silent underfoot.

"I dunno," observed Bookie Skarvan to himself. "I dunno—it ain't got much on 'Frisco, at that!"

The guide halted, and opened a door. A soft, mellow light shone out. Bookie Skarvan smiled knowingly. He was not altogether unsophisticated! A group of richly dressed Chinamen were absorbed in cards. Scarcely one of them looked up. Bookie Skarvan's eyes passed over the group almost contemptuously, and fixed on the only man in the room who was not playing, and, likewise, the only man present who was not an Oriental, and who, with hands in his pockets, and slouch hat pushed back from his forehead, stood watching the game—a man who was abnormally short in stature, and enormously broad in shoulder, who had hair of a violently aggressive red, and whose eyes, as he turned now to look toward the door, were of a blue so faded as to make them unpleasantly colorless.

Bookie Skarvan remained tentatively on the threshold. He needed no further introduction—no one to whom the man had been previously described could mistake Cunny Smeeks, alias the Scorpion.

The other came quickly forward now with outstretched hand.

"Any friend of Baldy Vickers is a friend of mine," he said heartily. "You want to see me—-eh? Well, come along, cull, where we can talk."

He led the way a little further down the passage, and into another room, and closed the door. The furnishings here were meager, and evidently restricted entirely to the votaries of poppy. There was a couch, and beside it a small tabouret for the opium smoker's paraphernalia.

The Scorpion pointed to the couch; and possessed himself of the tabouret, which he straddled.

"Sit down," he invited. "Have a drink?"

"No," said Bookie Skarvan. "Thanks just the same. I guess I won't take anything to-night." He grinned significantly. "I'm likely to be busy."

The Scorpion nodded.

"Sure—all right!" he agreed. "Well, we'll get to cases, then. Baldy says in his letter that you and him are in on a deal, and that you may want a card or two slipped you to fill your hand. What's the lay, and what can I do for you?"

"It's a bit of a long story." Bookie Skarvan removed the cigar butt from his lips, eyed it contemplatively for a moment, finally flung it away, fished another cigar from his pocket, and, without lighting it, settled it firmly between his back teeth. "I got to be fair with you," he said. "Baldy said he handed it to you straight in the letter, but I got to make sure you understand. We think we got a good thing, and, if it is, anything you do ain't going for nothing; but there's always the chance that it's a bubble, and that there's a hole gets kicked in it."

"That's all right!" said Cunny Smeeks, alias the Scorpion, easily. "If there's anything coming I'll get mine—and I'm satisfied with any division that Baldy puts across. Baldy and me know each other pretty well. You can forget all that end of it—Baldy's the whitest boy I ever met, and what Baldy says goes with me all the way. Go ahead with the story—spill it!"

"The details don't count with you," said Bookie Skarvan slowly; "and there's no use gumming up the time with them. The bet is that a nice, sweet, little Italian girl, that's just piked faster'n hell across the continent, knows where there's a hundred thousand dollars in cold cash, that was pinched and hidden five years ago by a fellow named Dave Henderson—see? Dave served his spaces, and got out a few days ago—and croaked—got blown up with a Dago bomb—get me? He didn't have no time to enjoy his wealth—kind of tough, eh? Well he stood in with this Italian girl's father, an old crook named Nicolo Capriano, and he went there the night he got out of prison. The way we got it doped out is that the old Italian, after getting next to where the money was, bumped off Dave Henderson himself—see? Then Nicolo dies of heart disease, and the girl hardly waits to bury the old man decently, and beats it for here—me trailing her on the same train. Well, I guess that's all— you can figure for yourself why we're interested in the girl."

"I get you!" said the Scorpion, with a sinister grin. "It don't look very hard bucking up against a lone female, and I guess you can telegraph Baldy that he don't need to worry. What do you want—a bunch to pinch the girl, or a box-worker to crack a safe? You can have anything that's on tap—and I guess that ain't passing up many bets."

Bookie Skarvan shook his head.

"I don't want either—not yet," he said. "The girl ain't got the money yet, and there ain't anything to do but just watch her and keep her from getting scared until she either grabs it, or lets out where it is." He leaned forward toward the Scorpion. "D'ye know a place, not far from here, that's called The Iron Tavern?" he demanded abruptly.

The Scorpion shrugged his shoulders.

"Everybody knows it!" he said caustically. "It's a dump! It's the rendezvous of the worst outfit of black-handers in America; and the guy that runs it, a fellow named Dago George, runs the gang, too—and he's *some* guy. But what's that got to do with it?"

"The girl's there," said Bookie Skarvan tersely. "Oh, she is, eh?" There was a new and sudden interest in the Scorpion's voice.

"She went there from the train with her grips." Bookie Skarvan's cigar grew restive in his mouth.

"Well, me, too, I'm for the same joint, only I don't want to take any chances of spilling the beans."

"You mean you're afraid she'll pipe you off?"

"No," said Bookie Skarvan. "No, I ain't afraid of that. She never got a peep at me on the train, and she only saw me once before in her life, and that time, besides it being dark and me being outside on the front doorstep, she was so scared I might have been a lamppost, for all she'd know me again. It was the night her old man croaked—see? No, I ain't afraid of her—but I couldn't afford to take any chances by blowing in there right after her. I wasn't afraid of her, but I had my fingers crossed on whoever ran the place, and I guess, after what you've said, that my hunch was right. It was a queer place for her to go right off the bat the minute she landed in New York, and she didn't go there instead of to a decent hotel just by luck—get me? I figured she might stand in there pretty thick—and if she did, and I blew in right on top of her, the betting odds were about one million dollars to a peanut that I'd be a sucker. I'm sure of it now that you say the fellow who runs it is a Dago in the same old line of business that her father was in. What?"

The Scorpion's pale blue eyes scrutinized Bookie Skarvan's face—and lighted with a curious benignity.

"You and Baldy make a pretty good combination, I guess!" he observed with dry admiration.

Bookie Skarvan indulged in his wheezy chuckle. "We've had a little luck together once in a while," he admitted modestly. "Well, you get me, don't you? I've got to get into that Iron Tavern joint just the same. That's the first card we play. I figured that mabbe this Dago George would know you by reputation anyhow, and that you could fix it for me without it looking as though it were anything more than a friend of yours, say, who'd got into a little temporary difficulty with the police down in Baltimore, say, and was keeping quiet and retired for a few days till the worst of it blew over—and that you'd picked out his joint as the best bet for me."

The Scorpion got up from his seat abruptly.

"Say," he said cordially, "I'm glad I met you! That listens good! Sure! I guess I can fix that! Dago George and me ain't exactly pals, and we don't love each other any more than you'd notice—but he knows where he gets off with Cunny Smeeks! You wait a minute, and I'll get him on the phone."

Cunny Smeeks, alias the Scorpion, of the élite of the New York underworld, left the room. Bookie Skarvan sprawled negligently back on the couch. He smiled softly—and chewed contentedly on his cigar. Things were working well.

"There's nothing like credit in this wicked world," Bookie Skarvan confided sapiently to himself. "I may have to run up quite a bill with Mr. Cunny Smeeks before I'm through, mabbe quite a fat little bill—but he can always send it to Baldy—if I'm not here! What? It's beginning to look good again. Five years I've been trying to get the grappling hook on that coin. It looks pretty good now, and I guess I can see it coming—and I guess I won't have to wait as long as Baldy will!" He wagged his head pleasantly. "I never was fond of San Francisco—and I always wanted to travel! Perhaps Baldy and Mr. Cunny Smeeks won't be such good friends by-and-by. I dunno! I only know that Bookie Skarvan won't be sticking around to see them go into mourning for their share of that hundred thousand that they think they're going to get—not so's you'd observe it!"

Bookie Skarvan's eyes swept the den indifferently and without interest. They fastened finally on the toe of his own boot. The minutes passed, and as they passed a scowl came gradually to Bookie Skarvan's face, and a fat hand in a sudden nervous gesture went to his forehead and brushed across his eyes. His thoughts seemed to have veered into a less pleasant channel.

"Yes," he muttered, "you can take it from me that I ain't sorry Dave Henderson's dead—not very! He never saw all my cards, and that's the one hold Baldy had on me." The room was apparently over-heated—for a fat man. A bead of sweat came out on Bookie Skarvan's forehead. He swore savagely. "You damn fool, can't you forget it! You're not afraid of a dead man now, are you!"

The Scorpion came back.

"Come on!" he said, from the doorway. "It's fixed! He put up a howl and wouldn't stand for it at first, and he kicked so hard that I guess he's in with the girl all right. He said he had no place to put anybody; but he came across all right—with a twist of the screws. You're a friend of mine, and your Baltimore spiel goes—see?" The pale blue eyes darkened suddenly. "You get what I've done, don't you? Dago George don't forgive easily, and if this thing busts open and Dago George tumbles to what I've handed him, I'm mabbe going to have a little gang war on my hands."

"I get you!" said Bookie Skarvan earnestly, as he joined the other in the doorway. "And that goes into the bill at a hundred cents on the dollar—and you know Baldy well enough to know what that means." The Scorpion laughed.

"Oh, well, it's nothing to worry about! As I told you, I've never been very fond of Dago anyhow, and I guess I can take care of anything he wants to start. There'd be only one of us in at the finish—and it wouldn't be Dago George! You can go the limit, and you'll find you've got the biggest backing—on any count—in little old New York! Well, come on over, and I'll introduce you."

"Sure! That's the stuff!" said Bookie Skarvan, as he accompanied the other to the street. "Baldy said you were the real goods—and I guess I got to hand it to Baldy!" He chuckled suddenly and wheezingly, as they went down the block. "The Baltimore crook—eh? Me and Dago George! Leave it to me! I guess I can handle Dago George!"

And twenty minutes later, in a room on the third floor of The Iron Tavern, Bookie Skarvan, "handling" Dago George, laid a detaining hand on the proprietor's arm, as the latter was bidding him good-night.

"Look here," whispered Bookie Skarvan. "I know you're on the level because Cunny Smeeks says so; but I got to lay low, damned low—savvy? I ain't for meeting people—not even for passing 'em out in the hall there. So how about it? Have I got neighbors? I ain't taking any chances."

Dago George laid his forefinger along his nose—and smiled reassuringly.

"Ah, yes!" he said. "Yes, yes, I understand—eh? But you need have no fear. I do not take guests, except"—he shrugged his shoulders—"except—you understand, eh?—to oblige a friend like Cunny Smeeks. Otherwise"—again the shoulders lifted—"I would not have the so-great honor of offering you a room. Is it not so? Well, then, there is no one here, except"—he jerked his thumb toward the opposite door across the hall—"my niece, who will not trouble you; and in the next room to hers a friend of mine, who will not trouble you either. There is no one else. You need have no fear. I assure you, you need have no fear."

Bookie Skarvan nodded.

"That's all right, then," he said in a cordial and relieved tone.

"It's only that I got to be careful."

He shook hands with Dago George, as the latter again bade him good-night. He closed his door, and sat down. The bulge of the protruding cigar butt metamorphosed what was intended for an amiable smile into an unlovely grimace.

"Niece—eh?" murmured Bookie Skarvan to himself. "Well, well—and in the room across the hall! I guess I won't go to bed just yet, not just yet—but I guess I'll put out the light."

V.
THE ROOM ON THE THIRD FLOOR

IT was pitch black. Dave Henderson opened his eyes drowsily. He lay for a moment puzzled and bewildered as to where he was. And then consciousness returned in fuller measure, and he remembered that he had thrown himself down on the bed fully dressed—and must have fallen asleep.

He stirred now uneasily. He was most uncomfortable. Something brutally hard and unyielding seemed to be prodding and boring into his side. He felt down under him with his hand—and smiled quizzically. It was his revolver. He would probably, otherwise, have slept straight through the night. The revolver, as he had turned over in his sleep undoubtedly, had twisted in his pocket, and had resolved itself into a sort of skewer, muzzle end up, that dug ungraciously and painfully into his ribs.

He straightened the revolver in his pocket—and the touch of the weapon seemed to clear his faculties and fling him with a sudden jolt from the borderland of sleepy, mental indolence into a whirl of mental activity. He remembered Millman. Millman and the revolver were indissolubly associated. Only Millman had returned the money. That was the strangest part of it. Millman had returned the money. It was over there now on the floor in the dress-suit case. He remembered his scene with Millman. He remembered that he had deliberately fanned his passion into a white heat. He should therefore be in an unbridled rage with Millman now—only he wasn't. Nor would that anger seemingly return—even at his bidding. Instead, there seemed to be a cold, deliberate, reasoned self-condemnation creeping upon him. It was not pleasant. He tried to fight it off. It persisted. He was conscious of a slight headache. He stirred uneasily again upon the bed. Facts, however he might wish to avoid them, were cold-blooded, stubborn things. They began to assert themselves here in the quiet and the darkness.

Where was that sporting instinct of fair play of his of which he was so proud! Millman had *not* gone to that pigeon-cote with any treacherous motive. Millman had *not* played the traitor, either for his own ends or at the instigation of the police. Millman, in blunt language, knowingly accepting the risk of being caught, when, already known as a prison bird, no possible explanation could avail him if he were found with the money in his possession, had gone in order to save a friend—and that friend was Dave Henderson.

Dave Henderson shook his head. No—he would not accept that—not so meekly as all that! Millman hadn't saved him from anything. He could have got the money himself all right when he got out, and the police would have been none the wiser.

He clenched his hands. A voice within him suddenly called him—*coward!* In that day in the prison library when he had felt himself cornered, he had been desperately eager enough for help. It was true, that as things had turned out, he could have gone safely to the pigeon-cote himself, as he actually had done, but he had not foreseen the craft of Nicolo Capriano then, and his back had been to the wall then, and the odds had seemingly piled to an insurmountable height against him—and Millman, shifting the danger and the risk to his own shoulders, had stepped into the breach. Millman had done that. There was no gainsaying it. Well, he admitted it, didn't he? He had no quarrel with Millman on that score now, had he? He scowled savagely in the darkness. It was Millman with his infernal, quixotic and overweening honesty that was the matter. That was what it was! His quarrel with Millman lay in the fact that Millman was—*an honest man.*

He sat bolt upright on the bed, his hands clenched suddenly again. Why hadn't Millman kept his honesty where it belonged! If Millman felt the way he did after going to the pigeon-cote and getting that money, why hadn't Millman stuck to his guns the way any ordinary man would, instead of laying down like a lamb—why hadn't he fought it out man to man, until the better man won—and that money went back, or it didn't! Fight! That was it—fight! If Millman had only fought it out—like an ordinary man—and——

"Be *honest*—at least with yourself!" whispered that inner voice quietly. "Millman was just as honest with you as he was with his own soul. He kept faith with you in the only way he could—and still keep faith with himself. Did he throw you down—Dave?"

For a moment Dave Henderson did not stir; he seemed mentally and physically in a strange and singular state of suspended animation. And then a queer and twisted smile flickered across his lips.

"Yes, he's white!" he muttered. "By God, the whitest man on earth—that's Millman! Only—damn him! Damn him, for the hole he's put me in!"

Yes, that was it! He had it at last, and exactly now! Over there on the floor in the dress-suit case was the money; but it wasn't the money that he, Dave Henderson, had taken a gambler's risk and a sporting chance to get, it wasn't the money he had fought like a wildcat for—it was Millman's money. It wasn't the money he had staked his all to win—he staked nothing here. It was another man's stake. Over there was the money, and he was free to use it—if he chose to take it as the price of another man's loyalty, the price that another man paid for having taken upon himself the risk of prison bars and stone walls again because that other man believed his *risk* was substituted for the *certainty* that Dave Henderson would otherwise incur that fate!

The inner voice came quietly again—but it held a bitter gibe.

"What is the matter? Are you in doubt about anything? Why don't you get up, and undress, and go to bed, and sleep quietly? You've got the money now, you're fixed for all your life, and nothing to worry you—Millman pays the bills."

"Five years!" Dave Henderson muttered. "Five years of hell—for nothing?"

His face hardened. That was Nicolo Capriano lying over there on his bed, wasn't it?—and plucking with thin, blue-tipped fingers at the coverlet—and eyeing him with those black eyes that glittered virulently—and twisting bloodless lips into a sardonic and contemptuous sneer. And why was that barbed tongue of Nicolo Capriano pouring out such a furious and vicious flood of vituperation?

Another vision came—an oval face of great beauty, but whose expression was inscrutable; whose dark eyes met his in a long and steady gaze; and from a full, white, ivory throat, mounting upward until it touched the wealth of hair that crowned the forehead, a tinge of color brought a more radiant life. What would Teresa say?

His hands swept again and again, nervously, fiercely, across his eyes. In the years of his vaunted boast that neither hell nor the devil would hold him back, he had not dreamed of this. A thief! Yes, he had been a thief—but he had never been a piker! He wasn't a vulture, was he, to feed and gorge on a friend's loyalty!

He snarled suddenly. Honesty! What was honesty? Millman was trying to hold himself up as an example to be followed—eh? Well, that was Millman's privilege, wasn't it? And, after all, how honest was Millman? Was there anybody who was intrinsically honest? If there were, it might be different—it might be worth while then to be honest. But Millman could afford that hundred thousand, Millman had said so himself; it didn't mean anything to Millman. If, for instance, it took the last penny Millman had to make good that money there might be something in honesty to talk about—but that sort of honesty didn't exist, either in Millman, or in any other human being. He, Dave Henderson, had yet to see any one who would sacrifice all and everything in an absolutely literal way upon the altar of honesty as a principle. Every one had his price. His, Dave Henderson's, price had been one hundred thousand dollars; he, Dave Henderson, wouldn't steal, say, a hundred dollars—and a hundred dollars was probably an even greater matter to him than a hundred thousand was to Millman, and—

He brought his mental soliloquy roughly to an end, with a low, half angry, half perturbed exclamation. What had brought him to weigh the pros and cons of honesty, anyway! He had never been disturbed on that score in those five years behind prison bars! Why now? It wasn't that that concerned him, that held him now in the throes of a bitter mental conflict, that dismayed him, that tormented him, that mocked at the hell of torture he would—if he yielded—have endured in vain, that grinned at him out of the darkness sardonically, and awaited with biting irony his decision. It didn't matter what degree of honesty Millman possessed; it was Millman's act, in its most material and tangible sense, that threatened now to crush him.

Both hands, like gnarled knobs, went above his head. He was a thief; but, by God, he was a man! If he kept that money there, he became a puling, whining beggar, sneaking and crawling his way through life on—*charity!* Charity! Oh, yes, he might find a softer name for it; but, by any name, he would none the less feed to the day he died, like a parasite and a damned puny, pitiful whelp and cur, on another man's—charity!

"Give it back—no!" he whispered fiercely through set lips. "I've paid too much—it's mine—I've paid for it with the sweat of hell! It's mine! I will not give it back!"

"Are you sure?" whispered that inner voice. "It begins to look as though there were something in life, say, an *honest* pride, that was worth more than money—even to you, Dave."

He sprang restively from the bed to the floor, and groped his way across the room to the light. He was in for a night of it—subconsciously he realized that, subconsciously he realized that he would not sleep, but subconsciously he was prompted to get his clothes off and obtain, lacking mental ease, what physical comfort he could.

He turned on the light, and the act diverted his thoughts momentarily. He did not seem to remember that he had ever turned off that light—but rather, in fact, that the light had been on when Dago George had left the room, and he, Dave Henderson, had flung himself down on the bed. It was rather strange! His eyes circled the room curiously, narrowed suddenly as they fell upon the dress-suit case, and upon one of the catches that appeared to have become unfastened—and with a bound he reached the dress-suit case, and flung up the lid.

The money was gone.

VI.
HALF AN ALLEY

MOTIONLESS, save that his lips twitched queerly, Dave Henderson stood erect, and stared down into the pillaged dress-suit case. And then his hands clenched slowly—tightened—and grew white across the knuckles.

The money was gone! The agony of those days and nights, when, wounded, he had fled from the police, the five years of prison torment which he had endured, seemed to pass with lightning swiftness in review before him—and to mock him, and to become a ghastly travesty. The money was gone!

The pillaged dress-suit case seemed to leer and mock at him, too. He might have saved himself that little debate, which he had not settled, and which was based upon a certain element of ethics that involved the suggestion of charity. It was settled for him now. He *owed* Millman now one hundred thousand dollars, only the choice as to whether he would pay it or not was no longer his, and— —

Damn it! *The money was gone!* Could he not grasp that one, single, concrete, vital fact, and act upon it, without standing here, with his brain, like some hapless yokel's, agog and maundering? The money was gone! Gone! Where? When? How? He could only have been asleep for a short time, surely. He wrenched his watch suddenly from his pocket. Three o'clock! It was three o'clock in the morning! Five hours! He had been asleep five hours, then! He must have slept very soundly that any one could have entered the room without arousing him!

His lips hardened. He was alert enough now, both mentally and physically. He stepped over to the door. It was still locked. His eyes swept around the room. The window, then! What about the window?

He felt suddenly for his money-belt beneath his underclothing, as he started across the room. The belt was there. That, at least, was safe. A twisted smile came to his lips. Naturally! His brain was exhibiting some glimmer of sense and cohesion now! It was evident enough that no one, since no one knew anything about it, had been specifically after that package of banknotes.

It could only have been the work of a sneak thief—who had probably stumbled upon the greatest stroke of luck in his whole abandoned career. It was undoubtedly a quarter of the city wherein sneak thieves were bred! The man would obviously not have been fool enough, with a fortune already in his possession, to have risked the frisking of his, Dave Henderson's, sleeping person! Was the man, then, an inmate of The Iron Tavern, say, that greasy waiter, for instance; or had he gained entrance from outside; or, since the theft might have taken place hours ago, was it a predatory hanger-on at the bar who had sneaked his way upstairs, and——

The window, too, was locked! It was queer! Both window and door locked! How had the man got in—and got out again?

Mechanically, he unlocked and raised the window—and with a quick jerk of his body forward leaned out excitedly. Was this the answer—this platform of a fire escape that ran between his window and the next? But his window had been *locked!*

He stood there hesitant. Should he arouse Dago George? He could depend upon and trust Dago George, thanks to Nicolo Capriano; but to go to Dago George meant that confidences must be led up to which he desired to give to no man. His brain seemed suddenly to become frantic. The money was gone—his, or Millman's, or the devil's, it didn't matter which now—the money was gone, swallowed up in the black of that night out there, without a clue that offered him a suggestion even on which to act. But he couldn't stand here inactive like a fool, could he? Nor—his brain jeered at him now—could he go out and prowl around the city streets, and ask each passer-by if he or she had seen a package of banknotes whose sum was one hundred thousand dollars! What else was there, then, to do, except to arouse Dago George? Dago George, from what Nicolo Capriano had said, would have many strings to pull—underground strings. That was it—*underground strings!* It wasn't a *police* job!

He turned from the window, took a step back across the room, and halted again abruptly. *What was that?* It came again—a faint, low, rustling sound, and it seemed to come from the direction of the fire escape.

In an instant he was back at the window, but this time he crouched down at the sill. A second passed while he listened, and from the edge of the sash strained his eyes out into the darkness, and then his hand crept into his side pocket and came out with his revolver. Some one, a dark form, blacker than the night shadows out there, was crawling from the next window to the fire escape.

Dave Henderson's lips thinned. Just a second more until that "some one" was half-way out and half-way in, and at a disadvantage and—*now!*

With a spring, lithe and quick as a cat, Dave Henderson was through the window, and the dark form was wriggling and squirming in his grasp, and a low cry came—and Dave Henderson swore sharply under his breath.

It was a woman! A woman! Well, that didn't matter! One hundred thousand dollars was gone from his dress-suit case, and this woman was crawling to the fire escape from the next room at three o'clock in the morning—that was what mattered!

They were on the iron platform now, and he pushed her none too gently along it toward the window of his own room—into the light. And then his hands dropped from her as though suddenly bereft of power, and as suddenly lifted again, and, almost fierce in their intensity, gripped at her shoulders, and forced her face more fully into the light.

"Teresa!" he whispered hoarsely. "You—Teresa!"

She was trying to smile, but it was a tremulous effort. The great, dark eyes, out of a face that was ivory white, lifted to his, and faltered, and dropped again.

"It's you, Teresa—isn't it?" His voice, his face, his eyes, were full of incredulous wonder.

Her lips were still quivering in their smile. She nodded her head in a sort of quaint, wistful way.

The blood was pounding and surging in his veins. Teresa! Teresa was here, standing here before him! Not that phantom picture that had come to him so often in the days and nights since he had left San Francisco—the glorious eyes, half veiled by the long lashes, though they would not look at him, were real; this touch of his hands upon her shoulders, this touch that thrilled him, was real, and— —

Slowly his hands fell away from her; and as though to kill and stifle joy, and mock at gladness, and make sorry sport of ecstasy, there came creeping upon him doubt, black, ugly, and bitter as gall.

Yes, it was Teresa! And at sight of her there had come suddenly and fully, irrefutably, the knowledge that he cared for her; that love, which comes at no man's bidding, had come to him for her. Yes, it was Teresa! But what was she doing here? In view of that money, gone in the last few hours from his dress-suit case, what *could* Teresa Capriano be doing here in the next room to his?

He laughed a little, low, sharply—and turned his head away. Love! How could he love—and doubt! How could he love—and condemn the one he loved unheard! He looked at her again now; and the blood in his veins, as though over-riding now some obstacle that had dammed its flow, grew swifter, and his pulse quickened. How could he doubt—Teresa!

But it was Teresa who spoke.

"We are standing here in the light, and we can be seen from everywhere around," she said in a low tone. "You—there is danger. Turn the light off in your room."

"Yes," he said mechanically, and stepping back into his room, turned off the light. He was beside her again the next instant. Danger! His mind was mulling over that. What danger? Why had she said that? What was its significance in respect of her presence here? The questions came crowding to his lips. "Danger? What do you mean?" he asked tensely. "And how did you get here, Teresa? And why? Was it your father who sent you? There is something that has gone wrong? The police——"

She shook her head.

"My father died the night you went away," she said.

He drew back, startled. Nicolo Capriano—dead!

Her father—dead! He could not seem somehow to visualize Nicolo Capriano as one dead. The man's mentality had so seemed to triumph over his physical ills, that, sick though he had been, Nicolo Capriano had seemed to personify and embody vitality and life itself. Dead! He drew in his breath sharply. Then she was alone, this little figure standing here in the darkness beside him, high up here in the world of night, with a void beneath and around them, strangely, curiously cut off, even in a physical sense, from any other human touch or sympathy—but his.

He reached out and found her hand, and laid it between both his own.

"I—I'm no good at words," he fumbled. "They—they won't come. But he was the best friend I ever, had in life, too. And so I——"

"Don't say that! Don't! You mustn't! Do you hear, you mustn't!" Her hand, that lay in his, was suddenly clenched, and she was striving to draw it away. "It isn't true! I—that is why I came—I came to tell you. He was not your friend. He—he betrayed you."

He held her hand tighter—in a grip that made her efforts to escape pitifully impotent. And, almost fiercely, he drew her closer, trying to read her face in the darkness.

"He betrayed me! Nicolo Capriano *betrayed* me!" His mind was suddenly a riot. Incredulity and amazement mingled with a sickening fear that her words were literally true—the money was gone! And yet—and yet—Nicolo Capriano—a traitor! His words rasped now. "Do you know what you are saying, Teresa? Quick! Answer me! Do you know what you are saying?"

"I know only too well." Her voice had broken a little now. "I know that the money was taken from your room to-night. Please let my hand go. I—you will hate me in, a moment—for—for, after all, I am his daughter. Will you please let me go, and I will tell you."

Mechanically he released her.

She turned half away from him, and leaned on the iron hand-rail of the platform, staring down into the blackness beneath her.

"Dago George took it—an hour ago," she said.

"Dago George!" Dave Henderson straightened. "Ah, so it was Dago George, was it!" He laughed with sudden menace, and turned impulsively toward the window of his room.

"Wait!" she said, and laid a hand detainingly upon his sleeve. "The money, I am sure, is safe where it is until daylight, anyway. I—I have more to tell you. It—it is not easy to tell. I—I am his daughter. Dago George was one of my father's accomplices in the old days in San Francisco. That letter which I wrote for my father meant nothing that it said, it contained a secret code that made you a marked man from the moment you delivered it here, and——"

"You, too!" There was bitter hurt in Dave Henderson's voice. And then suddenly he threw his shoulders back. "I don't believe you!" he flung out fiercely. "I don't understand how you got here, or what you are doing here, but you *wrote* that letter—and I don't believe it was a trap. Do you understand, Teresa—I don't believe you!"

She raised her head—and it seemed that even in the darkness he caught the sudden film of tears in her eyes, and saw the lips part in a quivering smile. She shook her head slowly then.

"It was not what I wrote," she said. "It was what my—what he added afterwards when he signed it. *Con amore*—that was the secret code, and——"

"But you did not know that, then—Teresa!" There was a strange, triumphant uplift in his voice. "I remember! It was while you were out of the room. Did I not say I did not believe you!"

Her lips were still quivering, but the smile was gone. "No, I did not know then," she said. "But his shame is my shame, nothing can alter that—I am his daughter. I did not know it until after you had gone—and then—my father had a—a sudden attack—and that night he died. I—there was only one thing that I could do. I had no way of warning you except to try and get here before you did, or at least to get here before Dago George had gone too far. There—there were things I had to do in San Francisco—and then I came as quickly as I could. I got here to-night. I found that you were already here—just a little ahead of me, and that you had given Dago George the letter. I had only one chance then—to make Dago George believe that I had come, since my father was dead, to carry on the plot against you where my father had left off. Dago George had no suspicions. He knew me." Her voice held a sudden merciless note. "I was a Capriano. He told me that you were upstairs here, drugged, and he gave me the room next to yours."

"Drugged!" Dave Henderson passed his hand across his eyes. That accounted for a great deal! He remembered the slight headache with which he had awakened; he was suddenly conscious of it now. "Drugged!" he repeated.

"In a way," she said, "I was too late. But Dago George, of course, did not know any details, and he had not gone any further than that. He had just left you in your room when I came. He had not, of course, heard from my father, since my father was dead, and he drugged you so that, during the night, he could have free access to your room and your belongings and find out what he could about you. I—I thought to turn him from that purpose by telling him enough of the truth to make him content to wait patiently and watch your movements until you had the money in your possession. Do—do you understand? He said the effects of the drug would wear off in a few hours, and I meant to warn you then, and—and we would both make our escape from here. I—that is why I told you there was danger. Dago George would stop at nothing. He has a band of men here in New York that I know are as unscrupulous as he is; and this place here, I am only too sure, has been the trap for more than one of his victims."

She paused. Her voice, though guarded, had grown excited, and a little breathless.

It was a moment before Dave Henderson spoke.

"And you?" His voice was hoarse. "If Dago George had found you out you wouldn't have had a chance for your life! And you knew that?"

"Yes," she said quietly, "I knew that. But that has no place here. There was no other way."

"And you did this for me?" His hands reached out, and fell upon the girl's slight shoulders, and tightened there. "You did this for me—Teresa?"

"I did it because there was no other thing to do, because—because"—her voice lost its steadiness—-"it was my father's guilt."

He drew her closer, with a strange, gentle, remorseless strength.

"And for no other reason—Teresa?" he whispered. "For only that? If it had not been your father? If he had had nothing to do with it? If it had been only me?" Her face was very close to his now, so close that the quick, sudden panting of her breath was upon his cheek, so close that her lips were almost warm upon his own.

She put out her hands, and pressed them with a curious gentleness against his face to ward him off.

"Don't!" Her voice was very low. "Have you forgotten that I am the daughter of the man who meant—who meant perhaps to take your life; that I am the daughter of a criminal?"

"And I"—he had her wrists now, and was holding the soft, trembling hands against his cheeks—"I am a thief."

"Oh, don't!" She was almost crying now. "You—you don't understand. There is more. I meant, if I could, to take that money from you myself."

In sheer astonishment he let her go, and drew back a step. She seemed to waver unsteadily on her feet there in the darkness for an instant, and her hand groped out to the platform railing for support; and then suddenly she stood erect, her face full toward him, her head thrown back a little on her shoulders.

"I meant to get it, if I could—to give it back to those to whom it belongs. And I still mean to." Her voice was quiet now, quivering a little, but bravely under control, "All my life has been a lie. I lived a lie the night I let you go away without a word of protest about what you were going to do. I do not mean to throw the blame upon my father, but with his death all those old ties were broken. Will you try to understand me? I must either now go on in the old way, or go straight with my conscience and with God. I could not bargain with God or my conscience. It was all or nothing. I had a share in enabling you to hoodwink the police. Therefore if you came into possession of that money again, I was as much a thief as you were, and as guilty. But I owed it to you, above all other things, to warn you of your danger; and so I came here—to warn you first—and afterwards, when you were safe from Dago George's reach, to watch you, and get the money myself if I could. Do you understand?

"When I came here to-night, I did not think that you had yet got the money; but something that Dago George said made me think that perhaps you had, and that perhaps he thought so, too. And so I sat there in my room in the darkness waiting until all was quiet in the house, and I could steal into your room and search, if I could get in through either door or window; and then, whether I got in or not, or whether the search was successful or not, I meant to wait until the drug had worn itself off sufficiently to enable me to arouse you, and tell you to get away.

"And then, I do not know what time it was, I heard some one steal up the stairs and go to the door of your room, and work at the lock very, very quietly, and go into your room, and move around in there. I was listening then with my ear to the partition, and I could just make out the sounds, no more. I should never have heard anything had I been asleep; there was never enough noise to have awakened me.

"The footsteps went downstairs, then, and I opened my door and waited until I heard them, louder, as though caution were no longer necessary, on the second landing; and then I stole downstairs myself. There was a light in Dago George's room. It came through the fanlight. The door was closed. But by leaning over the banister of the lower flight of stairs, I could see into the far end of the room through the fanlight. He had a package in his hand. It was torn at one corner, and from this he pulled out what I could see were a number of yellow-back banknotes. He looked at these for a moment, then replaced them in the package, and went to his safe. He knelt down in front of it, laid the package on the floor beside him, and began to open the safe. I heard some one moving above then, and I tiptoed back, and hid in what seemed to be a small private dining room on the second floor. I heard some one go quietly down the stairs, and then I came back here to my room to wait until I could arouse you. The money was in Dago George's safe. It would be there until morning at least, and on that account it no longer concerned me for the moment. And then after a long time I heard you move in your room. It was safer to come this way than to go out into the hall, for I did not know what Dago George might intend to do with you, or with me either, now that he had the money. He would not hesitate to get rid of us both if his cunning prompted him to believe that was his safest course. And I was afraid of that. Only you and I, besides himself, knew anything about that money—and he had got it into his possession. Do you understand? When I heard you move, I started through the window to go to you, and—and you saw me."

Dave Henderson had sunk his elbows on the iron railing, his chin resting in his hands, and was staring at the strange, fluted sky-line where the buildings jabbed their queer, uneven points up into the night. It was a long time before he spoke.

"It's kind of queer, Teresa," he said slowly. "It's kind of queer. You're something like a friend of—like a man I know. It's kind of queer. Well, you've given me my chance, you've risked your life to give me my chance, you've played as square as any woman God ever made—and now what are you going to do?"

She drew in her breath sharply, audibly, as though startled, as though his words were foreign, startlingly foreign to anything she had expected.

"I—have I any choice?" she answered. "I know where the money is, and I must notify the authorities. I must tell the police so that they can get it."

Dave Henderson's eyes, a curious smile in them that the darkness hid, shifted from the sky-line to the little dark figure before him.

"And do you think I will let you tell the police where that money is?" He laughed quietly. "Do you? Did you think you could come and tell me just where it was, and then calmly leave me, and walk into the police station with the news—and get away with it?"

She shook her head.

"I know!" she said. "You think it's a woman's inconsistency. It isn't! I didn't know what you would do, I don't know now. But I have told you all. I have told you what I intend to do, if I possibly can. I had to tell you first. If I was to be honest all the way with myself, I had first of all to be honest with you. After that I was free. I don't know what you will do. I don't see what you can do now. But if you keep me from notifying the police to-night—there is to-morrow—and after that another to-morrow. No matter what happens, to you, or to me, I am going through with this. I"—her voice choked suddenly—"I have to."

Dave Henderson straightened up.

"I believe you!" he said under his breath. "After what you've done, I'd be a fool if I didn't. And you're offering me a square fight, aren't you, Teresa?" He was laughing in that quiet, curious way again. "Well, I'm not sure I want to fight. Just before I found out that money was gone, I was wondering if I wouldn't give it back myself."

"*Dave!*" It was the first time she had ever called him by his name, and it came now from her lips in a quick, glad cry. Her hands caught at both his arms. "Dave, do you mean that? Do you? Dave, it *is* true! You're honest, after all!"

He turned his head away, a sudden hard and bitter smile on his lips.

"No," he said. "And I haven't made up my mind yet about giving it back, anyway. But maybe I had other reasons for even getting as far as I did. Not honesty. I can't kid, myself on that. I am a thief."

Her fingers were gripping at his arms with all their strength, as though she were afraid that somehow he would elude and escape her.

"You *were* a thief"—it seemed as though her soul were in the passionate entreaty in her voice now—"and I was the daughter of a criminal, with all the hideous memories of crime and evil that stretch back to childhood. But that is in the past, Dave, if we will only leave it there, isn't it? It—it doesn't have to be that way in all the years that are coming. God gives us both a chance to—to make good. I'm going to take mine. Won't you take yours, Dave? You were a thief, but how about from now on?"

He stood rigid, motionless; and again his face was turned away from her out into the darkness.

"From now on." He repeated the words in a low, wondering way.

"Yes!" she cried eagerly. "From now on, Dave. Let us get away from here, and go and notify the police that Dago George has that money, and—and—and then, you see, the police will come and get it, and return it where it belongs, and that will end it all."

It was a moment before he turned toward her again, and then his face was white, and drawn, and haggard. He shook his head.

"I can't do that," he said hoarsely. "There are more reasons than one why I can't do that." Her hands were clasping his arms. He forced them gently from their hold now, and took them in his own, and drew her closer to him, and held her there. "And one of those reasons is you, Teresa. You've played fair with me, and I'll play fair with you. I—I can't buy you with a fake. I——"

"Dave!" She struggled to free herself. "Dave,

"Wait!" His voice was rough with emotion. "We'll talk straight—there isn't any other way. I—I think I loved you, Teresa, that night, the first time I saw you, when you stood on the threshold of your father's room. To-night I know that I love you, and————-"

"Dave!"

His hold had brought her very close again to him. He could see a great crimson tide flood and sweep the white and suddenly averted face.

"Wait!" he said again. "I think I have learned other things as well to-night—that you care, Teresa, too, but that the stolen money stands between you and me. That is what I mean by buying you, and your love, with a fake. If I returned the money on that account it would not be because I had suddenly become honest—which is the one thing above all else that you ask for. It would not be for honesty's sake, but because I was a hypocrite and dishonest with you, and was letting the money go because I was getting something for it that was worth more to me than the money—because I was making a good *bargain* that was cheap at a hundred thousand dollars. I can't make myself believe that I feel a sense of honesty any more to-night than I did the night I first took that money, and I would be a cur to try to make you think I did."

He could feel her hands tremble in his; he could see the sweet face, the crimson gone from it, deathly pale again. Her lips seemed quivering for words, but she did not speak. And suddenly he dropped her hands; and his own hands clenched, and clenched again, at his sides. There was biting mockery at himself stirring and moiling in his brain. "You fool! You fool!" a voice cried out. "She's yours! Take her! All you've got to do is change your tune; she'll believe you—so if you're not honest, why don't you *steal* her?"

"Listen!" It seemed as though he were forcing himself to speak against his will. "There is another reason; but, first, so that you will understand, there is Millman. It is too long a story to tell you all of it. Millman is the man I spoke of—who is honest—like you. I told him when I was in prison where the money was, and I thought he had double-crossed me. Instead, he gave it back to me to-night—that is how I got it so soon." He laughed out sharply, harshly. "But Millman said if I didn't give it back to the estate of the man from whom I took it, he would pay it out of his own pocket, because, for me, he had been a thief, too. Do you understand? That's why I said I didn't know what I was going to do. My God—I—I don't know yet. I know well enough that if the police were tipped off to-night, and got the money, that would let Millman out of paying it; but that's not the point. I can't squeal now, can I? I can't go sneaking to the police, and say: 'There it is in Dago George's safe; I can't get my own paws on it again, so I've turned honest, and you can go and take it!' I wouldn't like to face Millman and tell him the money had gone back *that* way—because I couldn't help it—because it had been taken from me, and I was doing the smug act in a piker play!"

She stepped toward him quickly.

"Dave," she whispered tremulously, "what do you mean? What are you going to do?"

"I'm going to get that money—from Dago George," he said in a flat voice. "I'll get that money if I go through hell again for it, as I've been through hell for it already. Then maybe it'll go back where it came from, and maybe it won't; but if it does go back, it'll go back from *Dave Henderson*—not Dago George!"

She clutched frantically at his arm.

."No, no!" she cried out.

"Listen!" he said. "You have said you meant that money should be returned if it were within your power to accomplish it. I understand that. Well, no matter what the result, to Dago George or to me, I am going down there to get that money—if I can. But if I get it, I do not promise to return it. Remember that! I promise nothing. So you are free to leave here; and if you think, and perhaps you will be right, that the surest way to get the money back is to go instantly to the police, I shall not blame you. If the police can beat me to it before I settle with Dago George, they win—that's all. But in any case, it is not safe for you stay in this place, and so— —"

"I was not thinking of that!" she said in a low voice. "Nor shall I leave this house—until you do. I—I am afraid—for you. You do not know Dago George."

He did not stir for a moment; and then, with some great, overwhelming impulse upon him, he took her face in both his hands, and held it there upturned to his, and looked into the great dark eyes until the lashes dropped and hid them from his gaze.

"Teresa," he whispered low, "there are some things that are worse than being a thief. I couldn't lay down my hand now, if I wanted to, could I? I can't quit now, can I? I can't *crawl*. I took that money; and, whether I mean to give it back myself, or keep it, I'd rather go out for good than tell the police it's there, and see the sneer for an honest man—turned honest because he had lost his nerve, and didn't dare go after the money and face the risk of a showdown with Dago George, which was the only way in which he could stay *dishonest*. Teresa, you see, don't you?" His voice was passionate, hungry in its earnestness. "Teresa, what would you do—play the game, or quit?"

The lashes lifted, and for a moment the dark eyes looked steadily into his, and then they were veiled again.

"I will wait here for you," she said.

VII.
THE MAN WITH THE FLASHLIGHT

THE silence seemed like some uncanny, living, breathing thing. It seemed to beat, and pulsate, until the ear-drums throbbed with it. It seemed to become some mad, discordant chorus, in which every human emotion vied with every other one that it might prevail over all the rest: a savage fury, and a triumphant love; a mighty hope, and a cruel dismay; joy, and a chill, ugly fear. And the chorus rose and clashed, and it seemed as though some wild, incoherent battle was joined, until first one strain after another was beaten down and submerged, and put to rout, until out of the chaos and turmoil, dominant, supreme, arose fury, merciless and cold.

Dave Henderson crept along the upper hall. The pocket flashlight in his hand, one of his purchases on the way East, winked through the blackness, the round, white ray disclosing for a second's space the head of the stairs; and blackness fell again.

He began to descend the stairs cautiously. Yes, that was it—fury. Out of that wild riot in his brain that was what remained now. It drew his face into hard, pitiless lines, but it left him most strangely cool and deliberate—and the more pitiless. It was Dago George who was the object of that fury, not Nicolo Capriano. That was strange, too, in a way! It was Nicolo Capriano who had done him the greater wrong, for Dago George was no more than the other's satellite; but Nicolo Capriano's treachery seemed tempered somehow—by death perhaps—by that slim figure that he had left standing out there in the darkness perhaps; his brain refused to reason it out to a logical conclusion; it held tenaciously to Dago George. It seemed as though there were a literal physical itch at his finger-tips to reach a throat-hold and choke the oily, lying smile from the suave, smug face of that hypocritical bowing figure that had offered him a glass of wine, and, like a damnable hound, had drugged him, and——

Was that a sound, a sound of movement, of some one stirring below there, that he heard—or only an exaggerated imagination? He was half-way down the upper flight of stairs now, and he stopped to listen. No, there seemed to be nothing—only that silence that palpitated and made noises of its own; and yet, he was not satisfied; he could have sworn that he had heard some one moving about.

He went on down the stairs again, but still more cautiously now. There was no reason why there *shouldn't* be some one moving about, even at this hour. It might be Dago George himself. Dago George might not have gone to bed again yet. It was only an hour, Teresa had said, since the man had come upstairs and stolen the money. Or it might be some accomplice who was with Dago George. He remembered Teresa's reference to the band of blacklegs over whom Dago George was in command; and he remembered that some one had come down the stairs behind her and Dago George. But Teresa herself had evidently been unseen, for there had been no attempt to find or interfere with her. It had probably therefore been—well, any one!

It presented possibilities.

It might have been an accomplice; or a prowling guest, if there were other guests in this unsavory hostelry; or a servant, for some unknown reason nosing about, if any of the disreputable staff slept in the place at night—the cook, or the greasy waiter, or the bartender, or any of the rest of them; though, in a place like this, functionaries of that sort were much more likely to go back to their own homes after their work was over. It would not be at all unlikely that Dago George, in view of his outside pernicious activities, kept none of the staff about the place at night.

Dave Henderson's jaws closed with a vicious snap. Useless speculation of this sort got him nowhere! He would find out soon enough! If Dago George were not alone, there were still several hours till daylight; and he could wait his chance with grim patience. He was concerned with only one thing—to square accounts with Dago George in a way that would both satiate his fury, and force the man to disgorge the contents of his safe.

His jaws tightened. There was but one, single, disturbing factor. If anything went wrong, Teresa was still upstairs there. In every other respect the stage was set—for any eventuality. He had even taken the precaution, before doing anything else, to get their valises, hers and his, out of the place, since in any case they meant to steal away from this accursed trap-house of Dago George. It had been simple enough to dispose of the baggage via the fire escape, and through the yard, and down the lane, where the valises had found a temporary hiding place in a shed, whose door, opening on the lane, he had discovered ajar, and simple enough, with Teresa's help in regaining the fire escape from the ground, to return in the same way; but he had been actuated by more than the mere idea of being unimpeded in flight if a critical situation subsequently arose—though in this, his ulterior motive, he had failed utterly of success. Teresa had agreed thoroughly in the wisdom of first removing their belongings; but she had refused positively to accompany and remain with the baggage herself, as he had hoped he might induce her to do. "I wouldn't be of any use there, if—if anything happened," she had said; "I—I might be of some use here." Neither argument nor expostulation had been of any avail. She was still above there—waiting.

He had reached the head of the lower flight of stairs, and now he halted, and stood motionless. There *was* a sound from below. It was neither imagination nor fancy; it was distinct and unmistakable—a low, rasping, metallic sound.

For an interval of seconds he stood there listening; then he shifted the flashlight, switched off now, to his left hand, and his right hand slipped into his pocket for his revolver. He moved forward then silently, noiselessly, and, as he descended the stairway, paused at every step to listen intently again. The sound, with short, almost negligible interruptions, persisted; and, with if now, it seemed as though he could distinguish the sound of heavy breathing. And now it seemed, too, as though the blackness were less opaque, as though, while there was still no object discernible, the hallway below was in a sort of murk, and as though, from somewhere, light rays, that were either carefully guarded or had expended, through distance, almost all their energy, were still striving to pierce the darkness.

Tight-lipped now, a few steps farther down, Dave Henderson leaned out over the bannister—and hung there tensely, rigidly.

It was like looking upon some weird, uncannily clever effect that had been thrown upon a moving picture screen. The door of Dago George's room was wide open, and through this he could see a white circle of light, the rays thrown away from and in the opposite direction to the door. They flooded the face of a safe; and, darkly, behind the light itself, two figures were faintly outlined, one kneeling at the safe, the other holding a flashlight and standing over the kneeling man's shoulder. And now the nature of the sounds that he had not been able to define was obvious—it was the click of a ratchet, the rasp of a bit eating voraciously into steel, as the kneeling man worked at the face of the safe.

For a moment, his eyes narrowed, half in sudden, angry menace, half in perplexity, he hung there gazing on the scene; and then, with all the caution that he knew, his weight thrown gradually on each separate tread to guard against a protesting creak, he went on down the stairs.

It was strange—damnably and most curiously strange! Was one of those figures in there Dago George? If so, it would account for the presence of a second man—the one Teresa had heard coming down stairs. But, if so, what was Dago George's game? Was the man going to put up the bluff that he had been robbed, and was therefore wrecking his own safe? That was an old gag! But what purpose could it serve Dago George in the present instance? It wasn't as though he, Dave Henderson, had *confided* the package to Dago George's keeping, and Dago George could take this means of cunningly securing it for himself. Dago George had stolen it—and, logically, the last thing Dago George would do would be to admit any knowledge of it, let alone flaunt it openly!

At the foot of the stairs, Dave Henderson discarded that theory as untenable. But if, then, neither one of the two in there was Dago George—*where was Dago George?* It was a little beyond attributing to mere coincidence, the fact that a couple of marauding safe-breakers should have *happened* to select Dago George's safe to-night in the ordinary routine of their nefarious vocation. Coincidence, as an explanation, wasn't good enough! It looked queer—extremely queer! Where he had thought that no one, save Millman and himself, had known anything about the presence of that money in New York to-night, it appeared that a most amazing number were not only aware of it, but were intimately interested in that fact!

He smiled a little in the darkness, not pleasantly, as he crept now, inch by inch, along the hall toward the open door. He, too, was *interested* in that package of banknotes in the safe! And, Dago George or the devil, it mattered very little which, there would be a showdown, very likely now a grim and very pretty little showdown, before the money left that room in any one's possession save his own!

From ahead, inside the room, there came a slight clatter, as though a tool of some sort had been dropped or tossed on the floor. It was followed by a muttered exclamation, and then a sort of breathless, but triumphant grunt. And then a voice, in a guttural undertone:

"Dere youse are, sport! Help yerself!"

Dave Henderson crouched back against the wall. He was well along the hall now, and quite close enough to the doorway of Dago George's private domain to enable him, given the necessary light, to see the whole interior quite freely. The door of the safe, in a dismantled condition, was swung open; strewn on the floor lay the kit of tools through whose instrumentality the job had been accomplished; and the man with the flashlight was bending forward, the white ray flooding the inside of the safe.

There came suddenly now a queer twitching to Dave Henderson's lips, and it came coincidentally with a sharp exclamation of delight from the man with the flashlight. In the man's hand was the original package of banknotes, its torn corner identifying it instantly to Dave Henderson, and evidencing with equal certainty to its immediate possessor that it was the object, presumably, which was sought.

And now the man with the flashlight, without turning, reached out and laid the package on the desk beside the safe. The movement, however, sent the flashlight's ray in a jerky half circle around the room, and mechanically Dave Henderson raised his hand and brushed it across his eyes. Was *that* fancy—what he had seen? It was gone now, it was dark in there now, for the flashlight was boring into the safe again, and the man with the flashlight seemed intent on the balance of the safe's contents. It had been only a glimpse, a glimpse that had lasted no longer than the time it takes a watch to tick, but it seemed to have mirrored itself upon Dave Henderson's brain so that he could still see it even in the darkness: It was a huddled form on the floor, close by the bed, just as though it had pitched itself convulsively out of the bed, and it lay there sprawled grotesquely, and the white face had seemed to grin at him in a horrid and contorted way—and it was the face of Dago George.

The man with the flashlight spoke suddenly over his shoulder to his companion:

"You've pulled a good job, Maggot!" he said approvingly. "Better than either Cunny or me was looking for, I guess. And so much so that I guess Cunny had better horn in himself before we close up for the night. You beat it over to the joint and bring him back. Tell him there's some queer stuff in this safe besides what we were after and what we got—some gang stuff that'll mabbe interest him, 'cause he said he wasn't very fond of Dago George. I don't know whether he'll want to take any of it or not, or whether he'd rather let the police have it when they wise up to this in the morning. He can look it over for himself. Tell him I want him to see it before I monkey with it myself. You can leave your watchmaker's tools there. You ought to be back in a little better than ten minutes if you hurry. We got a good hour and more yet before daylight, and before any of the crowd that work here gets back on the job, and until then we got the house to ourselves, but that's no reason for wasting any fleeting moments, so get a move on! See?"

"Sure!" grunted the other.

"Well, then, beat it!"

Footsteps sounded from the room, coming in the direction of the doorway, and Dave Henderson slipped instantly across the hall, and edged in behind the door,-that, opening back into the hall, afforded him both a convenient and secure retreat. The smile on his lips was more pleasant now. It was very thoughtful of the man with the flashlight—very! He cared nothing about the other man, who was now walking stealthily down the hall toward the front door; the *money* was still in that room in there! Also, he was glad to have had confirmed what he had already surmised—that Dago George slept alone in The Iron Tavern.

The front door opened and closed again softly. Dave Henderson stole silently across the hall again, and crouched against the opposite wall once more, but this time almost at the door jamb itself.

The flashlight, full on, lay on the desk. It played over the package of banknotes, and sent back a reflected gleam from the nickel-work of a telephone instrument that stood a few inches further along on the desk. The man's form, his back to the door, and back of the light, was like a silhouetted shadow. It was quiet, silent now in the house. Perhaps five seconds passed, and then the man chuckled low and wheezingly.

Dave Henderson grew suddenly rigid. It startled him. Somewhere he had heard that chuckle before—somewhere. It seemed striving to stir and awaken memory. There was something strangely familiar about it, and——

The man, still chuckling, was muttering audibly to himself now.

"Sure, that's the dope! The Scorpion—eh? Cunny the Scorpion! Nice name! Well, we'll see who gets *stung!* I guess ten minutes' start ain't good enough; but if some one's chasing the Scorpion, he won't have so much time to chase me. Yes, I guess this is where I fade away—with the goods. By the time there's been anything straightened out, and even if he squeals if he's caught, I guess I'll be far enough away to worry—not!"

Dave Henderson's face had grown as white and set as chiselled marble; but he did not move.

The man leaned abruptly forward over the desk, picked up the telephone, chuckled again, and then snatched the receiver from the hook. And the next instant, his voice full of well-simulated terror, he was calling wildly, frantically, into the transmitter:

"Central!... Central!... For God's sake!... Quick!... Help!... I'm Dago George.... The Iron Tavern.... They're murdering me.... Get the police!... For God's sake!... Get the police.... Tell them Cunny Smeeks is murdering me.... Hurry!... Quick!... For God's——"

The man allowed the telephone and the unhooked receiver to crash abruptly to the floor. The cord, catching the flashlight, carried the flashlight with it, and the light went out.

And then Dave Henderson moved. With a spring, he was half-way across the room—and his own flashlight stabbed a lane of light through the blackness, and struck, as the other whirled with a startled cry, full on the man's face.

It was Bookie Skarvan.

VIII.

BOOKIE SKARVAN PAYS HIS ACCOUNT

THE little red-rimmed eyes blinked into the glare—it was the only color left in the white, flabby face—the red rims of the furtive little eyes. Bookie Skarvan's fat hand lifted and tugged at his collar, as though the collar choked him. He fell back a step and his heel crunched upon the telephone transmitter, and smashed it. And then Bookie Skarvan licked his lips—and attempted a smile.

"I," mumbled Bookie Skarvan, "I—I can't see your face. Who—who are you?" The sound of his own voice, husky and shaken as it was, seemed to bring him a certain reassurance. "What do you want? Eh—what do you want?" he demanded.

Dave Henderson made no reply. It seemed as though his mind and soul and body were engulfed in some primal, savage ecstasy. Years swept their lightning sequence through his brain; hours, with the prison walls and iron bars around him, in which he had promised himself this moment, seemed to live their life and existence over again. He said no word; he made no sound— but, with the flashlight still playing without a flicker of movement upon the other, he felt, with the back of his revolver hand, over Bookie Skarvan's clothing, located in one of the pockets Bookie Skarvan's revolver, and, with utter contempt for any move the man might make through the opening thus given him, hooked the guard of his own revolver on the little finger of the hand that held the flashlight, and unceremoniously jerked the other's weapon out from the pocket and tossed it to the far end of the desk. The flashlight lifted then, and circled the walls of the room. Bookie Skarvan's complaint had not gone unheeded. Bookie Skarvan would have ample opportunity to see whose face it was! The flashlight found and held on the electric-light switch. It was on the opposite wall behind Bookie Skarvan. Dave Henderson shoved the man roughly out of the way, stepped quickly forward to the wall, switched on the light—and swung around to face Bookie Skarvan.

For an instant Bookie Skarvan stood there without movement, the little eyes dilating, the white face turning ashen and gray, and then great beads of sweat sprang out upon the forehead—and a scream of abject terror pealed through the room.

"Go away!" screamed Bookie Skarvan. "You're dead! Go away! Go back to hell where you belong!" His hands clawed out in front of him. "Do you hear? You're dead—dead! Go away! Curse you, damn you—go away!"

Dave Henderson spoke through closed teeth:

"You ought to be satisfied then—Bookie. You've wanted me dead for quite a while—for *five years*, haven't you?"

There was no answer.

Dave Henderson's eyes automatically swept around the now lighted room. Yes, that was Dago George there on the floor near the bed, lying on the side of his face, with a hideous gash across his head. The man was dead, of course; he couldn't be anything else. But anyway, Dago George was as something apart, an extraneous thing. There was only *one* thing in the world, one thing that held mind and soul and body in a thrall of wild, seething, remorseless passion—that maudlin, grovelling thing there, whose clawing hands had found the end of the desk, and who hung there with curious limpness, as though, because the knees sagged, the weight of his body was supported by his arms alone—that thing whose lips, evidently trying to form words, jerked up and down like flaps of flesh from which all nerve control had gone.

"Maybe you didn't know that I knew it was you who were back of that attempt to murder me that night—five years ago." Dave Henderson thrust the flashlight into his pocket, and took a step forward. "Well, you know it now!"

A sweat bead trickled down the fat, working face—and lost itself in a fold of flabby flesh.

"No!" Bookie Skarvan found his tongue. "No! Honest to God, Dave!" he whined. "It was Baldy."

"Don't lie! I *know*!" There was a cold deadliness in Dave Henderson's tones. "Stand away from the desk a little, so that I can get a look at that telephone on the floor! I don't want any witness to what's going to happen here, and a telephone with the receiver off——"

"My God!" Bookie Skarvan cried out wildly. "What are you going to do?"

"Yes, I guess it's out of commission." Dave Henderson's voice seemed utterly detached; he seemed utterly to ignore the other for a moment, as he looked at the broken instrument.

Bookie Skarvan, in an access of fear, mopped at his wet face, and his little red-rimmed eyes, like the eyes of a cornered rat, darted swift, frantic glances in all directions around the room.

"Dave, do you hear!" Bookie Skarvan's voice rose thin and squealing. "Why don't you answer? Do you hear! What—what are you going to do?"

"It's queer, kind of queer, to find you here, Bookie," said Dave Henderson evenly. "I guess there's a God—Bookie. How did you get here—from San Francisco?"

Bookie Skarvan licked at his dry lips, and cowered back from the revolver that was suddenly outflung in Dave Henderson's hand.

"I—I followed the girl. I thought you'd opened up to the old man, and he'd bumped you off with that bomb to get the stuff for himself. I was sure of it when he died, and she beat it for here."

"And to-night?" Dave Henderson's voice was rasping now.

"I got the room opposite hers." Bookie Skarvan gulped heavily; his eyes were fixed, staring now, as though fascinated by the revolver muzzle. "She came downstairs. I followed her, but I don't know where she went to. I saw the package go into the safe. I could see through the fanlight over the door. I saw him"—Bookie Skarvan's hand jerked out toward the huddled form on the floor—"I saw him put it there." Mechanically, Dave Henderson's eyes followed the gesture—and narrowed for an instant in a puzzled, startled way. Had that dead man there *moved?* The body seemed slightly nearer to the head of the bed!' Fancy! Imagination! He hadn't marked the exact position of the body to begin with, and it was still huddled, still inert, still in the same sprawled, contorted position. His eyes reverted to Bookie Skarvan.

"You had a man in here with you at work on that safe, a man you called Maggot, and you sent him, with that dirty brand of trickery of yours, to bring back some one you called Cunny the Scorpion, with the idea that instead of finding you and the money here—they would find the police." There was a twisted, merciless smile on Dave Henderson's lips. "Where did you get into touch with your *friends?*"

Bookie Skarvan's eyes were roving again, seeking some avenue of escape, it seemed. Dave Henderson laughed shortly, unpleasantly, as he watched the other. There was only the door and the window. But he, Dave Henderson, blocked the way to the door; and the window, as he knew through the not-too-cursory examination he had made of it when he had come down the fire escape with the valises, was equally impassable. It had been in his mind then that perhaps he, himself, might gain entrance to Dago George's room through the window—only the old-fashioned iron shutters, carefully closed and fastened, had barred the way.

"Well?" He flung the word sharply at Bookie Skarvan.

"I—Baldy knew the Scorpion." Bookie Skarvan's fingers wriggled between his collar and his fat neck. "Baldy gave me a letter to him, and the Scorpion put one over on—on that fellow on the floor, and got me a room here upstairs. And when I saw the money going into the safe I beat it for the Scorpion, and got him to give me a box-worker, so he got Maggot for me, and——"

"You hadn't the nerve, of course, when you saw Dago George putting the money in the safe, to tackle the job alone before the safe was locked!" There was grim, contemptuous irony in Dave Henderson's voice. "You're the same old Bookie, aren't you—yellow as the sulphur pit of hell!" His face hardened. "Ten minutes, you said it would take them to get back. It's not very long, Bookie. And say two or three minutes longer, or perhaps a little more, for the police, allowing for the time it would take central to get her breath after that nerve racking cry for help you sent her. Or maybe the police would even get here first—depending on how far away the station is. I'm a stranger here, and I don't know. In that case, there wouldn't be even ten minutes—and part of that is gone now. There isn't much time, Bookie. But there's time enough for you and me to settle our little account. I used to think of what I'd do to you when I got out on the other side of those iron bars. I used to think of it when I couldn't sleep at night in my cell. I kept thinking of it for *five years*, Bookie—and here we are to-night at last, the two of us, you and me, Bookie. I overheard Runty Mott explain the whole plant you had put up to murder me, so there's no use of you lying, there's no use of you starting that—that's *one* thing you haven't got time to do. You'd better clean house, Bookie, for there isn't room enough in this world for the two of us—one of us has got to go."

Bookie Skarvan had crouched against the end of the desk again. He cringed now, one arm upraised as though to ward off a blow.

"What—what are you going to do?" The words came thick and miserably. Their repetition seemed all that his tongue was capable of. "What—what are you going to do?"

"I can't *murder* you!" Dave Henderson's face had grown set and colorless— as colorless as his tone. "I wish to God I could! It's coming to you! But I can't! There's your revolver on the end of the desk. Take it!"

Again and again, Bookie Skarvan's tongue licked at his lips.

"What do you mean?" he whispered.

"You know what I mean!" Dave Henderson answered levelly. "Take it!"

"My God!" screamed Bookie Skarvan. "No! My God—no! Not that!"

"Yes—*that!* You're getting what I swore I'd never give you—a chance. Either you or I are going out. Take that revolver, and for the first time in your life try and be a man; or else I'll fix you, and I'll fix it so that you won't move from here until your friend the Scorpion gets his chance at you for the pleasant little surprise you had arranged for him with your telephone trick, or until the police carry you out with a through ticket to the electric chair for what looks like murder over there on the floor. You understand—Bookie? I'll make you fight, you cur! It's the only chance you've got for your life. Now—take it!"

Bookie Skarvan wrung his hands together. A queer crooning sound came from his lips. He was trembling violently.

"There aren't very many of those ten minutes left, Bookie," said Dave Henderson coldly. "But if you got in a lucky shot—Bookie—you'd still have time to get away, from here. And there's the money there, too—you could take that with you."

The man seemed near collapse. Great beads from his forehead ran down and over the sagging jowls. He moaned a little, and stared at the revolver that lay upon the desk, and reached out his hand toward the weapon, and drew his hand back again. He looked again at Dave Henderson, and at the muzzle of the revolver that covered him. He seemed to read something irrevocable and remorseless in both. Slowly, his mouth working, his face muscles twitching, he reached again to the desk, and pulled the revolver to him; and then, his arm falling nervelessly, he held the weapon dangling at his side.

Dave Henderson's revolver was lowered until it pointed to the floor.

"When you lift your hand, Bookie, it's the signal," he said in a monotone.

Bookie Skarvan's knees seemed to bend and sag a little more—there was no other movement.

"I'm waiting," said Dave Henderson—and pulled the trigger of his revolver to put a shot into the floor.

There was the click of the falling hammer—no more. A grim smile played across Dave Henderson's lips. It was as well, perhaps, that he had tried in that way to startle, to *frighten*, this terrified, spineless cur who stood there into action! The cartridge that he had depended upon for his life had missed fire! He pulled the trigger again. The hammer clicked. He pulled again—his eyes never leaving Bookie Skarvan's face. The hammer clicked.

For the fraction of a second the room seemed blurred to Dave Henderson. *The chambers of his revolver were empty!* His brain seemed to sicken, and then to recover itself, and leap into fierce, virile activity. He was at the mercy of that cringing hound there—if the other but knew it. It seemed as though all the devils of hell shrieked at him in unholy mirth. If he moved a step forward to rush, to close with the other, the very paroxysm of fear that possessed Bookie Skarvan would instinctively incite the man to fire. There was one way, only one way—the electric light switch behind him. If he could reach that without Bookie Skarvan realizing the truth, there would be the darkness—and his bare hands. Well, he asked no more than that—only that Bookie Skarvan did not get away. His bare hands were enough.

He moved back a single step, as though shifting his position, his face impassive, watching the dangling weapon in the other's shaky hand, watching the other's working lips. The chamber of his revolver was empty! How? When? It had been fully loaded when he lay down on the bed. Yes! He remembered! It was queer that it had twisted like that in his sleep. Dago George! It came in a lightning flash of intuition. Dago George, cautious to excite no suspicion, had been equally cautious to draw, his, Dave Henderson's, teeth!

He edged back another step—and stopped, as though rooted to the spot. Bookie Skarvan, that dangling revolver in the other's hand, his own peril, all, everything that but an instant before had obsessed his mind, was blotted out from his consciousness as though it had never existed. That huddled form, that murdered man on the floor behind Bookie Skarvan, that he could see over Bookie Skarvan's shoulder, had raised his hand in a swift, sudden movement, and had thrust it under the mattress at the head of the bed, and had snatched out a revolver.

It was quick, quick as thought, quick as the winking of an eye. A shout of warning rose to Dave Henderson's lips—and was drowned in the report of the revolver shot, deafening, racketing, in the confined space. And, as though thrown into relief by the flash and the tongue flame of the revolver, a picture seemed to sear itself into Dave Henderson's brain: The up-flung arms of Bookie Skarvan, the ghastly surprise on the sweat-beaded face, the fat body spinning grotesquely like a run-down top—and pitching forward to the floor. And through the lifting smoke, another face—Dago George's face, working, livid, blood-smirched, full of demoniacal triumph. And then a gurgling peal of laughter.

"Yes, and you, too! *Con Amore!*" gurgled Dago George. "You, too!"

The man was on his knees now, lurching there, the revolver swaying weakly, trying to draw its bead now on him, Dave Henderson. He moved with a spring to one side toward the door. The revolver, as though jerked desperately in the weak hand, followed him. He flung himself to the floor. A shot rang out. And then, as though through the flash again, another picture lived: The revolver dropping from a hand that could no longer hold it, a graying face that swayed on shoulders which in turn rocked to and fro—and then a lurch—a thud—and, the face was hidden between out-sprawled arms—and Dago George did not move any more.

IX.
THE ENDING OF THE NIGHT

MECHANICALLY, Dave Henderson rose to his feet, and for an instant stood as though, his mental faculties numbed, he were striving to grasp as a concrete thing some stark and horribly naked tragedy that his eyes told him was real, but which his brain denied and refused to accept. Thin layers of smoke, suspended, sinuous, floated in hideous little gray clouds about the room—like palls that sought to hide what lay upon the floor from sight, and, failing in their object, but added another grim and significant detail to the scene.

And then his brain cleared, and he jumped forward to bend first over Bookie Skarvan and then over Dago George; and, where his mind had been unreceptive and numbed but an instant before, it was keen, swift and incisive now—the police who had been summoned—the Scorpion and his parasite yegg who were on the way back—there was no time to lose! There was no one in the house to have heard the shots—Bookie Skarvan had settled that point— no one except Teresa upstairs. But the shots might have been heard *outside*.

His ears throbbed with strange noises; those shots seemed still to be reverberating and beating at his eardrums. Yes, the shots might have been heard outside on the street, or by some one in the next house. Was that some one at the front door now? He held his breath, as he rose from Dago George's side. No, just the ringing in his ears; there wasn't any other, sound. But there wasn't an instant to lose; both Bookie Skarvan and Dago George were dead. There wasn't an instant to lose—only the instant he *must* take to make sure he made no false move here before he snatched up that package on the desk there, and ran upstairs, and, with Teresa, made his way out by the fire escape.

He stooped, and stretched out his hand to exchange his own empty revolver for the one that lay on the floor where it had fallen from Dago George's lifeless fingers—and, instead, drew his hand sharply back again. Fool! The police would investigate this, wouldn't they? Bookie Skarvan couldn't have been shot by an *empty* revolver! Well—he was moving toward the desk and back toward where Bookie Skarvan lay—suppose he took Bookie's revolver then? He shook his head. He did not need one bad enough for that. It was better to let things remain as they were and let the police draw their own conclusions, conclusions which, if nothing was interfered with, and he got away with the package of banknotes, would point no inference that, by hook or crook, would afford a clew which might lead to him. Was he so sure of that? Suppose the Scorpion had been let into Bookie's confidence, and that the Scorpion when he got here should happen to be caught by the police—and *talked* to save himself?

A grim smile settled on Dave Henderson's lips, as he thrust his useless revolver into his pocket, and, reaching out to the desk, picked up the package of banknotes. Well, if anything came of the Scorpion, it couldn't be helped! And, after all, did it matter very much? It wasn't only Dago George and Bookie Skarvan who were dead—Dave Henderson was dead, too!

It had been scarcely a minute since he had first risen: to his feet; it was his mind, sifting, weighing, arguing with itself, that had seemed to use up priceless time, whereas, in reality, in its swift working, it had kept pace with, and had even prodded him into speed in his physical movements. He was running now, the package of banknotes in his hand, for the door. Dago George was dead. Bookie Skarvan was dead. And if— —

He staggered suddenly back, and reeled from the impact, as a man from just outside in the hallway launched himself ferociously forward across the threshold. The package spun from his hand to the floor. Half flung to his knees, Dave Henderson's arms shot out instinctively and wrapped themselves around his assailant's body.

Came a snarl and an oath, and Dave Henderson's head rocked back on his shoulders from a vicious short-arm jab that caught him on the point of the jaw. It dazed him; he was conscious only that he had not let go his hold, that his hands, like feeling tentacles, were creeping further up the man's body toward throat and shoulders, drawing his own body up after them into a more upright position. His head sang with the blow. A voice seemed to float from somewhere out of the air:

"That's the stuff, Maggot! Soak him!"

Dave Henderson's arms had locked now like steel bands around his assailant and were tightening, as the other's were tightening around him in turn. The dizziness was leaving him. They swung, rocking, to the strain. The man was strong! A face, a repellent, unshaven face, leered into his. Twice they swirled around, and then seemed to hang for an instant motionless, as though the strength of one exerted to its utmost was exactly counterbalanced by the strength of the other; and over the other's shoulder Dave Henderson could see another man, a man who laughed with ugly coolness, and who had flaming red hair, and eyes of a blue so faded that they looked repulsive because they looked as though they were white.

Maggott and Cunny the Scorpion! There *had* been some one there in the front of the house—it had been Maggot and Cunny the Scorpion. And at any moment now there would be some one else—the police!

That nicety of balance was gone. They were struggling, lurching, staggering in each other's embrace again—he, and this Maggot, who snarled and cursed with panting breath. Their heads were almost on each other's shoulders. He could see the straining muscles in the other's neck standing out like great, purple, swollen cords. And as he whirled now this way and that, he caught glimpses of the red-headed man. The red-headed man seemed to be quite unconcerned for the moment with his companion's struggle. He picked up the package of banknotes from the floor, examined it, dropped it again, and ran to Bookie Skarvan's side.

A queer, hard smile came to Dave Henderson's lips. This panting thing with arms locked like a gorilla's around him seemed to be weakening a little—or was it a trick? He tightened his own hold, and edged his own hands a little higher up—and still a little higher. If he could only tear himself loose for the fraction of a second, and get his fingers on that panting throat! No, the man wasn't weakening so much after all! The man seemed to sense his intention; and with a sudden twist, each endeavoring to out-maneuver the other, they spun in a wider circle, like drunken dancers in some mad revel, and crashed against the wall, and rebounded from it, and hung again, swaying like crazy pendulums, in the middle of the floor.

The red-headed man's voice came suddenly from across the room:

"Soak him, Maggot!"

That was the Scorpion. The Scorpion seemed to be taking some interest at last in something besides Bookie Skarvan and the package of money.

A grunted oath from Dave Henderson's antagonist answered.

"Damn it, I can't! Curse youse, why don't youse lend a hand!"

With a quick, sudden wrench, Dave Henderson tried to free himself. It resulted only in a wild swirl in a half circle that almost pitched him, and with him the other, to the floor. But he saw the Scorpion now. The Scorpion had risen to his feet from Bookie Skarvan's side, and was balancing a revolver in his hand; and now the Scorpion's voice seemed to hold a sort of purring note, velvet in its softness.

"All right, then, Maggot! We might as well have a clean-up here, since he's started it. I guess we came just about in time, or he'd have had the money as well as our fat friend there—that he *got*. It looks as though we ought to even up the score." The revolver lifted in the Scorpion's hand. "Jump away, Maggot—I'm going to lead the ace of trumps!"

The eyes were white—not blue; there was no blue in them; they were white—two little white spots across the room. They held a devil's menace in them—like the voice—like the purring voice that was hideous because it was so soft. God, could he hold this Maggot now—not wrench himself free, but hold the man here in his arms—keep Maggot between him and those white eyes, that looked like wicked little plague spots which had eaten into that grotesquely red-thatched face.

Maggot was fighting like a demon now to tear himself free. A sweat bead spurted out on Dave Henderson's forehead and rolled down his face. The white eyes came dancing nearer—nearer. They circled and circled, as he circled—Maggot was the shield. He whirled this way and that. The muscles of his arms cracked, as they swung and whipped Maggot around in furious gyrations.

A shot rang out. Something sang with an angry hum and hot breath past Dave Henderson's cheek. The velvet voice laughed. Maggot screamed in a mixture of rage and fear.

"Curse youse, youse fool! Youse'll hit me!"

"I'll get him next time, Maggot," purred the velvet voice.

The white eyes kept too far away—that was what was the matter—too far away. If they would only come near—near enough so that of a sudden he could let go his grip and launch this squirming human shield full, like a battering ram, into those white eyes. That was the only chance there was. Only the Scorpion was too cunning for that—he kept too far away.

Dave Henderson swung madly around again, interposing Maggot's body as the Scorpion darted to one side; and then suddenly, and for the first time, there came a sound from Dave Henderson's lips—a low cry of pain. *Teresa!*

It was only a glimpse he got—perhaps it wasn't real! Just a glimpse into the hallway where the light from the room streamed out—just a glimpse of a figure on the stairs who leaned out over the banister, and whose face was white as death itself, and whose hands seemed to grip and cling to the banister rail as though they were welded there.

Teresa! He grew sick at heart as he struggled now. Teresa! If he could only have kept her out of this; if only, at least, she were not there to *see*! It couldn't last much longer! True, Maggot, beyond doubt, beyond shadow of trickery now, had had his fill of fighting, and there was fear upon the man, the fear of an unlucky shot from the Scorpion, and he was whimpering now, and he struggled only apathetically, but it took strength to drag even a dead weight around and around and that strength would not last forever. Teresa! She had heard those shots from up above—she had *seen* the Scorpion fire once, and miss, and she— —

The Scorpion laughed out. It looked like a sure shot now! Dave Henderson jerked Maggot in front of him, but his swirling, mad gyrations had brought him into the angle that the desk made with the wall, and, turn as he would now, the Scorpion could reach in around the end of the desk, and almost touch him with the revolver muzzle itself.

"I got him, Maggot!" purred the Scorpion. "I got him now, the— —"

The man's voice ended in a startled cry. The sweat was running into Dave Henderson's eyes, he could scarcely see—just a blurred vision over Maggot's shoulder, a blurred vision of a slim figure running like the wind into the room, and stooping to the floor where the package of banknotes lay, and snatching it up, and starting for the door again.

And then the Scorpion fired—but the revolver was pointed now across the room, and the slight, fleeing figure swayed, and staggered, and recovered herself, and went on, and over her shoulder her voice, though it faltered, rang bravely through the room:

"I—I thought he'd rather have this than you, Dave. It was the only chance. Don't mind me, Dave. He won't get me."

The whimpering thing in Dave Henderson's arms was flung from him, and it crashed to the floor. It wasn't his own strength, it was the strength of one demented, and of a maddened brain, that possessed Dave Henderson now. And he leaped forward, running like a hare. Teresa had already gained the stairs—the Scorpion in pursuit was half-way along the hall. And now he saw nothing else—just that red-haired figure running, running, running. There was neither house, nor hall, nor stairs, nor any other thing—only that red-haired figure that the soul of him craved, for whom there was no mercy, that with his hands he would tear to pieces in insensate fury.

A flash came, blinding his eyes; a report roared in his ears—and then his hands snatched at and caught a wriggling thing. And for the first time he realized that he had reached the head of the stairs, realized it because, pitched forward over the landing, lay a woman's form that was still and motionless. And he laughed like the maniac he was now, and the wriggling thing screamed in his grasp, screamed as it went up above his head—and then Dave Henderson hurled it from him to the bottom of the stairs.

He turned, and flung himself on his knees beside Teresa. He called her name again and again—and there was no answer. She lay there, half on her face on the floor, her arms wound around a torn package of banknotes. He rose, and rocked on his feet, and his knotted fists went up above his head. And then he laughed again, as though his reason were gone—laughed as his eyes fixed on a red-headed thing that made an unshapely heap at the foot of the stairs; and laughed at a slinking shadow that went along the hall, and scurried out through the front door. That was Maggot—like a rat leaving a sinking ship—Maggot who— —

Then reason came again. The police! At any moment now—the police. In an instant he had caught Teresa up in his arms. She wasn't dead—he could hear her breathing—only it was weak—pitifully weak. There should be an exit to the fire escape from this floor—but it was dark and he had no time to search—it was quicker to go up the stairs—where he knew the way—and out through his own room.

Stumbling, staggering in the darkness, holding Teresa in his arms, he made his way upstairs. The police—his mind centered on that again. If she and he were caught here, his identification as Dave Henderson, which would ultimately ensue, would damn her; this money, wrapped so tenaciously in her arms, would damn her; and, on top of that old score of the police in San Francisco, there had been ugly work here in this house to-night. If it were not for the money, the criminal hoax played upon the police in the disappearance of Dave Henderson would not be so serious—but the money was here, and in that hoax she had had a part, and the shadow of Nicolo Capriano still lay across her shoulders.

The night air came gratefully cool upon his face. He drew it in in great, gasping breaths, greedily, hungrily. He had gained the fire escape through the window now, and now he paused for the first time to listen. There was no sound. Back there inside the house it was as still as death. Death! Well, why shouldn't it be, there *was* death there, and— —

His arms tightened suddenly in a great, overwhelming paroxysm of fear around Teresa, and he bent his head, bent it lower, lower still, until his face was close to that white face he held, and through the darkness his eyes searched it in an agony of apprehension.

And then he started forward again, and began to descend the fire escape; and now he groped uneasily for foothold as he went. It seemed rickety and unstable, this spidery thing that sprawled against the side of the wall, and it was dark, and without care the foot would slip through the openings between the treads. It had not seemed that way when he had gone up and down when disposing of the valises. Only now it was a priceless burden that he carried—

this form that lay close-pressed against his breast, whose touch, alternately now, brought him a sickening sense of dread, and a surging hope that sent the blood leaping like a mill-race through his veins.

He went down, step after step, his mind and brain shrieking at him to hurry because there was not a single second to lose—but it was slow, maddeningly slow. He could not see the treads, not only because it was dark, but because Teresa's form was in his arms. He could only feel with his feet—and now and then his body swayed to preserve his balance.

Was there no end to the thing! It seemed like some bottomless pit of blackness into which he was descending. And it seemed as though this pit held an abominable signification in its blackness and its depth, as though it beckoned him on to engulf them; it seemed—it seemed—— God, if she would only move, if she would not lie so still, so terribly still in his arms!

Another step—another—and then his foot, searching out, found only space beneath it. He must free one arm now, so that he could cling to the bottom tread and lower himself to the ground. It was only a short drop, he knew, for the lower section of the fire escape was one of those that swung on hinges, and when, previously, coming up, Teresa had held it down for him, he had been able to reach it readily with a spring from the ground. But he dared not jump even that short distance now with Teresa, wounded, in his arms.

He changed her position now to throw her weight into the hollow of his left arm, lifting her head so that it lay high upon his shoulder—and with the movement her hair brushed his lips. It brought a sudden, choking sob from Dave Henderson, and in a great, yearning impulse he let his head sink down until his cheek for an instant was laid against hers—and then, the muscles of his right arm straining until they cracked, he lowered himself down and dropped to the ground.

He ran now, lurching, across the yard, and out into the lane, and here he paused again to listen. But he heard nothing. He was clear of that cursed trap-house now—if he could only keep clear. He ran on again, stumbling again, with his burden. And now, though he did not pause to listen any more, it seemed as though his throbbing eardrums caught the sounds at last that they had been straining to hear. Wasn't that the police behind there now—on the street in front of The Iron Tavern? It sounded like it—like the arrival of a police patrol.

He reached the shed where he had hidden the valises, entered, and laid Teresa tenderly on the floor. He used his flashlight then—and a low moan came from his lips. The bullet had cut across the side of her neck just above the shoulder; the wound was bleeding profusely, and over the package of banknotes, around which her arms were still tightly clasped, there had spread a crimson stain. He drew her arms gently apart, laid the package on the floor, and then, wrenching one of the valises open, snatched at the first article of linen that came to hand.

His lips trembled, as he did his best to staunch the flow of blood and bind the wound.

"Teresa! Teresa!" Dave Henderson whispered.

Her eyes opened—and smiled.

She made an effort to speak. He bent his head to catch the words.

"Dave—where—where are we? Still in the house?"

"No!" he told her feverishly. "No! We're clear of that. We're in the shed here in the lane where I took the valises."

She made a slight affirmative movement of her head.

"Then go—go at once—Dave—for help—I——"

Her eyes had closed again.

"Yes!" he said. His voice was choking. He called her name. "Teresa!" There was no answer. She had lapsed back into unconsciousness. And then the soul of him spoke its agony. "Oh, my God, Teresa!" he cried brokenly, and swayed to his feet.

An instant he stood there, then stooped, picked up the package of banknotes, thrust it into the open valise, closed the valise, carried it into a darker corner of the shed, and went to the door.

He looked out. There was no one in sight in the darkness. But then, what interest would the police have in this section of the lane? There was nothing to connect it with The Iron Tavern! He stepped outside, and broke into a run down the lane, heading for the intersecting street in the opposite direction from The Iron Tavern. He must get help! A queer, mirthless laugh was on his lips. A wounded woman in the lane was *the* connecting link with The Iron Tavern. And yet he must get help. Well, there was only one source from which he dared ask help—only one—Millman.

He ran on. Millman! Something within him rebelled at that. But Teresa was perhaps—was—— No, he would not let his mind even frame the word. Only one thing was paramount now—she must have help at once. Well, God knew, he could *trust* Millman! Only there seemed some strange irony here that chastened him. And yet—— Yes, this was strange, too! Suddenly he became strangely content that it should be Millman.

He reached the street, and looked up and down. It was four o'clock in the morning, and the street was dark and deserted except for a single lighted window that shone out half-way down the block. He ran toward it. It proved to be an all-night restaurant, and he entered it, and asked for the telephone, and shut himself up in the booth.

A moment more and he had the St. Lucian Hotel on the wire.

"Give me Mr. Millman—Mr. Charles Millman," he requested hurriedly.

The hotel operator answered him. It was impossible. A guest could not be disturbed at that hour. It was against the rules, and Dave Henderson was pleading hoarsely into the phone.

"Give me Millman! Let me speak to him! It's life and death!"

"I—I can't." The operator's voice, a girl's, was hesitant, less assured.

"For God's sake, give me Millman—there's a life at stake!" Dave Henderson cried frantically. "Quick! For God's sake, quick!"

"Wait!" she said.

It seemed a time interminable, and then a drowsy voice called:

"Hello! What's wanted?"

"Is that you, Millman?" Dave Henderson asked wildly. "Millman, is that you?"

"Yes," the voice answered.

"It's Dave speaking. Dave—do you understand? I—there's some one badly hurt. I can't tell you any more over the phone; but, in Heaven's name, get a doctor that you can trust, and come!"

"I'll come, Dave," said Millman quietly. "Where?"

Dave Henderson turned from the telephone, and thrust his head out of the booth. He had no idea where he was in New York, save that he was near The Iron Tavern. He dared not mention that. Before many hours the papers would be full of The Iron Tavern—and the telephone operator might hear.

"What's this address?" he called out to a man behind the counter.

The man told him.

Dave Henderson repeated the address into the phone.

"All right, Dave," Millman's voice came quickly; "I'll be there as soon as I can get my car, and pick up the doctor."

Dave Henderson stepped out into the night, and pulled off his hat. His forehead was dripping wet. He walked back to the lane, listened, heard nothing, and stole along it, and entered the shed again, and knelt by Teresa's side. She was unconscious.

He bent over her with the flashlight. His bandage was crude and clumsy; but it brought him a little measure of relief to see that at least it had been effective in the sense that the bleeding had been arrested. And then his eyes went to the white face again. It seemed as though his mental faculties were blunted, that they were sensible only of a gnawing at his brain that was almost physical in its acute pain. Instinctively, from time to time, he looked at his watch.

At last he got up, and went out into the lane again, and from there to the street. It was too soon. He could only pace up and down. It was too soon, but he could not have afforded to keep the doctor waiting if Millman arrived, and he, Dave Henderson, was not there—otherwise he would have stayed longer in the shed. It would be daylight before they came, wouldn't it? It was an hour now, a thousand years, wasn't it, since he had telephoned?

A big touring car rolled down the street. He ran toward it. Millman—yes, it was Millman! The car stopped.

"Quick!" he urged, and sprang on the footboard. "Go to the corner of the lane there!"

And then, as the car stopped again, and Millman, from the wheel, and a man with a little black bag in his hand, sprang out, Dave Henderson led the way down the lane, running, without a word, and pushed open the door of the shed. He held the flashlight steadily for the doctor, though he turned now to Millman.

"You've got a right to know," he said in an undertone, as the doctor bent, absorbed, over Teresa. "Hell's broken loose to-night, Millman—there's been murder further up the lane there in a place they call The Iron Tavern. Do you understand? That's why I didn't dare go anywhere for help. Listen! I'll tell you." And, speaking rapidly, he sketched the details of the night for Millman. "Do you understand, Millman?" he said at the end. "Do you understand why I didn't dare go anywhere for help?"

Millman did not answer. He was looking questioningly at the doctor, as the latter suddenly rose.

"We must get her to the hospital at once," said the doctor crisply.

"The hospital!" Dave Henderson echoed the word. It seemed to jeer at him. He could have summoned an ambulance himself! As well throw the cards upon the table! His eyes involuntarily sought that darker corner of the shed where the package of banknotes, bloodstained now, was hidden in the valise. The hospital, or the police station—in that respect, for Teresa as well as himself, it was all the same!

It was Millman who spoke.

"Wait!" he said, and touched Dave Henderson's arm; then turned to the doctor. "Can we move her in my car?" he asked.

"Yes; I guess we can manage it," the doctor answered.

Millman drew the doctor a little to one side. He whispered earnestly. Dave Henderson caught a phrase about "getting a nurse"—and then he felt Millman's hand press his arm again.

"It's all right, Dave. I guess I'll open that town house after all this summer—to a select few," said Millman quietly. His hand tightened eloquently in its pressure. "We'll take her there, Dave."

X.
GOD'S CHANCE

IT was a big house—like some vast, cavernous, deserted place. Footsteps, when there were footsteps, and voices, when there were voices, seemed to echo with strange loneliness through the great halls, and up and down the wide staircase. And in the dawn, as the light came gray, the pieces of furniture, swathed in their summer coverings of sheets, had seemed like weird and ghostlike specters inhabiting the place.

But the dawn had come hours ago.

Dave Henderson raised his head from his cupped hands. Was that the nurse now, or the doctor—that footstep up above? He listened a moment, and then his chin dropped back into his hands.

Black hours they had been—black hours for his soul, and hours full of the torment and agony of fear for Teresa.

From somewhere, almost coincident with their arrival at the house, a nurse had come. From some restaurant, a man had brought breakfast for the doctor, for the nurse, for Millman—and for him. He had eaten something—what, he did not know. The doctor had gone, and come again—the doctor was upstairs there now. Perhaps, when the doctor came down again, the doctor would allow him to see Teresa. Half an hour ago they had told him that she would get well. There was strange chaos in his mind. That agony of fear for her, that cold, icy thing that had held a clutch upon his heart, was gone; but in its place had come another agony—an agony of yearning—and now he was afraid—for himself.

Millman had tried to make him go to bed and sleep. Sleep! He could not have slept! He could not even have remained still for five minutes at a stretch! He had been half mad with his anxiety for Teresa. He had wanted to be somewhere where his restless movements would not reach Teresa in her room, and yet somewhere where he could intercept every coming and going of the doctor. And so for hours he had alternately paced up and down this lower hall here, and thrown himself upon this great, wide, sheet-covered divan where he sat now. And in those hours his mind, it seemed, had run the gamut of every emotion a human soul could know. It ached now—physically. His temples throbbed and hurt.

His eyes strayed around the hall, and held on a large sheet-draped piece of furniture over beyond the foot of the staircase. They had served other purposes, these coverings, than to make spectral illusions in the gray of dawn! Beneath that sheet lay the package of banknotes. It made a good hiding place. He had extracted the package from the valise, and had secreted it there during the confusion as they had entered the house. But it seemed to take form through that sheet now, as it had done a score of times since he had put it there, and always it seemed as though a crimson stain that was on the wrapper would spread and spread until it covered the entire package.

That package—and the crimson stain! It seemed to make of itself a curiously appropriate foreground for a picture that spread away into a vista of limitless years: An orphan school, with its cracked walls, and the painted mottoes whose scrolls gaped where the cracks were; a swirl of horses reaching madly down the stretch, a roar of hoarse, delirious shouts, elated oaths around the bookmaker's paying-stand, pinched faces on the outer fringes of this ring; a thirst intolerable, stark pain, the brutal jolting of a boxcar through the nights, hours upon hours of a horror that ended only with the loss of consciousness; walls that reared themselves so high that they seemed to stand sentinels against the invasion of even a ray of sunlight, steel bars, and doors, and bolts that clanged, and clanged, until the sound ate like some cancerous thing into the soul itself; and then wolves, human wolves, ravenous wolves, between two packs of them, the police on the one hand, the underworld on the other, that snarled and tore at him, while he fought them for his life.

All that! That was the price he had paid for that package there—that, and that crimson stain.

He swept his hand across his eyes. His face grew set, and his jaws locked hard together. No, he wasn't sure yet that even that was all—that the package there was even yet finally and irrevocably *his*—to do with as he liked. There was last night—The Iron Tavern—the police again. *Was* there a connecting link trailing behind him? What had become of the Scorpion? What story had the man perhaps told? Were the police looking for an unknown man— who was Dave Henderson; and looking for an unknown woman—who was Teresa?

Well, before long now, surely, he would know—when Millman got back. Millman, who had intimated that he had an inside pull somewhere that would get the straight police version of the affair, had gone out immediately after breakfast for that purpose.

That was what counted, the only thing that counted—to know where the police stood. Millman ought to be back now. He had been gone for hours. It was taking him an unaccountably long time!

Millman! He had called Millman a straight crook. He had tried to call Millman something else this morning—for what Millman had done for Teresa and himself last night. Only he wasn't any good at words. But Millman had seemed to understand, though Millman had not said much, either—just a smile in the gray eyes, and a long, steady clasp of both hands on his, Dave Henderson's, shoulders.

There was a footstep on the stairs now. He looked up. It was the doctor coming down. He jumped to his feet, and went eagerly to the foot of the stairs.

"Better!" said the doctor cheerily.

"I—I want to see her," said Dave Henderson.

The doctor smiled, as he moved across the hall toward the front door.

"In a few minutes," he said. "I've told the nurse to let you know when she's ready."

The doctor went out.

He heard the doctor begin to descend the outer steps, and then pause, and then another footstep ascending; and then he caught the sound of voices. And then, after a little while, the front door opened, and Millman came into the reception hall.

Dave Henderson's lips tightened, as he stepped toward the other.

"What"—he found his voice strangely hoarse, and he cleared his throat—"what did you find out?"

Millman motioned toward the divan.

"Everything, I guess, Dave," he answered, as he sat down.

"And——?" Dave Henderson flung himself down beside the other.

Millman shook his head.

"Better hear the whole story, Dave. You can size it up then for yourself."

Dave Henderson nodded.

"Go on, then!" he said.

"I told you," said Millman, "that I thought I could get inside information—the way the police looked at it. Well, I have. And I have got it from a source that is absolutely dependable. Understand, Dave?"

Dave Henderson nodded again.

"The police start with that telephone message," said Millman. "They believe that it was authentic, and that it was Dago George who sent it. In fact, without it they wouldn't have known where to turn; while with it the whole affair appears to be simplicity itself." He smiled a little whimsically. "They used it as the key to unlock the door. It's no discredit to their astuteness. With nothing to refute it, it is not only the obvious, but the logical solution. Bookie budded a great deal better than he knew—for Dave Henderson—when he used that telephone for his own dirty ends. It wouldn't have been so easy for the police to account for the death of three men in The Iron——"

"*Three!*" Dave Henderson strained suddenly forward. Three! There were—two; only two—Dago George and Bookie Skarvan. Only two dead—and a red-headed thing huddled at the foot of the stairs. Was that it? Was that the third one—Cunny the Scorpion? Had it ended with that? Had he *killed* a man? Last night he would have torn the fellow limb from limb—yes, and under the same circumstances, he would do it again—Teresa upstairs, who had been so close to death, justified that a thousand times over.

But——— "You mean Cunny the Scorpion—Cunny Smeeks?" he demanded tensely.

"Yes," said Millman. And then, with a quick, comprehensive glance at Dave Henderson's face: "But you didn't do it, Dave."

Dave Henderson's hands were clenched between his knees. They relaxed slowly.

"I'm glad of that," he said in a low tone. "Go on, Millman."

"The man had evidently revived just before the police got there," Millman explained. "He was shot and killed instantly by the police while trying to escape. He had bruises on his head which the police attributed to a fight with Dago George. Dago George, the police assume, woke up to discover the men breaking into his room. They attacked him. He managed to shoot Bookie Skarvan, and grappled with Cunny the Scorpion—the Scorpion's clothing, somewhat torn, and the Scorpion's bruises, bear this out. But in order to account for the time it would have taken to crack the safe, the police believe that the Scorpion at this time only knocked Dago George out temporarily. Then, later, while the Scorpion worked at the safe, Dago George recovered sufficiently to rush and snatch at the phone, and shout his appeal for help into it; and then the Scorpion laid Dago George's head open with the blow that killed him, using one of the burglar's tools as the weapon. And then the Scorpion, staying to put the finishing touches on his work to get the safe open, and over-estimating the time it would take the police to get there, was finally unable to make his escape."

"My God!" muttered Dave Henderson under his breath.

"That's not all," said Millman, with a faint smile. "There was known enmity between Dago George and the Scorpion. The Scorpion had come to The Iron Tavern earlier in the evening, one of the waiters testified, and had brought the fat man with him. The fat man was given a room by Dago George. The waiter identified the fat man, an obvious accomplice therefore of the Scorpion, as the man who was shot. It dovetailed irrefutably—even the Scorpion's prior intentions of harm to Dago George being established. There was some money in the safe, quite a little, but the police are more inclined to attribute the motive to the settling of a gang feud, with the breaking of the safe more or less as a blind."

Dave Henderson was staring across the hall. His lips were tight.

"That waiter!" he exclaimed abruptly. "Didn't the waiter say anything about anybody else who got rooms there last night?"

"I am coming to that," Millman replied. "The police questioned the man, of course. He said that last night, at separate times, a man and a woman came there, presumably to get rooms since they had valises with them, and that they saw Dago George. He did not know whether Dago George had accommodated them or not. He thought not, both because he had neither carried nor seen the valises taken upstairs, and because Dago George invariably refused to give any rooms to strangers. Lots of people came there, imagining The Iron Tavern to be a hotel where they could get cheap accommodations, and were always turned away. Dago George had gone out of that end of the business. The waiter inclined to the belief that the man and woman in question had met the same fate; certainly, he had seen or heard nothing of them since." Millman shrugged his shoulders. "The police searched the rooms upstairs, found no trace of occupancy except the hand-bag of the fat man, identified again by the waiter—and agreed with the waiter."

"There was Maggot." Dave Henderson seemed to be speaking almost to himself. "But Maggot was only a tool. All Maggot knew was that he was to get the safe open—for some money. I guess Maggot, when he finds out that the police don't know anything about him, will think he's lucky. I guess if there's any man in the world who'll keep his mouth shut for the sake of his own hide, it's Maggot. Maggot isn't going to run his head into a noose." He turned sharply to Millman. "But there's still some one else—the doctor."

"We have been friends, intimate friends, all our lives," said Millman simply. "I have given him my word of honor that you had no hand in the death of any one of those three men, and that is sufficient."

And then Dave Henderson laughed a little, a queer, strange, mirthless laugh, and stood up from the divan.

"Then I'm clear—eh—Millman?" he shot out.

"Yes," said Millman slowly, "as far as I can see, Dave, you're clear."

"And free?" There was fierce assertiveness, rather than interrogation, in Dave Henderson's voice. "It's taken five years, but I've got that money now. I guess I've paid for it; and I guess there's no one now to put a crimp in it any more, not even Bookie Skarvan—providing that little proposition of yours, Millman, that month, still stands."

Millman's face, and Millman's eyes, sobered.

"It stands, Dave," he said gravely.

"In a month," said Dave Henderson, "even a fool could get far enough away to cover his trail—couldn't he, Millman? Well, then, there's only Teresa left. She's something like you, Millman. She's for sending that money back, but she's sort of put out of the running—for about a month, too!"

Millman made no answer.

"Five years," said Dave Henderson, with a hard smile. "Well, it's *mine* now. Those years were a hell, Millman—a hell—do you understand? But they would only be a little hell compared with the hell to-day if I couldn't get away with that package now without, say, a policeman standing there in the doorway waiting for me."

"Dave," said Millman sharply, "what do you mean? What are you going to do?"

There was some one on the stairs again—some one all in white. Dave Henderson stared. The figure was beckoning to him. Yes, of course, it was the nurse.

"Dave," Millman repeated, "what are you going to do?"

Dave Henderson laughed again—queerly.

"I'm going upstairs—to see Teresa," he said.

"And then?" Millman asked.

But Dave Henderson scarcely heard him. He was walking now towards the stairs. The nurse's voice reached him.

"Just a few minutes," warned the nurse. "And she must not be excited."

He gained the landing, and looked back over the balustrade down into the great hall below. Millman had come to the foot of the staircase, and was leaning on the newel-post. And Dave Henderson looked, more closely.

Millman's gray eyes were blurred, and, though they smiled, the smile came through a mist that had gathered in them. And then Millman's voice came softly.

"I get you, as we used to say 'out there,'" said Millman. "I get you, Dave. Thank God! It's two straight crooks—isn't it, Dave—two of us?"

Millman's face was blotted out—there was another face that Dave Henderson saw now through an open doorway, a face that lay upon the pillows, and that was very white. It must be the great, truant masses of black hair, which crowned the face, that made it look as white as that. And they said she was getting better! They must have lied to him—the face was so white.

He didn't see the face any more now, because he was kneeling down beside the bed, and because his own face was buried in the counterpane.

And then the great shoulders of the man shook.

His life! That was what she had bought—and that was what she had paid for almost with her own. That was why she lay here, and that was why her face was so white. Teresa! This was Teresa here.

He raised his head at last. Her dark eyes were fixed on him—and they smiled.

She was holding out her hand.

"Dave," she said brightly, "the nurse told me she was going to let you see me for a few minutes—to cheer me up. And here I've been waiting—oh, ever so long. And you haven't spoken a word. Haven't you anything to say"—she was smiling teasingly with her lips now—"Dave?"

"Yes," he said. "Yes"—his voice choked—"more than I can ever say. Last night, Teresa, if it had not been for you, I—-"

Her finger tips could just reach his lips, and they pressed suddenly against them, and sealed them.

"Don't you know that we are not to talk about that, Dave—ever," she said quickly. "If I did anything, then, oh, I am so glad—so glad. You're not to say another word."

"But, I *must*," he said hoarsely. "Do you think I——"

"Dave, I'll call the nurse!" she said in a low voice. "You'll—you'll make me cry."

It was true. The dark eyes were swimming, full of tears. She hid them now suddenly with their long lashes.

Neither spoke for a moment.

"There's something else, then, Teresa," he said at last. "I'm going to give that money back."

There was no answer—only he felt her hand touch his head, and her fingers play gently through his hair.

"I knew it," she told him.

"But do you know why?" he asked.

Again there was no answer.

Dave Henderson spoke again.

"I remember what I said last night—that I couldn't buy you that way. And—and I'm not trying to now. It's going back because I haven't any choice. A man can't take his life from a woman's hand, and from the hand of a friend take the life of the woman who has saved him—and throw them both down—and play the cur. I haven't any choice." His voice broke suddenly. "It's going back, Teresa, whether it means you or not. Do you understand, Teresa? It's going back—either way."

Her fingers had ceased their movements, and were quiet now.

"Yes," she said.

Dave Henderson raised his bowed head. The dark eyes were closed. His shoulders squared a little.

"That—that puts it straight, then, Teresa," he said. "That lets me say what I want to say now. I've done a lot of thinking in the last few hours when I thought that perhaps you weren't—weren't going to get better. I thought about what you said last night—about God giving one another chance if one wanted to take it. Teresa, would you believe me if I told you that I was going to take that chance—from now on?"

The dark eyes opened now.

"I don't think God ever meant that you would do anything else, Dave," she said. "If He had, you would never have been caught and put in prison, and been through everything else that has happened to you, because it's just those things, Dave, that have made you say what you have just said. If you had succeeded in getting away with that money five years ago, you would have been living as a thief to-day, and—and you would have stolen more, perhaps, and—and at last you wouldn't even have been a man." She turned her face away on the pillow, and fumbled for his hand. "But it isn't just you, Dave. I didn't say that last night. I said God offered us both a chance. It's not only you, Dave—both of us are going to take that chance."

He leaned forward—his face tense, white almost as the white face on the bed.

"Together, Teresa?"

She did not answer—only her hand closed in a tighter clasp on his.

"Teresa!" He was bending over her now, smoothing back the hair from her forehead. The blood pounded in a mighty tide through his veins. "Teresa!"

She spoke then, as the wet lashes lifted for an instant and fell again.

"It's wonderful," she whispered. "God's chance, Dave—together—from now on."

Into his face came a great new light. Self-questioning and self-debate were gone. Teresa *trusted* him. He knew himself before God and his fellows henceforth an honest man. And he was rich—rich with a boundless, priceless love that would endure while life endured. Teresa! His lips pressed the white forehead, and the closed eyelids, and then her lips were warm upon his own—and then he was kneeling again, but now his arms were around her, folding her to him, and his head lay upon the pillow, and his cheek touched hers.

And presently Millman, coming up the stairs, paused abruptly on the landing, as, through the open doorway of the room that was just in front of him, his eyes fell upon Dave Henderson's kneeling figure. And he stood there. And Teresa's voice, very low, and as though she were repeating something, reached him. And creeping into Millman's gray eyes there came a light of understanding as tender as a woman's, and for a moment more he lingered there, and then he tiptoed softly away. And the words that he had heard seemed to have graven themselves deep into the great heart of the man, for, as he went slowly on down the hall, he said them over and over again to himself:

"From now on.... From now on...."